More Praise for Cynthia Bond's
Ruby

"Luminous ... a love story about pure-hearted patience conquering insurmountable odds. Many will compare *Ruby* to the work of Toni Morrison or Zora Neale Hurston, as Oprah Winfrey has ... but it may be most apt to compare Bond to Gabriel García Márquez"
—Guardian

"Stunning" *—New York Times*

"Bond proves to be a powerful literary force, a writer whose unflinching yet lyrical prose is reminiscent of Toni Morrison's"
—O, The Oprah Magazine

"A beautifully wrought ghost story, a love story, a survival story ... [A] wonderful debut" *—Los Angeles Review of Books*

"In Ruby, Bond has created a heroine worthy of the great female protagonists of Toni Morrison ... and Zora Neale Hurston ... Bond's style of writing is as magical as an East Texas sunrise"
—Dallas Morning News

"Channeling the lyrical phantasmagoria of early Toni Morrison ... Cynthia Bond has created a moving and indelible portrait of a fallen woman." *—San Francisco Chronicle*

"*Ruby* explores the redeeming power of love in the face of horrific trauma.... If the truth shall set us free, Ms. Bond shows us, in her story of grace, that love is truth." *—Pittsburgh Post-Gazette*

"If you love well-written historical fiction and multifaceted grown-up characters, put *Ruby* at the top of your beach bag."   —*Essence*

"Evocative, affective, and accomplished ... Bond tells the story of Ruby's and Ephram's lives and their relationship with unflinching honesty and a surreal, haunting quality."   —*Texas Observer*

"Bond is a gifted writer, powerful and nimble.... It's tempting to call up Toni Morrison or Alice Walker or Ntozake Shange. It should be done more as compliment than comparison, though ... Bond's is a robustly original voice."   —*Barnes & Noble Review*

"Lush, deep, momentous ... *Ruby* enchants not just with its powerful tale of lifelong quests and unrelenting love, but also with its exquisite language. It is a treasure of a book, one you won't soon forget."
—Edwidge Danticat, author of *Claire of the Sea Light*

"A stunning debut. *Ruby* is unforgettable."
—John Rechy, author of *City of Night*

"Cynthia Bond creates a vibrant chorus of voices united by a common struggle.... The prose's lyricism and Ruby's interaction with the dead call to mind *Beloved*."   —*The Rumpus*

"Cloaked in authenticity, *Ruby* is unlike anything else out there right now."   —*Windy City Times*

"The narrative is exquisite, juxtaposing horrific imagery with dreamy evocative lyricism."   —*Lambda Literary*

"[A] powerful, explosive novel. Bond immerses readers in a fully realized world, one scarred by virulent racism and perverted rituals but also redeemed by love."   —*Booklist* (starred)

Ruby

Cynthia Bond

www.tworoadsbooks.com

First published in Great Britain in 2015 by Two Roads
An imprint of Hodder & Stoughton
An Hachette UK company

1

Portions of 'A Conversation with Cynthia Bond' were originally published on
Amazon.com and BarnesandNoble.com in 2014.
'A Recipe for White Lay Angel Cake' was originally published in a newsletter from First Look
Book Club in 2014.

A CIP catalogue record for this title is available from the British Library

ISBN 978 1 473 62051 3
Ebook ISBN 978 1 473 62048 3

Printed and bound by CPI Group (UK) Ltd, Croydon, CR0 4YY

Hodder & Stoughton policy is to use papers that are natural, renewable and recyclable products and
made from wood grown in sustainable forests. The logging and manufacturing processes are
expected to conform to the environmental regulations of the country of origin.

Hodder & Stoughton Ltd
338 Euston Road
London NW1 3BH

www.hodder.co.uk

For Dr. Zelema Marshall Harris,
aka Mama

Ruby

Book One

Wishbone

Chapter 1

Ruby Bell was a constant reminder of what could befall a woman whose shoe heels were too high. The people of Liberty Township wove her into cautionary tales of the wages of sin and travel. They called her buck-crazy. Howling, half-naked mad. The fact that she had come back from New York City made this somewhat understandable to the town.

She wore gray like rain clouds and wandered the red roads in bared feet. Calluses thick as boot leather. Hair caked with mud. Blackened nails as if she had scratched the slate of night. Her acres of legs carrying her, arms swaying like a loose screen. Her eyes the ink of sky, just before the storm.

That is how Ruby walked when she lived in the splintered house that Papa Bell had built before he passed. When she dug into the East Texas soil under moonlight and wailed like a distant train.

In those years, after her return, people let Ruby be. They walked a curved path to avoid her door. And so it was more than strange when someone walked the length of Liberty and brought a covered cake to the Bells' front porch.

Ephram Jennings had seen the gray woman passing like a haint through the center of town since she'd returned to Bell land in 1963. All of Liberty had. He had seen her wipe the spittle from her jerking lips, run her still beautiful hands over the crust of her hair each day before she'd turned the corner in view of the town. He'd seen her walking like she had some place she ought to have been, then five steps away from P & K Market, stand pillar still, her rain cloud body shaking. Ephram had seen Miss P, the proprietor of the store, walk nonchalantly out of her door and say, "Honey, can you see if I got the rise in these rolls right?"

Ephram watched Ruby stare past her but take the brown sack filled with steaming yeast bread. Take it and walk away with her acres of legs carrying her, while Miss P said, "You come on back tomorrow, Ruby Bell, and help me out if you get the chance."

Ephram Jennings had watched this for eleven years. Seen her black-bottomed foot kick a swirl of dust in its wake. Every day he wanted nothing more than to put each tired sole in his wide wooden tub, brush them both in warm soapy water, cream them with sweet oil and lanoline and then slip her feet, one by one into a pair of red-heel socks.

But instead, with each passing year, he watched Miss P do her Christian duty from the corner of his eye. Watched the gray woman stoop to accept the doughy alms. He sat alongside the crowd of men parked on their stools outside P & K. Who read their papers, played dominoes and chewed tobacco. Toothpicks dangling. Pipes smoking. Soda pops sweating. Just as they had the day Ruby arrived back in Liberty. When she'd stepped from the red bus, the porch had crowded her with their eyes. Hair pressed and gleaming like polished black walnut. Lipstick red and thick, her cornflower blue sundress darted and stitched tight to her waist. Ephram had watched her light a cigarette and glare down at the crowd on the market porch in such a way that made folks feel embarrassed for breathing. Chauncy Rankin had said later, "Not only do her shit not stink, way she act, she ready to sell it by the ounce."

They had all watched, steadily, as she slipped into madness. Concern, mingled with a secret satisfaction, melted into the creases of their bodies like Vaseline. After a time they barely glanced up from their papers when Ruby walked up to the market. They yawned her existence away, or spit out a wad of tobacco juice to mark her arrival. A low joke might rumble as Miss P handed over her bread, followed by throaty chuckles.

But one end-of-summer day, Ephram Jennings took particular notice. One by one the men on the porch did as well. For instead of walking away with her bread, as she normally did, Ruby didn't move. Her body rooted to the spot. She stood there, holding the brown sack, hand quivering like a divining rod. And then she peed. A long, steady stream that hit the red dust and turned it the color of brick. She did it absently, with calm disinterest. Then, because no one knew quite what to do, Gubber Samuels pointed and hurled out a rough bark of laughter. Ruby looked down and saw the puddle beneath her. Surprise flowered on her face, then fell away leaving a spreading red shame. Her hands leapt to her eyes, but when she brought them down the world was still there, so she dropped the sack in the pool of urine and ran. But it wasn't running. It was flying, long and graceful, into the piney woods like a deer after the crack of buckshot. Ephram almost stood. Almost ran down the porch steps and into the woods after her. But the eyes of men were too strong, and the continued spitting and snickering of Gubber Samuels anchored him against the tug of mercy.

Because Ephram's mama had long since gone to glory, that very day, he asked his older sister Celia to make up her white lay angel cake because he needed to carry it to an ailing friend. Celia looked at him out of the corner of her eye but made it anyway.

She made it in that pocket of time before dawn, when the aging night gathered its dark skirts and paused in the stillness. She made it with twelve new eggs, still warm and flecked with feathers. She washed them and cracked them, one at a time, holding each golden yolk in her palm as the whites slid and dropped through her open fingers. She set them aside in her flowered china bowl. In the year 1974, Celia Jennings still cooked in a wood-burning stove, she still used a whisk and muscle and patience to beat her egg whites into foaming peaks. She used pure vanilla, the same sweet liquid she had poured into Saturday night baths before their father, the Reverend Jennings, arrived back in town. The butter was from her churn, the confectioner's sugar from P & K. And as she stirred the dawn into being, a dew drop of sweat salted the batter. The cake baked and rose with the sun.

Ephram slept as the cake slid from its tin, so sweet it crusted at its crumbling edges, so light little craters of air circled its surface, so moist it was sure, as was always the case, to cling to the spaces between his sister's long three-pronged silver fork. Celia Jennings never cut her white lay angel cake with a knife. "It'd be like using an ax to skin a rabbit," she'd always say.

The cake was cooling when Ephram awoke. It settled into itself as he bathed and dressed for the day.

Ephram Jennings smoothed the corners of his great-grand-daddy's hat for the tenth time that morning. His wide square thumbs running along the soft hide brim. The leather so thin in places the sun filtered through softly like a Chinese lantern.

The magical thing about Ephram Jennings was that if you

looked real hard, you could see a circle of violet rimming the brown of his irises. Soft like the petals of spreading periwinkle.

The problem was that no one, not even his sister, took the time to really look at Ephram Jennings. Folks pretty much glanced past him on the way to Bloom's place or P & K. To them he was just another thick horse brown man with a ratted cap and a stooped gait. To them there was nothing special about Ephram. He was a moving blur on the eyes' journey to more delicate and interesting places.

Ephram had become accustomed to this in his forty-five years of living. Slipping in and out of doorways without so much as a nod or pause in the conversation. At his job it was expected. He was a pair of hands carrying grocery bags to White folks' shiny automobiles. Taking tips and mouthing "Thank ya, Ma'am." Anger or kindness directed towards him indifferently as if he were a lump of coal. Ephram told himself he didn't mind. But with Black folks there were times when a man might expect an eye to catch hold and stick for a moment. Folks never did see his Chinese lamp hat, or his purple-ringed irises, or the way that they matched just perfectly the berry tint of his lower lip. They didn't see the ten crescent moons held captive in his fingernails, the way he moved, like a man gliding under water, smooth and liquid as Marion Lake. They didn't notice how the blue in his socks coordinated with the buttons on his Sunday shirt or smell the well-brushed sheen of Brylcreem in his thick hair.

They didn't notice the gracious pause he'd take after someone would finish a sentence, the way he'd give folks the chance to take air back into their lungs, before he'd fill the space up with his own breath and words.

They didn't see the way his pupils got wide when his heart filled up with pride or love or hope.

But Ruby did.

When her life was only a building long scream that faded into night. Even then Ruby noticed Ephram.

⁓

IT WAS after the big Brownsville hurricane of '67. After eighty-six-mile-an-hour winds crashed into Corpus Christi and rippled all the way east to Liberty Township. Splashing the edge of west Louisiana and flooding the banks of the Sabine. It was after the bending of trees, of branches arching to the floor of earth. After Marion Lake had swollen up and washed away Supra Rankin's hen house, and Clancy Simkins's daddy's Buick, and the new cross for the Church of God in Christ.

Hurricane Beulah had come Ruby's fourth year back in Liberty. It was then that she saw Ephram Jennings.

She had lain in the stagnant pools thick with mud and browning leaves. She had knelt before a cracked sugar maple tree and lain in the collecting waters, letting the thick fluid cover her like a bedtime blanket. She felt her skin melt and slip from her bones; her heart, spine and cranium dissolve like sugar cubes in warm coffee.

She had been muddy waters for three hours when Ephram found her. Her nose rising out of the puddle to inhale . . . and dipping back to release. Out and back. Out. Back. Rhythmic, like an old blues tune.

He did not scream. He did not leap over the tree. He did not scoop into her water center to set her free.

For Ephram did not see what anyone else passing down the

road would see: a skinny dust brown woman with knotted hair lying back flat in a mud puddle. No. Ephram Jennings saw that Ruby had become the still water. He saw her liquid deep skin, her hair splayed like onyx river vines.

As rain began to fall upon her, Ephram saw her splash and swell and spill out of the small ravine. Ephram Jennings knew. That is when Ruby lifted her head like a rising wave and noticed Ephram. In that moment, the two knowings met.

They stared at each other under the ancient sky with the soft rain and the full wet earth. More than anything Ephram wanted to talk to her and tell her things he'd kept locked in the storehouse of his soul. He wanted to talk to her about the way Rupert Shankle's melons split on the vine and how honeysuckle blossoms tasted like sunlight. He wanted to tell her that he had seen a part of the night sky resting in her eyes and that he knew it because it lived in him as well. He wanted to tell her about the knot corded about his heart and how he needed her help to loose the binding.

But at that moment Ruby closed her eyes, concentrated, and melted once again into the pool.

Ephram heard himself asking the strangest question, heard it before it left his berry lips. "Are you married?" But before it could lace through the air, he saw that she was once again water. And he couldn't ask that of a puddle, no matter how perfect. So he tipped his hat, and made his way back down the road.

E PHRAAAM! EPHRAM Jennings your breakfast is been ready!"
As he had nearly every morning of his life, Ephram heard his sister's call.

"Yes Mama," he replied.

Celia had raised him since March 28, 1937, when their mother had come naked to the In-His-Name Holiness Church Easter picnic. Ephram was eight, Celia fourteen. The thing he remembered was his sister running over to him covering his eyes. That next morning, their father, the Reverend Jennings, took their mother to Dearing State Mental—Colored Ward, then packed his own bags and began preaching on the road ten months out of twelve. Celia tended Ephram, cooked for him, cut his food, picked and ironed his shirts, blocked his hats, nursed him within an inch of his life when he came down with that joint ailment. She had paused only long enough to bury their father, the Reverend, when he turned up dead. Lynched a few days after Ephram's thirteenth birthday. Ephram had curled up and lost himself in the folds of Celia's apron where he stayed for the next thirty-two years.

"Ephram come in here boy!"

Ephram knew without looking that Celia was biting her inner cheek, a thing she did whenever a food item wasn't eaten at the proper temperature. The colder it got the more furiously she would gnaw. Then he heard her sweeping with a vengeance. Each morning of his life Celia swept bad luck out of the kitchen door. Every evening she sprinkled table salt in the corners, and every morning she swept it out again, full of any evil the night air held. The sweeping stopped.

"I know you hear me!"

"Inaminute," Ephram called as he smoothed the weathered brim of his hat once more and faced his sister's mirror. This morning, this crisp, end-of-summer morning, Ephram did something he had not done in twenty years. He looked.

He had always straightened the crease in his slacks on Sunday, or picked bits of lint from his Deacon jacket. He had held a handkerchief filled with ice on his split chin and lip, the one winter in his life snow had slicked the front walk. He had combed and oiled his scalp and plucked out in-grown hairs. He had shaved and brushed his teeth and gargled with Listerine. But in twenty years, Ephram Jennings had not truly looked into a mirror.

His greatest surprise was that he was no longer young. He assessed the plum darkness under his eyes, the grooves along his full nose, the subtle weight of his cheeks. Ephram pressed a cool washcloth to his skin, then he practiced a smile. He had tried on five or six when Celia launched her final call.

As Ephram sat down to eat, his chair scraped against the butter flower tiles.

"Sorry." Ephram managed.

"S'all right baby, just got to remember to pick it up instead of drag."

"I will, Mama."

"And remember not to leave your bad day cane out where folk can trip on it."

"I'll put it away after breakfast."

"Don't forget now."

"I won't, Mama."

Celia swept the long hall as Ephram dipped buttery biscuits into syrup. She straightened a wood-framed photograph of the Reverend Jennings as Ephram cut into the chicken fried steak. He had gotten the cutlet on special at the Newton Piggly Wiggly, where he worked.

By way of apology Ephram said, "You fixed that cutlet up real nice, Mama."

"That was a fair cut. Why don't you get me some more when you go into Newton today."

"I ain't going in today Ma'am."

"Oh. I thought maybe your sick friend was from Newton since you didn't say who they was."

"I'll pick up more of them cutlets on Tuesday, Mama."

Celia put *Andy Williams—Songs of Faith* on the phonograph while Ephram peppered his grits and four scrambled eggs. She finished sweeping salt from every corner of the house as "He's Got the Whole World in His Hands" smoothed across the furniture. Ephram chewed slowly and glanced at Celia's cake. Flaked white inside, the outside was all honey-gold. He imagined handing it to Ruby Bell and seeing something he had not witnessed in over thirty years—Ruby smiling.

Celia sailed into the room with her dustpan full of salt. "Well, if you ain't going to Newton, do your friend stay out by Glister's?"

"No."

"Cuz Glister got six of my mason jars if you goin' round that way."

"I can't today Mama."

"I was going to make Supra Rankin some of my fig preserves for her husband's great-uncle's funeral on Monday if you was going that way . . . Lord knows it's a shame that family don't believe in getting they people preserved right. And how they think the man will keep fresh while they waitin' on them Mississippi Rankins to get here I don't know."

"Shephard's Mortuary lay folk out nice, Mama."

"Shamed Mother Mercy last year with them red lips and rubbed-on fair skin."

"Mama . . ."

"Woman look like a peppermint stick, Lord know. You yet one of Junie's pallbearers?"

Ephram nodded yes. Celia opened the kitchen door to empty the dustpan, just as a strong wind blew a mouthful of salt into her face. She spit it from her lips, wiped it from her eyes and quickly swept what was left out of the back door.

Celia turned to face Ephram, "You know Baby Girl Samuels back in town."

Ephram took a bite of eggs.

Celia wiped the table with a damp rag. "Supra Rankin say Baby arrive from New Orleans three days ago, painted up like a circus clown, wrigglin' like a mackerel all over town."

Ephram lifted his cup and plate as she cleaned. "Mama—"

"I didn't say it. Supra Rankin did." Celia looked hard at Ephram, "Which is why I asked you to get my jars from Glister, since the Samuels are just past that way."

"Mama! I ain't taking that cake to Baby Girl Samuels! I ain't thought nothing about her in fifteen years." Ephram stood up. "I got to go."

"Finish your breakfast."

Ephram reluctantly sat.

Celia poured the steam back in his coffee. He ate the last of his meal as Andy Williams's rendition of "Battle Hymn of the Republic" syruped its way through the kitchen. Celia circled back to the sink, emptied water from soaking green beans, sat beside Ephram and began snapping the tips off the beans. With practiced grace she chucked the remaining pod into a pail with a hollow *TING!*

Without looking at Ephram she said, "Run into Miss Philomena yesterday at P & K. She asked after you."

Ephram ate quietly as the music curled under him. . . . *truth is marching on . . .*

Celia continued, "That Miss P always be so generous. Helping all manner of folk and such."

The song infused itself into the air.

I have seen Him in the watch fires...

Ephram breathed it in.

The beans echoed. TING.

Celia continued, "Way she give 'way that Wonder Bread to them folks flooded out in Neches."

Ephram nodded.... *of a hundred circling camps...*

TING.

"And her old jerky and pickles to them no count Peels."

TING. TING.

...builded Him an altar...

"And don't she help out that Ruby Bell quite a bit!"

...in the evening dews and damps...

TING.

"Now that Bell gal one sad case, ain't she!"

I can read his righteous sentence by the dim and flaring lamps...

TING.

"You knowed her as chirrun, didn't you! Pretty thang she was too, with them long good braids."

Glory glory Hallelujah!

TING.

"Look like"

Glory

"she was gonna"

Glory

"come to something,"

Hallelujah!

"being raised by that White lady after Papa Bell died."

TING.

"Going off"

Glory

"to New York"

Glory

"City like she done."

Hallelujah!

"Even going"

His

"to that White"

truth

"folks' school up there."

Is marching on.

TING. TING. TING.

The song faded into the wallpaper, but Celia sang on.

"It's more than a sin how far she fall. Hair nappy with mud, raiment's torn and trampled. Now I hear she take to doing her pee-pee in the streets! Beggin' for scraps with crazy scratched acrost her pate. And they say what happens at night with menfolk in old Mister Bell's house would set his bones to spinnin'."

Ephram felt little dots of sweat along his temples. "Ma—"

"But I don't blame them none. You know how men do. Nasty ring its bell and they come running like it's suppertime in hell. Devil got him a firm foothold in Liberty. I know. I seen firsthand what conjure can do. Folk cut down, men shriveled up like prunes. Leave a body empty of they spirit so they just a hollow thing 'til they lay down dead. Boy, I sat acrost the hearth from Satan, close as you is. Seen him stirring his big kettle a' souls over a lake of fire. I'm on a first name basis with the Devil, so I know how his mind be working, always looking out for another sinner to season his brew. So when Glister say her boy Charlie seen you eyeballin' that Bell gal ever day. Sniffin' after her, I say to her, No Sir. I raise my boy better than to eat at no Jezebel's table and I *know* he ain't bringing dessert."

"Ceal—"

"I ain't got flippers."

"Mama—"

"What?"

Ephram noticed his wrist trembling. Just barely, but there it was. He set his cup down.

"Mama—it's just cake."

"Bait more like it."

"She just—"

"Tell me you ain't lie your own mama into making ho-cake?"

Ephram breathed in a huge gulp of air, as the sleeping pain in his fingers yawned to waking. Far away Andy began singing "Amazing Grace."

"Your bones botherin' you today baby?"

"No." The pain stretched itself into his knuckles, wrists and arms.

Celia took his hand. "Ephram, you always been simple. When you was a boy you'd come back with half a pail a' milk instead of whole. Couldn't never figure out how to stop that cow from kickin' it out from under you. But that's all right. God love simple, but so do the Devil. Cuz simple ain't got the kind of mind to withstand temptation."

Ephram's bones began to shoot through with fire, the very marrow sizzled under his skin. It was the bad day pain, the worst he'd felt in years. He began to perspire. His legs began to shake as a dot of sweat dropped onto the kitchen table. Ephram stood.

"You need your bad day cane!"

He didn't look at her when he said, "I'm not going out today Mama." Ephram walked to the doorway as Celia took a cloth and wiped away the drop of sweat. He walked past the narrow hallway as she stood and plopped her green beans into a waiting pot on the stove. He crept into his bedroom, slipped off his polished shoes, took off his jacket and hat, then lay back flat upon the iron bed.

Celia called in from the kitchen, "You want a slice of cake, baby?"

"Not now Mama."

"Well, I'll cut you a piece. Leave it out for when you get up."

Ephram prayed against the pain. It came anyway, sizzling like a pit fire. Rising, burning, sucking. Ephram gritted his teeth against it. Sweat poured into the curve of his ear, onto the pillowcase. It began receding. Ephram took in a breath. He felt the bedsprings coiled beneath him. The ceiling low and bumpy from when Celia hired the Pastor's son to scrap stucco gray over the wood.

It started again, clanging like a fire alarm, wrenching his stomach. Ephram balled his fists so hard, all ten crescent moons disappeared to white. It passed. He gasped for air.

The spells were getting worse. Lately, he'd felt like his bones were God's kindling. That God must be awfully cold to set so many fires. As Ephram waited for the pain, he saw Ruby as she used to be, the first time he'd seen her. The sweet little girl with long braids. The kind of pretty it hurt to look at, like candy on a sore tooth.

Ephram gasped in. He could tell this wave would be big. The hurt rose up, and the world crashed down. Ephram's last thought before passing out was of sorrow, that Ruby would never taste Celia's angel cake.

His body grew limp upon the chenille spread, his bones grinding even in slumber. The Saturday sun ruffling his curtains, sending fingers of light across the floor. Outside something cawed from atop a tree. Something shiny and black. It flew from its perch and made lazy eights over Jennings land, then it drifted down from the sky into a patch of yard just outside Ephram's room. Scratching and strutting until a broom-toting woman yelled at it from inside the house. At that the crow tilted her head, spread her wings and caught the wind. Then she cawed.

Chapter 2

The piney woods were full of sound. Trees cracking and falling to their death; the knell of axes echoing into green; the mewl of baby hawks waiting for Mama's catch. Bull frogs and barn owls. The call of crows and the purring of doves. The screams of a Black man. The slowing of a heart. All captured, hushed and held under the colossal fur of pine and oak, magnolia, hickory and sweet gum. Needles and capillary branches interlaced to make an enormous net, so that whatever rose, never broke through to sky. The woods held stories too, and emotions and objects: a tear of sleeve, bits of hair, long-buried bones, lost buttons. But mostly, the piney woods hoarded sound.

Like the sharp squeak of a wheel from a child's wagon turning round and round. A rusted Radio Flyer, being pulled by a little brown boy, rattling with a lunch pail of chicken and dumplings, biscuits with fig preserves stuffed inside, collard greens and a special dessert wrapped in a red and white napkin.

The boy named Ephram pulled the wagon with great anticipation. He guessed what dessert his big sister had put in his pail. She'd made one just like it for his eleventh birthday four months ago. The white lay angel cake. His mouth watered so that he stopped under the big trees and opened the cloth. He was right. He nibbled one corner and covered it. He paused for a second, opened it again, then crammed the slice into his mouth. It was like eating sweet air. When he was done he shook the napkin over his face to catch any crumbs, brushed off and walked until he smelled the water.

There were two suns at Marion Lake, the one high above and the one floating on the surface. The water was a blue mirror, surrounded by a hundred trees and a million frogs. Ephram took off his shoes and cooled his toes first thing. He loved Marion Lake, especially on Sunday morning when nobody else was there. He used to go on Saturdays before his mama had gone, but only after he'd finished his chores. She was very firm about that.

Ephram watched the water swirl and skim not too far from shore. He knew the fish would be biting. He baited a bent nail with a bit of fatback from Celia's slop jar. Then hoisted his branch pole between two rocks and sat down to eat his dinner. Ephram knew he might sit there for hours and never catch a fish. Sometimes, he'd feel one tussle with the line, he'd pull it above water and see those invisible teeth still grabbing ahold of the bait. Scales flashing silver, tail twisting . . . single glass eye staring straight ahead until they realized the spot they were in and let go. *Flop! Splosh!* Down into the sky water until it was out of sight. His real mother had called it "feeding," not fishing. He guessed that was true. Otha Beatrice Jennings always took notice of the little things. Maybe that's why she'd been such a good lace-maker. Ephram wondered if they let her make lace up where she was now. He sure hoped so.

The chicken and dumplings were good. Not as good as Mama's, but Celia was a good cook, even though she was too bossy about it. She was bossy about everything since their father, the Reverend, had been asked to step down by the Elders. He would mumble at bedtime, to no one in particular, "That was a mighty unchristian thing for a pack of Christians to do."

To make matters worse, the acting preacher was Elder Rankin's cousin and a part-time janitor at the Piggly Wiggly in Newton, who had only recently heard the call. The Reverend renamed it "the Piggly Service," then bade Celia and Ephram to never cross its threshold. "We'll have church in our own house, fifty-two Sundays a year whether I'm here or no." Celia had kept the faith, making Ephram memorize huge sections of Leviticus and Revelation and recite them perfectly each Sabbath. When the Reverend was in town, Sunday mornings before breakfast and after chores, Ephram and Celia would kneel and he would preach while eggs turned to yellow glue and pancakes shriveled and died. Long. And sometimes, he would pour two fingers of rye, and slip a sip between Ephesians 1 and 2, until he dozed off. That had happened that very morning in fact. Celia had scraped their breakfast into the bin, made the Reverend some coffee, then fixed Ephram's dinner and told him to go play.

He had just finished eating and was sitting with his pole when he spotted them—Maggie Wilkins and the quiet little girl beside her. They were across the lake. The girl tiptoed and leaned in, her nose almost touching Margaret's cheek. She was caramel brown with her hair up and fancy, grown-up eyes in a heart-shaped face. She held shining black shoes with white stockings balled into the toes. She wore a pink dress and looked about eight or nine. Margaret was dressed like a farmer. She was one of those grasshopper children, with legs almost as thin as their arms and twice as long. There were six tall rough girls in the Wilkins family including Margaret. All lanky and black brown with a constant sheen of ash on their knees, elbows and shins. Every one of them known for being bad, but Margaret had the worst reputation. The Wilkins were the Bells' no count relations and they lived just on the edge of Liberty.

Ephram had heard of Margaret—Maggie's right hook getting her kicked out of school long before he'd seen her fight. None of the Wilkins girls stayed in school for long. Most left after half-killing some student or teacher.

After each of the girls spilled a good amount of blood, they stayed home and helped their mother, Beulah Wilkins, farm her twenty-seven acres of cane and cotton. Beulah Wilkins was bigger than all her children put together, a mountain of a woman who made the earth shake just a bit when she walked. Beulah had been his mama's good friend and Ephram had heard his mama saying that staying out of school might be fine for Samella and the other girls, but not so fine for Maggie, since she was the smartest of them all.

Still, he'd never met Margaret face to face. He remembered just last month he'd seen her fight Chauncy Rankin's younger brother Rooster—so named for the rust color of his hair, and the way he liked to crow. He was built like all the Rankins. Big. Maggie was ten, Rooster was fourteen and he'd picked a fight with her because, he said, he wanted to "see if she could really fight." He'd made her take off her boots because they were pointed at the end. She'd beaten him in bare feet. Beaten him bloody. Ephram had seen this horrible thing she had done to Rooster. Seen his pride water down to a puddle, and he couldn't help feeling a little sorry for him. Maggie beating Rooster was all anyone had talked about for weeks. So when Ephram saw Margaret on the other side of the lake, he had no desire to cross paths.

Just as he thought of retreating into the brush, he saw the

quiet girl pointing in his direction. Maggie turned fiercely and cut her eyes at him.

"What you staring at?" she called across the lake.

"I'm not staring."

"What you doing then?"

"Fishin'."

"Well you best not be staring at nobody if you know what's good for you."

Ephram nodded. "I'm just fishin'."

"Well see that's all you do."

Ephram watched the other girl whisper into Margaret's ear. The two began to approach, walking along the water's edge. As they got closer Margaret asked, "You catch anything?"

"Naw."

"How long you been here?"

"Awhile."

"You ain't fishin', you feedin'."

Ephram paused and looked at Margaret. Although he was a year older, Margaret towered above him.

"Gimme that pole."

Ephram handed it over before she asked twice.

"You Celia Jennings's brother, huh?"

Ephram nodded.

"You got a name?"

"Ephram."

Margaret slipped a bobby pin from the other girl's hair and bit off the tip. The girl's two plaits fell past her shoulders.

"What you using for bait?"

Ephram handed her more salt pork.

She took one look at it and rolled her eyes, "No wonder." She walked straight to the lake's edge, dug her hand into the soft earth until she retrieved a long earthworm. She walked over to the pole, fastened the black pin to the string and bent it back. Then she pierced the moving worm with the sharp end of the pin and cast it easily in the water. Ephram and the little girl winced.

"Ruby ain't never had no catfish. This here's Ruby."

Ruby nodded at him. Ephram nodded back.

Margaret continued, "Ruby stay up in Neches most the year with a White lady. They ain't got no catfish where she from."

Ephram ventured, "Ain't they got catfish ever where?"

"What I just say?" said Margaret. The three of them fell silent.

They sat on the lake's shore, Ephram to the left, Margaret in the center and Ruby to the right of her. Out of the corner of his eye, Ephram saw Ruby's sleeve barely touching Maggie's coveralls. Then Ruby leaned back and let her head rest against the soft moss grass. Ephram did the same and they looked into the identical swatch of sky. He hadn't noticed it before but the blue had blown away and a dark flannel had taken its place. Maggie took a cigarette from her left ear and struck a kitchen match against the wedge of her belt.

"Ain't your mama up at Dearing?" Maggie asked out of the corner of her mouth, her eye squinting against the smoke.

Ephram didn't make a sound. Maggie went right on.

"Thought that was you."

Ephram saw Ruby nudge Maggie as if to stop her.

"Naw, I ain't sayin' nothin' bad. Papa Bell usta say some of the best people he know be up there. Say world be better off if them inside come out, and them out go in. How long she been there?"

Ephram cleared his throat. "Three years."

"See then? She not bad off as some. I know a lady who mama

been there fifteen years. Ain't no reason to be shamed." She sucked her teeth. "So, why they send her up there anyway?"

Ruby finally spoke, "It's gonna rain."

Maggie slipped off her overshirt and handed it to her. Ruby covered her shoulders with it.

"What she do?" Maggie repeated, flicking an ash without removing the cigarette from her mouth.

"Nothing."

"She had to do something big else she wouldn't be there. I ain't gone tell nobody, and Ruby going back to Neches this afternoon. I'll tell you what I hear and you tell me if it's right. Say your mama come out naked to the church Easter picnic. That so?"

Ephram just stared ahead at the water. He didn't want to talk about his mama, and he surely didn't want to talk about her to this rusty butt girl.

"Say all them church ladies near wet theyselves. Samella was there for the free food and said they was trippin' over theyselves to throw some clothes on her back and she just took off running, titties flappin' 'til the Rev, your daddy, catch up with her and knocked her cold. Next day she up at Dearing. You was there, huh? When it happen?"

Ruby parted her lips and there was a scream at the edge of her words, "Mag, *stop!*"

"Hush now, s'all right. I'm just sayin' what happened is all. Just tryin' to find out why the boy's mama done that. Seem like if anybody know it be him."

Ephram was standing now. Some flood of courage nearly drowned him, and he found his hands pushing up his sleeves and knotting into two tight fists. "Don't talk about my mama no more."

Maggie started laughing. "Boy, don't make me hurt you. Sit your scrawny butt down. I ain't mean no harm." Just then a fish tugged at the line. Small at first, and then harder. Maggie stood up and just when it seemed it was about to escape she jerked hard and fast on the line. The fish came up wriggling with the black pin sticking through its nose. "Y'all 'bout to make me lose my supper."

Maggie swung the wriggling fish to the earth and popped its head on a smooth stone. Of all the fish in that lake, luck brought Maggie a catfish. She flicked out her jackknife and split him down the center and ripped out his insides.

Ruby turned away, "Maggie . . . what you do that for?"

"You say you want catfish. So I catch you some catfish." Then she turned to Ephram. "You, go get us some twigs so we can make us a fire."

"It's gonna rain," said Ruby.

"Not before I cook me some fish. Go on." Maggie scaled the small fish and chopped off its head and tail as Ruby started to cry. Maggie stood up and looked into her eyes. "There, there, gal. I ain't did it to hurt him. That fish know what he gettin' into, swimmin' in that lake. He ain't the first fish been caught and fried, and won't be the last. That's how he live. That be his life. Swimming and knowin' that any day, *whoosh*, he gone be on somebody plate." Ruby cried harder and Maggie wrapped her in her arms. "All right now. See up there! See that wind moving at the top a' those trees!" Ruby looked up. "That fish be swimming up there now. He ain't got to stay stuck in some ole lake size of a dime. See! That's how it be. He come to us. He wants us to make a nice fire and eat him so all his memories of that lake be inside us. See Ruby! You see that fish up there?"

Ruby looked back at Maggie. "You just saying that."

"I am not. I swear to it. And your Mag-pie don't lie. Not 'bout catfish anyway." Maggie winked and grinned.

Ruby smiled back and showed perfect white teeth. Ephram had never thought of the life of a fish like that. He picked up the bits of wood just around them, then gathered a few more behind a wall of thick trunks. He brought them back and Maggie made a fire with her great match sticks. She took out a jackknife and whittled a sharp point on a stick and pierced it through the fish. Then she roasted it, turning it this way and that until its fat sizzled into the fire. When it was done they all sat around that small fire and munched on that fatty, crunchy fish, careful to avoid the bones.

"See what I tell you! It's good, huh!" Ruby nodded and winked at Maggie. Ephram chewed. He wished he had something to offer up as grand and soulful as that catfish. His heart sank when he thought about that slice of cake he'd gobbled in the woods. Celia's cake stood up to Maggie's fish any day. He guessed Celia was right about that gluttony sin after all. When they were done eating, just as Maggie had promised, the wind picked up and it started to sprinkle.

Ruby stood to go but Maggie said, "We got to do one thing first." Then she took the fish head and dug a small hole beside the water. She placed the head so that it was straight up and she covered it over. The rain was misting the tops of their heads, their noses and shoulders.

"Now we got to make a wish on this good fish we just ate. But you got to make it quick so it'll come fast." So they all closed their eyes and wished. Ephram opened his and watched Ruby's lips say very softly, "Tanny." Ephram couldn't imagine what that Maggie would be wishing for, but he cast his for his mama.

Ruby slipped on her shoes, then Maggie took her by the hand and the two walked quickly into the woods. Maggie turned back, "Hope your mama on the mend."

"Uh-huh."

Ruby half waved, but Maggie pulled her along and they were gone. Ephram stared after them. He put his dinner pail into the Radio Flyer, thought to leave but got snagged by the rain on the lake instead. By the blue and the gray. It looked like the drops were falling up, catapulted from a thousand tiny explosions. He thought about Ruby Bell. He had heard about her plenty too, but he'd never seen her before today, the Colored girl being raised by White folks up in Neches. Where did she get those eyelashes and that beauty spot on her left cheek? Ephram let himself get bone wet as the rain found the parts on his scalp and trickled down his face. A piece of thunder broke off and rolled about on the forest floor.

Ephram hadn't heard anyone behind him until he felt her hand on his shoulder. He spun around quickly and there she was. That little girl Ruby. She was completely soaked and she was talking. But he missed it. Only seen the movement of her lips and the smell of Dove soap. That and the scent of Dixie Peach and something else he couldn't quite place in the rain. There, he had missed it again. He tried to catch her words in midthought—

"—just ain't called for. See?" She had finished. She was looking up at him and he had no idea where to start or end. Was she chiding or comforting?

She stood for another moment then said, "Well, I gotta go."

He had to say something before she turned. All he could come up with was, "I was thinking . . ."

She stayed, her face screwed up a bit. "What?"

"Nothing." He looked down into the mud to hide the lie. "Just thinking about what you said."

"What about it?"

Scrambling: "About things not being called for."

She eyed him a moment then seemed to relax. "Thanks. But it ain't just me who says it. Papa Bell says it too, all the time."

He was lost again, but nodded his head anyway.

Margaret called from the rise, fenced by post trees and grass. "Ruby we got to be going!"

Ruby called back, "Said I'd be along!"

"Ain't leavin' you in all this rain. 'Sides she gonna be waitin' on us."

Ruby screamed and her voice lifted like the wind, "*I said go on!*"

Maggie stood there quiet against the bark of a long-needle pine. Walls of water between them, her head bent down just a bit. She moved away, like a puppy who'd been scolded, until only the top of her head showed above the rise. It did not budge.

"She get jealous a' everybody. It ain't just you."

"Why she act like that?"

"Why you act like you act? Why do your mama?"

"I didn't mean no harm."

"Don't be talkin' 'bout her. Or askin' after her. You ain't nobody to be questioning her."

Ephram was silent and he was starting to get cold. He wanted to find some shelter but he didn't want to leave. Instead, he felt himself leaning into her—this girl—and before the idea could gel, he knew that he wanted to kiss her.

Suddenly Maggie appeared beside them. Her eyes sliced into Ephram as if she could read his thoughts, then she took both of their hands.

"Come on, y'all gone catch your death." They were walking, then running through the wet forest.

"Where we goin'? I'm cold," Ruby whined.

Ephram and Maggie began speaking at the same time.

Ephram: "They's a cave on yonder side—"

Maggie: "Ma Tante expecting us Ruby."

Ephram: "—of Marion, by that clearing."

Ephram watched Ruby savor their attention. The way her head tilted up in something akin to pride. The way she let them wait for just a beat longer, weighing more than their suggestions in the rain. Finally Ruby looked at them and said, "I hate that old clearing. 'Sides, Ma Tante's just around that bend."

Ephram stated, "My daddy say he don't want me goin' over there."

Maggie jumped in, "Well, then, you ain't got to go, do you, Preacher son?"

Ephram said simply, "I'm going."

They all walked, then ran, to Ma Tante's door.

A row of dead trees, chopped and dragged from the forest, fenced Ma Tante's hut. Twigs, moss, mud, cloth and bits of hair had been stirred together and smoothed between each post. The fence door was made of wood and clay. The sky grumbled low as Maggie hauled back her fist and hit the heavy door. It croaked open.

Inside the yard Ruby and Ephram stopped in spite of the torrent. There were mirrors everywhere, glinting and winking, next to open jars collecting wet sky. The entire yard smelled of myrrh. Ephram's heart tightened as he saw small mounds of earth covered with soaked crimson flags. Smoke churned out of the hut's stovepipe as what looked like badger and fox skulls clattered on a clothesline. Spades were jammed into the soft earth and the severed dried wing of a red-tailed hawk stretched across the porch awning. Strange herbs crept up twine and sticks, next to tomato plants with their fuzzy, acrid scent. At the edge of the yard a Gall Oak stood tall, its branches ripe with bottles of colored water, swinging like plump figs. Purple. Green. Red. Black. Blue. Yellow. Tapping against one another.

Maggie pointed to the tree and whispered, "That there's a soul tree. They's souls in them bottles."

"Nuh-uh," Ephram managed.

"Break one and find out."

Ephram hurried on. They were soaked through when they reached the porch. Maggie knocked. The sound was dull and flat in the rain. She knocked again, waited, and then pushed the door open and slipped into the hut.

Maggie spoke from inside of the dark, "Come in. She ain't here."

Ruby shook her head no. "Uh-uh."

Maggie urged, "She won't care none. You just being scared."

"I ain't going in there."

From the black Maggie said, "I won't let nothing happen to you girl."

Ruby shook her head no.

The rain picked up speed and strength. It whipped against Ruby's calves and patent leather shoes. Her white lace socks were soaked through. Ephram's trousers clung to his skin as he slipped his hand over Ruby's. He held her hand as she looked up at him. Before she could smile, Maggie grabbed her by the wrist and yanked her inside. Ephram followed.

They were swallowed in the inky gloom. Maggie patted her

inside pocket and swiftly lit a candle. "I can keep a match dry in a hurricane."

In the sudden light, Ruby gasped and Ephram's mouth fell open like a fish. There were knives everywhere, on every surface and wall. A dagger hung over the fireplace. A leather strapped machete hung against the wall. There were bolo knives and jack-knives, hunting and butcher knives, broadswords and tomahawks, and blades they had never seen before or since. Some shining and clean, others orange with rust, all cramming the insides of Ma Tante's hut.

Ruby spun about to go and almost slipped on the puddle they had made.

Maggie grabbed her arm hard. "Ruby she just keep them blades, she ain't got much cause to use 'em."

At that moment a strong breeze pushed open the front door. It swallowed the flame and knocked the dead candle to the floor. Maggie scrambled for the taper as the wind spun about, lifting the black curtains, letting in peeks of gray only to smother them again. Papers were lifting, rustling, flapping like wings. Then the door banged shut and the room settled against itself. Maggie felt the candle in the darkness, struck a match against a dry floorboard and lit the wick.

All three children screamed as they saw Ma Tante standing above them. She was burnt cork black with yellow eyes, rake thin and tall as God. She glared down at them.

She asked in a thick Creole accent, "Ever heah of *méchant* stew?"

Ephram, Maggie and Ruby remained deathly silent.

"Answer." Her eyes cut into Maggie.

"N-no Ma'am." Maggie answered.

"It is good. Start with onions and salt pork. Twelve carrot. Some potato ... then you slice three naughty children into quarters and throw them in a pot."

The candle began shaking in Maggie's hand, causing shadows to wriggle along the wall of knives. All three children held their breath as Ma Tante, all sharp dark angles stared down upon them. Six watery eyes looked back.

Finally, Ma Tante griped, "Too bad you all too skinny. Be a waste of good potatoes."

"I-I'm sorry Ma Tante—"

"Yes, you one sorry-ass rude child. Gaiwn make that fire so I can have my tea." Maggie went to the kettle as if she lived there and stoked the wood in the stove. Ruby and Ephram stood, their shoes and clothes drunk with the storm, tributaries widening the pool around them. Ma Tante sneered at Maggie, "Dry up and quick. My plancher not no basin." Maggie ran and grabbed well-used flannel towels, tossed them to Ruby and Ephram, then sopped up the water on the floor. They all fearfully patted and blotted as best they could.

Ma Tante lit a corncob pipe, lowering her lids as she puffed. Eyes closed she added. "And tell the *méchants* to sit down. Standing make me nervous."

Ephram and Ruby quickly sat at the table, facing Ma Tante, cold and damp. Maggie lit candles and fed the stove until the room was aglow. As the dark woman smoked, Ephram snuck looks at her. She was so black she was almost blue. He'd heard his father say that she was the Devil's midwife and stitched evil into night's coattails. The Reverend had preached for his congregation to stay away. Still, everyone in Liberty knew about Ma Tante. Her late night visits into the piney woods to forage for animal bones and secret plants. Her trips to the graveyard. Her penchant for pulled baby teeth.

Ephram had heard she was born in a place called Jamaica, but that she had moved with her people to Louisiana when she was five, into a community where every tongue was thick with French Creole. She had left there at twelve to begin her "ministry." No one in Liberty admitted to following her, but Christian or not, folks lived their lives according to a set of rules nobody spoke out loud but everybody understood. Never hanging panties on a clothesline, lest someone steal them for hexing. Be ever watchful for red powder in your shoes or crossing your path. Never borrow or lend salt. Good church women with straying husbands knocked at her gate after prayer circle. Sisters and missionaries came with dollar bills folded in their bra straps. Came with clippings of their fathers' hair, their husbands' fingernails, a placenta from a still-birth folded in newspaper. Came with awe, trepidation and hope. And once there, Ephram had been told, Ma Tante would glare at them with her yellow eyes and smoke her mustard pipe. Those who came without money would be sent away. Still others with money were turned away if they had a bad, what she called, "*odeur spirituelle.*" The rest she kept, inspecting their palms, the soles of their feet and ears. She would look at their tongues and the whites of their eyes. Then she would give them a colored powder, potion or gris-gris. For stirring into coffee, for boiling up with tea leaves, for folding into egg whites with a touch of sugar and molasses, for leaving out at suppertime sprinkled onto a full plate, for hiding under the bottom porch step, for sleeping under a pillow. For dusting the house only to sweep it out again.

Ephram had heard how she had told a man, "If you go home now you be dead in three hours." Sure enough the foolish man got hungry for supper and walked the fifteen minutes it took him to get home. Upon arriving, his wife shot him in the thigh for cheating. It took him exactly two hours and forty-five minutes to bleed to death while his wife mended and pressed his good suit for his upcoming funeral. There were many such stories told throughout the piney woods. Ephram wondered if they were all true. Especially about Ma Tante and the story Gubber had told him about the black bird, and the horrible thing the conjure woman was said to have done.

Ma Tante suddenly opened her eyes. "Don't stahr at me boy. I bite." Then, "Come heah." Her eyes caught him, like a hook through a fish's gills. He wobbled over.

"Your name."

"E-Ephram Jennings."

Ma Tante's eyes gentled. "Ah. Otha's boy."

"Yes'm."

"You got her eyes."

Ephram let his head drop, so Ma Tante picked it back up again, his chin resting in the crook of her hand.

"Hope you ain't got her luck." Ephram wanted to run out of the room, but something in the midnight face held him. She touched the back of his head, her fingernails scraping softly along his neck.

"You ain't nothing but a wishbone. See there!" She touched the base of his skull—tapped at a small bump. "That say you lives on wishes."

She pressed into the nape. "Thing 'bout wishbones? They got to snap in two to give up they wish. And somebody always lose. But still . . ."

Ephram felt his heart quicken as she stared hard into him.

Little dots of perspiration bloomed along his forehead and temple as she twisted her face into his. Then Ma Tante turned away, shook her head, sucked at her teeth and said, "Girl, where my tea?"

Maggie clanged and fussed by the stove. "Almost, Ma'am."

Ephram remained beside Ma Tante.

She suddenly turned upon him almost snarling, "Why you standing there?"

He cleared his throat. "I—thought you wasn't through talkin' Ma'am."

"You got money?" she snapped.

"No'm."

"Well come back when you do. I done give you what you git for free. You pay if you want more."

Ephram stood still. His ears hot with shame.

"You want tea?" Ma Tante asked him.

Ephram shook his head no.

"What you say?"

"No'm."

"Margaret, fix him some. And the girl too."

Ephram slipped back to his seat and tried not to look too hard at anything. Maggie slid a bowl of hot tea across to him. He followed the steam up and spied an entire wall of the hut. Besides the knives it was stocked with shelves upon shelves of mason jars, some filled with small bones, others with brightly colored powders. There were dried frog legs, snake rattles, apple cores, fuzzy rabbits' feet. Many jars were stuffed with herbs and roots. One seemed to be full of children's teeth, a huge glass urn was full of black raven or crow feathers, another with bits of what looked like gristle.

An ember popped in the oven. Ephram let a shiver take hold

of his spine. He knew he had to leave, but how to maneuver Ruby out of this place? Maggie handed him a steaming bowl of tea for the girl. The smell was strong, different than his. He felt a twang of concern as he passed it to Ruby, but was soothed by the sweet of her smile as she took the cup.

RUBY SMILED at the chocolate boy as he handed her the cup. She liked the way he grinned all droopy when she did. She smelled the hot tea. It was as black dark as the old lady. The left side of her dress, closest to the stove, was warming against her skin, but her shoes were squishy. She softly pried them off with her toes. She sipped and saw the boy Ephram frown, and her Maggie give Ma Tante a nervous look. Ruby tried to trace everything with her eyes so she could tell her friend Tanny later on.

Maggie pointed scared-like, "And that there's Ruby Bell, the one I tole you 'bout."

"I see." Ma Tante breathed out a curl of smoke.

Ruby looked first to the left. Then the right. Then settled, like a divining rod, into the woman's face.

Ma Tante hissed at her, "Drink."

Ruby blew across the lake of tea, then took a big sip. It was bitter. Still she took more. When the cup was almost drained Ma Tante reached over, took it and studied its well. Her eyes like coal set in butter.

"You got company." Was what she said.

Ruby felt her breath coming in shallow bursts.

"You was born with a glaze over you face. Come out the womb with the white gel what let you see into the gray world. Yes?"

Ruby just barely nodded in agreement.

Ma Tante reached out and grabbed Ruby's right hand. She

turned over her palm and pointed. "You got da mystic star. There." She took her other hand. "There too. Lord child you ain't nothing but a doorway. How many haints you count at your heels?"

Ruby stopped dead. It was the first time anyone had seen. It meant she couldn't pretend it was a game anymore, or a piece of a bad dream. Finally she answered, "Three."

"Your count be off. And more on the way."

Maggie and Ephram stayed still, but Ruby began trembling from somewhere near her heart.

Ma Tante's voice quivered deep and quiet. "Child, they ride you like a chariot ride a horse." She spit like popping grease into the girl's hand. Ruby felt frozen in place. Ephram pushed his seat back and stood. Maggie stayed strangely quiet.

Ma Tante leaned into Ruby, staring, fingers digging into her wrist. Ruby could smell the old woman's pipe breath as she came close. And something that smelled like rotten meat. "Legba, Legba, *libérez cette enfant de douze mauvais esprits.* Legba, Legba, *libérez cette petite fille, s'il vous plaît.*" Ma Tante drew back her hand and slapped Ruby across the cheek.

Ma Tante explained to no one in particular, "Sometime they need a good exsufflation to make them leave the livin'." She spoke to Ephram and Maggie, "Y'all go outside. I got work to do."

Ruby started crying. With one frightened step, Ephram put himself between Ma Tante and Ruby.

Through her tears Ruby saw Ma Tante look at him as one would a gnat. "This child gots a powerful hex *sur son esprit,* done by peoples who knows how. Make her flypaper for all manner of traveling haint. May already be too late. Now get."

Ruby watched Ephram give way. She couldn't stop crying, her

face slick. Even still, Maggie took Ephram by the hand and led him outside. Leaving her alone with the knives, the pulled teeth and the yellow eyes.

~

M AGGIE AND Ephram stepped onto the damp porch and caught the tail end of the rain. The sky was an ashen pink. Ephram heard Ruby's hollow sobs and put his hand back on the doorknob.

"Where you think you going?" Maggie edged.

"Inside."

Maggie ducked under his arm, leaned against the door and said, "Nah-uh you ain't."

"I is."

"That right?"

Maggie squinted at him, mouth tight. Then never taking her eyes from him, she retrieved a Lucky and lit a dry match against something inside of her pocket. She breathed it in like air, then said, "Try."

They stared at each other. Maggie, coiled tight beneath a lazy smile. Ephram trembling.

He was afraid to push past her, ashamed to sit down, so instead he asked. "Why you bring us here?"

"I didn't bring you."

"Why you bring her?"

"She needed bringing. Now shut your black ass up and go."

Ephram reluctantly released the doorknob. Ruby's sobs were softer now, blending in with the last bit of rain. Ephram left the door, looked towards the gate and instead sat on the damp step, his face burning—a red shame staining the brown of his skin.

Maggie sat beside him. The trees, the fence, the little glass bowls, everything around them was shining and wet. Maggie blew clouds of smoke into the sky.

She picked a bit of tobacco leaf from her tongue, and said softly, "You don't look nothing like him."

In the silence, she answered for him, "Yo daddy, the Reverend Jennings. Walk like him, stink like him, talk like him." Maggie turned to face him, bitter. Then, "You best do like he say and stay way from round here. I ain't 'bout to let no harm come to Ruby . . . not while I'm yet livin'."

EPHRAM FELT a sudden, unspoken fury crackling in his throat like hot grease. Some of it popped, " 'Cept leave some old lady to beat on her."

Maggie cut her eyes against his face, her fists tight in her lap. "Beatin' ain't the worse can happen to a body." The orange tip of her cigarette devoured the white. " 'Sides she ain't no concern of yours. I looks after Ruby."

They both sat in silence. But Ephram answered her behind his eyes. No words just loose thoughts floating like the tea leaves caught in his teeth: *Girls don't look after girls.*

Maggie answered as if he had spoken aloud, "You more girl than I'll ever be and I'm more man than you ever gone grow into." Maggie scanned Ephram from top to toe and let out a guffaw.

He looked at her. The cock of her head, the way she threw her bony shoulders back and puffed her chest out like a rooster. This horrible girl seemed to think she was somebody's boyfriend. Ephram swallowed the thought as another steamed into his temples: *Ain't no way to magnetize when it's the same between the thighs.* It was something he'd heard his daddy say low to Gubber's Uncle Clem. Both men had chuckled into their collars, but neither

Gubber nor Ephram had known what it meant. Now the under-standing made Ephram feel sick.

Maggie sneered. "Now get yourself home for I whoop you into next week Sunday school."

Ephram didn't move his head one inch. He sat still as earth, afraid to swallow his spit.

Maggie let out an angle of smoke. Then, quick as a rattler, she punched Ephram across his jaw. Stunned, he felt her pinkie fin-ger like a stone as it cut into his neck, her ring finger gouging just under the jaw. Blood collected where his molar met the lining of his cheek. He tried to swing with his right but she was on top of him, cigarette pinched between her tight lips. He tumbled down the porch stairs. She sprung after him like a cat. Ephram tried to block his head from Maggie's assault, but she was in high gear. There were no words.

From inside the house they heard Ruby scream. Then Ma Tante's voice booming: "Lâchez! Lâchez!" Maggie stopped for a second, fist midair. She and Ephram turned in the direction of the door. Then Ephram tried to push up to run to the house, as Mag-gie smashed into his nose with a hard left.

She looked straight into the boy's eyes. He was easy to polish. Poke into his right eye, pop against his left ear. Solid like she used on Rooster Rankin. The boy didn't know the first thing about blocking. Skin on wet skin. Smack into his lip. Blood between the crack of her fingers. Mud everywhere. She heard her Ruby cry out again. Her Ruby. Pam! Jab into the boy's nose. More blood. Pam! Same hit again. It sprayed against her lip and cheek. His weakness made her angry, his softness lit a fire under her lungs. The ciga-rette never leaving her lips, she puffed deep and breathed dragon smoke into the wet air. *Pam!* Against the boy's ear. Teeth. The next hit skidded on blood and bent back his nose. *Pam!* Maggie felt something like tears squeezing out of her eyes. *Pam!* She knocked them away with a blow to his chin.

Suddenly, the door of the house shook. Glass tinkled against wood. Ma Tante's words were blades cutting wood and nails and air: *"Relâchez cette enfant ... Maintenant!"*

Right cut. Upper cut. Full on. Maggie would not let herself look towards the door. Not even when she heard whimpering on the other side. He was almost finished, a few more and he would be out cold.

Ephram squinted at Maggie through the blood in his eyes. The world was fists and red and the orange of her cigarette, but somehow, he caught her fist with both hands. Brought it to his mouth and bit hard. He saw her draw in deeper on the cigarette. And then she kicked.

Ephram felt something rise up inside of him. Something brewed and steeped and lining the edges of his soul. It entered his left shoulder then jolted down his arm and shot into Maggie's chest. *Pow!* It landed firm and back she went. Surprised. Cigarette still tight. Orange tip drawing brighter as she hopped back and kicked Ephram in the side. The man boot connecting before the foot inside brought pain. He grabbed her foot and down she fell again. He jumped on top of her, his blood sliding into the narrow part in her lips wetting the cigarette. Maggie flipped him over. They were tumbling into the small mounds of earth, tangling the red flags. Ephram shot off three crunches into her ribs. Only one made a clear connect. Maggie's cigarette broke off, the orange dying in wet dirt.

Inside the house, Ma Tante gathered Ruby in her arms amid the clutter of glass and stone. The child's eyes fluttered white. Ruby tried to speak but a low croak hissed from her mouth. Ma Tante held out a painted knife to an invisible something in the gloom. *"Passez cette enfant! Trouvez un autre cheval à monter!"* Then Ma Tante began speaking in tongues, spit arching from her mouth into the darkness. *"Schoon Netwaye li Tiszta Bersihkan Garbitu Bersihkan . . ."* God's gibberish lifted and filled the room.

Outside Maggie rounded back against Ephram. She held the nap of his hair and hit his jaw with all of her might. Ephram began speaking in tongues. Strange words muttered into the gray world. Maggie paused for a moment. Leaned in. *Pam!* Ephram hit her face. He was on top of her. He crashed into her head. Her neck. The mud. Maggie had rolled away just in time. He heard a hairline snap as his fingers crashed into stone.

Inside, the walls leaned towards the two. *"Rompre le lien! Rompre le lien!"* Ma Tante snarled. Ruby looked up as Ma Tante lifted the knife and brought it down hard, halving a pomegranate on the floor beside them.

Ephram grabbed at his hand, the pain cutting like nails. Maggie was up in a flash, wheeling back her foot then *pop* into Ephram's cheek. Ephram lay still, moon eyes walled, then fluttering, then soft and still. Head tilted into the mud.

The juice dribbled down the part and into Ruby's hair. Ma Tante tore open a glut of seeds and squeezed the fruit until a crown of red streamed down the young girl's face.

Maggie walked back to the porch as the wind brought another blanket of feathery rain. The sky sweetened and thinned as sunlight sprinkled through. She took note of the fact that Ephram was still breathing.

Ruby held the juice against her tongue and the roof of her mouth while the old woman smoothed it into her skin, still clucking words from a fold in the black of time: "*Tumulong potrebno . . . Duboko haja Gu-semerera esivanemad . . . O-negai shimasu. min faDlik Apsaugoti savo . . . en smeken Era berean seo Faoi deara . . .*"

Maggie lit a new cigarette from her porch vantage. Bent but still intact.

"There, there, child . . . there, there . . ." Ma Tante hoisted Ruby upon her lap. Ruby looked into her yolk eyes. "I don' mean no harm."

Outside, Ma Tante's yellow cat found its way from under the house, hopped onto Maggie's thighs and purred into her chest. Maggie petted the cat, blew out smoke and pretended not to shake.

Ma Tante petted Ruby's head. "I try to make it harder fo' them to steal your soul's purse. They's things that happen out in them woods under the blood moon. Nights when a child like you need to stay behind locked doors. But it's too late for that, ain't it!"

Ruby nodded yes.

"They already dragged you out to they pit fire, ain't they?"

Ruby nodded again.

"Already cracked open your spirit like a walnut and try to stuff they rot in there. Dat's why them spirits pester you so. They like openings and you a sieve. You got to know they two kinds of spirits—haints is like leeches, hang on, but can't swallow you whole. Dyboù something different. Ain't content with nothing but snuffing out all you is—smell like a burned out candle when it come.

"I try to suck the poison of the pit fire out. I try. Girl, you got to fly off next time they take you down there. Don't hold fort in your body, surrender it so you can come back when they done. I'm afraid they'll whittle you down to nothing if you keep on fightin' 'em. Won't be nothing left of you." She motioned towards the door. "You tell her?"

Ruby shook her head no.

"Good. Don't. She too stiff a tree to take that weight."

Ruby let her long neck soften and bend. Let her lungs push air out and sat there empty, until nature nudged her to breathe in.

Ma Tante rubbed Ruby's back, lifting only an ounce of the weight in her chest—but it was something. "Lawd, Lawd. Man and magic wasn't never meant to go together. Dey got to rule ovah things. And magic be the ocean say you ride my wave. But when you know man be content to ride nothing 'thout breakin it first?"

She petted Ruby's head. "Child, they's a rainbow of doings in this here world, but man, he only see the black and the white of it. Do good work with his right, and the Devil work with his left. Stay way from that left hand as much as you able." Ma Tante spit into her apron and wiped Ruby's skin clean like a mother cat.

"Me? I am not long here, you see that, yes? I take in too many people sin when I was young and didn't know where to put them down. So my nails and eyes yellow like piss in the sun. Some things you cannot be fix. Some can. Too early to tell how it turn for you." Ma Tante wrapped Ruby in a furry blanket.

She rocked her like a baby against her chest until Ruby had fallen into sleep, then set her gently on the daybed and opened the front door.

Ma Tante looked onto the porch through the screen. "Maggie, help dat boy up and quick."

Maggie rose and walked to where Ephram lay, surrounded by flashing stars. "Get up." Maggie puffed and reached her hand under the crook of his shoulder. Ephram wobbled up, leaning against Maggie. Ma Tante supervised from the porch. The rain had started again. Harder than before. The crows were complaining in the trees as Maggie sat Ephram down on the steps. For Ephram, the world was dizzy with lights and the sound of waves.

"Come in boy." Ma Tante waved him in. "N', Margaret, you best sit out there 'til you can think to act right." Maggie flicked her cigarette into the rain. Got up to leave and turned around.

"I ain't leavin' 'thout Ruby."

"Then I guess you ain't leavin'."

Maggie huffed as Ephram stumbled alongside Ma Tante into the house.

RUBY WOKE up to the smell of cocoa. Her face sticky with dried juice and the old woman's spit, her cheek swollen from where she'd been slapped. Miss Barbara would be mad about that. So would her grandmother. Ruby peeked out from the moldy-smelling daybed. She would fake sleep a little while longer. Ruby couldn't get a proper look at the boy from where she lay but she saw Ma Tante rattling around, her skirt swishing against the floor like a broom. She was fiddling with something on the table— Ruby hoped she wasn't slipping the bones out of a live bird, as Maggie had seen her do, or cutting a hex out of a horny toad. After what she had seen, Ruby didn't doubt a word Maggie had said. Those yellow eyes had seen the thing Ruby hid, even from herself. And when two people see a thing, for better or worse, it becomes real. Ruby felt that knowing smooth over her like tree sap and fill in a little of the ache.

The boy Ephram fidgeted in a chair. The light caught his face and Ruby saw him, eye purple and swollen shut. Two fat lips. Nose busted for sure. Cotton balls stuffed up in it. Hand bandaged. He sat like he'd wet himself in front of class. Shamed like that. *Damn Maggie.*

"Hot chocolate, y'all share," Ruby heard Ma Tante say to Ephram. Ruby could smell the sweet bitter before it reached her and she pretended to wake.

Ma Tante set the cup down on a side table and wiped Ruby clean with a wet towel.

Then she handed the cup over to Ruby and turned to Ephram, "Come on over here, son." Ephram carefully lifted himself onto the far end of the bed and sat there quiet. Ruby caught the tail end of his silence and let it settle across her lap. She sipped the hot cocoa. There was a knock on the door.

"You ain't ready yet," Ma Tante called and Ruby could hear Maggie stomp across the porch and sit hard. Ruby handed the cup to Ephram.

He waited, then took hold of the handle with his good hand. "Thank you."

"Maggie give me this," Ruby said after a pause and pulled a silver thimble from her dress pocket. "From P & K. She got that five finger discount."

"Hmmm."

"She do that for me sometime. Steal me treasure. She ain't always like that, how she were with you. She get jealous is all . . . that, and she ain't too fond of your daddy, the Reverend."

He was quiet in a way that seemed to say that he understood very well how someone might come to dislike his papa.

Ruby took in the wreck of his face up close. Bits where Maggie's knuckles had busted the skin on his cheek wide open. His limp right hand swollen and wrapped like a splint.

Damn.

Ruby felt the lonely before it came. Knew that for all she'd have to face when she left this tiny shack, the lonely would be the worst of it. She knew too that it was the thing each of them shared, only it was waiting for them in different places. For Ruby it was a room at Miss Barbara's. For Maggie it was the minute after Ruby said good-bye. And for Ephram, it was right here, right now. She felt how the lonely never left him, not even sitting beside her.

Her throat squeezed until her lashes got wet. But she never cried, not since moving away. Not since she'd gotten her room at Miss Barbara's. She swallowed it down.

He looked right at her. "I'm fine."

"It hurt?"

"Little bit," he lied.

He handed the chocolate back to Ruby and she slid in close to take it.

"Who look after you?" Ruby asked.

"My sister Celia—who look after you?"

"Mama's up in New York City. She's gonna send for me next month she misses me so bad. But 'til next month and since my grandmama got all that work to do—this White lady up in Neches take me in."

"You working for her?"

"Sometime."

"What you do?"

"Stuff. Pick up after folk. Take care of her other children too. But she sends me to school and such. She gone a lot. Own a couple a' shops in Lufkin and Newton."

"What kind?"

"Miss Barbara Brides."

"Miss Barbara's Bridal Necessities?"

"Think so."

"There is where my mama usta work!"

"Naw! What did she do?"

"Stitching hems and such. And she a lace-maker too. She real good at it."

"Miss Barbara be there?"

"Sometime. Usta be."

"Your mama worked with her! Ain't that something. Was she—nice to work for?"

"Miss Barbara was nice enough, I 'spose. She give me candy sometime. Do she you?"

"Oh yes."

"What she give you?"

"Them gumballs mostly."

"I like those. She mostly give me Tootsie Rolls."

"I like them."

"Yeah, they real good."

They sat quiet for a minute. Then Ruby added, "But, if you see her, don't tell her I said nothing 'bout her. She don't like being in people's mouths. She say it uncouth."

"I won't. Promise."

"Thanks."

MA TANTE walked to the front door and swung it open. "Come on." Maggie walked in like a scolded puppy. She watched Ruby and Ephram lean against each other on the edge of the bed for a moment. She looked to Ma Tante, busy pulling the black drapes from the windows, then slowly sauntered over to the bed, hoisted herself up and tickled Ruby in her side. Ruby laughed.

"What y'all doing?"

"Talking." Ruby said, "He know Miss Barbara. Say his mama usta work for her."

Maggie loosely put her arm around Ruby's shoulder, drawing her away from Ephram in one easy move. "Now ain't that something."

Ephram looked away and saw that the sky had turned a soot black. Ma Tante lit a kerosene lamp and walked over to the three of them and scooted them from the bed like chicks.

"Y'all got to leave. I got me a paying customer comin'." She took the empty cup from Ephram. "Open yo' right hand to the sky." And all three turned their right hands up.

Ma Tante looked down at the three of them. Stupid as dirt before God blowed across it to make up some humans. Dumb as dishwater, light on suds. Three ignorant children with grown up sorrow living inside they eyes. They wasn't worth her time. Didn't know why she'd wasted so precious much of it.

Ma Tante sighed and felt suddenly old. Her whole life a drop of water in a pool. Make a little wave and then fade away to nothing. The eyes were still looking up at her. Palms raised. So she answered them.

"Ain't nobody ever gone answer you cries. You can fill a well with tears, and all you gonna get is drowned. You sit there long enough and the crazy man find you. You weep too long, your heart ache so, the flesh slip off your bones and your soul got to find a new home. You wait on answers 'til the scaredy-cat curl up in your belly and use your liver for a pin cushion. And that's just how you die. Ascared and waiting. And death find your ghost wailing for help. In this life, if someone promise you aid, they a lie. If someone offer they hand, check five time ten to see where they hide the bill. You ain't nobody but alone. And God come to those with the fight to find It. Ain't nothing easy. Not for the likes of you."

The sky groaned outside. The storm was not over. In fact, it had not yet begun.

Useless, Ma Tante thought. To give them the gris-gris she'd made. What difference could it make? Didn't have the juice time would have fed them. She'd made them up quick when she'd smelt the children coming through the rain. Couldn't stop nothing. Still, it was a sin not to paddle your boat, even in a lake of fire.

So, into each hand Ma Tante put a teeny Black doll with red cross eyes. No bigger than a child's pinkie.

"Don't peek," she warned.

The doll with the crow's wishbone stitched to its heart she gave to the boy. The one with a woman's silver ring sewn about its waist she handed to Maggie, and the third—the one with the oval lodestone tied on its back—was for Ruby.

After a beat she pointed to both Ephram and Maggie and said, "You two. Trade. Don't look just trade."

And Maggie gave over her secret and Ephram did the same.

"Me make a mistake sometime. Rare. But sometime."

There was a knock on the door.

Ma Tante hissed, "Get!" as she opened the back door and pushed the three into the night.

The oak, pine and maple trees heard the heavy thud of the witch's door and took note.

They watched three children pause, then, one by one peek into the hole of their palm. The piney woods heard a growling scream, "*I said get!*" Then watched the children bolt out of the yard stumbling. The tall lanky girl jerked ahead. Ruby stayed at the gate with Ephram. He whispered something into her ear, something so soft that even the smallest saplings could not catch. Then she answered, "I already got me a walk home Ephram Jennings and a beau." She turned to go, then spun about and gave the boy a kiss on his left cheek. The old trees watched as she ran away from him and into their arms. The dark boy stood still as the rain washed his scalp clean. He stood staring after the girl for a very long time. Then, with a crack of thunder he jumped and ran through the woods, to the lake, and grabbed a rusting red wagon. It squeaked double time as he ran all the way home. The old forest caught every tinny creak, only to echo them back some thirty years later, to an old house perched on the edge of the great wood, to a man sleeping inside, curled in the sun like a kitten.

⌒

EPHRAM NEARLY leapt from the bed, leaving all thoughts of pain tangled in the covers. Shrugging off sleep and memory he lifted a nearby floorboard and retrieved a small flask for his right stocking garter and a tied white kerchief. He gently placed them in his right pocket. He then laced his waiting shoes and moved with determination into the kitchen. The wall clock read 3:27 P.M. So much time had passed. There he saw the slice of cake Celia had cut with her special wire blade. It had a white cloth napkin draped over it like a flag of surrender. He carefully removed it, lifting it with both hands at the corners, slipped the three-pronged silver fork under the slice and fitted it like the last piece of a great puzzle into the whole.

The afternoon sun reached in through the window and slanted against his hands. He felt his breath quicken. He turned and Celia was there, standing behind him.

"You going somewheres?"

"Yes'm."

"In that shirt? You wrinkled it sleepin'. Take it off and I'll pass the iron over it."

It was a moat he had to leap over. "It'll be fine."

"You sure you ain't feelin' too poorly?"

Tingling began to creep into his left hand. A ring of fire to hurtle through. "I'm quite well." He took the cake and reached for the glass cake cover.

Celia spat, "I'ma need that cover later." She took it out of his hands.

Ephram swept into an open drawer and retrieved a plaid cloth. The sun pulled at his sleeve. "I'm going Mama."

Celia turned quickly and whisked down the hall, tripping and falling into the wall, tilting the Reverend's portrait. "I told you 'bout this cane!" Drawbridge lifting. He would have to jump. "Help me with this here." She held the portrait up.

With the cake perched in one hand he jerked down the hall-way, lifted the framed picture and righted it, then leaned and kissed Celia on the cheek. "Love you, Mama." He unlocked the door with one hand. "What about this here cane? EphRAM!" Drawbridge rising higher. He leapt free onto the front porch, but stumbled on the bottom stair. A pillar of will sent the cake up and out of his right hand. It was falling, flat and hard towards the earth. Time slowed. The yard spun before him. Then he swooped under the falling circle, fell to one knee and caught it in two steady hands. The cake quivered under its cloth but did not crumble. Ephram could have sworn he heard a holy jubilation, a swell of cheers from the passing clouds.

He turned and it was only Celia. Doubled over in the blackened doorway, guffawing into the open air.

He lifted himself and almost ran to the front gate.

"Cain't make it out the yard much less down the road." Her laughter barked and cut through the air like flying bullets as he unfastened the latch and scurried down the road.

"Goin' courting 'n' cain't walk two feet 'thout fallin' flat. Oooooo hoooo! Ooooooooo hooooo! Even crazy gonna throw that fish back. Ooooooooo hooooooo!"

Moving. Steady. Moving away. A slim tear in his pants leg, knee bleeding in slow tender drops. Ephram heard her porch laughter as he walked stiffly down the road. It didn't fade until he had covered nearly a mile in distance, the clay pathway gathering small drops of his blood like bread crumbs.

Chapter 3

Ephram felt the sun warm the back of his neck. It glowed against his dark skin, calling forth a thin sheen of sweat. His breath was slowing some. The faint scent of Johnson's Baby Powder kept him company. Calmed the rocket in his chest.

He sat on a tree stump beside the road and situated the cake on a tuft of grass, tucking the corners of cloth under the plate, a Maginot Line against red ants. It was then he realized he'd left his old hat. Maybe, he thought, it was best to keep the thinking that had been ground into it, right where it was. Ephram took a quick sip from the flask in his pocket—felt the warm liquid burn and smooth the rough of his throat. He opened the kerchief he'd hidden for over thirty years, and saw the same two dusty Black dolls with red cross eyes. One with a silver ring about its waist, the other with a lodestone tied to its back. He tried not to think about how he came to have Ruby's in his possession. He closed his eyes against the why of it and pushed it back into a well in his mind. He then slipped the dolls into his front pocket. Still bleeding, slacks torn, he caught sight of his Timex. Three forty-five. Late. But there were still a good three and a half hours of daylight left. He picked up the cake and began walking southwest towards Ruby. Late. But if he hurried, still time enough to stop by P & K for a bit of iodine and cotton. Maybe a needle and some brown thread.

A few of the Rankin brothers were out working their seventy-two acres when he passed. From this distance, little men in dark coveralls lifted hoes only to let them fall. But up close all seven of the Rankin men towered above six feet. Chauncy Rankin, whom Ephram had secretly envied the whole of his life, was the tallest, boldest and most handsome of all the Rankins. "Six foot fo'," he often bragged over dominoes and cola. Then said, winking, "Then add two mo'."

Supra Rankin, the matriarch, rang the dinner bell. Every man stopped dead still, dropping hoes and bags, and strode like small giants to the Rankin house. Ephram kept walking.

He saw the stretch of road before him. Narrow and red—too small in fact to fit most four-wheel cars. It had been cleared when the town lived on horseback and bootheels. Most folks viewed it as impolite to go barreling down the road. So the people in Liberty traveled by foot, horse, or mule save when supplies were brought in to P & K and a few other locales. The Red Bus to Newton, taking janitors and housekeepers to work, was another exception.

He passed the In-His-Name Holiness Church, Pastor Joshua wielding chalk and board in the front yard. Each Saturday the Pastor wrote some headline of scripture pertaining to God's judgment on the old blackboard and rolled it out to the road, where folks on their way to Bloom's Juke would be sure to stumble upon it and rethink their almost-sin.

In Liberty, Pastor Joshua was one of two men well-known for stammering, but if Paul could withstand a thorn in his flesh, like in Second Corinthians, Pastor Joshua was more than happy to oblige God's will.

The Pastor was dabbing his forehead against the heat as the

cloud of chalk dust settled into his skin. He had almost finished an abbreviated, hard-hitting bit of scripture:

> *Because I have called, and ye refused; I have stretched out my hand, and no man regarded . . . I will mock . . . when distress and anguish cometh upon you. Then shall they call upon me but I will not answer; they shall seek me early, but they shall not find me.* Proverbs 1:24–28.

It was one of Celia's favorites.

Pastor Joshua turned from his work. "Good afternoon Ephram."

"Afternoon Pastor."

"Where you off to with one of Celia's cakes?"

Ephram stared into the Pastor's eyes and, for the first time since he'd known him, uttered a bold-faced lie, "Mo's wife is poorly."

"Her dyspepsia flaring again?"

"I believe so."

"Well, you give Bessie and Mo my best. They haven't had a Sunday off since they started working for them Goldbergs in Burkeville."

Ephram nodded yes lest he give voice to another lie.

The Pastor, reviewing his own handiwork, eulogized, "Sh-sh-shame 'bout old Junie Rankin. Donated more than p-p-plenty to the church fund when he c-come last Easter. He will be missed."

"He surely will." Ephram's heart pinched at the thought while his feet itched to keep walking. He kept his lips pressed tight, lest he inspire one of the Pastor's on-the-God-spot sermons.

Thankfully the Pastor said, "Now you boys come nice and early Monday morning to set up for the funeral."

"I will Pastor. I got the whole of Monday off from the store."

"Good. Good."

"Well good evening to you," Ephram managed as he edged away.

"Good evening." Then he paused a moment, his eyes finally taking Ephram in fully. "You always such a help to this church. Set a fine example."

"Thank you Pastor."

"See you tomorrow son." At that the Pastor patted Ephram's back, chalk dust billowing about and sticking to his warm neck.

Chapter 4

Five steps away from the church Ephram saw the rooftop of Bloom's Juke. It stood just across the road and down the rise, brazenly selling bootleg Saturday night straight through to Sunday morning so that good church folks on their way to service passed the weaving and the drunk on their way to bed. As Liberty had been situated in a dry county since Prohibition, it was desperately in need of Ed Bloom, otherwise known as Liberty's "pocket apothecary." Ephram remembered how Bloom, a tobacco brown bootlegger from Livingston, had come to Liberty after his brother, Shep Bloom, had been run off by the lobster red sheriff from Newton. But only after Shep had cheated the sheriff out of his 50 percent. So Ed had come in his brother's stead, with a renegotiated 60 percent cut in the lawman's favor.

The whole town of men made their way there on Saturday nights. Gathered against stacked lumber and around the pit fire. Inside the one room house, thick with sweat and smoke, men bellowed at the roll of a seven or turn of an ace. Knives lined the backs of trousers and for the men who worked at Grueber's, or in Newton or Jasper, Friday pay bulged inside work shirts or front pants pockets. Nearly once a month, a few of the working girls from Beaumont would ride down with one of Bloom's cousins. A Falcon or a Tuscadero with Beaumont plates would alert the men not to spend all of their money on craps and liquor. Bloom partitioned off what had once been a pantry at the back of the house. He'd tacked up a line of string and draped black fabric over it for a door. Put a small kerosene lamp in the corner of the room, which men turned up or down depending on their mood and their need for visuals. Mostly, the lights stayed down. The "girls" were gristle whores, too old for Fair Street in Beaumont, broken from decades of trade. They were two-dollar prostitutes, five with the tight market in Liberty. But sometimes if a man were particularly drunk, they'd go as high as seven dollars. They knew they could get away with it in Liberty. They also knew about the needle of lust that pierces the heart of small church towns. Where Bible quotations were stitched into the lining of panties. And Jesus plaques stared from the headboard of marital beds.

While the inside of Bloom's main room was loud and light—full of smoke, the sour scent of new alcohol and old sex—outside was for the quiet drinkers. The men who sipped their rye and whiskey under naked branches and whispering stars.

Ephram paused as he recalled last Saturday. He had been resting against the flat tire of Bloom's rusted Buick. He had thrown his hip out while loading groceries into Mrs. Gregory's mint green Skylark. And the pain had started making the usual rounds to his sacrum, coccyx and femur. The clear rye helped. Bourbon was his favorite. But Bloom didn't always have that in, and when he did it was a dollar for one small shot. Ed's home brew was the economical selection. The first sip cleared his nose and watered his eyes. It tingled against the crown of his skull. The second fell deeper, burning hot down his tongue and sizzling against the acid of his belly. The third loosened the girder of his pelvis, let the spring of pain ebb like a pint of peach ice cream in August. By the sixth and seventh he melted against the flat of the wheel. One half a bottle and he could grin at the shades of grass and the lady bugs tucking into the shadows. The crickets whittled in the dark ushering in something akin to peace.

Ephram softened, like corn bread dipped in warm milk, as Gubber, Charlie and Celia's former beau, K.O., stumbled onto the lawn. K.O.'s younger brother Jeb was heaving up his first ten drinks.

"That's the way, boy," K.O. called out. Firm and dark as stone. The only sign of age a crisping of white along his temples. "Got to lay it out before you can play it out." Then to the other two men, "He's seventeen tonight, going to have his first taste when Mabel gets through with Chauncy."

"Best get sick here than in her lap," Charlie scolded, in his thin nasal voice. "Say she ain't comin' back next man do that." He wiped the bald of his scalp, then slapped his narrow thigh to emphasize the point.

Gubber Samuels, a butter cream lump of a man, wall-eyed since birth, turned up his whiskey and smacked when it came down. "Best she don't bring her black ass back nohow. One mo' drop a' ugly in Liberty and we gone have us a flood."

"Mabel's all right. She know her business." K.O. lit a Lucky.

Rooster Rankin, nearly dead drunk beside the well, slurred out, "Sh-she sho d-d-do!"

"But the woman too fat!" Gubber countered. "Lord, ain't seen that many rolls since the Michelin tire man won a pie eatin' contest."

"Aw no," K.O. crossed, "if that's not the pot callin' the kettle. Gubber so fat when he die they'll take him to the River Jordan and jes' set him down."

Charlie answered the call, "And why is that?"

"Hell, ain't nothin' mighty 'nuff to tote his big ass over."

A few good sized chuckles skitted across the yard.

"Well, I ain't got no 'for sale' sign tacked on my behind," Gubber countered.

"Already got a 'all you can eat' one takin' up space."

The men broke into laughter. Rooster hollered so something gave way in his throat and he took to coughing.

K.O. threw Gubber a rope, "But you right 'bout one thing, Gub. Town full a' spinster virgins and old married women. Ain't no bona-fine-in-they-prime women like we usta have."

Mabel appeared in the doorway. She was a chocolate Easter bunny filling out a blue ribbon dress. "Y'all ain't much to look at neither."

K.O. pointed at his brother. "Hey Mabel. He's next."

"Not 'til I have my Lucky. Girl need a break. Gimme one K.O."

He handed it over while Gubber muttered, "You sure ain't a girl no more."

"Wish I could say the same 'bout you Gubber Samuels." And the men roared. Gubber sipped his bottle in silence.

Ole Pete, a white haired man with burnt almond skin, spoke from the shadow, "Too bad y'all ain't ole enough to remember them Bell girls. Lord, they was some pretty women."

Charlie jibed, "Aw Pete, you too ole to 'member what your own mama look like."

Pete cut back, walking towards the pit fire and settling before it, "But not too old to 'member what your mama like."

Charlie mocked anger, "Man, you so old if I told you to act your age you'd be in the grave."

"You know boy, I coulda been your daddy, but the fella in line behind me had correct change."

Charlie feigned rising in protest. K.O. sat him back down. "Hush." Then to Pete, "Naw, I remember them Bell girls. There was three of 'em. I wasn't but a young boy, but I was old enough to know they was some fine women. What was they names?"

Pete looked into the fire. "Girdie was the youngest with them long Indian braids, the redhead was Charlotte, then the eldest Neva."

K.O.'s brother Jeb, a spindly boy all teeth and legs, came to life against the stairs. He wiped his mouth and slurred, "K.O., ain't that crazy gal livin' out at the Bell place they kin?"

Pete replied, "That's Charlotte Bell's daughter Ruby out there."

"She ain't nothing to look at." Jeb shrugged.

K.O. said quiet, "Usta be."

"Well," Jeb tried to focus, "she look like the scarecrow now."

Mabel asked between a slow drag, "Wasn't that them three sisters had that trouble with the law?"

Pete shifted before the fire and shook his head. "Yes, but Neva make out the worst."

Jeb leaned forward. "Who?"

"Neva Bell, Ruby's Auntie."

K.O. started, "Yes, yes I remember. I remember hearing what they done to that child."

Charlie nodded. "It were a sin before God."

Jeb's face squeezed tight with interest. "Well—what *happened* to her?"

Pete shifted in the firelight. And the whole of the front yard seemed to lean into him. As he spoke, the ash on Mabel's cigarette grew.

"TROUBLE COME the year of Mister Bell's bumper cotton harvest. Nineteen and thirty-two. When the crop grew so tall and white, folks said it dusted the heaven. That year Mister Bell bought brass bells up in Jasper and tied them to his chinaberry tree. So that on a windy day at picking time the air was full of ringing and bits of cotton all the way to P & K.

"Now most of them Bells passed for White. Left the South on buses, boats and trains . . . flew up north just like them bits of cotton, but not Mister Bell, who was whiter than milk from a white cow in winter. Folks always speculating if Neva would take that train up north, but they knew just as well that she wouldn't, she loved her daddy so.

"Now, Neva was the kind of pretty make the sun jealous. Not just because she was strawberry blond with her daddy's blue eyes. And it wasn't just her figure, though it looked like God must have been tickled with hisself with that handiwork. It were her smile. Lord help the men in Liberty when that child took a notion to smile. It were a miracle of nature, the apple that come into her cheeks. So we didn't get mad one at the other for loving her cuz there wasn't no escaping it. Still, we keep a distance from her, all Colored folk did, cuz she was different. We watch Neva Bell like we do a star just a-twinkling. Which made it all the harder when Mr. Peter Leech yank her down to earth.

"She'd kept house for them Leeches in Newton two years before when the rains had drowned most of her papa's crop. Mr. Leech were Viceroy of the First National Bank. Folks say he look like Lincoln 'thout the whiskers. His wife, Missus Julie Leech, were a mean scrawny thing with a Adam's apple. One day after

Neva had put they three horse-faced children to bed, Mr. Leech tried to jump her. Neva up and quit the next day.

"Know how some men won't work hard at nothin' 'cept doing wrong? Well that man, who could barely lift his head to say hello to folks, who wouldn't raise a hand to catch it if his soul was driftin' off—somehow got the wherewith to chase Neva Bell up and down that red road in that black Fairlane of his. She say no ever' way she could think of, but yet he chase and chase for months on end. Chase all the Black fellas away. Chase 'way what few friends she had. Chase so she didn't feel safe walkin' with her own sisters. She make them follow a mile behind. He chase her 'til she didn't know where to turn. Chase her 'til that apple left her cheeks. Chase away her hope, and any dreams she might have been kindling 'bout that yella English teacher from Louisville. Mr. Leech chase her 'til she was tired enough to let him catch her, one Sunday after church in a ditch out by Marion Lake.

"Some folk say after time she come to love him. Others say she jes' give in to shame. Me, I don't know much, 'cept that he chased her all the way to lonely. And once you make it there, ain't too many choices left.

"Things was easier for her after that, 'cept folks wouldn't look her straight in the eye. They'd look at her new hat, or her paten' leather shoes. She and her sisters was still invited to the same church socials, husking bees and melon splittings—only when the fiddle come out, didn't nobody ask her to dance 'cept her daddy. He don't never reproach her. Treated her like a princess, like he always done.

"All went long smooth 'til that man up and build her a house in them piney woods. Mr. Leech spent three months raising that place, hired my daddy, who was a sawyer and carpenter, to build it. I helped haul lumber from the mill and seen Mr. Leech there. Hands on his hips, his left foot jest a tappin' 'til the last plank was painted. He fixed that house up with real glass windows, running water, and a icebox to keep his root beers cold, but not one single door lock. Not even a screen hook. Now he ain't got to share her with nobody. Call her Bluebell cuz of her eyes.

"Now, she don't go nowhere. Weddings, barn raisings come and go without Neva Bell. He only let her out once a week for church and her daddy's Sunday supper after, but the rest of the time Mr. Leech have her stay in that little white house.

"Now they up there together most weekends. Smoke just a-churning out that chimney. Him leavin' his wife and chirren ever Friday and not coming back 'til Sunday mornin' in time for service. Sneakin' off middle-week too. His black Fairlane kickin' up clouds a red dust at noon while folk workin' they fields and then kickin' it back up in the opposing direction less than an hour later.

"'Til the day come when he pack up two steamer trunks and land them on Neva's front porch. She'd been out working her little vegetable garden, her sister say, and pushed her spade down in the soil by her radish tops. She look at him and just knew trouble on its way. Say she could taste it in the back of her throat. Seem like a White man can do anythang on earth to a Black woman—rape her, beat her, shame her. But he show her a ounce of respect and all hell break a loose. And that day, he give her just a drop and tell her he leavin' his old life on the side of the road to Liberty. So Neva, in spite of something holdin' its breath in them woods, accepted that little drop. She left that spade planted in the earth and opened her unlocked door.

"Now Missus Julie Leech, who didn't much mind having her

husband out her hair and her bed on weekends, thought another thing altogether when her neighbors seen him putting his trunks in his Fairlane. Then that little Adam's apple took to jumpin' and she call on her family. First she call her mama, Lucy Levy, who tole her husband, Mr. Jeffrey Levy, president of First National Bank, who tole his son, Sheriff George Levy, who called on his sister where she cried into his collar 'bout shame, niggah whores and Black witches, and not bein' able to show her face nowheres.

"I 'member that were late September and all them acres of Bell cotton been picked, baled and levied. Fetched a fair price so that Mister Bell's purse was chock-full for a change. That Saturday— naw, it were a Sunday. I remember 'cause I'd seen Neva in church that morning, with her two sisters. Preacher'd been in fine form, and the sun shine soft on the fields, the road and the faces of folk after church. Especially on Neva Bell. She was wearin' something with little purple flowers. The wind danced with that dress like a beau. She was talking to her sisters, they heads leaning one to the other like does.

"I wasn't but seventeen but I swore God if he let her look my way I wouldn't sin a day in this life. God pitied a liar and she did just that. Turn and smile all big and pretty right into my eyes. Then her sister Charlotte, 'bout seventeen her own self, with them evergreen eyes and pretty red hair, look over too, and the two of them start giggling like young girls do. Then they walk on off. And that's the last I seen of Neva Bell ever on this earth.

"Neva stayed late at her papa's for Sunday supper since Mr. Leech been called to Austin for bank business. She sat round the hearth with her sisters and watched her daddy play 'Clementine' on his fiddle. Afterwards, Papa Bell he say he gone treat his three girls to a soda pop, so he give each a nickel and they take off walkin' to the store. Many a day I wonder how he live without them nickels. The hollow they yet make in his pockets.

"It happened a mile from P & K. When Sheriff Levy on his black quarter horse, come upon them three girls. Him and eleven of his deputies. One, two, six won't do. He need all eleven for the job. That night they hauled the two youngest girls, Charlotte and Girdie, off to the Newton County jail sayin' they got to question them about Claud Jackson's missing cattle. Girdie wasn't but ten.

"That leave Neva alone with the rest. If she thought to run, she musta chose against it. They wasn't no place on earth to go, so she laid her hope on mercy instead.

"Them lawmen drag her out to that hill past Marion Lake. It musta been then they slide on they white hoods. The moon, it was nearly full and bright. From up there Neva musta been able to see her daddy's land. All them fresh-harvested acres. Maybe that's where she fix her eyes while them Klux keep her out there for hours—doin' what God ain't got the muscle to look at.

"Then when they was done, out there on that hilltop, time stretch itself out like molasses. Crickets slow they crik. Owl drag her 'hoo's.' That's when Sheriff Levy click the safety off that Remington Sport rifle of his—the one he brag on so, its barrel catching a piece of moon. Then each every man take his firearm to his shoulder and aim at that child. What they see through them deluxe ta'get sights they think need shootin'? Only Neva Annetta Bell. Eighteen and a half year old. Knees on the dirt. Her hope broke like water round the edges of her skirt. But them the kind use to firing into gentle things.

"Twenty-seven blasts we count by the fallen shells next morning. They shoot her so many times couldn't nobody recognize her. Then they strung her up. Her little body swinging from that choctaw jes over yonder. The front of her flower dress stiff with blood. We find a hood crumple behind them snakewood bushes. Papa Bell cut Neva down before the sun had the nerve to show itself. He carry her all the way to his porch rocker and held her like a five-year-old with a scraped knee.

"All of us knew who done it. Ain't no secrets in Liberty. Not with Colored sweeping every White floor in the county, including the Mason Clubhouse, where Mr. Peter Leech hide himself away that whole night drinking his Wild Turkey. Seem he didn't have no business trip after all, only a long talk in President Levy's office instead, 'bout a White man's responsibility, and how Viceroy jobs be mighty hard to come by. Then how, if he know what's good for him, he best choose to stay put somewheres 'til sunrise. And that's just what he done. Then come morning, he's crying and slipping on his piss, saying how he sorry, how it ain't his fault. Saying, 'My little Bluebell,' 'til he pass out cold on the floor.

"They let the other two girls out the Newton jail that next morning, Girdie's eyes like beets, Charlotte, brassiere in her fist, red clay streaked down her back. Ten miles of shame them girls walk, past White folks' Monday morning and they yellow school bus. When they make it home and see they sister, Girdie hiccup and faint dead-limp. Charlotte scream like ax cutting pine.

"For all of that, all that Devil harvest—that still weren't the worst of it.

"It wasn't 'til Neva made it to the Shephard's Mortuary 'til anyone noticed the empty pool in her chest. Edwin Shephard seen what was missing, but since only White corpses went to county, he packed his secret in sawdust and wax between the girl's cracked ribs. Then he clean and dress her. Since he couldn't do nothing with her face, he closed that coffin up nice and sealed it with them silver nails. Took him five years to tell his mama what he seen, took his mama five minutes to spread the news like bacon grease all round the town.

"Say Klux do that evil to kill Neva's spell over Leech. Me, I don't know what they do in the black of them woods. What they put in they red neck pouches, and why we find all manner of beast with they entrails cut out.

"In God's tightfisted mercy Papa Bell spent eight more years on this earth. He lived long enough to see Leech drink 'til he drown face deep in a mud puddle and for Sheriff Levy to fall off his quarter horse, and break his neck in a dry well.

"Mister Bell stared up at that choctaw 'til he was a five point star withering on his bed. When they close his eyes they last, folks say he yet looking at that tree."

THE YARD seemed to hold its breath. Ephram's head had grown clear leaning against the flat of the tire, turned towards the story and the teller. Mabel held her burned out filter between curled fingers. She hadn't taken a single puff.

K.O. paused and turned to Pete. "Mr. Jeffrey, I got to thank you for tending to that telling." Pete nodded back and gently kicked a bit of dust into the fire. He hadn't been called by his proper name in nearly fifteen years.

Jeb broke the spell with, "So that crazy gal up there got Charlotte Bell for a mama?"

"And a jailhouse for a daddy." Old Pete let out a weary breath, "Charlotte had her baby girl Ruby in June that next year. They say she willed that baby brown. Eatin' coffee grounds, chocolate cake, even brown eggs from a black hen. Wouldn't eat nothing white while she was with child. Sure enough, out come that gold-brown baby girl, Ruby. Prettiest child in Liberty. Even jealous mamas had to admit that. Still Charlotte up and run off to New York City when Ruby wasn't yet a year, like she chased by the Devil—ain't been seen alive nor dead since."

Gubber scowled. "Always say that Ruby better off locked up at Dearing."

K.O. cut Gubber with, "They all kinds of crazy. Some folk drink theyselves to stupid. Others so empty, gluttony take they belly hostage. And some get so full up with hate, it like to crack they soul. Hell, ain't nothing strange when Colored go crazy. Strange is when we don't."

Then K.O. ushered Jeb up with his words. "Go on boy. Mabel ain't got all night to waste." Mabel stooped just a bit, then straightened her shoulders, spit and said, "Come on little big man." Jeb wobbled up to the porch and followed Mabel into the house. The door swung open, letting sound and smoke into the night air.

The porch was quiet for a while, each man climbing out of the well of memory. As they did they touched upon stones—recollections of other lynchings—family and friends slain in open fields, dragged on the backs of cars, swinging from a low branch. Ephram's mind caught on his father dying alone in the piney woods.

The men outside of Bloom's had drunk from that well plenty—knew it was a dangerous place where water could suddenly rise from all sides. A man could drown like that.

Rooster pushed back his thoughts with, "Hear they n-n-never could cl-cl-clean that blood stain off the floor."

Charlie added, "I hear ain't nothing but haints on Bell land."

Gubber coughed up a wet laugh. "Hell, only thang livin' in that house is one butt-ugly, crazy-assed heifer."

Pete rose and retreated into the wall of shadow. He stopped and looked at Ephram. The two men shared a gaze.

"Rumor say them White folk up in Neches who take Ruby in wasn't right," Charlie sent back, "that lady draggin' her around like she own her."

K.O. shook his head. "Why anyone hand over they child to slave for White folk is beyond me."

"Plenty folk done had trouble," Gubber spit, "don't mean they got to walk around with no man's pants on they knucklehead. We just sitting round playing dominoes and here she come wearing them soiled pants—then just walked blind into that ditch."

Charlie snorted. "Folks was laying bets on whose pants they were."

Rooster jumped in, "W-well we kn-kn-kn-know they wasn't G-g-gubber's, 'less she got a head the size a' barn door."

Gubber took aim. "Watch out Rooster, or I'll find some little girl to whoop yo' ass." A direct hit.

Rooster's hand reflexively touched upon the scar a nine-year-old Maggie had torn across his cheek.

Gubber rallied, "I come up on her whiles she was butt naked, wrapped around one a' them mother pines."

Charlie's mouth flew open. "Ain't so!"

"My mama seen her humping rocks on the ground." Gubber kept on, "Cleary seen her grinding herself into the clay road. She just throw that used toothpick she call a body at anything happen by livin' or not."

Rooster found his voice, "And wh-what she be buryin' out th-there every n-n-night!"

Charlie added, "And all that screaming and hollering. Something got to make her do that."

"M-my m-mama always say it's some evil th-thang living inside of her."

"That ain't all she wants up inside of her, you catch my meaning." Gubber smacked out a grin.

K.O. lifted himself from the stairs. "Even that stump catch yo' meanin' Gubber." He spoke to an unseen ally. "Lord please do something 'bout these ignorant Negroes!" Then to the men behind him, "I need me a drink."

Charlie and Gubber reluctantly rose and followed him into the house. Ole Pete looked after them, then back at Ephram and the rest of the men hidden in shadow. Then walked onto the red road into a bath of moonlight.

THE CLOTH trembled against the cake in Ephram's hand. The hot wind pressing it close. Ephram turned back and saw the steam from Bloom's mash rising just over the low trees. He shook his leg and felt the cool flask between sock and skin. He took it from its hiding place. Not much left. Enough for a quick shot of courage before knocking on her door, but no more.

He looked down the long road in front of him and thought of Ruby at the end of it. Each step he took was a question. How would she answer? Would she laugh at him as Celia had done? Would she slam the door? Would she kiss him? Raise her skirt for him? Would she remember Ma Tante and Marion Lake when he showed her the little dolls? Ephram felt a root of fear spike into his belly so he unscrewed the flask's cap and took another sip.

He turned quickly, flask slipped back into his sock. Bloom's wasn't far. Just a few shaded yards away now through the trees. A sudden thirst caught hold as he crossed into the open yard.

"What chu' doin' there boy?" Ephram looked over and saw Bloom and Sheriff Levy, Junior, Sheriff Levy's only son, standing just to his left. Folks called him Sheriff Junior, though he was well past fifty. Ruddy faced with a beefy build, his mustard hair spread thick across his forehead.

"Sheriff Junior, you 'member Ephram Jennings. Live with his mama just up the way. Work up there as bag boy at the Newton Piggly Wiggly."

He stared blankly at Ephram. "Sure do." Then, "You ain't spying are you?"

"No, Sir."

"Stealing?"

"No."

"Well you didn't come over this way for spirits did you? Newton's a dry county and jail's the place for drinking men round here."

"No, Sir."

"Well that's good." He stared at Ephram for a long moment. "Can't be too careful." His mouth smiled, slow and steady, but his eyes stayed fast on Ephram.

Ephram noticed Sheriff Junior's patrol car hidden behind the back of Bloom's Juke.

"What kind you got there?" The Sheriff nodded towards the cake.

"Angel food. I'm—taking it to a sick friend."

"Can't be too sick if they eating cake." He laughed at his joke. Bloom joined in.

"Don't suppose you could spare a slice for a working man. Y'all got me so busy I plain missed my dinner."

Ephram paused. He tried to imagine handing Ruby a half-eaten cake, then imagined saying no to this Sheriff Junior. The moment yawned uncomfortably.

A sudden clank to Ephram's left. The Sheriff wheeled in that direction and pulled the forty-five from his holster. A large crow lifted in flight from Bloom's trash can, perched in a nearby tree and cawed. The Sheriff laughed nervously, gun in hand. He looked at Ephram again.

"Can't be too careful now 'days."

"Yes, Sir."

"Later, Bloom."

"Thanks fo' stoppin' by."

The Sheriff walked to his car with the gun loose in his hand, got in and rolled away. When he had cleared the distance of vision, Bloom walked swiftly to Ephram, finger poking hard into his chest. "What is *wrong* with you!"

Ephram stepped back holding tight to his cake.

"What I tell y'all 'bout comin' here daytime Saturday?" Bloom turned back towards his house. "Y'all gone git me and your own stupid ass kilt over this shit! Man lets me be. Just don't want nobody foolin' with his business." He paced, raising dust. "Then wouldn't give him a piece of cake! Get away from here Ephram Jennings and you best stay 'way fo' a month."

Ephram stood as if punched, then turned and walked swiftly to the road. He was breathing quickly. A sticky musk stained the underarms of his shirt. His shoes were dusty, his pants torn. How could he face her now? He felt the tug to turn back but fought against it. He looked at his Timex. Ten after four. He was losing the day. But, he figured, he could still stop at P & K, stitch his pants and reach Ruby's before nightfall if he was careful. And Ephram Jennings was a careful man. He was careful of the cloud of sweetness he carried on Celia's fine plate, careful not to let the August breeze blow dirt under the cloth. Careful not to hope.

Suddenly, a cool sludge plopped onto the dome of his scalp. It dribbled mulberry and white down his temple, his cheek and onto his clean collar. Ephram looked up and saw what appeared to be the same black bird from Bloom's making lazy circles in the air above him. As he retrieved his handkerchief to wipe the bird's waste from his face and neck, the bird began to fly south over the Samuels farm. Ephram watched as it veered west towards Bell land.

Chapter 5

The crow caught a cross current and gained altitude as the man grew small and then vanished behind a rise in the earth. She tilted with the curve of the horizon. The sun warmed her hollow bones, her blackest feathers holding its heat. She flew over thatches of land, gold, green, brown, following the red river road until she reached the town square. Far below she saw a knot of men crowded onto the store's steps, the women fanning their faces and looking on, headscarves tied. A woman chasing three boys off with a broom. She saw the different roofs, black tar, shingled, wood. She flew on. More farms. Wide, wild pines spearing the clouds. Pockets of green. Bony fences leaning into the road or boxing in pigs, chickens, cows. A woman in white hanging white sheets out to dry. A berry cobbler set out to cool. A red melon split on an outdoor table, children gathering around it like flies. The crow saw two men plodding home, carrying empty pails. Smoke from the mill in the distance. She flew past Marion Lake and the tangle of woods beneath, a wealth of beetles, grasshoppers and other legged insects, until she finally reached Bell land. The dried grass and empty hard field. Figs and apricots wormy on the earth. Gravestones littering the hillside. The house with holes poked through the roof. Rain and sun cutting them larger each day until now the foot of the girl's bed was in view. She was asleep on her belly, her black soles facing the sky. The crow landed outside of her window, feathers light with ruffled wind. She spread her wings and cawed.

Inside the old house Ruby was sleeping, which was rare. Ruby did not sleep—much. For her mind tangled like a fine gold chain, knotted, she was certain, beyond all repair. Still she tried each day to trace the links, only to lose them again and again.

Ruby had lost much more than that. She had lost the 562 dollars she had brought to Liberty, tucked inside the change pocket of her Etienne Aigner purse. A week later, the purse had gone missing. Then, inexplicably, four pairs of capri pants, six madras blouses, three shirtwaist dresses. Most of her shoes, including her favorite pair of Beth Levine red stiletto pumps. Her hot comb, her Royal Crown hair oil, her lipstick, makeup bag, and the suitcases they had all come in.

She began losing time as well. It folded in on itself so that hours passed in minutes, weeks in days. She would start walking, eyes on the road, and suddenly find herself eight miles away, outside of Newton; or in a ditch; or once, chin high in Marion Lake, water filling her mouth, coughing, rasping.

Sometimes Ruby would wake on the forest floor—her clothes hiked above her waist, the sour milk scent of a man on her thighs. Her ribs aching with each inhalation, plum bruises on her face. The burning scrapes on her back made her cry out when she tried to stand. Still she would lift herself, smooth her dress and walk back to her Granddaddy's land.

She lost the rising curve of her shape. Already thin, she wasted to a sliver, her clavicles like handrails. The plump in her calves and thighs disappeared. Her breasts drew close to her chest. Her wrists withered to blades of grass, bones knobby and hard under her skin.

Impervious to her monthly blood as it dried in fresh smears down her legs, until the loss of weight caused her womb to stop its monthly orbit.

More than all of this, Ruby had lost her train ticket home to Manhattan. She had lost New York.

She remembered wearing black stockings clipped into place, red lipstick and hair hot-combed and slick. The parties and whispers in her ear about so-and-so and what he painted, what he wrote, who he slept with and the heady rush of the drinking, clinking crowd.

She'd remember the telegram from Maggie, pulling her trump card and calling Ruby home.

Ruby remembered the crush of a dark Manhattan penthouse loft, flooded with women in black tights and false lashes, a few Chanels and Ceil Chapmans in the crowd like lights on a Christmas tree. The men in skinny slacks and ties, or leather jackets with pony caps. The room was filled with a gray cloud of smoke where people appeared then floated away. There were the magnet men who walked with headlines fluttering over their heads, who carried a circle of human bodies, tight to their arms, their voices. Who waited with ready laughter and deference. Then there were the falling men, who had slumped out of the limelight, who sat with a glass resting on their crotch, a stringy female threaded through their arms and Ruby gliding through it all. One of four brown faces who were not famous—each a footnote in the Bohemian Guide to Entertaining.

That she looked like Dorothy Dandridge was the compliment

most often paid her. Makeup like Sophia Loren, heels adding two and a half to her five eight so that she looked down when she was introduced to the poet Gregory Corso and the painter Robert Motherwell. Quite far when she spoke briefly to James Baldwin—about Texas and little Liberty and the victory of Brown over Topeka's Board of Education. He told her she was beautiful in that pure way that only gay men can, and peeled generously away only when the hostess, Mrs. Gladdington, called for him.

And for a moment after, she had become a magnet, as if mere proximity had gifted her with the power of attraction, and a circle had orbited her, until they realized she was not an author, a famous man's girlfriend or a singer—only a pretty Negro girl who worked for the hostess, and all had drifted away. Still from across the room, she caught a supportive, conspiratorial wink from James Baldwin and felt, for a moment, seen and known by sparkling brilliance.

In a second she was back in Liberty. Ruby looked down at the browning mattress and could feel his crinkled grin fading. Her dresser mirror in Manhattan, her bras, panties, stockings, cigarettes, the bottle of Chanel 19, her English-French dictionary, for the trip she was to have taken with Mrs. Gladdington. Gone.

But for all that Ruby had lost, there were many things she had found.

A rising growl that rumbled out of her belly. Drool that wetted her lips and slid down the angle of her jaw. A jerking, rhythmic contortion of her face. Because these often happened without her permission and in view of the town, Ruby found what it was to no longer be seen as human.

She discovered that she could hammer her pride so wafer thin that she could accept alms like a beggar.

Then, one late afternoon, Ruby found a new pitted terror, as she sat on her bed watching dust swim in the light. She heard the slow creak of the screen door, a flutter of sparrows outside. She listened as a cup of water on the kitchen table turned over, and a thin cascading splash, like a man urinating, poured onto the floor. Ruby waited—it would not be the first time someone had come unannounced. But instead of a man, she saw a weighted, umber thickness slide into the room.

It shifted, moving along the floorboards. It darkened the corners, adding mass to the shadows. Ruby whispered, softly to herself, that there was nothing there, just the coming evening. Still her skin tingled hot, her mouth dry as it crossed the space between them and pressed against her, flattening her dress against her chest, her legs.

Ruby did not know why she sat on the bed, then lay down, but the old curtains ruffled towards the window frame, not away. Then something fell upon her chest. The scent of a dead candle filled her, making it hard to breathe. When the mattress sank deeper, Ruby thought to scream, but whatever lay upon her whispered the creaks and groans of the house into her ear, it smoothed and relaxed her until she felt a soft pressure upon her groin. To her fogged surprise, her body responded, a swelling excitement that ebbed through her thin frame. Ruby felt compelled to turn onto her stomach and push her pelvis into a mattress spring just under the padding. The bed seemed to roll under her, its legs grating, rubbing on the floor. Ruby knew this was a Dyboù— what Ma Tante had spoken of so long ago. A heat pulsed around her, then entered her. The house seemed to shake.

She spoke, but it was not Ruby speaking. In a low graveled voice she grunted, *"Bitch,"* hot air escaping her lips, *"Whore."*

She ground harder, faster, with mechanical precision until, in the building heat, an explosion roared through her. Her scream filled the room, the house suddenly still. Her sex spilled, chest empty, Ruby had fallen into sleep.

The Dyboù had come the next night, shifting the pillars of her grandfather's home, entering her pores, her follicles, until it moved like oil under her skin. Soaking, filling every second of her heartbeat, each rise of her breath, night after night until she felt that she became what he called her. Slapping at her own buttocks, grabbing handfuls of her hair and smashing her face into the bed. In this way, Ruby found the Dyboù. In this way, Ruby learned to rape her body each night.

She was exhausted and drained when she found it—heard the sound of a child crying, faint, like wind through the tall pines. It was not the cry of a living child, Ruby knew that much. She had seen and heard the ghosts of children before. She followed the sound, and found a cloud of a girl weeping in Marion Lake. She was clear as glass, cinnamon brown, and no more than seven. She rippled the water with each sob. When she saw Ruby looking at her, relief loosened her shoulders.

She flowed towards Ruby until she was inches away. They locked eyes and Ruby felt, knew that the girl had not merely drowned in that lake—someone had held her under. Ruby put her arms around her, but because she could not hold air, the child walked inside of her body, curled there and settled into her womb. Ruby held her belly and rocked. She hummed and said softly that everything would be all right now, and the girl let out a little burp and fell asleep.

Ruby knew something about ghost children. Along with the hundreds of ghosts, they too had passed through her body. Seven had even taken up residence, but had been scared and wily enough to hide inside of her marrow. This new child was not so lucky.

That night, when the Dyboù slid into Ruby's bedroom, it stopped at the door. It seemed to grow larger. The air became electric. Spider cracks spread across the panes. Instead of reaching for Ruby, the Dyboù lifted above her, the whole of the ceiling in shadow, then it dropped down upon the new spirit sleeping within her.

In seconds the girl was gone, inside the creature, screaming, terror flashing in her clear eyes, small arms reaching for Ruby, as the Dyboù slithered across the floor. It paused and turned as if it suddenly sensed the other spirits Ruby had hidden deep inside her years ago. Ruby shouted out and quickly it turned away and was out the door. Ruby followed, ran outside into the black. The trees were hollow, the shadows between them empty. She did not know what to scream. She did not even have a name. So she shrieked, howled into the woods—wailing like a distant train.

Then, from the big thicket, the spirit of another child appeared, a boy, about twelve, with a noose about his neck. Then another, a little tan girl, hands bound. Then another. And another. One with blood soaked through her clothes. One child, naked, eyes red. More came, walking slowly across the earth towards her, with stories of their deaths hanging just above their heads. Ruby remembered a word she had heard Maggie's mother say once— "tarrens," the spirits of murdered children. Tarrens. All of the children who had been killed in those woods. They were speeding towards her. Their faces washed in horror. They were running from the creature between the pines. At first she was scared. Then she heard them, a hundred little whispers, each voice a thread, weaving such a sorrowful blanket.

So she waited on the porch. Then, one by one they slipped into her body for protection. One by one she let them in.

Ruby walked into the house and sat with her back against the wall in the kitchen, her eyes on the front door, her empty stomach grinding, heart banging beneath her ribs. She felt the Dyboù in the ink of the pines. Watching, shifting the branches. Ruby waited. She waited with nothing but her hands and her fear to save them—but if he came, she would try. Sweat dripped down her neck and collected in the hollow at the base of her throat. It streamed down her sternum. As morning broke, Ruby knew, like a nail rusted in her sternum, that sooner or later, he would come again and try to take them.

Mixed in the cacophony of all she had lost, and all she had found, Ruby stumbled into a merciful sleep.

That night the old crow perched just above her on the rooftop. She would stay and watch over her until dawn.

Chapter 6

Ephram walked quickly into the heart of town. Four-forty. Time slipping. He saw the congregation of men at P & K, laughing, frowning, faces ripe with sweat. They loomed ahead on the porch. He'd hoped to miss their evening game but the day had grown old on him.

Verde May Rankin, Chauncy's younger sister, was picking out dried goods and discussing the latest *Ebony* with Miss P. Ephram faded into the spice shelf and waited, his hand keeping a soft, anxious beat. Verde May, the unfortunate recipient of the Rankin males' bulk and height, leaned into Miss P and paused just above Billy Dee Williams and the "Pretty Black Men" article he was featured in.

"If he was a grapefruit, I would squeeze him dry."

Miss P chuckled. "Girl, you greedy, I be set with one little drop."

Both women shared a laugh.

Leaning against bottles of cayenne and cinnamon, Ephram remembered the day Ruby had arrived back in Liberty. Eleven years ago, in August of 1963, hundreds of thousands of Negroes had marched in Washington, D.C., exactly two days before Ruby showed up at P & K. Ruby had bucked the tide and made her way behind enemy lines. Ephram had seen her standing in the exact same spot Verde May stood today. She'd worn city shoes with straps and height, carried four sleek pink bags. Thick black lines framed her questioning eyes, a nervous smile on her red lips. Her hair was pressed straighter than some White folks' and twisted up high on her head. It was the first time Ephram had seen Ruby properly since they drank hot cocoa at Ma Tante's.

Before that, Ephram had spotted Ruby twice from a distance. At thirteen he'd seen her one Sunday through the church window. He'd wanted to bolt up and call out to her, but Celia had shot him a look that kept him nailed to his pew. He'd had to wait five years to see Ruby again. She'd been with Maggie at sunset. He was nearly a stone's throw from them on the road. Maggie in men's coveralls, Ruby pretty in white lace. They were arm and arm. He'd watched Ruby once again tiptoe and press her forehead against Maggie's chin on the quiet road, just as he had seen her do at Marion Lake so many years ago. They stayed that way for a beat, then two. It was a soft simple thing that felt like a paw resting on his heart. Then they'd turned and walked towards Bell land.

That August of '63 in P & K, Ephram had seen the girl he'd known right away. Everyone knew her, but were taken aback by the thick of her perfume and the clip of her speech. Ephram heard Miss P say later that Ruby sounded like a radio broadcaster. It seemed to Ephram that in the thirteen years she'd been gone, she'd ironed Liberty right out of her voice.

There'd been a crowd on the porch peeking in, men and women, a row of children hiding behind the pickles and candy. It wasn't until Ruby asked about Maggie that she softened like cotton candy. It was then the porch seemed to see her as Charlotte Bell's daughter, Papa Bell's grandbaby. In that open door, Ephram watched as Miss P went to give the girl a hug. Ruby bristled and inched back, shaming the older woman into converting her gesture into straightening Tabasco bottles on a nearby shelf.

Then Ruby spoke slowly, as if addressing a group of first graders. She asked if someone could carry her to *her* land. Not Papa Bell's, not her dead grandmama's, but hers. It looked as if folks took note of that right away. She said she'd be willing to pay twenty dollars for the courtesy. Before anyone could answer, she purchased Clorox, a mop, a broom and a stack of dishcloths as if someone giving her a ride had already been decided. And although each and every person within earshot looked offended, she was right. Twenty dollars was twenty dollars. Charlie Wilkins volunteered.

Ephram had been getting Celia a Sunday paper when he heard her. Saw her. Saw the circles of sweat under the blue of her sundress as he came close to lay the dime and nickel down on the counter. He was careful not to brush her as he swept silently from the store.

She tried to tip Percy Rankin two dollars for gallantly carrying her bags to Charlie's car and opening the door for her, without an inkling that she was insulting both the family and the man. Then she drove away, leaving a cloud of disdain behind her like an unpleasant scent.

Ephram had seen all of this and did not know why he'd felt pierced through with a crushing sorrow. He had kept to himself the rest of that day. He forgot to wish Celia a pleasant sleep. He did not brush his teeth or put on fresh pajamas. He lay in his thin bed, fully clothed, staring into the night. He did not fall asleep until dawn.

"WHAT YOU need today, Ephram?" Miss P asked him warmly. At sixty-nine, everything on her was round and smooth, her eyes, cheeks and jaw. Her fluffy white hair rounded to a bun in back. Her neck rolled into her full breasts, which gave way to even fuller hips and thighs. She always reminded Ephram of bread fresh out of the oven.

"Didn't see you there. Me and Verde discussin' serious business here." She winked at Ephram.

Verde May had retrieved her copy of *Ebony* and was leaning over Billy Dee, who smiled up at her from the counter. She ignored Ephram completely.

"So what you need?"

"Bit of iodine and cotton, brown thread and a needle, please Miss P."

"Give me a minute, baby." She disappeared into the back as Chauncy strode into the store, opened the glass cooler and retrieved a Pepsi-Cola. He studied his sister, Verde May, as he opened the bottle against the counter.

"Look like the canary drooling after the cat."

Verde answered without looking up, "Look like yo' fly is open."

Chauncy quickly zipped up and slumped out to the porch.

Miss P reappeared with his items. She punched them into her ancient register.

"That'll be four ninety-five, Ephram."

Ephram glanced at his wristwatch, minutes melting, disappearing. He edged around Verde May to get to the counter. It was awkward with the cake. She shifted in an angry huff. He reached into his pocket and realized he'd left his wallet sitting on the corner of his dresser.

"Er-uh. Forgive me Miss P. I gone and left my wallet on my dresser. I'll get them things tomorrow."

"I wouldn't hear it. You pay me tomorrow after church. Look like we getting a new Church Mother." She winked at Ephram and smiled.

Verde cut her eyes at Ephram, put her money on the counter. "I'm gone take me a Crush out the cooler." At that she rolled Billy Dee and all the other Pretty Black Men under her arm, grabbed a soda and sauntered out of the store and down the street.

Miss P smiled and her voice dropped low, "Verde's just mad cuz she wants her mama to win instead of yours. Supra Rankin ain't got a chance. Celia as good as Church Mother already."

"Thank you for saying so, Miss P."

"No thanks needed, it's us need to thank her for all she do round here with her Sanctified Saids, her ministering to them drunks down at Bloom's and sprinkling holy water over pit fire ashes fools been burning in them woods. Don't know what we'd do without her." Then Miss P looked at Ephram and then at the cake resting in his right hand. "Where she sending you this late with one a' her cakes?"

"Mo Perty's wife sick again."

"Lord that dyspepsia can be a burden."

"Yes it can Miss P. Thank you kindly."

He crossed the doorway onto the porch of men and took care to edge past them. The game over, they were mid-conversation.

Ephram had successfully made his way to the bottom stair when there was a loud creak. All eyes on the porch turned to him.

"Hey Ephram," Gubber called out, "where you going with that cake?"

"Mo Perty's wife is sick."

Moss Renfolk spoke out, "Naw she ain't. I seen her take the Red Bus into Newton this morning."

Gubber laughed. "Then you going nowhere but Hades fo' lying. Bring your black ass up here so I can get a nose full."

Such was the holy adulation of Celia's cakes that the whole of the porch waited, so Ephram reluctantly walked up a few steps and lifted the cloth.

"Damn that shit smell good!" Gubber let out a wolf whistle. "How 'bout a little taste," he half teased, half asked.

Ephram quickly covered the cake.

Chauncy instigated, "Ephram, put up yo' dukes. I believe Gubber 'bout to tackle you for that confection." Then, "What she making fo' my Uncle Junie's repast day after tomorrow?"

"One angel cake, two sweet potato pies and some of her fig preserves."

"That's why you and me gone be friends fo' life Ephram Jennings."

Charlie grinned. "I'm damn happy when I take ill, cuz I know Celia Jennings soon come knocking."

Gubber said wistfully, "Woman can cook like a mule can piss."

Ephram eyed the open forest and began his escape.

Percy tensed with unspent gossip. "Speaking of piss, did y'all hear what that Bell gal done yesterday?" He had their attention. "Sat up in the middle of the road and peed all over herself. Like all that midnight hooping and hollerin' wasn't enough."

Gubber sneered. "Somebody need to put her out her misery."

Chauncy leaned back in his chair. "I wouldn't be so quick. Just cuz a toad got warts don't mean he ain't taste good when you fry him up."

Ephram watched Moss draw the door to the store closed. He always did this when the talk turned unchristian.

Gubber spat back, "I don't eat no toads."

Percy nudged Gubber, winked at his brother. "Maybe you should start. Somebody tell me they got nice, long tongues and knows just how to use them."

Moss shook his head. "I ain't never heard such."

"Mouths too . . ." Percy put a stamp on it.

Chauncy added the postscript, "A man ain't no better than a fly, so what he gone do if a juicy frog come along and beg to lash him with her tongue? The Devil hisself wanna do that I'd be hard-pressed to say no."

Moss shot out, "No suh! That happen, sho' nuff?"

"May God strike me."

Moss fell into wonderment—like he'd just watched his dog sit up and moo.

Percy added, "Just last Thursday night. I know cuz I was there."

Moss mouthed, "Lawd-a-mercy."

Ephram couldn't move. He felt his legs growing into the rail on the step. His feet were the planks, nailed tight to the beams. He couldn't walk away now, not if God had ordered him to. He stood on the stairs like solid wood until Gubber handed him a proposition.

"Play me a game."

Ephram felt the wood in his legs tingle and walk up the stairs. A familiar dull ache began just above his knee. There was nowhere else to walk. No road to follow. No door to be knocked on and opened. Once he was sitting Gubber added, "Put yo' money down. Fifty cent a game."

Ephram felt his lips moving. "I ain't got no money on me, Gub."

The two had been fast friends at thirteen, but the memory of that had long since faded into the wallpaper. Now they grunted at one another if they happened to pass on the street.

"Then play me fo' that cake."

Percy interjected, "Cake worth more than two bits."

Moss added, "I seen it go for as high as seven dollars at the Juneteenth auction."

Gubber relented. "Hell, I'll give you five whole dollars if you win, which you ain't 'bout to do." Suddenly Ephram wanted to be rid of the cake. Wanted it stuffed between Gubber's large teeth, so he nodded yes and the porch leaned in to watch. Moss eased the store door open again and Miss P peeked out of the screen, ever grateful for Moss's timely gallantry. It was almost closing time, but she would let the boys finish their dominoes.

The "cake game" lived in the mouths of men until suppertime. It wasn't an event of great consequence, but it was something. Gubber Samuels had lain down the gauntlet and Ephram Jennings had picked it up. They'd had Moss hold the cake while the two men played. Gubber won the draw. They'd chosen their seven bones and quick as lightning Gubber slapped down a double six. Ephram hadn't one single six and that fast had to *knock*. Gubber put down a blank/six combo. Again Ephram had to pass. So Gubber had started talking dirt about Ephram's luck and added something about his flat feet. At one point Gubber was down to four bones before Ephram laid a single tile. Everyone talked about how steady and solemn Ephram had played Gubber, how even when they were down to one tile each, Ephram hadn't once looked up from the game. When he laid out that four/two and Gubber had to admit that he was beat, Gubber got so mad that he messed up his cussing. "Fucker-mother, bitches of sons." Until the whole porch laughed. In the end after Ephram won, folks talked about how he walked from the porch in a kind of daze.

How Gubber Samuels had followed after him and whispered something that made Ephram yank away, cake teetering, then stomp down the road. How Gubber made his way back to his seat and grinned, "Don't mess with a man ain't wet his wick in twenty year."

Charlie eased the door closed as Miss P counted out her register. He bent low. "Ain't natural."

"Been knowing his crusty butt too long," Gubber expounded. "Lying, carrying angel cake, sweating aftershave! Mule out courting."

Chauncy Rankin stated fact. "Nothing more pitiful than a grown fella lose track his manhood."

Gubber added, "Shit so backed up he like to kill some poor bitch when he let loose."

Charlie looked out towards the darkening woods. "Who he sparking out that'a way? Ain't nothing but Rupert Shankle's and a patch of headstones."

A flash glinted in Chauncy's eye. "And Ruby Bell."

"Jesus wept." Charlie blanched.

Miss P easily put the game away inside of the door, then walked out of the store and put her key in the ancient lock. Her movements ushered the men from the porch.

As he stepped onto the road Chauncy whistled and said, "Like collecting brimstone in hell. Man hit the jackpot."

Gubber spit. "Waste a good cake, you asked me."

The men gathered close like old hens for one last scratch of sundown gossip—then scattered, each to his own dinner table to fill their bellies with the steaming, spiced handiwork of women.

⁓

For ephram Jennings the game had been a kind of water torture of the mind. He remembered a picture book that Charlie and Lem passed around at Bloom's some Saturday nights, of women doing all manner of things. It made him both ashamed and excited. Naked and twisting, mouths open, kneeling, waists bent, bodies like feed bags, fit to each man's liking. Then he put Ruby's face on each of those mind pictures and lost the fight against embarrassment, Devil lust and jealousy. And worst of all, fear. He knew in the moment that he could never, even in his dreams, fill the well of Chauncy Rankin's voice, the gait of his stride, or the practiced slide of his touch.

So a hope that had lived in Ephram for thirty-five years against odds even Job couldn't fathom died. Right there on the steps of P & K. With the sun yawning towards night and eleven grown men laughing around him.

It wasn't that Ephram hadn't sampled some bit of life for himself. When he turned sixteen K.O. had lied to Celia about a Young Men's Bible Conference, and instead dragged Gubber and him down to Fair Street in Beaumont. He'd said it was something a boy's daddy ought to do, but since neither boy had one, he had taken on the job.

The woman had been banana pudding yellow and as fat as a prize hog, with a pink corset pushing and shoving her flesh into place, but her face was smooth and sweet as a child's doll, and her top lip had been painted into two little red triangles. She'd smelled like sweat, ammonia and Tootsie Pops. He'd fumbled and tumbled until her impatient hand guided him to her soft center. The release had been magnificent. Almost as great as the shame that followed.

Many years later there had been Gubber's cousin, Baby Girl, fast, young and shaped like trouble. His one true girlfriend. She never removed her panties but let him do whatever was possible with the benefit of loose elastic around her full, plump legs. He spent every dime he made on her, until they were discovered behind P & K, where Celia had followed him. She yanked them apart so hard and fast, Baby's panties, at long last, fell to the ground. After a night of demons being prayed from his flesh by Celia and ten good church members, that was the end of that.

Ephram walked farther into the piney woods and felt a low ebb tickling his joints, his knees. As he crossed the clearing Ruby's gris-gris slipped to the ground and was covered by a puff of dust.

This thing Chauncy had spoken of, like in Lem's book—this deed. Ephram tried to push this new act away from the picture of Ruby he had hanging in his chest, the one with her rising like a wave out of a mud puddle. But it stayed like a scratch on polished wood, until she became all things in his mind. And being a simple man from East Texas, Ephram Jennings did what any man would do. He walked down to Marion Lake and had himself a sleep.

Chapter 7

Ruby sat on the soft earth under the chinaberry tree and let her fingers strum the soil. She looked down the turn in the road. The evening shadows had stretched across the pathway and it seemed to fade into the black tourmaline of the forest.

Ruby had felt something coming through the pines all day. She knew it was not the Dyboù, it was not Chauncy Rankin, nor his brother Percy. It was something salted sweet like pomade and sweat.

So she had spent the day waiting. She had pushed back her hair as best she could. Gone to the pump, pulled the handle with all of her might and splashed the cool well water on her hands, then wiped it across her face. Her fingers came back dripping black, so she rinsed her face again. That was the best she could do.

Then she had pulled up a chair, wiped off the kitchen table with her forearm and sat. That day, the house was not unkind. She was used to the smell—the low dank sugar of rotting things and waste. It was a kind of comfort. The cicadas had been singing, too loudly outside her door in anticipation.

When the morning heated into afternoon Ruby had walked across the road and retrieved a fallen long dogwood branch. Back inside, her fingers slowly began pulling the leaves and peeling off the thin little squares of bark, as if she were plucking a chicken.

Ruby remembered her grandmother saying, before she died, that the dogwood had blood at the roots since it was used to crucify Jesus. Ruby figured that the scale of righteousness had long since broken, and one more little curse couldn't do much harm.

By evening she had a mound of leaves and bark on the table. Some had fallen on the floor. A low hum had begun that had caused her fingers to tap on her legs. The little spirits in her belly shifted, causing an unsettled pressure on her diaphragm. Nausea spread to her stomach, wetting her mouth. She was grateful that today she did not regurgitate—but many days she did—and many days, in the tilt of her world, Ruby could not clean the waste and eventually it dried, hard as bark, into the floor.

She had gone to the door and pressed her forehead gently against the screen and looked into the cobalt sky. The sounds of twilight had called to her—the crickets and the whippoorwills and a few impatient owls, so she pushed out the front door and made it to the chinaberry tree.

Then as evening fell into night, Ruby knew nothing was coming. A rocking sadness filled her. The air was dead and the wind had stopped. Of all that happened in her grandfather's small house over the years, the lonely had been the worst of it. Words unspoken for so long. Only the trees to listen.

But then again, there were her children. A little over a hundred now. Soon the midnight would come and the screaming, the pushing, the birthing of another soul. But now it was quiet.

Ruby felt the chinaberry's roots twisting three feet under her hand. She rubbed until she could feel a small bit of tan root with her thumb. She was on a first-name basis with those roots. She felt them hollowing under her palms. It was those roots that had kept her alive. It was the roots that had saved her.

She remembered six years ago when she had made a clear decision to take two large bricks she had found near Rupert Shankle's fence, bind them to her feet with willow branches and leap into the deepest part of Marion Lake. As strong as she was, as much as she loved her children, Ruby could not bear the weight of her days. Perhaps, she thought, if she left, she might pull them all with her, like the tail of a kite.

Before walking to Marion she had come to say good-bye to the chinaberry and the old crow when she felt the old roots whispering, telling her to dig her toes into the soil. She had pressed her thick eyelashes together, lid to lid, and concentrated. Suddenly she had felt her toes stretching, running wide along the topsoil. Her toes were thin, tendril roots that wrapped like yarn about stones and the abandoned roots of the nearby field of sugarcane. Her skin became reddish brown and hard, her body narrowed and stretched. She felt sweet sap thick within her. Her breasts and buttocks became gentle, knotted swells in the tree's trunk. A thousand lavender flowers erupted from the edges of her fingers. They played a delicious melody that scented the wind and called striped bees and hummingbirds.

Ruby had felt it then. The audacious hope of rooted things. The innocent anticipation of the shooting stalks, the quivering stillness of the watching trees.

For the next weeks Ruby walked through the Big Thicket, becoming. The loose black clusters of muscadine grapes on the vine. The egg-shaped seeded maypop fruit. Pecan trees, horsemint, stones and mud puddles.

She felt the call of the red road and so she became that as well. She felt herself stretching from the dusty passageway that ran through Liberty, Texas, and her grandpapa's five acres, to access roads, to paved yellow-lined promenades with streetlamps, to Burkeville, to Prairie View, to Katy, to Houston, to Austin, to Galveston and beyond, snaking along the Gulf of Mexico.

She could feel a pair of soft child shoes stepping five miles away in Newton County, ten miles down in Burkeville the thick, callused feet of cane field workers at dawn. Faintly she heard the skipping step of a man who still had the sweet ripe smell of a woman on his fingers. Far away the hushed step of two teenage braided cousins rustling skirts and practicing kissing each other against a shaded tree. She felt the rumble of diesel engines, and a hundred pairs of black rubber wheels barely touching asphalt.

Ruby remained red road long past the owl call of midnight. She slept with gravel for a twining mattress and woven cotton and starlight as her covering quilt.

She had slept and awakened on that same road for four mornings until dusk of the fifth day when Chauncy Rankin's horse Millie almost kicked her in the head. She rose, covered in dust and straw, to the sound of his cursing crazy women left alone to get themselves killed. She turned to enter her yard as he slid from his worn saddle. But a part of her was still the road, still alive with men and machines and rabbits scurrying at its edges.

Chauncy grabbed the thin fabric about her waist. His angled brown chin tilted down as he studied her blank eyes. Her eyes still holding the road. He called her. He jostled her. He shook her. He turned his nose at the smell of her. Then Chauncy Rankin spit into her face. Her face remained vacant and still. He saw flecks of his saliva dot her dust-covered cheek. The thick fluid slid down her face, revealing feather brown skin. He took his shirt sleeve, licked the corner and began wiping. He then began patting dirt and grass from her dress, her arms, her buttocks, her stomach, her legs.

He peeled off her gray dress and rubbed at her nakedness, wiping her with the damp edge of the shirt. He felt himself rise in his stained trousers, tent the looseness by his zipper. He dragged her to the pump and cranked the handle until water poured, rust brown at first and then clear. He filled a bucket and doused her with it. Once, twice, three times. When she was sufficiently clean, he half carried, half dragged her to a ditch only three feet from the open road. His maroon face twisted above her as he globbed saliva into his palm, wetted his penis and crammed into her.

And yet to Ruby, her dress empty and flat two feet away, the small of her back scratching on a smattering of pebbles, her pelvis and ribs crushing under a sweating full weight, this was a mere irritation. Like an ant crawling on freshly baked corn bread before being flecked away.

Chauncy Rankin could not know that he was only a cinder in her wandering eye, much more preferable to what waited at the bottom of Marion Lake and the shadow in the woods. For Ruby, men were a slight discord that she waited to pass.

She simply kept her limbs numb and her eyes empty as she had since she was fifteen. Since she was twelve. Seven. Six. Five. When the first man had ripped the cotton of her panties, explaining that this is what happens to very bad little girls. When the first man had sun smiled, "Training time . . ."

When Chauncy Rankin finished he patted her head absently, then left, mumbling a stale warning about lying in roads that grown men had to travel. He climbed on the old horse and trotted down the road.

The road held him as it had the children and the cousins and the hundred spinning black wheels. It did not buck him, or open up and chew him to pieces. The betraying road held him in its open palms. It led him home. It led him to his bed. It would lead him back to her door whenever he cared.

RUBY LOOKED up at the moon high in the sky. The road was still empty and the pains were beginning, the labor that robbed her senses and ripped through her. A little girl, swimming in her body, waiting, gently, tiny hands open. With each birth, she lived the murder of that child. The snap of a neck. The rape of a tiny body. Beatings, bones cracking. Skull smashed against a speeding fist.

She had, over the many years, released them one by one, night after night, her body twisting with pain. Ruby looked at the tiny graves dotting the hill. She had often thought of the small mounds at Ma Tante's and wondered if the old woman had buried souls there as well. It was time. Ruby screamed with each contraction that ripped through her. Howled and saw a pillow smothering the child as she slept. She wailed and whipped the tall trees around her.

Chapter 8

The reaching pines knew that there were legions of spirits tromping through their woods, trapped in thick underbrush, bound beneath the crisscross of branches, in places on the other side of Marion, where sunlight never hit the earth. Some were haints still hanging from the tree they'd been lynched on. Some let the wind roll them like tumbleweeds from one side of the woods to the other. Some were angry and smelled of burned candles, like the rolling dank shadow haunting Bell land, swollen with such hate that it bent the new saplings aside when it passed. It shifted the cush of brown needles and leaves beneath it.

It was this one—Ruby's Dyboù—who watched Ephram drop into sleep on the bank of Marion Lake.

Yes, the spirit had watched, had seen a thing drop from the man's pocket as he walked from P & K, a gris-gris doll with a lodestone tied to its back. It smelled of the girl who hid ghosts in her belly. The Dyboù let out a groan, coughing up a swirl of dust, burying the doll before the fool could notice it missing. Then it had followed Ephram, slipping under each foot before it fell, shooting fingers of doubt and shame through the man's arches, collecting in his testes.

It despised the man and his body still sparking with fireflies of hope, so it crushed the twinkling light between its fingers. Then sat across from him as he slept. Looked into the old, stupid face. *Weak*, it thought: *Fool always been flesh weak.*

The Dyboù contemplated Ephram for hours, watching drool steal down his chin. It scorned the fat back of his earlobes. Then it started looking for chinks in his spirit, little holes to jimmy and crack, until they were just wide enough to lean in and sip.

The biggest tear was near the heart, like a run in a woman's stocking. The Dyboù's tongue snaked, playfully poking its tip into the tear. Tasting. It wondered why innocence always tasted like peach cobbler. The ghost swallowed deeply. A shudder ran through Ephram's sleeping body.

That is when the first crow landed. It fluttered down, its talons curling around a branch. Then came another. Another. A parade of black settled about the tree, cawing and purring under the stars. In the jubilation of call and response, the Dyboù thinned and stole away.

Ephram awoke. The first thing he saw was the white moon waving upon the black lake. Then he heard the soft clucking of crows lacing through the trees. He felt the pine on his back and an ache in his chest. The cake was still intact. He glanced at the tear in his slacks. He dabbed iodine on his knee, by moonlight, and began the slow process of threading the needle—just the way his mama had taught him.

Then he heard it. The midnight wailing.

It was high-pitched and long like a train whistle. It screamed through the air like a spinning knife. It cut into his pride and his resolve. He was running, cake in his hands. Past Rupert Shankle's place. Past the spring oaks. When he reached Bell land he stopped. A silence stopped him.

He walked softly. He could feel the brittle crisp of the grass beneath his shoes. The place was a weed. The house, the well, the porch, the top of the chinaberry tree in the distance, everything on the place jutting and dry. His heart rang like a cowbell in his chest. Ephram stepped under the splintered porch awning and knocked. Silence. He knocked again. Silence. Again. Again. Again.

Tentatively, he circled the house. Nothing. No one. He peered into the blackness. He called out her name, a small plea under the weight of the sky.

Then he heard her scream.

Ephram ran towards the haunted sound, balancing the angel cake. Guided by moonlight, he made it over the rise. There he saw her clawing into the dry earth with her bare hands. He saw her jerk and rip at a solid root. He walked silently closer and saw that her thumb was cut and bleeding, her fingers raw.

She dug with a fury, a whipping wild might, and she wailed until the roots and the branches shook. In that second she looked directly at Ephram. She poured her anguish into the black of his eyes. *"Jesus! My babies! Jesus Lord! Jesus Lord!"*

He took it in and held it close.

Saliva spewed from the knot of her mouth and she spread her legs and pushed absolutely nothing into the shallow grave of earth. But Ruby knew that she had just released the hidden soul of one of the murdered children. Ephram saw and felt a gush of warmth against the cuffs of his slacks, his ankles. Somehow a tiny slant of light grew brighter upon that soil.

Ephram watched Ruby bury and consecrate with her tears.

"There, there," she whispered like wind, "you safe now. The womb or the earth. The womb or the earth. Only two places children be safe." Ruby patted the mound of soil, her body gulping air and releasing it tattered. Ephram looked and saw dozens of small graves. The branches of the chinaberry cast shadows that stretched like arms over the hill.

"There, there . . ." she whispered again. Her red eyes finding him. Ephram knew that he had seen the breaking of the storm. He looked at the hem of her gray dress. How a corner had been ripped away and a clean fold of blue lay across her thighs.

He wanted to tell her it was the color of a robin's egg. He wanted to take her in his arms. He wanted to tell her about how Celia's cake was best with iced milk. He wanted—Ephram caught his breath. He wanted. Had held wanting at bay for the stretch and girth of his life.

So Ephram reached out for the first time since his mama left him. He reached out to smooth down Ruby's dress.

She laid on down, hiked up her skirt and waited. The quicker he began, the quicker he would end. And he had brought what looked like cake, which was more than most, more than all. So when he pulled her up and lifted her injured hand she bared her teeth and glared, because if he didn't want to take her body, then he must want something more vile.

When he took out the bottle of iodine, she snarled and then she kicked him. Hard. Kicked the waiting moon cake. Kicked his lips and nose so that blood trickled down his chin. Then she crouched and waited.

The cake in ruins about his feet, Ephram felt a lump rise in his throat and then he began to sob. Soft little whimpers like a child. She looked at him. Then she caught the jagged tear of her breath. Her lungs calmed and she leaned over and let her hand pat his back. Gentle like burping a baby. She said, "There, there." They stayed like that for a little while in the dark, until she reached over and grabbed a handful of cake from the ground.

She chewed and she gave him a soft nod.

So he gave her one right back.

Ruby ventured, "You know, you've got to stop letting yourself be beat on by women."

"I know," Ephram replied.

The night shifted her horizon and contemplated the kindling of dawn. Ruby and Ephram sat in silence and ate the most amazing white lay angel cake, made theirs with bits of dirt and grass, while the piney woods watched from the shadows.

Book Two

Two Bits

Chapter 9

Celia Jennings had not slept in her bed. She had fallen asleep at the kitchen table waiting for Ephram, and awakened at four o'clock in the morning alone, still sitting upright. She had not leaned, or even slumped, onto the polished wooden table. Had not let saliva trickle onto the grain. She was stiff even in sleep, clean in slumber.

Celia had been fourteen when her mother had shamed her entire family by walking up to the Easter Day picnic naked. Ephram was only eight, but the stain still spread over each and every one of them. It was the burden God had decided to fit upon their shoulders. That and their mother having a new home from that day forward—Dearing State Mental. The fact that their daddy, the Reverend Jennings, was politely asked to leave his own church was yet another weight to bear. He took to preaching on the road ten months out of twelve, in even smaller, dingier churches along the Sabine.

The first day the Reverend folded up his tobacco pouch, grabbed his bag and left, Celia started cleaning. She cleaned the smokehouse and the attic and all the jars in the root cellar, the lard-oil lamps and the grandfather clock. She cleaned the parlor and the water closet, scoured the cookstove and scooped its ashes, bleached the walls, the cabinets, and between the tines of every fork. She made Ephram help her drag out all three mattresses, one feather, two barley straw, and then she beat them into submission. She then scrubbed every floor with lye soap and water until her fingers withered and burned. She pumped water into three large tins and a kettle. Lit a pit fire. Took a washboard to seven sets of sheets, ten towels and a house full of clothes. Rinsed them in the second tin, boiled them in the kettle, with the last tin for bluing whites, then hung them all out to dry. When she finished, two weeks had passed.

After that, Celia was surprised that she had ever had time for classes; for spelling competitions; for A's in Arithmetic and History; for boys like Chauncy Rankin and K.O. Charles, when there was so much to be done at home. Besides Chauncy and them had never made much time for her until her sophomore year, when her chest and hips had swollen up so that students actually pointed the first day of the school year. That was also the day Chauncy and K.O. began their friendly rivalry over the handsome, brown-skinned preacher's daughter at number 8 Abraham Road.

Chauncy and K.O. fought over everything. Dominoes, dice, marbles, baseball, grades, rows plowed, races run, lakes swum and, most of all, girls won. Chauncy Rankin, at sixteen, stood six feet four inches, skin smooth and toasted almond, black hair that had the nerve to curl up and wave. His smile finished off most, perfect white with a twisted dimple under his left cheek. K.O. was the scholar, shale brown and only one inch shy of Chauncy's height, but built for speed and strength. Angled jaw, cheekbones high, K.O. looked as if he'd been chiseled with a sharp blade.

The fall of '36, Chauncy and K.O. descended upon Abraham Road. Since Celia's father did not allow her to date, they came to her house, bringing Hershey bars and RC Colas. Sitting in the parlor for hours at a time until the Reverend made whichever one was there leave. Chauncy would tease her, blow bubbles in the soda and say, "I'm a huckleberry above K.O.'s persimmon any day."

K.O. read her bits of *Nature* by Emerson, and when they were alone, leaned into her ear and asked her, if he could, in two years, ask her to marry him. When Chauncy got word he plain out asked her. Celia said yes, as long as long engagements were all right with him. Chauncy said they were his favorite kind. K.O. took the news as best he could.

They'd planned to ask her parents' permission that Easter Sunday. At the picnic, Chauncy held her hand tight, until folks started laughing and talking and pointing. Chauncy let go of her hand and pointed too. Celia followed his arm, his index finger, and saw her mother at the end of it, walking over that hill naked save her Easter hat, her light blue shoes and her lacing tat. Chauncy would never take hold of Celia's hand again.

At fourteen, Celia gathered her wits and stitched them into her apron. She gladly quit Lincoln High School and looked after Ephram, and their father when he came into town. In a year of chopping wood, and plowing ten acres of land, her arms grew thick and corded. Scars wrapped themselves about her shins and knees. At fifteen, her hair grew brittle from soap and steam, and her velvet eyes began to film with grease and onerous routine. At sixteen her full lips started their descent towards her jaw and grew tight with the anger of responsibility. At seventeen, Ephram came down with a sickness of the joints and she had to drag him back and forth from the County Hospital in Galveston for nigh on two years. She was nineteen years old when her father was found murdered out by Marion Lake. Ephram was only thirteen. And she'd tried the best she knew how to explain to him why Mama was still far away, and why awful men did bad things to good men. But looking at Ephram's face, the only answers she could think of were not hers. They were found in God's house, kneeling at His throne. She took Ephram by the hand, walked back into the church doors and began her new life in Christ. Where she stayed for the next thirty-two years.

And she was grateful. Of course she was. As she often said during testimony, "Satan set his hounds agin' me, with a powerful mind to win me. But he chase me so high-hard, I run straight to the arms of God." Celia had invented hundreds of what she called "Sanctified Saids" over the years. Different members of the congregation had their favorites and put in requests before service. Never a jealous man, the Pastor called upon Celia to testify often, said she had a gift.

It was only on rare spring nights, when the wind carried a pinch of jasmine into her window just before she fell asleep, that Celia would press her lips against her cupped palm . . . and wonder what it must be like to actually kiss.

THE DAY had long since broken its yolk and was high above the horizon. Ruby felt the morning tickling her fingers, tickling and biting. She opened her eyes and saw red ants scattered across her hands. She quickly brushed them off, wiping her palm across the ground killing an entire battalion. Then she saw the man. He was innocent with sleep. What was left of his cake lay in crumbs between them.

She watched the rise and fall of his broad chest. His head lay upon a shoulder of earth. A bit of wind crossed her lap and

Ruby noticed her eldest child as she leaned up from her grave. She pressed her waxy hand on his chin. Then came the others, like Lilliputians to sleeping Gulliver. Some held back, while some went boldly over and sat on his chest, plucked at his eyelashes and played with his ears.

He didn't move and Ruby liked it that way. He was nice enough. If only he had been a sweetbay magnolia or a thistle blossom and needed only rain and sun. But he was a man and would require much more than that. Most of the men she had ever met had been devils or boys, and she already had enough of both.

Ephram rose quickly, brushing ants from his hands, his slacks and shirt sleeves. But his movements swept the ghost children away as well. They tumbled and fell on the grass. Ruby glared at his carelessness.

Ephram saw the fear in her eye and looked slowly at the ground lest he startle her, his body still, his breath soft.

Ruby felt his practiced calm and lashed out, "Ain't you got somewhere you need to be?"

She watched him chuckle. "Not anymore I don't."

Ruby stared at him. He looked at his watch and then up at the orange blue sky, shaking his head and grinning.

"Who you laughin' at?" she spat.

A bittersweet relief stole across his face. "Myself."

"Then don't let me interrupt you." Ruby rose abruptly. The children gathered behind her like clouds.

She was set to spring. Ephram knew the signs. He wanted something akin to the salt lick he'd used to call a young doe when he was twelve. Then, "I go get us some of Miss P's tea cakes. Made fresh yesterday."

Her eyes pulled to him. His voice easy, "P & K open an hour

on Sunday before church. I be there back in no time." He waited, couldn't push.

"Suit yourself," Ruby sniped.

Ephram wiped the sweat from his forehead, and set down the road he'd traveled only a few hours before.

Ruby watched him walk away, back wide, collar wet. The man was patient—like he'd learned sweets after spinach early in life. He would come for her after breakfast—of that Ruby was sure. Scared, then frantic and quick. Then leave ashamed. Shame was best—it was as pliant as biscuit dough.

The old crow perched on the white fence and cawed.

"Shut up," Ruby managed, closing her eyes.

It fluttered across the road and the short distance into the yard, gently scolding.

Ruby growled, "None of your damn business."

It was the same damn bird—big. So big it snapped the skinny branches it sat upon. The same one who'd been clamoring about the place nigh on eleven years. Some might call it a raven, but they would be wrong. Ruby could tell by the caw and the way it purred when it was lonely.

Her youngest began to fuss, so Ruby rocked him. She tried to settle all of her children. They were restless so she sang to them:

"*Hush-a-bye, don't you cry—*

"*Go to sleepy little baby.*"

The black crow hopped down into Ruby's yard, so she stretched her song across the ground.

"*When you wake,*

"*you'll have cake*

"*and all the pretty little horses.*"

Voice soft so she wouldn't scare them. It was their favorite.

"Way down yonder,

"in the meadow

"there's a little baby crying."

Her voice almost a whisper.

"Birds and butterflies,

"Round his eyes,

"Little baby finds his mama."

Ruby felt them calm, their hands tucked under their cheeks, knees folded. Soon they were asleep.

She looked at the crow scratching the ground softly, then picking up a cluster of hard green berries and flapping up to a low branch. In two weeks the tiny fruit would be yellow, in a month it would ferment, making all the birds and squirrels tipsy. Ruby and Maggie had watched them as children, the robins gorging themselves and then flying off like drunken pilots. Chickens, pigs and goats would nibble the shrunken brownish beads and wobble as they walked away, only to come back the next day. Maggie and Ruby had laughed and giggled in the front yard, saying they should open a Chinaberry Juke.

Years later, when Ruby returned to Liberty she had watched the tree in late August and smiled, especially at the large crow who seemed to have imbibed more than most—flapping and falling, stunned in the front yard. When the Rankins' foxhound happened by, Ruby had decided to go outside and sit near her to keep the dog at bay. They had been friends ever since.

The bird cawed once more. Ruby looked around. The land felt different. The man's footprints were still in the dust and the hill had not yet covered them. She looked down at her hands. The cut in her thumb, clumped with dirt. She thought about the polish she had worn into Liberty. The manicure Mrs. Gladdington had taken her to have in a private salon in Chelsea. She had chosen Lost Red by Elizabeth Arden. Ruby saw the clean taper of her hands folded in her lap as she took the train from New York. The brilliant scarlet of each perfect nail.

IT WAS the wrong Liberty. One hundred and four miles south-west from its Colored namesake, Liberty Township. Ruby should have known it the moment she bought the ticket at Penn Station, but the air about her was charged, and her thinking had flared and dimmed like a faulty fuse. Colors had flashed so bright that she'd had to wear her sunglasses inside, and sometimes the sound of static had fizzed and scratched in her ears.

It was 1963 and a world full of Negroes were making their way to Washington, D.C., to stir some change into the batter of the world. Taking trains, buses, some stuffed into the backs of pickups and some riding their thumbs, hitching five, six hundred miles. Like a lone salmon Ruby had taken the road south.

She should have known when the train stopped in Shreve-port, Louisiana, instead of Lufkin, Texas, that she had overshot her Liberty.

But Ruby had been mean behind the train's window. A low steady buzz shooting through her body. A voltage overdose that had amplified her spite and made it impossible to notice anything as benign as the world rolling and flashing in front of her. Instead she had twisted matchbook covers, unpeeled cigarette butts and shredded the moist filters. She had not spoken to the oozing woman across the aisle, although she had been given gentle leads to do so from the woman's cow eyes, from her chubby hand waving a chicken drumstick like a baton, holding out the grease-stained bag as a communal offering. Ruby had shaken her head no in one clean glide. Ruby's smile had been a wince. Even her hellos had been a reproach.

She'd sniffed at the elderly conductor as he walked by, silently impugning his personal care and hygiene. He had pretended not to notice, but the next time Ruby saw him he'd smelled strongly of balsam.

Ruby had not suspected that she was off-course until the conductor called out "LIB-er-ty next stop, LIB-er-ty," and something tickled her. That something prompted her to truly look out the window. When she saw the flat prairie land of Central Texas instead of the piney woods, a panic rose then settled in her chest. She suddenly remembered the road to Liberty. Catch the *Carolina South* to Lufkin, Texas, change to the *Buxton Limited* until you reach Newton. Then take the Red Bus the thirty-seven miles to Liberty. She had not followed the bread crumbs she'd left over a decade ago and she had unfathomably forgotten her way home. She had only been able to spit out "Liberty," the ticket was issued, and the train had barreled south.

Twenty minutes later, angry and confused, she pushed two fat quarters into the Red Cap's hand as he helped her from the train. The weight of her mistake pushed her down on her luggage, where she sat and contemplated her next step.

That is how Ruby came to be sitting on the train platform amidst a fortress of new pink Samsonite bags. Her black hair swept straight and high, pressed within an inch of its life. Lipstick

Persian red. The beauty mark on her right cheek darkened. The buzz in her head quieted to a hum as she secretly primped without benefit of mirror. When in distress, Ruby was certain, it was a matter of survival to look one's best.

The last of the White folks and Negroes crisscrossed the platform to step aboard the train she had just vacated. The little stairs pulled up and the doors closed as a blue-black uniformed man walked up to Ruby, cap stiff, with a rail insignia brassed along the front. "Need help with your luggage Miss!"

Ruby raked through her purse—the Etienne Aigner purse—carefully avoiding the telegram from Maggie. The platform began to clear save a few men and women running to the train. She didn't look at the Red Cap. Then she did. This was a man whose back had been used as a bootjack for the greater part of his life. Ruby realized that she had not breathed in this particular odor of obeisance for nearly a decade.

"Not exactly," she answered. Her manner claimed unquestionable authority. It was one of the many things she'd learned on the Upper East Side of New York, how to use the tilt of a head, the jaunt of a chin to dictate and persuade. She found her cigarettes as the doors of the train sighed and closed. Leaving only Red Caps, the Station Master and little clusters of reunited families, lovers, White men conferring as they stepped away.

The Red Cap leaned in closer. Ruby felt the push in his voice. "Ma'am, you got somebody coming to get you?" he asked, his face creased with concern—a grandfather, an uncle, or a man with plenty of daughters.

His voice fell to a whisper, "Cuz with all this Colored March hullabaloo, Station Master ain't gonna let no Colored woman set out here for too long without a ticket going somewheres."

Ruby's eyes settled on the man. The protectiveness of his voice was an affront to her. That and the bend-down-low in his carriage.

She pulled a Dunhill out of her purse. She placed the cigarette between her dark red lips, stared at the old man and waited. Ruby knew that years of habit would take his match and light the damn thing. He did just that. Ruby did not know why, but her eyes squinted in anger. She did not thank him. Just like a White woman. Just as Mrs. Gladdington had taught her—that some things were her right. That she no more had to thank the waiter or the cab driver than she would thank the air that she breathed.

Mrs. Charlise Gladdington had pulled Ruby from The Pony, a Village bar, and situated her in the maid's quarters of her Upper East Side cooperative. Ruby was to be her companion—and that quickly, she escorted her to Bergdorf's and brought home a world of Chanel and Emilio Pucci. Camel splashed with maroon and gold to better complement Ruby's skin. She began taking her to the Met, the Museum of Modern Art and to quiet West Side parties where the women dressed in suits and ties. She sent Ruby, who had never gone to high school, to the City College of New York by the sheer weight of her position and the fact that she sat on the board. Ruby was one of a handful of Negro students, but the only one to be picked up by a driver at day's end.

Ruby emptied glasses and ashtrays at the old woman's parties, where the literati, artists and composers of the day gathered with benefactors, friends and would-be patrons. She lit cigarettes for Bukowski, Ginsberg and artist Elaine de Kooning. She brought gin and tonics to Ezra Pound, whom she had read, and Chivas on the rocks to John Hersey, whom she had not but pretended that she had.

Mrs. Gladdington's only recompense for her largesse was the

time spent reading to Ruby in the evenings, seated on the Charles Lane love seat, her clothed thigh just barely resting against Ruby's knee.

"Miss?" The Red Cap was still standing there.

Ruby clipped her words. "I need to reach Newton, then on to Liberty Township." The train spit and jerked to a start a few feet away.

"Liberty Township. Ain't that that Colored Liberty by the Sabine?"

"Yes."

"Ain't no direct way there this time a day 'cept by car, Miss."

"I don't have a car. When is the next train?"

"Won't be a train going that way 'til morning lest you catches the one you jes got off. It was Beaumont bound. From there, Newton's a Greyhound bus away."

The train pulling away from the station spit a spark of malice that landed in the tinderbox of Ruby's throat. It conjured a wall of black soot and flames that filled her mouth, making it difficult for her to speak in full sentences.

"Is there a—where can I—is there a hotel I might—"

"Ain't no place like that round here, Miss."

Of course there isn't, Ruby thought. *Of course*. Ruby realized that she had been out of the South for too long. She looked past the man at the slick green awnings, the red of the benches and the pinched face of the Station Master when his gray eyes landed upon her. It didn't matter that she wore an original Mary Quant sundress, sky blue linen. It didn't matter that she had winced at the spreading Negroes around her—sweating under flowered hats as they had stepped around her to get to the Colored car. None of that mattered. In his eyes she would always be a nigger.

One he might be more likely to want to fuck, but a nigger all the same.

Ruby snapped back to the moment at hand. "Then can you arrange a ride? I'll pay twenty-five dollars."

The man jumped to attention, "See what I can do. I'll be back directly, Miss."

She looked back at the COLORED WAITING AREA sign. Nine years after the Brown decision and it still creaked boldly. Before she'd left Manhattan, her friend Billy, a costume designer at the X Theater in Greenwich Village, had been weeping. He'd equated the South for Northern Blacks with Nazi Germany for Jews. That it was insane to go. He'd said that Ruby hadn't seen Maggie in nearly a decade, and that she should be as dead to her as the pickaninny, backwards town. For which Ruby had slapped him.

She had met him at The Pony in the East Village one night and after three dirty martinis apiece, Billy, a pale redhead from Boston, told her he was queer. She told him she was a rich woman's platonic whore, and the two had become fast friends. They had crashed downtown "tea parties" and smoked weed with artists who had rambled for hours about abstract expressionism versus pop art. Billy had slept with an unnamed famous on-the-road writer who pretended to be straight, and they were both in love, from afar, with the short, pudgy author famous for being gay. At night, when Mrs. Gladdington was out of town, the two had slept together in Ruby's narrow bed, whispering their dreams, her head on his shoulder.

Ruby breathed the smoke in—hard. She was a wet smoker, filters always damp and shit brown when she crushed them. Maggie was the opposite, even though she inhaled like she was sucking in air after a hard run, the tips were as dry as straw. But everything

Maggie did was clean. She made rolling her own cigarettes with one hand an art form. Each one perfectly like the next.

Ruby tapped the ash, her lipstick bright along the end, then brought it back to her mouth. *Fucking Maggie,* she thought, *Fucking Maggie and that goddamn telegram.* The fact that she had never wanted to come back home was another matter. It was Maggie's fault she was there. Maggie yanking her back to Liberty Township, where Black folks waved the heat away with Jesus fans. Everyone was slow. Blood flowed in veins like molasses, sweat stuck to clothes like blessing oil.

Fucking Maggie. How she stood over Ruby before she left for New York, stiff as cast iron but crying in spite of herself. It had been the first time, to hear Maggie tell it, that she had ever cried. Ever. It was, in any case, the first time Ruby had ever seen it. She'd told Maggie she despised the town—what it had taken and how it had used her as a spittoon.

Ruby remembered how Maggie's own mama Beulah Wilkins had hated Liberty Township. How she used to say, nearly every Sunday when they were children as she cleaned her shotgun, "Town cursed."

She'd continue, "Not one of them fools had the gumption to incorporate with the county. So Liberty ain't under America, God, nothing. Hell, place tweren't never baptize by nobody's law." Then she would push the oil rag down her barrel. "Which is why the Devil write it down in his book, got many Liberty men soul on his roster."

Ruby had known that Maggie would never leave. She'd known that Maggie would take in wash, catch striped bass and catfish at Marion Lake, that she would work like a plow horse, drink herself stupid, get into scuffles at Bloom's, and cheat at poker. That over time, creases would be smoothed like damp clay into her face, until bit by bit they would dry and harden; that her hair would become dusted gray, cheeks sinking into her teeth, her muscles shrinking to her bones. Ruby knew that one day some fevered complaint would steal through Maggie's proud body until she could barely lift her head to swallow a spoonful of soup; that she would light cigarettes in spite of the shouts and condemnations of the sisters she had yet living. That those same sisters would crowd around her as she sipped in her last breath; they would be her pallbearers and only mourners. That Maggie would lay in a coffin, under sugar sand and red clay, until her bones blanched and her flesh wormed away. And that she would never leave the piney woods.

They had met at the edge of a cotton field when Ruby was three and Maggie five. Ruby's grandmother and Maggie's mama sweated oceans under the Texas sun as the two children sat under a faded umbrella and sucked on sugarcane. Ruby remembered how everyone said that the two of them had locked eyes and hearts in the time it took a star to twinkle. As they grew older, they all but lived in the chinaberry tree. The branches were low enough for a seven-year-old to easily pull herself up. Legs dangling beneath the branches. Maggie would always find her there. Even through the worst of it, when Ruby was caught like a bird under the claws of a great cat, Maggie would climb up and sit beside her. Give her gifts she'd stolen from P & K, and even more boldly, from the five-and-dime in Newton, where they would have beaten her raw. Thimbles and Butterfingers, barrettes and embroidered handkerchiefs, Cracker Jack—Maggie would always let Ruby keep the coveted prize inside the box. They would pull taffy and wrap it around

their wrists like soft bracelets before eating it. Maggie would find
her clear stones down at Marion Lake, or a bluebird feather. She
would bring her Clem Rankin's peaches, because Ruby didn't have
the stomach for his buckshot. In the evening, before Papa Bell died,
they sat under that tree staring into the blueberry sky, listening to
his fiddle—the horsehairs thick with resin, and metal strings cast-
ing a line of sound that sailed through the trees and caught their
hearts. Ruby would then put her head against Maggie's wide chest,
and feel her arms like supple steel around her. There had been a
comfort to the way Maggie smelled, like Juicy Fruit and tobacco.
When she got older and she began smelling like the wash she was
taking in, Ruby saw it crush something inside of her. For Maggie was meant to be the king of something. She was meant to puff
out her chest and conquer worlds. But Ruby watched her join the
army of Black folks dragging off to Newton, their souls crumpled
in their handkerchiefs until suppertime. And while Maggie didn't
droop her head as much as the rest, it still fell a bit to fit through
the door of servitude.

But before that, when they were free under the chinaberry,
Maggie told Ruby that she wished she had a fine ring to give to
her. She said she wished for a steeple someplace that would hold
them up high in the eyes of God. But Maggie could not steal a
ring good enough for Ruby, for they kept them under glass at the
five-and-dime, and the only rings in Liberty were on the hands of
some married ladies. So Maggie had wrapped Ruby all the closer,
always holding her like she was made of lace and glass, and promised she would get a ring befitting her Ruby Bell. Not long after,
she had gone to work, and not long after that, Ruby had lost her.

To leave Maggie, Ruby had had to forget the chinaberry and
the blueberry sky, the crickets and cicadas who accompanied Papa

Bell. The mockingbird, who came after the fiddle was put away, and sang every birdsong in the forest, the wood thrush's and the pine warbler's, even making up his own tunes. Ruby had to push all of that away and turn into that hard clear river stone. She had to turn her tongue into a sharp stick—otherwise she would have stayed. She had to all but kill Maggie to leave her. She had been too young to know she could have kissed her good-bye. She had been too young to know that a person can still hold on to the shared secret of love and walk away. She hadn't known, until she reached Manhattan, that she had murdered a part of herself as well. That it would be years until that part came to life again.

RUBY FELT her eyes grow wet, a knot form in her throat. She swallowed it down—as she had done the whole of her life.

Then she grew angry. If Maggie had left, even for a trip to Houston, she would not be on that platform. *Fuck Maggie.* She saw the Red Cap helping a young blond woman with her bags. New passengers had begun to congregate on the platform waiting for the next train, both Negro and White. *Fuck Maggie and fuck the Red Cap. Slow-ass Negro.* She flicked her dead cigarette onto the tracks and as she lit another, her jaw started aching. Over the past week she had been pressing her molars together so tight that at times the mandible had begun to throb. She wished she had brought her aspirin, or Mrs. Gladdington's sleeping pills, or both. Ruby could not remember the last time she truly slept. Even before the telegram, many nights a low scraping sound had kept her awake—like a man sanding a wooden floor. Ruby's hand shook a bit as she took another long puff of her new cigarette.

The train platform was sparse and clear. She had to think. Wait. She pursed her lips and pushed the smoke out of her lungs. *Where was the goddamn porter!* Suddenly a dark curve between her bags shifted and moved. Ruby ignored it, as she had ignored it for weeks, as she had ignored so many things lately. But the nothing that lived on the periphery of her vision had been the worst of it. The nothing with small chubby fingers that sifted through the weave in her clothes—that sometimes had the outline of pigtails. Ruby hated her. Hated her need, the way she tried to curl on her chest when she slept. Hated that she knelt beneath the apple bins and ruffled through the bok choy in the fresh-air markets in Chinatown. Ruby saw that the dead nothing was hollow and imagined that was why it had affixed itself to her left femur.

Once anchored, she had trailed behind Ruby like a helium balloon, drifting back down to earth, only to rise again. Ruby had tried to shake her, take sharp turns, or leap into subway cars seconds before they closed, to no avail. Once she had gotten the telegram from Maggie, once she was headed home, the spirit floated above her in Penn Station near the newsstand, fluttering the folded papers with images of the young Buddhist nun guilty of self-immolation. She had settled near a cafeteria radio while Ruby got a regular coffee, and swung her legs in time to "It's All Right."

She'd cozied beneath Ruby's seat on the train, tickling the inside of her knees. Now on the platform she crept out of her hiding place. Ruby refused to look down. In answer the puff of air leapt onto her shoulders. Ruby stood quickly, knocking over two of her bags. Four faces turned her way. A shock of fear shot through her. She sat back on the bag but the little spirit clung tight to her neck. Desperate now, Ruby felt it trying to enter at the base of her skull. She quickly put her hand there, a thin sweat filming her forehead. It then slipped under her arm and was pushing now against her chest, softly at first, then roughly, almost knocking Ruby onto the platform boards. Ruby wanted to run, to scream and kick the cloud of a girl away.

Now, Ruby was trapped on the mountain of pink bags. The day tilted. The horizon slipped blue to prairie brown to cut-outs of green. Too green. An electric spinning green. The black of the tracks, the wash of the ties. Her fingers were on fire. Ruby flicked her orange cigarette to the ground then sucked at the fleshy burns. She smelled the remnant of a cigar burning somewhere, some salty thing like ham, perfume. And sweat. All left behind on the platform. The child was weeping now, so strong that the air crackled. In moments, Ruby knew she would scream. In a few moments she would break through the mirror of convention and the White men would come running, their hands twisting her thin wrists, eyes too red, faces too white. The Black folks would cower as they hauled her to jail or worse. So Ruby prayed. She prayed for the illusion of sameness.

As if in answer, the spirit grew smaller. Younger. A toddler. Younger still until she was six months old, three, until she was a small baby newly born. Ruby recognized her for the first time. Heart-shaped face. Long tan body. Her breath stopped when she saw it was her girl. Her baby who died without a name when Ruby was fourteen.

She was swaddled and tiny, there on the wooden planks, so of course Ruby lifted her into her arms. The child began crying. Bawling so loud, so scared, coughing something out of her lungs, trying to breathe. Ruby held her and rocked back and forth. Her girl. Her lost girl. Ruby tried to hide her from the people at the station, some of them turning to look. Ruby pretended she had a chill and was merely wrapping her arms around her body, but her child could not stop—the sound tearing through Ruby.

There on the platform Ruby bade her to enter. The girl hushed and looked into her eyes. Ruby could hear the echo of her tiny heart and suddenly the baby slipped as if soapy from a bath, and fell hard into Ruby's chest.

Ruby stumbled back, tripping over her bags. She struggled to right herself and her feet caught the handle of a bag and she fell down again. Then Ruby wept. Huge black tears that plopped onto the sky blue of her dress.

The Red Cap was back, hand on her arm, face crunched like a fist with worry, the Station Master was looming behind him. A small crowd of White folks pushed forward.

The Station Master boomed over her, "What's the problem here, Jonah?"

Ruby looked around, liquid liner running down her cheek.

The Red Cap, Jonah, knew something. Was it about the child? Had he seen it too?

Jonah threw out a rope. "She just trip and fall is all Suh."

Ruby took it. "Yes, I'm sorry, I just tripped. Over my bag. I'm so sorry." Ruby began standing, straightening her dress.

The Station Master took a step forward.

"You drunk, gal?" The White man was less than a foot away.

Ruby knew if she looked at him she would be taken. So she stood, slumped her shoulders, stared at the ground and answered the White man, "No, Sir, No. I'm sorry, so sorry." She spit out, "I'm on my way home—my cousin is dead." Ruby cut the truth out of her gut and sliced it up to save herself. "She—her funeral was a month ago. I just found out, Sir. Yesterday, Sir. I'm just—just got upset is all."

The air was close to boiling. Ruby searched the platform. Her purse lay on its side. She reached down and grabbed the telegram, the one Western Union had tried to deliver to three old addresses before they found her. She pushed it in the Red Cap's face. He handed it over to the Station Master. He scanned it, lips tight.

Jonah put the nail on the thing. "You know how emotional we be sometime, Suh."

Nearly satisfied, the Station Master stepped away, throwing the telegram in Ruby's direction, "One thing I don't need is another drunk nigger. They been leaving from here all week for that monkey march, I swear to God as drunk as Moses." His associates chuckled. The rest of the White folk turned on his cue, retreating into cool shade and ice cold soda pops of the Whites Only Waiting Area.

Ruby took a breath. Her hand on Jonah's arm. "Thank you."

"No need, Miss. How old was she?"

"Thirty-three."

"What happened?"

"Cardiac arrest, they said."

Off of his confounded look, Ruby said, "Heart attack."

He shook his head, "I'm sorry for you."

"Thank you. Can you—did you find a car?"

He looked to make sure no one was around. "No. I'm sorry Miss, but you best get yourself out this here station if you gots to walk. They be looking for somebody to lynch since Minister King started this here. My nephew be up there. Young men's church group. Ain't never had a drop of liquor in his life." Then he bustled into the station.

Ruby watched his back walking into the building. *Fucking Maggie.* Ruby collected her pocketbook and walked and sat on the bench next to a withered plum-colored man chewing a wad of tobacco. A bit of the brown juice dripped onto his chin. He wiped it with the edge of his sleeve. She started crying anew. *Her fucking heart. Her fucking weak-ass heart.* Ruby pulled out her compact, looked in the mirror. Crazy stared back. Black lines like soot across her face. Crimson lipstick on her teeth, chin. Cheeks. Her perfect hair unpinned and sticking straight up. But it was her eyes that finished the job. Blood red, but more than that, there was a new, empty terror spreading from the center. Her eyes had disappeared and these new dead things had emerged. The old man handed her a handkerchief. She silently thanked him and began to wipe her face with shaking hands.

She had cleaned her face as best as she could when the man said, "I ain't got a car," then gave her a wink, "but I got me a truck."

"I can pay you—"

He smiled, bashful but certain. "Yo' company be payment enough."

Ruby's eyebrows lifted a bit. He looked to be about seventy. The few teeth he had left were dark brown with tobacco. He smelled musty with age. She tried to conjure her smile, the one that used to send the New York boys and girls reeling. She tried, but all she managed was a nod.

The old man caught his breath and began dragging her largest bag across the platform, looking back as if he'd just stumbled upon a free steak dinner.

Her little girl shifted inside of her chest and Ruby was forced to step out of the dark room of her mind. Step out and turn off the projector, the one with an old truck pulled over on an abandoned Texas road. And a not so young girl with her head in an old man's lap, destroying the girl and corrupting the man, whose biggest temptation in all his years had most likely been hard apple cider in his wife's basement.

Ruby looked up. Gray, when had the sun become so gray?

"You're in luck lady," Jonah said. "Train's coming back."

"What happened?" the old man with her bag asked plaintively.

"Seems the Rail Manager for Southeastern line's wife done fell asleep and forgot her stop."

The railway platform filled with people, surprised at the returning train. The Station Master ran to the doorway flagged by a conductor as the train screeched to its stop, and everyone watched as a drowsy-eyed White woman stepped down. Angry. Embarrassed. Flustered.

Jonah said gently, "Colored car in the rear. Get yourself on and quick." Ruby flew from the bench, and with his help, gathered her bags and climbed into the designated car. She pushed a ten-dollar bill into his hand. He tried to push it away, but Ruby won out. In seconds the train cranked into movement and headed for the heart of the Black folks' Liberty.

AN HOUR passed before Ephram returned with two bags of groceries. His forehead was wet and there were dark stains under the arms of his shirt.

Ruby stood, bones stiff from sitting, and nodded towards the house. He waved back and walked towards the porch.

Ruby knew what he would find just inside the door. Refuse,

soiled clothes, feces in the corners, caked dirt, flies breeding. Ruby had found that nursing and battling ghosts and the hell of memory was hard work, and keeping house while doing it had proved to be impossible. She was anxious to see how Ephram's flag of hope fared in such desolate waters. She would not raise hers until she was sure.

She felt saliva rising in her mouth like anger so she spit. Not raise her flag! She'd have to make one first. Hope was a dangerous thing, something best squashed before it became contagious. She looked at Ephram inches from her door and felt a low growl in the pit of her stomach. She doubted he would last the day.

Chapter 10

Celia looked at the rooster clock on the kitchen wall. It was now nine on Sunday morning. The In-His-Name Liberty Township chapter of the Holiness Church was beginning service across town and Celia had not put on the navy dress she had ironed the day before. It rested like a grounded flag on the bed in her room—the fabric, napped and pleated just under the bodice, the scooped high collar and sleeves trimmed in duchess lace—starched hard and pointed.

Two minutes after nine. Her eye began to twitch in anger. Celia stood to make breakfast then sat back down. There wouldn't be time to eat once Ephram arrived home. They would have to hurry and dress. Celia knew that, whatever else he may have done, her boy would be home this morning, because in forty-five years, Ephram Jennings had never missed Sunday service. He certainly, absolutely would not miss today, the day she had patiently waited for the last twenty-five years. The day of the election for Church Mother. Her name was one of only three on the ballot. She began to pace.

For four months Celia had planned to wear her new Star-of-Bethlehem brooch to church this morning. Only members of the congregation with the proper discernment would see the dark-sky dress and the pear-cut rhinestone pin and know the symbology, the statement the dress was making. But when Celia stood in church to bear witness before the election, she would weave the brooch into her testimony, lay it out with such clarity that even Melonie Rankin, her opponent's own daughter, would give one of her little sighs. May, the Pastor's wife, would be moved to call out a strong "Hallelujah!" followed by echoes of "Preach on, Sister Jennings!" "Tell the truth and shame the Devil!" "Seraph," and of course, "In His name!"

The fellowship often said that Celia bore witness to God better than her father, the Reverend Jennings, ever had. That it was a shame she hadn't been born a man so that she could stand in the pulpit as preacher. Celia, who often watched as Pastor Joshua stumbled midsermon, due to his nearly conquered stuttering habit, never allowed herself the blasphemy of envy. She knew she was born exactly as God intended, to do the work He assigned her.

Celia looked at the clock once more. 9:07. She slammed the kitchen chair under the table, walked to her sitting room window and looked down the red road. Empty. Celia willed Ephram over the hill. The wind whipped up little dust devils on the road in response. Celia gnawed at the inside of her mouth and thought of the matching tri-cornered hat she planned to wear today. It was, she'd noticed when she first saw it in the Spiegel catalog, a holy trinity hat, complete with tall cream and navy feathers. Its illusion lace scooped around the circumference of the hat and her Page Boy wig in silver/black would shine under it bone straight.

Celia pushed the flat of her palm against the windowpane. The wig was waiting for Celia on one of her five foam wig heads. All of Celia's good hair lived above her dresser mirror. Ephram had nailed up a perfect shelf for them a year ago, so that Celia could look in the mirror, then above at the selection of wigs to determine which one would be best for the garment she was wearing. Her Ephram had done that and so much more. He loved her wigs almost as much as she did. He knew, for instance, that the Charade in Fancy Black was her favorite—long bangs, hanging curls in the back—but that the Misty Page Boy would look best with her new hat.

Celia walked back into the kitchen. 9:15. The fixed frown line between her eyes deepened and she bit deeper into the soft flesh inside her cheeks. A question flashed through her mind: Had he somehow taken his Sunday clothes and planned to meet her there? Celia nearly ran into Ephram's bedroom. The navy suit still hung where she'd left it yesterday afternoon. The white shirt, washed and ironed, with the blue tie she'd chosen for him, was still draped over the hanger. Celia sat down on Ephram's bed, anger rising like steam from her wide sturdy body.

Monday through Friday Celia lived in head rags, her scalp oiled with Camber's Hair Food each evening, then seasoned with a crisscross of bobby pins. She wore housedresses from the Salvation five-and-dime and slippers with the fluff mashed out of them. She cooked Ephram's meals: breakfast, dinner and supper, plus a nighttime snack. Wrung the necks from chickens and cracked their fertile eggs. She made Ephram's bed and sprinkled his sheets with rosewater to draw good dreams, then put epsom salts in the corners of his room to keep out haints. Gave him a teaspoon full of ipecac when he had fever and Bayer aspirin when his nerves shot through his arms and legs. Cod-liver oil every weekday morning. Celia scoured and Cloroxed and Lysoled the house at number 8 Abraham Road during the week, and managed the money Ephram earned from bagging groceries at the Piggly Wiggly. Celia kept all of the tips he made taking the groceries to White ladies' Buicks. Monday through Friday Celia did all this and more for her boy.

She sat on the bed, her heart knocking against her sternum, growing more enraged as she recounted her weeks upon years of service.

Saturday was upkeep and preparation. Cutting and chopping for Sunday supper. Making sweet potato pies and 7UP cake. Keeping the stove wood dry then lighting the fire. Ephram had bought her a Sears gas model ten years before but it added a funny aftertaste to her pies and she wouldn't stand for it. Loading the washing machine. Then rewashing what the machine didn't catch on her scrub board, using liberal amounts of bleach. Hanging everything out to dry on the line then taking it all in. Heating the iron on the stove and pressing the sheets, the pillowcases, then Ephram's work and Sunday clothes. Only then would Celia attend to her own church attire. Take her hair out of the kerchief. Wash it. Oil it. Then pin it up again so that it would stay snug under the wig of choice. Once in bed she would read Deuteronomy, her favorite book of the Bible, until she fell quickly to sleep.

Sunday was Celia's only day. Celia gnawed more rapidly at her left inner cheek. She bit down on the soft flesh until she tasted blood and she clutched at the quilt on Ephram's bed. He must, must remember. He couldn't *forget* that today was her day to share counsel with the most Holy. To teach others by example: by demeanor, testimony, by speaking in tongues, and certainly by her attire. What better way, Celia and Ephram had agreed, to glorify God than to wear a mantle worthy of him! They always wore matching colors to service. As a pair, thought Celia, they had always been exemplary. Today's navy outfit had cost Ephram $55.68 of his tips, without the wig. But it was worth it. Her standard Sunday best would not have sufficed on this special day.

Celia stood in rage. *For today*—Celia ripped the quilt off the bed. *Was the day*—She ran to the cupboard and grabbed a handful of baking soda then dashed it on his sheets as a calling prayer. *Celia Jennings would be voted in as Church Mother.*

The white powder made a small cloud above the bed. Celia crossed herself and spat over it for luck. Ran back to the kitchen. 9:25. Then back to his bed. She spread her face and arms over his sheets. Holding the bed she began praying her boy home.

Celia had dreamed of holding her rightful position as Church Mother since she was a little girl. After her mother was taken to Dearing Mental, and the Reverend was lynched, she'd held on to the picture of herself seated in the Church Mother's place, the corner pew with the white ribbon. Not the pews that faced the preacher where the general mass of the congregation sat, but one of the special two flanking the pulpit on either side like an open ended square. The ones people had to look past to see the minister, and the Church Mother's seat was the most visible.

Celia stood from her prayer bristling. Baking powder on her cheek, neck, arms and breast. She picked up Ephram's suit and walked into the kitchen. 9:40. The election was to be held after service so . . . *If* Ephram came home, *if* they made it to church before the end of service, *if* she won the election, she would be given the brilliant white sash to wear each Sunday with the words "Church Mother" written in silver glittering cursive.

Celia folded Ephram's suit carefully, and put it in a Piggly Wiggly sack. She went into her bathroom and wiped the soda from her sturdy face, her body. She slipped off her housedress and wetted and soaped the washcloth in the sink and just like that she knew Ephram was not coming home this morning. Celia began to cry as she washed between her legs. She sat on the toilet and wondered if it was God's will that she let this cup pass from her lips. Perhaps He was trying to spare her the responsibility and sacrifice that being Church Mother entailed.

But then hadn't He helped her all along to win the post?

Hadn't He started two years ago when it became apparent that Mercy Polk, Mother Mercy she was called, would soon be unable to fulfill her Church Mother duties due to old age and incontinence? At God's heeding, Celia had secretly campaigned, had made special entreaties to the Pastor's wife, May, and others of influence on the board. However, the rules of removal had been more stringent than those of Supreme Court justice. Once in office, a Mother simply could not be supplanted. Even after Mother Mercy passed away, her seat had remained empty for six whole months. Four was the usual protocol of respect shown to each Mother. Mother Mercy's tenure had been such that she had been given two additional months for the congregation's mourning.

There had been no doubt that Celia would win the election. The competition was weak. Supra Rankin and Mother Mercy's granddaughter Righteous were lackluster at best. All of Mother Mercy's heathen grandchildren had been given Holiness names at birth. It hadn't helped. Praise B., the middle boy, had spent the last five years in Burkeville Federal Corrections for stealing stamps from the post office. Salvation was rumored to be dating secretly Pastor Joshua right under his wife's nose. The twin girls, Milk and Honey, had each gotten pregnant, out of wedlock, by the same itinerant preacher. Their baby boys, born within two weeks of one another, were both cousins and brothers at the same time.

Then that horrible thing had happened to Honey after she left her child, moved down to Beaumont and was said to have gotten mixed up with a lesbian homosexual and a life of drugs. The fruit, thought Celia, never falls far from the tree.

There was also the fact that none of the other nominees for Church Mother had committed Genesis through Nehemiah to memory. Not to mention Psalms, Proverbs and Lamentations. Forget that she knew Matthew through John. Corinthians one and two. And of course Revelation. Who else could say that? Supra Rankin's tongues were a joke, painted-on things to impress the multitudes. Righteous Polk had only her grandmother's glory to push her into a nomination. None of them had her following. The women who gathered about her after Bible study to ask questions. Leaning into her every word. Not one had her pious nature. Her humility, the years of missionary work in Kountze County, Beaumont City and Nacogdoches. Who else had traveled to the convention in Hardin County in '55 or Galveston in '57? Taken their own child's money and spread the word from little Liberty Township? Who had put their small church on the map at the '59 convention in Raleigh by being voted chair of the Preparatory Basket Committee? Who else had had a vision of Jonah and angelic visitations from the twelve Apostles or the gift of prophecy? Certainly not Righteous Polk with her hanging slips and scuffed shoes. Did the woman not a have a mirror to look into before going to church on a Sunday morning?

Who else had not married and remained God's holy vessel? No. It was His will. It was God's will that Celia Jennings take her rightful place among all of the other women whose pictures hung on the ladies' lavatory wall. The lobby was for past preachers, but when the lavatory was moved indoors in 1945, the In-His-Name

Liberty Township chapter of the Holiness Church's Women's Auxiliary had decorated it with pink and beige rose wallpaper. Hung chintz curtains and two framed pictures of past church mothers over the sink.

Celia thought to go to church alone to claim her prize but stopped. For what would she have said to their questions?

"I hope Brother Jennings isn't feeling poorly," Supra Rankin would have said slyly. And what if she had lied, "Yes, he is a bit under the weather today," then Ephram had shown up? Or walked by the church from his night of sin? Still smelling of—her. That Bell woman. It was unspeakable. The shame she would feel as the assembly discovered the truth, that her child, her good boy, had fallen as surely as Adam fell, as surely as Samson. Fallen like fruit, not far from her tree.

Celia heard the truth as clearly as Gabriel's trumpet booming above her head. This was the Devil's work. Who else had a vested interest in the downfall of her church—which was sure to happen if Supra Rankin were elected and used her influence to put more pushy, bossy Rankins on the church board? Who else would tempt him who was closest to her? And who best to do it if not one of the Bells? Those fair-skinned harlots who brought shame and unrest on the community over forty years afore. That blond, blue-eyed Neva Bell, who fornicated with a White man and got herself shot because of it? No matter this one was brown. This Ruby Bell carried the same blood, and that blood carried the same sin. And the sin had risen like a flood to carry her good boy away. She would not allow it! Not now. Not ever.

Ephram was going to church today, and she would become Church Mother.

Celia Jennings rushed into her bedroom, slipped off her

house sheath and donned her new blues. She put on her Star-of-Bethlehem brooch, fastened the wig tight on her head, then attached the hat with T-shaped pins. Her shoes—she hadn't lain them out. She went into her closet and found the patent leather blues. She grabbed her matching purse, the Piggly Wiggly bag with Ephram's suit, and set out down the road. The same red road Ephram had ventured down not twelve hours before.

The streets and fields were Sunday morning empty, filled with the sound of her feet crunching clay, kicking dust and gravel behind her. She passed Rankin land, the scarecrow waving straw hands in the breeze. The world was in church. Still, it wouldn't hurt to walk along the low path to stay out of sight. She winced as she passed Bloom's Juke, still smelling of Saturday night. Then she was back on the main road. Her steps took on a rhythm. A grinding beat. Celia saw the large black bird flutter down on the fence up ahead. Its wings stretched wide as she walked quickly by and it followed her with its oil eyes. It cawed three times, then rose up in flight. Celia walked faster. The beat of patent leather speeding her closer. She reeled past P & K, dark and silent. By the time she passed Rupert's melon patch and the pathway to Marion Lake she was almost running, the tall pines pushing her along.

When she reached Bell land her breath was deep and sharp. Her knock sounded louder than she expected on the dry rot door. No answer. She knocked again. A face darted in the window then disappeared. She lifted her hand to knock again—

Ephram opened the door.

He looked crumpled. His morning beard growing in, sleep crusting in the corner of his left eye. This wasn't like her son, who never left the house unshaven, unwashed. He held a wet rag in his hand. His knees were soapy wet and Celia spied a full sudsy bucket over his shoulder, in the kitchen of the filthy house. Had he been—*cleaning?* And on the Sabbath? The place was a room out of hell. Cobwebs and black dirt, layers thick. Dust everywhere. The house reeked of human waste. Celia's face went numb with disgust and fury.

Between bared teeth she said evenly, "Ephram. You late for Sunday service."

Ephram looked down at her, his face kind but hardened. "I ain't going today Celia."

She heard what sounded like a bedspring in the next room. Celia craned her neck around Ephram and saw that thing sitting on a soiled mattress. Eyes like a swamp lizard. Evil mark on her cheek. Her legs spread out in that foul gray dress she always had on.

Celia lost track of speaking for a moment. Then a noise between a yelp and a cry stabbed up from Celia's throat. "NO! Ephram, you comin' with me now."

Ephram bent his head, scraped at his chin with his hand. "Mama, I'ma stay here for a bit longer." He tried to put his hand on Celia's shoulder. She pushed him off.

"Your soul in jeopardy boy."

"Ceal ain't nothing in jeopardy—I swear."

"Look how it started, you already cleaning on a Sabbath."

"Luke chapter fourteen. 'The ox was in the ditch,' Ceal."

"You twistin' the Bible already; besides church done started."

"You go on then. I'll see you directly."

"When?"

"When I get there Ceal." He sounded harder, the softness gone. The nasty thing was standing behind him now.

"Go on," It said. "Go on home to your mama."

Celia saw her Ephram turn to the creature and get soft like

saltwater taffy. Get soft and sweet and whisper, "But I don't *want* to go nowhere Ruby."

Celia backed away into the front yard. She conjured with gospel—the one thing that never failed to bring Ephram in line. "'. . . though your sins be as scarlet, they shall be as white as snow!'" Celia pointed to the sky and continued, "'Though they be red like crimson, they shall be as wool.' Isaiah 1:18."

The thing got quiet. Ephram stared dumbly at Celia from the open doorway. Celia felt an electric power building within her, guiding her words. "Ephram, you best to remember Leviticus chapter twenty-six, verse twenty-one: 'And if ye walk and will not hearken unto me; I will bring seven times more plagues upon you according to your sins. I will also send wild beasts among you, which shall rob you of your children, and destroy your cattle.'"

Celia lifted both of her arms high to the heavens to finish the job. She had chosen the perfect passage. Ephram blinked as if he were about to weep. Celia held out the grocery bag with his Sunday suit. She would instruct him to change behind P & K after she delivered the final words. He would enter In-His-Name on Celia's right arm and they would give testimony together today. About Leviticus. About family and the blood of Jesus. Celia felt her eyes wet with joy as she charged dramatically: "'And if ye will not be reformed by me then will I punish you yet seven times for your sins.'"

Celia stood smiling with the outstretched bag.

Ephram shut the door and went inside.

Celia staggered back, slipped on a stone and nearly fell over. She could not breathe, not in nor out, as if a great and mighty wall had crashed into her. She paused for a moment, then ran wildly in shame for home.

She got as far as Marion Lake when she stopped dead, a smile sliding across her teeth. Celia very methodically took off her brooch and placed it in her purse, then rested the purse on the side of the road.

Then Celia threw herself to the ground. Hard. Using one hand to secure her hat and wig, she thrashed herself against the cracked clay. Ripped at her collar . . . some, but not enough for impropriety. She tore at the lace along the sleeves and inadvertently bloodied her ankle. When she stood she was covered in dust, her brunette skin ashy with scrapes and dirt. Then she reached into her purse, retrieved the brooch and pinned it close to her heart.

When Celia turned onto the church road she had a mission, a holy war she would not only fight, but win. She practiced the first words she would utter upon entering the gate. Upon opening the door to a seated congregation. Upon the singular note of awe she would conjure from the crowd.

She mouthed the words, "I just had a fight with the Devil—" The rest, Celia knew, would spring forth from her mouth like a deep well gushing in the desert. "I just had a fight with the Devil," she practiced, "and I needs your help to win."

Chapter 11

The man's flag was still waving, but it was filthy as hell. Ruby sat on the bed and ate the third tea cake Ephram had given her that morning. He'd also brought her head cheese, which she had promptly ignored.

Little charges flashed through her body, then settled. She sipped coffee that he had valiantly prepared on the hearth with a small kettle he'd bought from P & K. The bitter smell connected, then exploded. She hadn't had a cup of coffee in ten years. And she loved coffee, loved it like air. The fire he'd made danced in the warmth of the day, flecks of blue and gold. He was still cleaning. It had been two hours and he had not stopped to sit, that is, if there had been a clean inch to sit on.

When he had first stepped foot in the door Ruby had seen him falter. Stumble over the black of his shoes. Then he had held his handkerchief near his nose, paused and looked about the house. Then he seemed to be methodically planning his attack.

Ruby watched him survey the five solid rooms: the kitchen, its black potbelly stove thick with grease, dried batter, bits of food and a pan holding stagnant water that had long since sprouted maggots. The wood pail was filled with rotted dewberries she had picked and forgotten. The counter, ripe with molded bread and peaches slick brown surrounded by swarming fruit flies. Ruby had not truly seen the house, but now, through Ephram's eyes the filth and waste echoed.

He pushed the rounded oak table away from something crusted and black and noted the mound of leaves and bark on top. He made a left from the kitchen and walked into an empty living room that not one person had sat in since Neva died. Ruby knew it was unusually clean, as was the back bedroom he disappeared into. They did not belong to her.

Ruby had heard all three girls, Neva, Ruby's mama, Charlotte and her aunt Girdie, had shared that room, slept some nights back to back like spoons, giggling like a waterfall.

Ephram went through the kitchen into the small bathroom and stumbled out, a bit of fear washing over him. Ruby knew that what he had seen might send him out of the door for good. Instead he stepped out onto the generous porch and walked down to the pump.

Before Neva died, Ruby'd heard that Papa Bell had started fitting the house for running water. He'd bought long iron tubes and loops of wire. He'd gotten as far as the bathroom. Then later, he had sold every last pipe for pennies on the dime.

Papa Bell would have liked him. He did not slip. Ruby had heard that her grandfather had built the steps a little slanted. "To keep out shaky, crooked folks," he used to say. "Straight-minded folk can walk up any kind of stairs."

Back when the house was young, Ruby had heard, often visitors ended up in the sugar snap peas just to the right of the porch.

When Ephram came back she watched as he turned left and walked into her room. It was the worst of them all, but it had been built square and spacious. The windows so wide they needed special panes of glass. It had been her Granddaddy's, and for all the ghosts who had haunted her, Ruby often wished he would come. He never did. Perhaps, Ruby thought, he had no great desire to spend one more second on earth. Maybe he had finally found a bit of rest sitting beside Neva on a star, paying the world no mind.

Once Ephram had taken on the job, he began in earnest.

The supplies were meager but he improvised well and worked steadily. He'd bought a can of Comet at P & K and added that to the few things she'd bought when she first arrived. He'd swept the floors with an old mud-caked broom he'd found out back. He'd held it under the pump until the water ran clean, then made it through two rooms, sweeping all manner of things into a central pile when his sister had come to the door.

Her eyes had bulged, the vein on her temple had leapt and strained. Celia Jennings stood at Ruby's door spitting like a raving lunatic, screaming down curses in the way of verses. So Ruby had started giggling, and then she started laughing. She hadn't meant to, but when she peeked through the window and saw the froth collecting in the corner of Celia's mouth, that Popeye-the-sailor-man hat bobbing on top of that ridiculous zebra wig, Ruby had stuffed her fist against her mouth and laughed until her eyes grew wet. Ephram tried to shush her with his eyes, which made her laugh harder.

Finally Ruby had gone to the door just to mess with the woman's head. Let her see him choose her. He had. Of course he had.

After his sister left he appeared lost. He had wiped his hand over his face and paused before turning back to Ruby, rubbed his arms and shaken out his legs. He'd seemed beaten for a moment, then he'd apologized for the interruption, and he started cleaning again. She would be ready for him when he finished.

Now he was using Chauncy Rankin's pail. Chauncy had filled it with water and doused her with it two nights ago in the back-yard when he'd come with his brother.

Moss had left the Dove soap whittling into slime in a broken bowl. Ephram was reaching for that now to wash his hands.

In the beginning, when Ruby first moved to Liberty, there had been many visitors and they had been more industrious. It had been harvest time, corn gold and tall, cotton flying and catching on tree tops. The chinaberry tree had sprouted the yellow berries all of the birds loved to pluck. It had been sweet, hot fall when the first—a slanted, tall man with a small keloid scar on his upper lip—had wandered down the road. She was scrubbing the old stain on the porch at the time—the one she'd heard her Auntie Neva had left when she died. When the man asked if she was little Ruby Bell, she'd told him yes. He said he'd known her grandfather, and her mama and aunts, and had seen her go to church on Sundays. He said he'd heard she was back in town, and he'd come by to offer his help. The fact that he was a janitor by profession proved convenient and so he had gotten down on his hands and knees and taken over washing the stained porch. Ruby couldn't remember his name—Jeffers, Jefferson, and didn't want to be rude by asking again, but he was polite and said thank you when she offered him a glass of water. He worked at the Colored High School in Jasper, and said he had a special cream cleanser at work that could get that up. He almost bowed when he left. When he came back a week later, Ruby had been growling in a corner, her clothes stripped and balled in the center of the floor. He had led her to her bed and taken her, simply and politely. He'd left the cleanser on the nightstand when he exited.

Word travels fast along the Sabine when it comes to unmarried women who offer horizontal refreshments. Three others came shortly thereafter. A tall, seal-colored man with a pious expression who'd quoted the Bible during and after. A fat, yellow sloth of a man and an old dark grandfather with a creased face. But then the high school boys from Jasper had made their pilgrimage. They came in bunches and they came drunk. Sometimes they came mean. Sometimes they hit, and worse, sometimes they laughed. As time passed, as her skin seemed to sink tight about her bones and she lost every remnant of sanity, fewer came. As the house piled high with human waste and garbage only the diligent remained. Old-timers like Chauncy and Percy wiped here and there before doing their business, always taking her outside. Sometimes under the chinaberry tree with the old crow staring down on them, calling out, blaming. Sometimes they brought a rag, or a box of lye and a jar of bacon grease to mix for soap. Sometimes they brought food.

What she never articulated, not even in adjoining thoughts, like train cars linking for a journey that she never let herself take, was that, of late, she had enjoyed these visits. Had found her own reflection in their routine. There was no other mirror in the house. These men, and their eyes—wide, slitted, beetle black, hazel green, repentant, fearful, angry, joyous, wet with lust—saw her. Not her grace, nor her strength. Not the plow horse of her soul, but they saw something. They held someone. They ached for her legs to part, for her to receive them. For in that instant, before release, the world could have split in two and they would have continued. Pumping steadily. Furrows deepening. Sweat washing. All hypocrisy silenced. And while they might have gone out and found a better, saner, prettier girl with full breasts, in that instant, nothing else on earth would suffice and subsequently Ruby knew the only power she had ever known on earth.

Ruby kept her screen door unhooked most nights.

Ephram had found the white box of lye and was sprinkling it like powdered sugar on the swept floors.

Ruby said softly, "You good at that."

"Thank you." He let a smile tickle the edge of his lip.

Ruby looked down at her foot. It had involuntarily started to become the grain of the wood. She felt herself grow too hard, too stiff to move. Small splinters formed a fuzz along the toes. Ruby ardently shook her leg and foot back to flesh. Ephram politely looked down at the floor as Ruby asked, "Your sister teach you?"

"She did as a matter of fact."

Now a familiar buzz started again, this time in her belly. The food smelled too strong, the cheese too bitter and orange. She couldn't eat such a bright aching color. She put it down on her soiled mattress. She was still hungry so she bit into the bread, but it caught as she tried to swallow. She coughed it into her hand and rubbed the chewed mass into the mattress.

Ephram noted it, but only said, "How's that coffee?"

Ruby picked it up and took another sip. The coffee stole down her tongue and secreted into pockets of her mouth before spilling down her throat. It was a friendly dull brown. Ruby chose not to answer his pushy question. Instead she took aim.

"Why you call her Mama?"

"Celia raised me."

"Wonder how your real Mama would feel about it."

It was Ephram's turn to be quiet.

"And what's all that you were talking about at the door . . . the ox in a ditch on a Sunday. What's that all about?"

The buzzing grew louder. Her stomach turned in on itself and Ruby felt the food rising into her throat.

He glanced at her. "It's a Bible verse, Book of Luke."

"What's it mean?"

The food spewed out of her mouth, covering the mattress, her throat raw. Ephram didn't pause. He took her hand but the sound was louder. His touch hurt her skin. She yanked away and walked to the window.

Ephram took the broom and swept the vomit into a pail. Then went to dump it. He came back in with his jacket wetted.

Ruby was relieved. He was to now take what he'd come for. She knew he would clean her up, wipe her down. The world tilted back to normal. The sound stopped as she imagined Ephram—a lonely, docile man who jacked off behind his "Mama's" bathroom door and hated his sin later. Ruby just stood there and waited.

He handed her his jacket and said, "Interesting you asked 'bout that ox. It's what Jesus say to the Pharisee when they give him a hard time 'bout healing a man on the Sabbath. Jesus say, if your ox fall down in a pit, whatever the day, you'd fetch him out. If it's important enough you got to do it."

She nearly yanked the jacket from his outstretched hand. "So my house is an ox."

"I'd say so."

She began cleaning her face and mouth in a kind of shock.

Ephram dipped the broom into the pail of lye water and commenced to scrubbing the bed. Then with a simple ease, he moved back to the floors.

Ruby watched Ephram cleaning and could feel the old house stretching under his hands, sighing and adjusting itself to better meet his efforts. The broom all but fell apart as he worked, but he mopped on with the handle and the shredded nub until Ruby could see the tan of the floor. Then he tackled the ceiling with a found rag. Small cubbies of dust and web disappeared from the corners, carrying with them the carcasses of forty or fifty houseflies. The stilt legs of spiders flew to the floor.

Ruby watched as Ephram disturbed the coiled shadows of men and women lining the baseboards. The homeless dead had been using her place as a squat for the past nine years, fully grown spirits who were not Ruby's kin. While they were a nuisance she had let them stay, no reason to refuse their entrance. They insulated the rooms and cushioned the alone.

Ephram began humming as he cleaned. Ruby gasped at his knowing. Perhaps a preacher's son knew something about haints. Maybe it was the lavender rings around his pupils or a lucky coincidence. Ruby watched as his voice vibrated against their parasitic intrusion. He did not stand up or billow out his chest. He simply hummed and the treble of his voice said, "Get." They yawned awake and slowly filed out her door.

Fuck, Ruby thought. He was more than she had imagined. This was not the man she had seen approach last night, the frightened man with only a puddle of life in his chest. Something had grown wide in him. It had a tide and a rhythm to it. *Fuck*. It smelled acrid and bitter, like the mattress. The scent was heavy in the room. Why was this man here? What did he come to take? Ruby's eyes squinted tight to better see him. What right did he have to flip her home over like a flapjack?

Ruby almost barked, "Hey."

He looked over.

"Hey." She smoothed the cut of her voice to better fit her purpose.

He was starting to tackle the potbelly stove. Something sticky and tar black had cooked to the iron years ago.

"You ain't got to do all that."

"Yeah, I do." He kept scrubbing.

"No, you don't." Ruby walked up to him. Once she was there, he turned to face her. She was close enough to smell his salt, and placed her hand over his. It burned yet she held it. She put her chin in the crook of his neck and slid her arm around his back. She tiptoed and pressed her groin ever so gently against his. Felt his lungs catch. Would he push into her with temerity? Or would he aim higher? Unzip his pants over the apple of her throat? A jaded anger rose from her gut. She wanted to swallow him whole and when he was properly trained she would release him.

The room creaked as the day brought warmth under her arms, between her legs. Ruby felt Ephram's hands around her waist. He all but lifted her off him and half carried her to the lone chair in the place. He leaned over her, lips close. She could see the oil that had collected along the curves of his nose. She closed her eyes.

"We already got one ox in the ditch. Let's leave it at that for now."

Ruby blinked. In that instant she saw what he saw. Her rib cage loose with skin. The spirit of meanness poking out of her like nails. The corrugated filth of her hair. But more. The broken femur of her soul, reset without a proper splint. She could accept anything on earth from a man except his pity.

"Faggot," she spat out, and ran from the house.

He caught up to her on the first step of the porch, his hand firm about her wrist.

She tugged against him, "Let me be." But he did not. He held tight to her arm so she spit out: "You ain't the only man I know."

"I know that."

"You just scared."

In kindness he said: "Maybe."

But Ruby knew that that was only partly true. Shame spread under her skin as she smelled the stench that rose from her dress, her scarecrow body. Blood caked in her thumbnail, sludge caught in the creases of her palms. And if that were not all Ruby was suddenly aware of the twisted knot of her features, the madness streaming out of her eyes.

For a moment Ruby grasped at the girl she had been, the one who had arrived in New York, fresh from Neches, scrubbed and eighteen. Haunting eyes, beauty mark painted by God, angled jaw, a tight sway in her hips. A dipping smile that men and women were drawn to, collided with one another to be near, handing over money and liquor and ready drugs. All that and more.

The year was 1950, when the town's literati adorned themselves in token colorful accessories. Ruby had been a bright bangle on the arm of one of their esteemed patrons. But that came later; first Ruby had had to kneel at the city's gate and decide what she would sacrifice for admittance. Her culpability had been an easy choice.

Chapter 12

It hadn't been difficult for Ruby Bell to find the ripe center of the city. Having never fully entered the house of her body, she had no difficulty finding boarders. Mr. Hubert Malloy was the first man to offer her ten dollars and change for sex. She had been sitting in Brewster's, a small jazz piano bar in the mid–West Twenties, listening to a tepid rendition of "Lush Life." That morning, Ruby had spent six of her remaining twelve dollars on the brushed satin dress that cinched midnight at her waist. She sipped water with an olive and a wink, until Mr. Hubert Malloy joined her.

He was a fur merchant whose second-floor business peered across Seventh Avenue to Penn Station. Monday through Friday he watched women and men crowd into its belly at dinnertime. Today he had stayed late and watched his mother-in-law, his wife's son from her first marriage, and his wife Bea, swarm down with them to the A train, Far Rockaway bound. He had entered the bathroom near his office, wetted a ball of toilet paper and wiped himself extra clean below. Then made his way to where Colored girls and White pretended to be equal in the creamy black hollow of a basement bar.

He had slipped his hand onto the small of Ruby's back and when she hadn't moved it, even to see who he was, he knew he'd found his girl. He was too round and belted to be hip, but the dark gave him courage. He'd bought her a Manhattan, because she said she'd never had one, and he fucked her two hours later by a threaded Blaster machine, mink pelts half stitched under its needle. Feet swinging inches above discarded black pumps. Bent at the waist, breasts scrunched against the giant spool of thread. Panties school girl white. No stockings. The scent of cured skins beside her white fingernails. He loved the feel of her. Nasty black and tight. The way she arched her young buttocks to allow him. The way her head never turned when he farted low and sticky. How he pulled her then to the floor upon scraps of rabbit and wolf, her face almost in the dustpan. Mouth open on still hide. She had no tits. Her padded bra lay like small lace hills on the ground beside her. It had been his one disappointment. But she was stringy and astringent and felt like a young boy with lipstick smeared down his throat. She was a nigger drag queen with a pussy. So it was easy to fuck her mouth and her anus. She opened to all of it and drank in his wadded semen. He gave her a rabbit stole and a whiskey kiss on her cheek. After. He pressed a folded ten-dollar bill to her palm, wrapped neatly around a "Bea's Furrier" card. Then he gave her two bits—a quarter, "for fare home," he explained. "Ten cents to spare."

It was the easiest money Ruby had ever made.

Ruby walked home. She carried the quarter close to her, then opened her palm. The word "Liberty" hung like a banner over the White man's head, which made it easy for Ruby to know whom it was promised to. Both word and coin. With God's trust and blessing.

Then she thought about the other Liberty, her Liberty. Red roads and piney woods. The sun yawning across the Texas sky, too tired to keep pace with the rolling earth. She thought about the *Carolina South*, which had taken her to Manhattan, the same train that had taken her mama seventeen years before. But her mother had chosen to pass. She'd stepped on Colored and walked off White in New York, shedding Liberty along the way, including her Blackness, her papa and a brown-skinned baby named Ruby Bell.

Ruby was constantly amazed by the gush of life pressing against her on the street. The theater marquees towering over her head. The bands plunking away on corners, crooning jazz, Southern blues and swing. The scream of taxi drivers, the sounds of rubber on concrete and hundreds of feet landing on pavement, then pushing off again with purpose. The eyes that raked over her, some approving, some not. The crush of Colored and White pressing shoulder to shoulder on streets, buses and subways. The enormous billboard with a stunning Negro woman named Katherine Dunham surrounded by Black men in feathers and masks, books standing tall in shop windows with the brown-skinned writers Richard Wright, Gwendolyn Brooks and J. Saunders Redding smiling back. And the people! Sure Ruby passed Colored men and women with their heads bowed, dressed as maids in loose overcoats, or men in coveralls with ashen, scraped hands. But there were also the immaculately groomed Negro women in matching olive skirts and scarves, cigarette holders and poodles on green leashes, hair coiffed and pressed perfectly under leaning hats. There were dapper chocolate men in brown velvet suits with piles of books stuffed under their arms. Along with hot dog vendors and pretzel men who glared at her, there were also thin White men with goatees who smiled warmly at Ruby and young, young White men with

shaggy hair and baggy slacks and stark women in loose skirts, passing out pamphlets about socialism and social reform, looking her
right in the eye and inviting her to meetings. Ruby was lost and
found, all at the same time. She scanned the many, many faces as
she had for five months, looking for the red hair, cream skin and
green eyes of her mother, Charlotte Bell, like the painted photograph that had lived above Papa Bell's mantel. She felt her mother
there, closer to her than air, on the periphery of her gaze. Since
Ruby had arrived she followed each woman she spotted with red
hair until she saw her face. This hope kept Ruby in Manhattan
after months of fruitless searching, that and a new seeded liberty, a
sharp-edged freedom that seemed to have taken root inside of her
when she first arrived in the city.

Ruby held the furrier's coin tighter. When she reached the
maid's room she rented in the Roger Williams Hotel on East
Thirty-first she clinked the man's quarter into an empty Band-Aid
tin in the medicine cabinet, behind the aspirin and the Dixie Peach.

After the furrier, Sherman Monty, the owner of Monty's
delicatessen on Fifty-third, gave Ruby a case of provolone and five
dollars for a blow job. The night manager of the Roger Williams
Hotel gave her free towels and sheets for the use of Ruby's hand
and her bottle of lotion. Her neighbor Mr. Moskowitz gave her
five pairs of panty hose for Vaseline sodomy. She gathered their
change as well.

Ruby thought about walking along the Hudson, but the other
women had razors, better shoes and pimps. She had seen the
women on corners, dangling like coat hangers—wearing deep
V-necks, red bandannas around their necks, and purple bruises
barely hidden from view.

Unwilling to trade sovereignty for the brutality of protection, she passed three years walking into bars where, sitting on silver gray stools, she could hide her feet in the shadow of the bar. She learned what to wear, how to speak, and shifted and slipped into and out of the mouths of men and darkened her beauty spot and lips and brows and uncovered the night Village throb. It was 1953. The hip and the beat crowd pretended to pretend that skin color was a frock you donned for the evening. Ruby was more than beautiful, causing men and women to pause in their stride, to bump into light posts and whistle long and low. She was younger than everyone and dangled easily and brightly from ears and throats. Until one night a stocky White woman at a table in Jim Atkins's Restaurant invited her to Julia's Place, a hidden, second-string lesbian club. There she learned about Swing Rendezvous, Stonewall, select house parties and the Pony Stable, where women in seersucker suits smoked like steam rising from a boiling kettle.

Ruby would never have discovered Page Three and Abby, had it not been for the ease of older women. Nothing to wash. No gummed knots to comb out of her hair. No lipstick cum on her gloves. And they were kind, most of them, and when they were not, how easy to defeat them. One glance at a man, a pair of slacks, a pillow of breath in the right direction and they crumbled. The slackest, firmest mountain would quake and the avalanche always brought compensation.

Then there were the arms. Firm, cuffed, creamed, soft, wide, beneath crisp white and linen. Elbows bent against brass or wooden bars. Or stretching for a filterless behind a ducktail, pomade darkening a narrow strip of tobacco roll. Reaching for bourbon and melting ice. Arms rising, banded, weighted and swift. Ready for protection and pain.

Then there were the hands. The old dykes carried countries in the valley of their palms. Rivers ran from the rise of their fingers, the blunt of their nails. Thumbs jutting out, peninsulas coasting the sweat of a glass or thigh. Pinching the edge of a Camel or clit. They walked sex in the crook of their smiles, in the cut of their eyes. Ruby discovered that they were the best men she had ever known. For their manhood coagulated in the raw shimmer of spirit, not groin. It electrified the thrust of their tongues and fingers.

Abby Millhouse, the Page Three's bouncer and the club manager's best friend, was tall, plain and crackled white. She had let Ruby into the club after barring her for a long nice beat. Ruby had flashed the kind of smile that let her know that tonight, if Abby played it just right, she might have company. That night Ruby called Abby her "Little Jack Horner." Because at forty-seven, Abby was the first woman to slip her wide, crooked thumb past Ruby's panties, bury it and twist slowly, steadily and with firm deliberation, until, in a gush of slick awareness, Ruby learned the true magic of opposable thumbs. Ruby loved to trace the mighty chip in Abby's front tooth with her tongue. She kissed the healed carvings along Abby's legs, and her missing kneecap, which Abby revealed with pride after four bourbon and sodas. She'd nearly been beaten to death by the infamous Batman and Robin, two cops notorious for attacking and killing old butches, fairies and drag queens near Washington Square, and in hidden alleys of the West Village. The doctors had told Abby she would never walk again. Ruby smiled at the thought of such a pronouncement over the angry body of her Manby, Ruby's word for Abby, which she would caw softly during sex, as the gristle warrior became melted cheese under the dome of Ruby's thighs.

When Ruby told Abby that she'd come to New York to find her mama, Abby pressed into her heart and said, "Maybe you already have." So one week after they'd met Abby came to the Roger Williams Hotel and watched as Ruby packed her life into two paper grocery bags. She filled them with: one midnight dress, one rabbit stole, one pair of black pumps, two Peter Pan padded bras, three pairs of panties, one pair of capri slacks, a black turtleneck, hair supplies, toothbrush, makeup and an old clinking Band-Aid tin filled with quarters. Abby carried the tan bags seventeen blocks to 275 East Twelfth, apartment 7. Ruby rented her body to Abby now, curled her life into Abby's warm lap.

Inside Abby's skinny railroad apartment, there was a naked mattress lopsided on the floor tiles, a single ceiling bulb skitting dim then bright. One foldout tin chair and a card table with one weak leg jimmied against the wall to keep it from spilling over. Only a hot plate and a pot for boiling. Ruby quickly spent Abby's savings on a Westinghouse stove, and ate the meals that Abby prepared for her. She took down Abby's torn sheet and hung new mint voile curtains instead. Introduced Abby to installment payments and finance charges in only four weeks. They painted the walls Pistachio. Ruby decided. Abby painted.

Ruby chose many things. Under her tutelage Abby went to a barber for the first time in her life, instead of snipping her own brindle-colored hair. It lay down and cooed against the width of her neck. She began sporting ties and jackets that Ruby had selected, and took on a new distinction at Page Three. Ruby played her part so well that all the girls in the club saw Abby in a new light. Ruby glittered against her in the dark. And when the police came at two o'clock one Saturday in June, as Abby and

Ruby were leaving after closing, it was Ruby who chose to give the boys a blow job in the backseat so they'd leave Abby alone.

Abby waited against the shadowed wall, trying not to look into the car's cloud windows. Car 224—Batman and Robin. When they'd called Abby over and opened the door of their squad car, Ruby had walked up to them in her stead, giggling like she was a bit tipsy, which she wasn't. She'd leaned into the car until the red-faced Irish Batman grinned. He had glanced over at Abby, whispered to Ruby then laughed out loud. Ruby had slipped in and the windows had been rolled up. But Batman squeaked the window down to stare in Abby's direction as soon as Ruby's head slipped out of sight.

After a time, Ruby stumbled out laughing, waving good-bye. Until 224 drove around Avenue A. Then her face fell. Abby and Ruby walked home in silence, their feet crunching on the sidewalk, walking into the spill of lamplight and out of it again. Laughing cars rolling past them, then fading. The sky fogged black.

Abby put a cigarette between her lips and lit it. The spin of flint and flame cast light on the puff red of her eyes. She quickly snapped the Zippo shut and inhaled deeply as they walked. As was their custom, Ruby reached out and took the cigarette from Abby's lips and took a long drag, coughing just a bit as she always did when she puffed Abby's Camels.

Ruby was drawn to the bright red hair of a magnificently bedraggled queen as she stumbled towards them, beyond drunk, mascara streaked to her chin, black hose torn at the knee and ankle. She winked at Ruby.

"Got 'nother cig?"

Abby motioned to the cigarette in Ruby's hand. "Last one."

The drag queen paused and wavered. "S'right. Got a nickel?"

Abby reached into her pocket and gave her a quarter.

She winked now at Abby. "Thankzz, honey-pie."

They parted ways. The redhead teetering on sky high heels. Ruby took another deep puff of the Camel as they walked. Then reached to replace the cigarette between Abby's lips. Abby paused. Averted her mouth for just a fraction of a second. Then took the cigarette, wiped the butt clean, of Ruby, of the fogged police car. Watching, Ruby felt her face flush hot. Before Abby could bring the cigarette to her mouth, Ruby snatched it from her, turned around and called out to the queen half a block away, *"Hey!"* Then walking swiftly to her, reaching her. "You want it."

The woman nodded. Her lips furry pink. Eyes blood red, rimmed in spider black.

"Thankzz, pretty." The queen reached for the cigarette.

"Trade." Ruby motioned to the quarter.

"That's not right." Then looking at the cigarette longingly she handed Ruby the quarter. She grabbed the cigarette, inhaled hard, swallowing the smoke in. She stumbled away mumbling, "Know that's not right."

Abby had stopped by the light. Ruby walked quickly past her, then had to wait on the stoop for her to open the door. When they walked into the soft green apartment, Abby asked Ruby, "What did that queen say to you."

Ruby lied without blinking, "She asked me if I missed dick too."

Abby stood bone still. "What. Did you say."

Ruby started undressing. She unzipped and peeled off her dress in a quick easy movement. "I said, 'Sure I do,'" she kicked off her shoes. "'—but I got a fix tonight so I'm cool.'"

Ruby unsnapped her bra. Stepped out of her panties and sauntered into the bathroom.

Her hand shook as she locked the door and climbed naked into the comfort of the empty white bathtub, Abby's quarter still in her palm. She turned the knobs and watched as the steaming water rose. Ruby opened her hand, looked at the coin and thought of the furrier. Remembered then how quickly she had thrown away the man's card. But his quarter had been something else. So were all the quarters now filling her Band-Aid box.

They were the calling cards she kept. She'd been given the first in 1939 at the Friends' Club in Neches County, Texas, when she was only six. Ruby set the quarter on top of her pubic hair as the water rose covering her belly. The water reached her breasts, her heart. Ruby could hear Abby clunking around outside the room. She heard her open the cupboard, heard a glass shatter in the kitchen sink. She imagined Abby drinking straight from the bottle. Then Ruby let her mind wander past a gated East Texas lot in Neches.

THE FRIENDS' Club was comprised of abandoned offices of corrugated tin. There was no grass for miles, as if a large boot had stomped its grilled sole upon the land and demanded nothing grow. Miss Barbara had been the hostess. She was plaster white and hard, poured wet into her skin dress and solidified in gooey mounds. She wore her inky wig high. Frost pink lips circled a gnash of rotting incisors. She smiled with her lips tight in camouflage, until some random act of cruelty caused her to laugh, exposing the corrosive brown. This was the woman who Ruby was handed over to periodically when Papa Bell was sick, and then more often after he died.

The first time the Reverend Jennings had taken her to Neches, she was dressed in her Sunday pink fluff dress, black patent leather shoes with lacy socks. Her Grandmother had heeded the Reverend's suggestion that Ruby work that summer for a nice White woman who ran a children's boarding school in Neches. Ruby would get paid for keeping the younger ones company and bringing in wood, washing dishes and such. She was to come back for a visit home every two weeks, then back to work until school started. Grandma Silvia had pressed her hair and tied it in a fancy bun on her head and packed a satchel with clothes and a traveling supper. The Reverend told her he was going to Nacogdoches to preach at the Faith Temple Revival and wouldn't mind at all dropping Ruby off in Neches.

After an hour of driving they stopped in Zavalla, near Rayburn Lake, to have their supper. Ruby felt nervous being with the Reverend but he was very polite and asked the kinds of questions grown-ups like to ask. They talked about the Reverend's children, Ephram and Celia. Ruby asked if they went to Lincoln Elementary School where she was to start in the fall. The Reverend said that they did. Ruby ate the drumstick and corn fritter that her Grandma had made her. The Reverend shared a cup of fresh milk that tasted funny and they talked until Ruby's eyelids got so heavy they dropped right down to her cheeks. She fell into a crashing sleep.

When she woke up from a very strange dream, the sky was pitch black and the Reverend was sitting across from her, smiling.

He said she seemed over-tired, so when she'd taken a nap, he just let her go on sleeping. The Reverend packed his tin and poured what was left in the milk bottle into the earth.

They had driven another hour to Miss Barbara's, then turned

down a crooked dirt road in the woods towards an old building with a red porch light. There was a flag nailed on the side that Miss Barbara later told her stood for "the Confederate States of America."

A strange little White man was waiting outside. He was just a head or so taller than Ruby, but his legs were shorter. He wore a plaid blue cap but his hands and boots were dirt black. When he saw the Reverend he gave a nod and knocked once on the porch door.

Miss Barbara appeared. Her whole body seemed to be smoking when she opened the door. She took a puff of her cigarette and rubbed Ruby on the head. The tiny man disappeared.

"Hey, y'all."

Ruby just nodded, awestruck by the sight of her.

The Reverend introduced Ruby to Miss Barbara, then the two adults took a few steps away from the porch and whisper-spoke, close, his mouth almost on her ear. Ruby watched Miss Barbara hand him an envelope. The Reverend looked inside then Ruby heard him say quiet, "You short by ten."

RUBY MADE little waves in the bathtub with her knees. She picked up her washcloth and a bar of soap. A brindle-brown hair curled on it. Ruby lathered the cloth and washed the makeup from her face, then under her arms. She'd forgotten to put on her shower cap and accepted that tomorrow her hair would be nappy. Ruby slid down and dunked her head under the water.

Miss Barbara was there just under the surface, offering Ruby her hand.

HER NAILS were bright pink and long like possum claws so Ruby hung back. When she smiled it frightened her more. Ruby could not stop staring at her teeth. It looked like a rat had gnawed at their dark edges.

"Gawd don't like a scaredy-cat." Her voice was high and sweet like they were old friends. Then she winked at Ruby and held out her hand again. Since there was no place else to hold on to Ruby gave her two fingers and Miss Barbara pulled her into the building. The room was a cloud of smoke, as if the chimney flue had been closed. Then there was the stink of it. It smelled just like a well that a water moccasin had died in, with something sticky sweet sprayed over it. The ashtrays were full of butts and empty Coca-Cola bottles sat beside them. The lights buzzed and flicked over her head and a gray sofa sat in the middle of the floor like a cat with crumbs on its whiskers. Magazines were spread out on the coffee table, *Life*, *Look*, *Movie Time*. A half-eaten sandwich let Ruby remember that she was hungry. Ruby didn't know for sure but it seemed to be some kind of a waiting room, but Miss Barbara kept walking through into a long dark hallway. Ruby felt her chest moving fast as she followed. She felt like she was getting smaller the farther she went into the hall. The smell got stronger. The floor was sticky and black under her feet. There were doors on either side, most closed. The first open one Ruby walked by she saw a little White girl's legs dangling from the edge of a bed. Ruby peeked around and saw her face. She looked like a baby doll Ruby had seen in the window of the Newton five-and-dime, same blue eyes and long blond hair except the girl's was tangled high and wild. She looked bored until she noticed Ruby and stuck out her tongue.

Miss Barbara patted Ruby's back to hurry her along. There were sounds coming from behind the closed doors. Cottony voices that made Ruby's throat close tight. Miss Barbara led her to a little room then spoke to the smoke rising up from her hands.

"This here's your room sweetheart. Bathroom's down the hall but seeing how you're Colored you'll have to use the one outside. Mighty inconvenient if you ask me, but thems the rules, you just got to ask permission first. And don't go touching this here lamp, it lets folks know what's what, all right? I'm gonna call you Bunny. You got any questions just ask for me, Miss Barbara."

She gave Ruby a good long look then she walked away. Ruby was alone in the tiny room. Something about the alone took all the air out of her so she fell down to her hands and knees, gulping in and out. She got light-headed until her gut told her to slow her heart. Ruby put her hands over her chest and pushed in there, stroking like she would a cat and after a time her heart slowed itself to normal. She kept doing this as she took in the room. It was almost empty save a strange bunk bed with its top half sawed away. That is when Ruby decided she was having a dream. Then the nightstand was a dream nightstand. With a dream ugly lamp without a shade. A dream empty candy dish beside it too. The dream walls were tall and dark yellow with paper bubbling all the way up to the ceiling.

After a while Ruby grew tired of standing and started biting her mouth. She'd discovered it was a way to pass the time while she sat in church, nibbling at the soft inside of her mouth. She placed her crooked finger on the outside and pushed the soft inside into her teeth. Then she stopped because she could feel it, and in a dream you can't feel anything. Her tummy grumbled a make-believe dreamy rumble, then started flipping and her legs got tired so she sat in the only place there was to sit. Climbing up onto the bed and letting her legs hang over the edge, her shoes thumping lightly on the wooden frame. When the door creaked. Ruby's heart pushed up into her mouth.

A tan mulatto girl was standing in her door, no more than seven. She slipped in and stood eyeing Ruby, then looked in the candy dish. Her hair was reddish like Ruby's mama's but with sparks of blond. Her eyes were light gray and she had a dimple under her left cheek.

"Ain't you had no friends yet?"

Ruby looked back in answer.

"You get to keep your change. Don't let nobody tell you different. Tried to take mine 'til I learned better."

They stared at each other for a long stretch.

Then the girl said, "Don't never tell them your name."

Ruby didn't understand but something inside her felt like she'd just heard gospel.

Ruby nodded back as Miss Barbara stepped in the door with a lampshade. Her face tight she said, "Tanny now get back in your own room." Tanny ducked under her arm and made a funny face, which smoothed out the terror rising like water. Then she ducked out of the door.

Miss Barbara's eyes stabbed into Ruby. "Mind you keep that one out of your room. She's a bad influence."

Then Miss Barbara let a smile land upon her face as she fitted the shade over the lamp and quickly disappeared. A man with a big square head came in—the top and the bottom of it almost had corners. He was paste white with red-water eyes. He smelled sour like the rye Papa Bell kept for Sundays. His necktie was loose. Ruby thought about how it looked like a scarf her Auntie Girdie used to wear before she moved to Kansas to marry that porter and how dreams made you think of all kinds of funny things from all kinds of places. Like how real-life men didn't walk around with tiny little bodies or with square heads. The man nodded that he wanted to sit beside Ruby so she let go of the scarf and Auntie Girdie and scooted over. Her heart was beating behind her eyes so hard she was sure she would wake up. And then she wanted, needed to wake up, because something in the quiet man beside her was more terrible than any monster she had ever imagined, and so she started pinching her arm. She started pinching it harder and harder but still he kept sitting, hands pressed together between his legs, head down. Ruby pinched again and again, her eyes watching his fingers, his square thumbs, the brown stains along the inside of them. Ruby wiped away the little welts of blood as they popped through her skin and kept pinching as they sat and sat and sat. She stopped when she saw his body begin to shake, saw his hands fly up to his face as if to stop a running pump. He was bawling, snot and tears running through his fingers, down his arms. Loud like a little baby. Singy song cries and big gulps of air. Ruby thought it would stop, but it got worse until he crumbled up on himself, clutched at his belly like someone had punched him, and hid his face from the lamplight. He cried like the whole wide world had split in two, cried like he had lost his first child and his mama and his best friend. Ruby had never seen a body that sad, not even Great-Uncle Tippy after he lost his dog Pete after sixteen years. Or even Papa Bell when he talked about Neva. The square-head man's sorrow broke through her. Ruby breathed in the sweet and the sour of him, so that it filled her lungs and pushed tears from her own eyes. Until she felt so sorry for him that she made the mistake of reaching out to help him, and he turned on her.

The things he did to her hurt worse than anything she knew,

than any way she imagined she could be hurt. But the things he called her hurt worse, words she didn't know the meaning of but felt slugging through her, moving into her like poison. *Slut*, and *cock-tease* and *whore*. His stained fingers grabbing, opening, licking all the while, moving his hand inside of her pants, then pushing her down, hands like lobster claws. Anger sweating from his body, entering hers, his words spoken to the center of her own skull. *Horny bitch. Fucking slut.*

Then . . . then Ruby searched the dark of her own body and found a hiding place, thick in the branches of the chinaberry. It held her safe. The leaves full, always green. The sky all stars and crickets. There were sounds above her, horrible sounds, so she pulled herself closer and prayed to the tree. The tree answered, and she saw her hand turn to bark, broken mahogany ridges, her fingers tiny living twigs, with golden beads dangling from them. Her torso melted into the trunk and her toes lay safe underground. The sky shook over her head but Ruby was now the tree. She stood there safe and waited for the storm to pass.

But the girl still on the bed, trapped under the weight of a giant, had no such refuge. The thick tide of his hate poured over her, filled every inch until she had no choice but to swallow it down.

You nigger cunt. You little Black whore.

And so that is what Ruby became.

A firefly inside of that girl fought it. Then as if he knew, felt it, he slapped her like a father disciplining a child. Just hard enough to set off a lightning of fear that nearly lifted her off the bed, until she shattered, pieces flying like glass and landing all across her body. Each holding a fractured picture of the moment. The ceiling, his red eye; the wallpaper, his mouth stretching open; the lampshade, and the firefly. That last piece sank deep within her flesh, deeper than she could know, and lay dormant for the many years that followed.

Ruby did not unfold from her hiding place until the man was weeping beside her again. Holding her to his wet face, fumbling to put her clothes back on, crying so hard and so long that when he asked if she thought he was a bad man, Ruby knew to answer no. As he was leaving he smiled like a boy who had broken his mama's lamp. He reached in his pocket and put two bits into the candy dish—a quarter. Her first tip from her first Friend.

Miss Barbara stepped back into the room, removed the shade and handed Ruby a damp towel and a blue dress. "Clean yourself up now Bunny, we got another friend coming for a visit in about ten minutes."

So that is where Ruby waited each night for the next two whole weeks with grown White men entering the small of her room. As they left, they clinked a quarter, sometimes more, into the empty candy dish. She learned how some mothers and grand-mothers brought change purses for their girls. On her fifth night there, one man, who Miss Barbara said had paid extra, told Ruby she was her own change purse, pushing the quarter into her and whispering, "Ching, ching."

Ruby had wished the visitors would give them sweets instead of tips. How in the entire building there didn't seem to be a sliver of Wrigley's Spearmint Gum or Pixy Stix or Chunky Bars to unwrap themselves into the hands of a little girl. "But plenty of jawbreakers," she'd heard Miss Barbara joke.

Tanny and Ruby were the only Colored girls with Miss Bar-bara. Miss Barbara once said, "You girls are important here because gentlemen can do things with a Colored girl they simply can't bring themselves to do with a White girl." Ruby knew that the White girls were always good girls, even when they were bad, but Negro girls started bad and could be anything after that.

One long night, after Ruby had had more than eight Friends visit her, she had fallen into the twilight of sleep. She was awakened when her door creaked open and the little man with the hat crept in, reached his hand into her candy dish and scooped out $3.25. Without thinking, Ruby sprang from the bed. She was on him, arms and legs flying, speeding through the air like bullets, balled-up little fists pounding hard, fast. He held her at bay laughing, then pushed her to the bed.

"All right, all right, I was only counting it."

Ruby was out of breath, heaving on the mattress.

He was turning to leave when he said, "Miss Barbara was right. You're a born whore."

But he hadn't needed to tell her. Ruby already knew. Already knew she was a whore. A nigger whore who could make $3.25 in tips in a single night.

RUBY KNEW who she was as she stepped out of the tub of cool water, fingers puckered, body shivering. She realized that she had somehow forgotten that fact, playing house at 275 East Twelfth, looking for a mother who knew well enough to leave trouble early. Ruby wouldn't forget it again.

She reached into the draining tub and pulled out the coin, then dried herself and climbed into bed. Abby curled at the far end of it. Ruby knew Abby had cried herself to sleep, but Ruby didn't cry. Evil things seldom do.

One week later, Ruby traded up, almost fucking a dyke of

better means on the Page Three dance floor as Abby watched. Abby ran up and slapped Ruby hard. Ruby skidded across the floor into a table leg. Stood up, leaned back on the bar and dabbed the blood from her mouth. She smoked a cigarette without coughing as the two women fought. Hard. As they tumbled out bloody into the street. Outside, Ruby glimpsed a tall redhead walking away from the commotion, a unique grace in her step. Ruby didn't bother to turn her head.

Chapter 13

Ruby blinked and in an instant the past eleven years washed down her cheeks. Ephram led her back into the house and sat her on the edge of the bed. The day was slipping into evening. She looked at where she had lived for over a decade. Late. When, she wondered, had it become so late? New York, Liberty, the slide into hellfire. All forty-two years broke across her body, knocking her into a waiting chair.

She managed to push words out of her mouth, "What year is this?"

He didn't skip a beat. "Nineteen seventy-four."

She had wasted eleven years walking the red roads of Liberty. Without her noticing, age had stolen into her joints, under the ash of her skin. She sat quite bare before Ephram, looking into his soft, sad eyes.

"Nineteen sixty-three . . ."

Ruby shook her head. She looked down at her hands and barely whispering said: "I ain't the woman I once was."

He smiled. "You plenty woman Ruby, don't you never think different."

She looked off towards the window.

Ephram took her hand, "But I'll tell you what. I'm most interested in the woman you have yet to be."

Gratitude flooded through her limbs. For the first time in eleven years, that future woman held interest for her as well. The room was almost copper in the afternoon sun. Ephram found her hand and held it soft in her lap. Something like a small window opened in her throat and the first tears began to pour down her cheeks.

Neither she nor Ephram heard the first knock on the door, nor the second. When the windows started rattling and a shrill voice started calling, "Yooo-hooo. Yooooo-hoooo . . . anybody home?" Ruby and Ephram broke out of the spell that had surrounded them. She heard a small crash and a yelp.

Ruby found the weight of her legs, got up, opened her door and stepped out onto the porch, coming face-to-face with Su pra Rankin, Righteous Polk, Moss Renfolk's wife, Tressie, and Supra's daughter, Verde, pulling herself out of the vines, sputtering, "Damn steps." Ruby fell back and inadvertently closed the door behind her. They seemed to loom over her, bearing deluxe Tupperware containers of potato salad, blackberry cobbler, cod peas and smothered chicken, a look of grim determination on each of their faces.

Supra was a wide, square woman with a matching wide, square bosom. She wore a simple green dress. Her hair, silver with generous streaks of taupe, was pulled so tight it lifted the corners of her eyes. She stood a half-inch above five feet, which caused folks to joke that if they didn't know any better, they'd doubt that she was the Rankin boys' mama. Her comfortable brown shoes were covered in dust.

The women descended upon Ruby like chicks on a handful of corn.

Ruby turned and ran into the closed door. She felt as if the house had punched her. The women spun her about.

Ephram called from behind the closed door, "Ruby! You all right?"

"Child, how you keeping yourself?" Supra started, her hands petting Ruby along her shoulders until Ruby felt a snarl at the base of her gut.

"Yes, how you been making out?" Righteous twilled in a remarkably high voice.

Ephram tried the door but the women pressed against it.

Tressie Renfolk, a girl-faced matron, kept her lips in a tight line and awkwardly handed the potato salad to Ruby. "We brung this from the Women's Auxiliary."

Righteous gentled the thing. "Was already cookin' aplenty what with Junie Rankin's wake tonight, so we figured we bring some on over to you."

Verde Rankin added, "This too." She thrust a worn Bible into Ruby's hands.

Righteous produced her Bible from her purse. "Figured we might do a little study while we're here, if that's all right with you."

Ephram pushed against the door until they all peeled away. He took Ruby's hand: "What y'all want here?"

All four women, as if on cue, slit their eyes at the sight of him. Supra put her arm around Ruby and stepped past Ephram as if he were not there. These four women had petted and praised Ephram since he was a child. He had stood, in his forty-five years, as a perfect example of Christian manhood. Ephram felt their cold shoulder like ice cream on a cavity.

As the women crossed the threshold, they stopped and took in the state of the house. A broom lay by a bucket, black with God knew what. Scraps of filth still affixed themselves to the floors. Rags lay used, every inch the color of tar.

Righteous let out a "Lord have mercy!" Verde pulled out her handkerchief and held it tight to her nose and mouth.

Supra mumbled a prayer against the demon filth. "Create in me a clean heart, O God; and renew a right spirit within me."

She looked at Ruby, distracted, the Bible and salad tilting in her bone arms. "Child, we been meaning to come out, check to see how you doing. See you surely in need of ministering."

Righteous fell in step on Ruby's left flank. "Yes we sho' been meaning to do that. How *are* you doing girl?"

Verde looked about the house. "I see you been doing some cleaning."

Ruby's lip was twitching, her eyes full and wild. Her body began to shake then, began to topple. Supra caught her before she slipped to the ground.

Ephram took Ruby's elbow, eased her away from Supra and said, "I'd like to thank you ladies for stoppin' by today to visit with Ruby but as y'all can see she awfully busy—"

Supra shot back under her breath, "You already done enough busy-making last night, ain't you?"

Tressie pelted him with disgust. "We'll take it from here, Ephram."

Righteous spit out softly, "Ain't you got a home to go to?"

The shame caught Ephram by surprise and made his tongue grow thick in his throat.

Then Supra set Ruby's potato salad down on the sideboard. The other women followed suit. She took Ruby's hands in her own and started, "Ruby, I knew your mama and I called your grandmama my friend so I hope you know I'm speaking from my heart when I say this. The Devil got ahold of you and he's just like a tar baby, anyplace you touch him he stick, and if you tries to unloose him with your own hand you just gonna get more twisted and stuck."

"Amen," Righteous whispered.

Supra looked hard at Ephram. "And them who come up to that tar baby with good deeds on they lips but sin in they heart gone git stuck just the same."

Ephram saw Ruby try to say something with her eyes but Supra rolled right over it. "Now mores the shame we ain't been out here sooner, but livin' in a world of sin you get tired of fighting fires with thimbles and just start tending to your own backyard, your own good family. But when my friend Celia break down and cry her heart out in church, well then we talk to the Pastor and he agreed to meet us down to the lake."

Tressie's girlish face cut through with concern. "We would greatly appreciate your company to the lake for a baptism. Wash your spirit clean in the blood of the Lamb."

Verde grumbled under her handkerchief, "Washing her ass clean be a start."

Righteous piped in, "We got three deacons and our new Church Mother Celia waiting down there as well. She don't bear no grudge for nobody for nothing. That's just how she be."

Tressie added, her face somber, "They praying down there while we come up here to get you. If we ain't down there directly, they might just come up here and take you."

Ephram broke in, "Ruby—she's not going nowhere."

The women promptly ignored him.

"Celia say that the Devil been content with your soul, but now," Righteous shook her full face in concern, her skin as smooth as a river stone. "He's interested in pulling the rest of Liberty, one by one, down into hell and can't nobody let that happen. She say when he can grab hold a good man like Ephram Jennings, then ain't none of us safe."

Supra pulled Ruby towards the door. "Come on now, child, it ain't a matter of if, it's a matter of when."

Ruby found herself, felt Ephram's eyes strong against her, yanked her hand out of Supra's. The woman's fingers were like ice. Ruby felt the whole of her arm growing into one long icicle. In a moment she knew she would smash her fist into the woman. In a moment she knew she would scream.

Ephram quickly swallowed the silencing shame into his gut where it belonged. "I'm sorry but y'all got to leave."

Supra took a stand. "I wasn't talking to you Ephram Jennings. You sound like you been batter-dipped and fried in wrongfulness. I was talking to this poor bedeviled child."

"Excuse me, Mrs. Rankin," Ephram managed, "but it took y'all eleven years to get here, another day or two won't make no difference."

"How long it take you?" she shot back.

He looked at Ruby. She let him catch her eye. "Too long." A calm washed over her and the ice melted.

Verde whined through her kerchief, "Mama, can we just go? You can cut the funk up in this place with a knife."

Supra then put her hand on Ruby's face. "Child, your mama might of fallen from grace but that don't mean you got to follow. You got to choose right, else evil win every time."

Verde started stacking the Tupperware tubs against her chest.

Supra glowered at Verde. She turned to Ruby and said deathly quiet, "Folks ain't going to leave this thing to buckle the weave of the town. You come to us or we come to you, but we gone have your salvation come Sunday." Then between gritted teeth to Verde, "Leave them things."

Ruby finally spoke. She turned to Verde and said, "Leave everything but the cod peas."

Verde greedily eyed the cobbler and the chicken, then her mother, who nodded yes. Verde fumed out of the house with the cod peas, followed by Righteous, Tressie and finally Supra.

When the door closed Ruby looked at Ephram. She breathed out, let the floorboards steady her and managed, "I always did hate cod peas."

"They never did one thing for my salvation neither."

Ephram put on a smile, so Ruby found hers and dusted it off. They looked straight at each other long enough for her grin to settle.

Then Ruby pulled away from Ephram, from Papa Bell's house, and walked into the pines. She found the narrow pathway she had taken so many times as a child, all the way to the far side of Wilkins land, where they buried their kin, even after they had all moved to Beaumont. All but Maggie. Ruby saw the grave in the distance, flecked with thin, curling willow leaves. She wished Maggie had a headstone. She deserved at least that, with something sweet and secret etched on the front—but the sisters had built the cross nice and sturdy. Ruby knelt there for a time, her hand flat upon the soil. Then she lay down not three yards away, near a waving cluster of jonquils. She had come there for answers, but since she wasn't sure of the questions, she breathed in the sweetness—then erupted into a hundred little yellow blossoms and slept the afternoon into evening.

THE REST of the day the road in front of Bell land had more business than it had in years. Ephram walked the road exactly four times, once to borrow a bath tin and a change of clothes from Rupert Shankle, once to find a trim of fallen cedar to chop into cooking wood, twice to buy things on credit at P & K. He'd already used up the ten dollars he'd won from Gubber and he wasn't yet ready to face Celia for his wallet. He cursed himself for having forgotten the lamp oil the second time. Both times he walked past the crowd at P & K in silence, each time causing a stir as he left.

Then there were the children who'd been in church that morning when Sister Jennings—now Mother Jennings—had told the congregation that the Devil was living out on Bell land. Never having seen the Devil in person, about six of them perched on the fence across the road from the Bell house and waited for him to show his face.

About twenty other people found themselves wandering the back road to Bell land that day to see if Ephram would fall down and start foaming the evil out of his mouth. Instead they watched a lone man clean and tote and haul. But it was still more than enough. It wasn't just the exhibition of sin that Celia Jennings had painted so beautifully during testimony that morning, it was the pure, unadulterated, juicy, unholy spectacle of the thing. The scarecrow crazy whore of Liberty had taken up with the township's mule of a deacon. It was the best piece of gossip the town had had to chew on in twenty-three years.

Chauncy Rankin and his brother drove by slowly as evening

gave way to night on the way to their uncle's wake. They parked just up the road and watched the glow of the house. Chauncy wondered why it hadn't occurred to him to clean the gal and the place up proper so that he and Percy could have her on tap whenever they got the itch. He quietly cursed Ephram Jennings, and realized he hadn't, in all the years he'd known him, given the man his due.

Evening found Ruby leaving Maggie's grave. The perfume of tiny cream flowers still drifting from her pores. Then she made her way through the silent, watching pines. When she reached her home its windows shone with amber light. The water pump held moon light.

Ruby imagined Ephram inside and felt a gentle hand upon her heart. But her children were calling to her, so she went to the chinaberry and knelt. Their voices rose like music from the earth, violas and flutes, weaving into one song. Then she felt the many small ghosts who were still hidden in her body. The ones she had yet to give birth to. They turned and shifted within her. Ruby looked at the last whispers of dark blue evening and felt compelled to dig not only one grave, but another and another. Then she waited for the pain, the pushing to begin—seeing yet another murder.

Suddenly each child, still roaming her body, looked towards the small graves of sifted earth. Something was different. They moved in unison. Ruby knew it was time. They did not tear through her as they had every night for years. Instead each one simply floated from her belly, soft as a puff of talcum powder. It was not a birth, but a gentle exodus.

The last to leave was her own baby. The one who had followed her from New York, who had come to her on the train platform.

Her own child. The sweet baby girl she never named. The child Ruby had at Miss Barbara's when she was fourteen. When, pregnant and round, men still took her body gently, or sometimes with an amazing brutality, in spite of, and at times because of her condition.

Ruby looked up. It seemed that there were more stars peeking above her, moving into position, the Dipper and the Southern Cross.

The little spirit paused at the small precipice. She looked at Ruby. She wanted Ruby to remember, so Ruby saw it all. Her old room, after a man had left, before another entered. Ruby remembered how she had felt, full of hopeful life. The morning sickness had stopped. Now, at eight months, her girl was strong within her, in spite of the fact that Ruby had never seen a doctor. It was as if the child knew she would have to build and grow without a kind or knowing hand. Ruby's child was the strongest part of her, until one night Ruby was knocked down by a crushing punch into her gut by a john, who paid a little extra. Always a little extra. Ruby curling, holding, protecting as he kicked with a brown boot. Again and again. Then acted out a rape, a brutal rape of a soon-to-be-mother, which is what he had come for. One day after he left, the contractions came. The ripping unbearable pain. No hospital. Nothing. Pushing, screaming, with not a single soft eye upon her. Still her baby fighting, then slipping out of her. Someone caught her child and dropped her onto Ruby as if the infant were soiled laundry. Ruby saw the top of the baby's head, wet, red dotted with white. Little hands . . . ten little chubby miracles. The child was crying, laying upon her. Crying. Then coughing. Coughing as if she had swallowed Marion Lake. Hands taking her away. Ruby reaching out. Her baby coughing so hard. Then soft. Then little gasps of air. Then she was quiet in another person's arms. Until the silence grew heavy with meaning.

The only words Ruby heard were, "She dead." Which is how Ruby knew she was a girl.

On the rise of the hill, under the sky, the little spirit turned away from Ruby. She seemed satisfied. Her mama had not forgotten her. She lay herself down and let herself be covered with earth.

Ruby kept her hand upon the mound for a long time. She let out a sigh. It was safer there—the womb or the earth. The womb or the earth. Ruby realized sitting next to all of her children that the soil was both. The world would hold them.

Ruby knew they would still leap and play. She would still visit them come sundown, have them lean up and listen to bedtime stories. Even play hopscotch and freeze tag during the day. But at night they would sleep in their graves. At night they would be safe. She bent down and kissed the kind earth and went towards the warmth of the house.

When Ruby walked through the doorway the first thing she noticed was that the house smelled of cedar.

There were two kettles of water boiling and a huge tin tub full of bathwater on the floor. Ephram stood in the center of the kitchen, washed and wearing a pair of overalls two sizes too big.

The house was clean. A few furtive stains remained in the grooves of the floor, but the walls, the baseboards, the window frames, all of the wood seemed to glow like bronze. The belly of the stove was alive with flames. The six kerosene lamps threw saffron rays onto the walls. A full plate of chicken and potato salad sat on the sideboard. The steam rising from the bath and the kettles was doing something magical and luminous with the light. Crickets and owls harmonized in the blackness outside.

There was a clean sheet folded near the tub.

Ephram motioned towards it. "I'll be outside drawing plenty water. You eat your fill, then get in that water, have yourself a good soap, then drape that sheet over the tub. I'll be in directly." And he stepped into the night. Ruby did just that. The food, though seasoned a little heavily with judgment, went down just fine.

The water was almost too warm against her skin and its waves held her. She looked and found the Dove soap on the floor. The white turned tan where it touched her skin. She washed her face. Her neck. The water was just right now, so warm under her arms and between her thighs, her long, long legs, her breasts, her cocoa nipples, her belly. She dunked her hair under its surface and brought it out steaming, stretched the sheet over the tub and softly called to him.

Ephram walked in and looked at Ruby. He poured an alchemy of oil, steam and well water into a pitcher and poured it over Ruby's thick hair. It seemed to drink the water like desert sand. Ruby sighed.

He arranged his supplies on the sideboard: two large tins of Crown Royal hair dressing. Casey Farms peanut oil. Ginger root. White Rain Shampoo and Conditioner. Hair bands, small blue worlds attached to black elastic eights, like children wore to Sunday school. And a wide-toothed comb and scissors.

Her hair was hard in places like thick plastic. It had matted so that scabs had formed along the scalp, bled and dried into scars. Some of the hair had tangled into ropes, so dense, so solid that it would have been easier to shave her head and start fresh. As if she could read his thoughts she said, "It might be easier to cut it off."

But she said it the way pretty women say things they know

people will disagree with. He smiled at the weight of her pride. The roots of her belief in her beauty ran deep, had lasted through over a decade of drought. Maybe, he thought, the tips of her hair remembered.

Ephram had always thought of a woman's hair as living testimony to her life, her memories. Celia kept hers twisted tight under bobby pins, bound by headscarves and wig nets. His mama had kept hers free and puffy, until, he'd heard, they had made her tie it back at Dearing. He'd silently watched women and the complexity of their hair all of his life. He knew that some memories were better cut out, amputated. He'd seen women freed that way. But his bones told him that Ruby needed her past to find her way home. So he spent the night tending to her hair.

He had no one to ask so he supposed. He started with soap. The first suds turned black. He rinsed her hair with a pitcher, pouring the water into a separate bucket to spare the clear moving warmth of the tub. Then he washed it again and again. By the seventh rinse, the water almost ran clear. It felt like heavy, black wet wool.

The hair started whispering to his fingers. It showed him where to part and what to leave alone. It told him to crush wild ginger and mix it with the peanut oil, to warm it, to slip into the tunnels beneath the tumult and work that concoction along her scalp with his fingertips. He suddenly realized that it had been speaking to him all day while he was cleaning, telling him what to buy, what it needed. It frightened him. He wondered if Supra hadn't been right after all, that maybe devilment was catching. Maybe crazy was a cold you caught. But then the fear left him and he realized that the whole wide world had been talking to him for years, only he'd stuffed cotton into his ears, packed it tight until a rail thin storm of a woman had knocked it out with a kick to his head.

So he opened himself up and listened as it told him how to work the conditioner into each corded knot. How to aim not to free the bond, but be content with loosening it bit by bit. It led him to eventually comb the fringed edges, then helped him to work like a craftsman, extracting strands one, two, three at a time.

He kept the kettles on the stove so that the air stayed heavy and moist. He heated the water in Ruby's bath as slow hours passed. He worked steadily, courteously. He worked in love.

Around two in the morning, he stepped onto the porch as Ruby emerged from the bath naked and golden, and lay herself under clean linen atop the mattress. Ephram covered her with another sheet, slipped a grocery bag under her head and continued working. She tumbled into a sleep so deep, that she forgot to be afraid.

White Rain and oil at the ready, Ephram combed and soaked, teasing out the stubborn fists. At about four in the morning, three-quarters was free. It twisted and curled and waved like a river set loose from a dam. Down her neck, across her shoulders and dripping past her angel blades. Then Ruby's hair began to do more than guide Ephram's hands, it began to guide his heart.

It spoke to him in feelings. Each strand holding a story, each knot an event. Trapped bundles of thought, released. Her youth lived at the ends of her hair. Her present life near her scalp. He was midway down her back when suddenly the words *Where is my baby?* seeped into his hands. He felt an empty hollow in his belly. His throat clenched tight. Then *Where is my baby? Where . . . is . . . she? What happened?* Then a scream, spreading like a grease fire, until it exploded. *Where you put her body?* Gone.

Taken. Ephram parted her hair through his tears. He worked in fractions.

Exhausted, eyes red, Ephram freed a coiled spool of black. It seemed to bounce lightly between his fingers. He felt his skin soft as gardenia petals. The froth of silk against knees. Lips coated in thickly spread color. He heard the thump of music and felt the sway of his hips keeping perfect rhythm. A man's firm hand, spinning him, skirt swirling, lifting. Then the eyes of men pausing, watching. He felt a confidence, a certainty in the power of beauty, as the music swelled and laughter bubbled from his throat.

He loosened another strand and felt the blue flame of life in his belly. His body yielding, accommodating, and like a sweet gum tree come autumn, filling with milk. He felt his torso stretch, making way for the building, spinning matter, until it was as heavy as a planet in his womb. Until a sixty-foot wave crashed into the thimble of his body and there the child was, like a damp feather upon his breast, weighted as a new world.

He reached a knot, too tight, too large, it tugged free in his hand. His face grew hot. A terror so strong it busted the wall of reason. Felt himself entered, torn, ripped, bleeding. Felt sweat slick, spit hurtling against his cheek. He felt himself gag, choke then accept. He felt what it was to be mute earth. A dull ache wound through his fingers until he tackled another mass.

As he held tight to Ruby's hair, his palm itched and then was tickled, so he was forced to smile. Then laugh. Then gasp as his pelvis warmed like honey in the sun, as hot sticky waves swirled, as his entire body tightened, contracted, as a lightning rod of bittersweet ache buckled his flesh. Too, too sweet, embarrassingly so, like a roller coaster crashing to the dip, only to discover it had another hill to climb and dip, and climb and dip. Exploding again and again and again. When it ended he didn't know how to fix his face. He wilted like a week-old rose. He released the reins of her hair. He looked up and saw the moon reaching in through the window. Ruby still sleeping and the caw of a lonely crow breaking up the silence.

So this is the life of woman, he thought, and kneeling beside the bed, head on the mattress he fell asleep.

Book Three

Revelations

Chapter 14

Under the blackberry sky, the impartial moon shone on night phlox, evening primrose and lone houses with slanted steps. It also cast upon wolf cubs caught in traps, hidden bones long buried and burning crosses—with the same indifferent grace.

That night, the Dyboù stretched along a ridge of pines moving towards a glowing light in the distance. Dead pine needles shifted under his belly; above him the branches and needles shivered. He liked the way the old trees bowed and groaned, pushed by a stolid might.

When he reached the pit fire, he saw the men in the distance. Eyes on something they had just cast into the fire. It yowled. He smelled the thing being burned alive.

As he slid forward, he could taste the screams of the cat. See her black fur catching and her fangs, screeching, green eyes covered over, then eaten by the hungry flames. It took a while for her to stop fighting, then he gulped in the shaking spirit of the creature, still locked in its scorched body—barely alive. It disappeared inside of him forever. They could have burned something larger. But he had been hungry. It was enough.

One man stood before the others, the leader, soot and blood in the crease of his palms. The others were waiting in the waving heat. The Dyboù lifted high above them, higher, then blasted down like a grenade upon the circle. They all stumbled and fell back. He lifted again and chose the horse he would ride. They all wanted him, their mouths open, teeth bared and wet, saying the old words until their lips grew white in the corners. He chose the strongest man among them and fell like an anchor upon him.

The Dyboù looked out of the eyes of the man. His man. His horse. He felt the strength of his muscles, the heat of his crotch. He had chosen well. The man was shaking violently on the earth, nose bleeding, drool down his neck, trying to fit the Dyboù into the acorn hull of his human body. The man's spirit folded smaller and smaller to make way.

The Dyboù waited. Like fucking a virgin, the Dyboù took his time until the man became accustomed to his size. Then he plunged in deeper. He felt the man's likes, his dislikes, his penchant for menthol tobacco, his favorite tie and suit. He did not smother the man's soul—he welded to it.

Soon he lifted the man to his feet. He looked at all of the living men, their dumb faces glowing yellow. He smelled the pines. Then he drew back and bit into the skin of the man he was wearing. The man bucked, so the Dyboù sunk his teeth through the muscled arm until he had the faint taste of blood, until it ran down his forearm and his hand. He had been branded.

The circle of men gave him the red bag and a black bottle. It was the reason they had called him. They thought. But it had been his idea all along, planted like brackle in their minds while they slept between white cotton sheets.

Now he felt the soles of his feet on the forest floor. The hush of owls, the quiet of the crickets. The living thicket watched.

The red bag in his palm was heavy with magic, made more powerful by the wet blood that had streamed into it.

Before the powder had found its way into his hand, it had been a mandrake root, baking and drying in the West Texas sun. It had then been gathered when the moon was void, by a left-handed man, and had never since seen the light of day. Then made its trek across Texas earth to its new home in the east, where it had been soaked in gator urine and cooked over a fire. It had been shaved into an open pot then boiled with things such as graveyard dust, red pepper, stagnant water, RIT red dye and things so secret they had only been thrown in during the pitch of night and not looked upon by the thrower. But the strongest ingredient was intention. The ill-will of man whittled to a sharp point, then stirred for forty days in a mash, laid out for one week to dry, and then pulverized to a fine powder. The Dyboù was pleased.

Soon he saw the girl's land. When he reached it he stepped back. The honey of the earth filled him. So sweet, the land shifted under him. The grass flattened before each footfall, and a dog somewhere began to moan. It smelled like persimmon and apricots stirred with cane syrup. Hundreds of little beings beating, throbbing. The Dyboù bent down and clutched a lump of soil and stuffed it into the man's mouth. It was like a sugar teat, cotton soaked in the white granules and milk, then given to a baby to suckle. He calmed himself. He knew patience. Whatever small shield the girl had mustered would be washed away come morning.

The house was cracked, soul splinters where it had been blasted apart by sorrow. The Dyboù looked through the window, through the torn curtains, and saw to his surprise that the girl was not alone. The man was asleep, his body draped like a rag against the side of the bed, knees on the floor, his acorn head resting on the pillow. The girl was spread like a starfish on the mattress, hair like frothing black water all around them. He scooted to get a better view and saw it was the fool he had been following for years, who had dropped the gris-gris and his manhood like a harlot drops her drawers.

He fingered the veined glass and zigzag lines spread beneath his hand. He felt his member swelling, his hand on the weave of the pants rubbing. Fast. Faster. His hand inside of his boxers now, until he grew thick and hard against the thigh. Pleasure rising . . . saliva pouring down his chin. Almost bursting. The house began to shake. The table bounced and the girl shifted and almost lifted her head.

The Dyboù stopped moments before release. Eyes bulging. The chinaberry shook in the distance. The girl curled onto her side. An old crow cawed.

He walked to the door, creaked it open, then dropped to the floor, knees cutting into a splinter, the Dyboù grinding it deeper. Bleeding. The left hand, spilling the contents of the black bottle upon the threshold of the house, molasses and ox blood. The length of him straining against his zipper. He heard something whispering, calling *to stop*. To stop what he was doing. *To stop. Stop. STOP*—and he looked, it was only the old crow—good for nothing, not even boiling. The Dyboù rumbled low. Then he spilled the contents of the red bag over the sticky dark. He bent to smell the mix and a thick surge of power shot through the body. Yes. It was good and strong. It would weaken the soul of anyone who stepped upon it. Cause their courage to drain from their feet. Cramp their guts and twist their resolve.

The Dyboù pushed open the door and walked into the house. He stood in the doorway. He stepped onto her bedroom floor and grinned. This boy, this mule, was meant to protect the whore!

Like two pill bugs facing a praying mantis, there was no chance they would survive.

He walked away, out the door, down the steps and towards the pines. The man's nose started bleeding again, his heart pounding too fast. He would not last long, so the Dyboù walked him back to his home, slipped him into his bed, and oozed out of his body. The man would remember only a little, but he would awaken stronger, with a bit more spite and fire in his veins. The Dyboù liked the size and cut of the man. He would ride him again soon.

Chapter 15

Ephram woke to tapping. The sun was only peeking over the horizon when he saw Gubber Samuels standing outside Ruby's door, shifting one foot to the next, and when he caught Ephram's eye he motioned for him to join him. Ephram slipped his head from the bed and tipped outside.

"Why you clean that whore's house?" was what he said when Ephram greeted him.

"Gubber go home," Ephram managed. The day was soft blue and coral pink, too pretty and new for the likes of Gubber. So he repeated, "Go home."

"Man I know she got good pussy." Off Ephram's look he added, "Least that's what I hear."

Ephram grabbed Gubber by the shirt sleeve and pulled him away from Ruby's door. But before Ephram could open his mouth Gubber cut in, "Look Ephram, we been friends too long for me to keep quiet. Folks 'bout to run y'all out of town after what Celia say at church yesterday. Ain't no joke."

Ephram looked at Gubber Samuels, his boyhood friend and ally. He was tipped to one side to balance his considerable weight. His creamed corn skin wet with the strain of walking so early. His right hazel eye steady, his left floating, traveling right then left on its own volition. Walled.

"I don't want to hear you say nothing like that again."

"What?" Ephram looked at him sideways so Gubber said simply, "All right man."

Ephram knew Gubber Samuels had never talked around things. He'd always spoken like rocks falling. When Ephram thought about it, Gubber hadn't been up before 10:00 A.M. on a weekday since he could remember. So Ephram pointed to a stump across the road and the two men walked over and sat down.

"So what did Celia say?"

"You know how Celia be when she testify. Talk a fly off a fresh pile a' shit."

"I know." Ephram looked back at the house to make sure Ruby was still sleeping. He rubbed his fingers. Their soreness made him smile.

"It ain't funny. She come in church all tore up right before elections, look like she been ravished. When she commence to talking, you couldn't knock folks over with a dick."

A cock crowed somewhere off in the distance as if to emphasize Gubber's point.

"First she say how she can't sleep all that night what with hearing demons scurrying across her floor. Then she wake up and find you ain't sleep in your bed. Then how before she make her Folger's, one a' them demons slither around her living room floor on her nice shag carpet with the plastic covers. That demon just keep saying, We done got him. We done got him. When she ast who was they and who they got, that demon start laughing and points to that picture of you when you was little, the one with your daddy up on the wall. Then she say she look at that picture and damn if it don't bust into flames."

"Well that's easy to prove a lie."

"Oh, she one step ahead, boy. She say when she look back them flames disappear. That's when she say it's a warning. Say it means they's still time."

"Jesus."

"Yes nigger, why you think I move my fat ass up here this early in the morning?"

Daylight spit yellow across the heavens while Gubber told the rest of it. "Then she starts out to see you, and see the Devil three times before she got there. Each time he take a different form. First time he a crow, second, a jackal and third, he a toad. And you know how she tell it with that flourish and rhyme and all her Sanctified Saids. Each, every time the Devil say, 'Don't mess with that girl, she be my special pearl.' But she say she keep on walkin' 'til she get out to Bell land, where she see a snake slithering backwards crost the road. 'Til up she come to the door and touch the knob and it's cold as ice.

"Then she tell how she begs you leave cuz she seen the Devil's mark appear, spreading across your left cheek. She paint it so good them niggers was ready to run out the goddamn church and get you. If she'd told 'em, some of them fools would have burned that girl house down to the ground. But then she calm them, tell them it best to trick the Devil with kindness. Try to baptize them under his snare. Try to bring her boy back to Jesus. That the mark faded as quick as it came. There was still time."

Ephram shook his head against stupidity. "They believe that mess!"

"The best part I ain't told you. Some folk not saying Amen like she want. So she say the Devil told her he was gone sneak into the minds of the weak in the congregation before she got there and tell them not to believe her. So then, you know ever body was up and stomping and clapping and yelling Amen by the time she talks about the fight she had with the Devil."

Ephram looked back at the house again. A light purple cloud was arranging itself just above its roof. Gubber let out a belch, cracked his knuckles and said, "If I was you I'd put my johnson back in my pants and get my ass home."

"I ain't going back. Don't know if it's safe for her with me here, but—I'm not going back."

"Damn, you always been a hard-up ignorant nigger. You can still fuck her, if the pussy that good. Hell, ever'body else do."

Ephram gave Gubber a look that let him know it was past time to stop. The look that said his fist could and would connect hard with Gubber's slack jaw.

Gubber backed down, "Man, do what you want." He stood to leave. "Only you better be at Junie Rankin funeral this afternoon. You already done missed the wake yester-evening. Supra and them expecting you to stand pallbearer and they gone be hell to pay you don't cover your corner."

"Junie were a good man."

"Only one used to keep them rude-ass Rankin boys in check."

"I can't say I'll be there Gubber. Maybe. Maybe not."

"I ain't say no more. Only, you best think long and hard else your next step might lead you off a goddamn cliff."

Ephram watched Gubber struggle up from the stump then sit back down with a thud. "Damn. Need me a minute, all that walkin' only to turn round and walk right back. I gots to catch my breath." And he pulled a pack of Newports out of his pocket, lit one and sucked it into his lungs.

A school of swallows took flight from a tall pine, their complaints little pinpricks in the stretch of dawn. Both men looked up and watched them freckle the sky. Ephram thought about a wide-toothed comb inside the house, furry with black hair. Gubber thought to spit. But he did it in such a lazy, will-less way that it clung in streaks to his cheek. It seemed an effort even to wipe. He waited until he brought the cigarette back to his lips to give a halfhearted try. Ephram fought the urge to take out his handkerchief and hand it to him. It was hard for him to remember sometimes the boy Gubber had been, but sitting close to him on the stump, Ephram could yet see him peeking through.

Gubber Samuels's snaggle-toothed grin, stretching full, pride bursting. Gubber, the skinny, yellow boy that he'd learned to pee standing up with. Ephram had been five, Gubber six. Ephram's mama and Gubber's grandmama had taught both boys to pee-pee like girls to avoid sprinkles on their new indoor toilets. So one day Ephram and Gubber had ventured into the woods near the lake, aimed away from their fallen trousers and peed and peed and peed until they could not muster another drop. Then they'd run to the well and filled the dipper so many times their bellies sloshed when they moved, and they'd waited eagerly to try their aim again.

Ephram remembered it clearly because later that same year, in June of 1934, the two boys had watched as water and mud swoll up and swallowed the Reverend Jennings's new church. It was meant to be the star of Liberty, with twenty new pews, red velvet carpet in the aisles, brass handles on the front door and a stained glass window gotten half price because the White First Baptist in Jasper thought Jesus had mistakenly been crafted with a harelip. Reverend Jennings had gotten him for a song. After the storm Ephram and Gubber sat perched on the fallen steeple and watched the Reverend kick at the mud, cursing the hurricane until he slipped and fell face down right on top of the harelip Jesus. Split it clean in two. The boys held in their laughter until he'd started crying, big, ugly sobs. Then Ephram started crying too, at the sight of his daddy weeping, which is when the Reverend leapt up and slapped him off the steeple.

Easter of '37 when Ephram's mama had walked over the hill as God had made her, Gubber was the only person at the picnic who had the wherewithal to pay Ephram any mind, walking up to him, while all the women were running to put a tablecloth over Otha's sin, and patting his friend Ephram on the back.

The next day Ephram's daddy beat his mama for one whole hour before dragging her screaming and begging to Dearing State Mental Hospital. Wouldn't even let her say good-bye to her son. Beat Ephram with a hair brush when he tried to defy him and come out anyway. His mama clawing at her own face until the Reverend stopped and punched her. Gubber was waiting in the tall grass through it all. He crept up to Ephram's window to find his friend's face under the pillow, fat from crying, his body sore, his spirit broken. He climbed into Ephram's locked room and offered him a piece of sugarcane. The two boys sucked and gnawed in silence while the Reverend drove an unconscious Otha all the way to Dearing.

After that Gubber tended to the splinter that had lodged itself in Ephram's heart. Not by any direct thing, but by just knowing it was there and acting like it wasn't, both boys could pretend that life had unfurled itself in a different way. Together they found that they could ignore the pelting looks and questions directed at Ephram. Gubber Samuels knew something about hard looks too, because of his walled eye and the shenanigans with his own mama, who'd had four children by four different papas and hadn't stayed around long enough to raise a one of them. Over the next few years the boys knitted their unique brands of forgetfulness into a shield against the folks of Liberty.

They decided that Gubber's dancing free eye was a good thing. It meant that he could see not only what was right in front of him, but the whole of the sky and stars at a glance. They whispered into freshly dug wells to stay cool and not grab any small children. They reminded crooked saplings to straighten up their act.

That shield gave them a new boldness so they ran wild up and down Liberty Township, adding unflattering letters to lovers' names carved into tree trunks, swimming and splashing in Marion Lake, snatching Sarah Geoffrey's drawers from the line and taking turns smelling them. They stole so many of Clem Rankin's peaches that the man was forced to shoot buckshot at them or go broke at harvest. They hid brilliantly from the seven rowdy Rankin boys, standing up to them only when a church elder was present.

In 1939, the boys watched with the rest of their neighbors as thousands of White soldiers pitched tents in the woods and on the embankments of Liberty Township and Shankleville—the only Colored towns in the vicinity. Watched as they tromped through the woods in full battle regalia, with what they later learned were M1 Garand rifles high on their backs. Ephram and Gubber secretly and courageously moved the red or yellow cotton ties marking the boundaries for the battalion's army maneuvers. They hid as soldiers, wearing faded yellow or red armbands, crept closer, and held in their terrified giggles as the soldiers stopped, checked, then double-checked their maps. Kicked a tuft of grass, whispered, then turned back cussing. Two years before

Pearl Harbor and the one year after, over ten thousand men came to occupy that little corner of the piney woods, camped in tents, some not twenty yards from Black folks' back doors. Like any occupied town in the world, mothers and fathers kept their daughters locked indoors and their fighting-age boys out of sight. More than one girl had run home in tears, clothes torn; more than one boy had become the butt of regimented, orchestrated cruelty. K.O.'s older brother Taylor had been found shot to death. His daddy went to the Funeral Home in Jasper to dig the army-issue bullet out of his boy himself when no one else would do it. Taylor's mama walked all the way into Newton to show the Sheriff, who'd taken the bullet, looked her in the eye, said he'd investigate. He had then promptly thrown it in the trash receptacle.

In 1940, Mussolini decided to join Hitler against France and Britain, France surrendered to Germany, Leon Trotsky was assassinated in Mexico City and Ephram Jennings almost died from eating a persimmon. Ephram and Gubber had been plastering the bright orange fruit across their faces, into their mouths, until one of the seeds lodged itself in Ephram's nose. Gubber tried to fish it out and managed to jam it in so deep that blood began to spurt. Gubber ran screaming into his house. With the Reverend preaching out of town, Gubber's daddy had to drive Ephram, Celia and Gubber the forty-three miles to the Leesville County Hospital, the only medical facility in a hundred miles with a Colored wing. He lost so much blood on the way the intern said it was a miracle he was still living. Apparently the persimmon seed had punctured the "lower dorsal artery" and Ephram could have easily bled to death. They took a special pair of tweezers and, with great pain, retrieved the seed. The inside of Ephram's left nostril needed twelve stitches. He remained in the hospital for one night, until word got through to the Reverend, after which he promptly yanked Ephram out of the hospital bed so that he could convalesce at home.

One year later, in the summer of 1941, the boys had seen Sarah Geoffrey's visiting cousin Lily take off her bra for Percy Rankin in the Geoffreys' blue barn. Percy had told them to hide up there and for 5 cents each, he'd show them what big titties looked like. Gubber had been thirteen and Ephram twelve and they had stopped moving, even to breathe, as the lipsticked girl slipped off her blouse and unbuttoned her bra. It wasn't the way Percy squeezed her breasts or the way she laid down on fresh sweet hay with her panties around her ankles that Ephram remembered most, or the way Percy moved over her and she pushed up to meet him. It was the way her breasts fell out of her bra, the way they spilled like sugar cookie dough onto the flat of her stomach.

He and Gubber snuck into the same dry barn early Sunday mornings before Gubber attended the Piggly Service. There, as dust floated in slatted sunbeams, the boys would "play Lily," they called it. Gubber laying carefully on the same golden hay, Ephram over him, hands running the length of Gubber's body. They kissed, Ephram's full lips to Gubber's warm mouth. Discovering the use and need of strength in pleasure.

That was the year, the moment in Ephram's young life, when he'd felt a tickling desire, a wish for the things that other men hold dear, that called forth secret winks of approval on Saturday nights. He had wished for a straight-haired, light-skinned woman to love him. He had wished for height and a loud, echoing voice. A mist green Lincoln Continental Cabriolet. He wished for Sarah Geoffrey to giggle high and sweet at him like she did with Percy's brother Charles. For friends to crowd about him and reel out their laughter over a pint of whiskey and a smoke.

But even then there were things more dear to him, and their dearness made him different. He loved the smell of honeysuckle, so much he'd wear it in his ear when he slept at night. He'd watch a spider weaving its web for hours at a time. He loved the way Gubber kind of gurgled when he laughed. He enjoyed lying on his back with his friend in the evening and painting big dreams against the starry sky. Moving up north. Joining the merchant marines and sailing to Alaska. Playing baseball in the Negro Leagues.

None of which had set well with Ephram's father, the Reverend Jennings, who followed his son to that barn loft one early Saturday morning, and after the shock of seeing the two boys kissing on the hay, beat Ephram to within an inch of his life. He busted his lip, cracked two ribs and sent his last two baby teeth, the right upper canine and the molar beside it, down his gullet.

Ephram had taken it in silence and shame, accepting each kick and punch with only enough shielding to save his father from a jail cell or worse. Gubber had heroically remained until the Reverend snarled that he would kill them both if he didn't "GET!" The Reverend Jennings had dragged Ephram home and thrown him on the hall rug for Celia to tend to. "No hospital this time" was all he said. In fact that was all the Reverend would ever say on the subject. He also never looked directly at his son again.

One year later the Reverend found a small parish in Farrsville where the minister was ailing and he lived in and preached there three weeks out of four. Although Reverend Jennings had strictly forbidden it, Ephram snuck into the woods and met up with his friend Gubber most days. It was autumn, hot yet morning cool. They were heading to Marion Lake for a dip. It had been so hot of late that they'd planned to swim in the cool water until supper, so they'd run through the woods, trees making stepping-stones of sunlight ahead of them on their path. They'd leapt from sun patch to sun patch, laughing if they touched shadows, when Ephram felt a sudden shade across his body. He looked up and saw the Reverend standing high above him. He threw his hands up to block a blow. A flash of sun stole off his daddy's face, the Reverend so high, mouth so wide that Ephram lowered his hands, opened his mouth to say what he was doing there. Then he saw the rope. Then saw his daddy turn in the air. Gubber peed down his leg. A cloud passed in front of the sun. There was blood on the floor of leaves beneath his daddy's feet. One of his shoes was flung off way over there. His bare sock had a hole. All turning two feet above the earth. The sound of Gubber crying thick snot and water. The way his daddy's head was like a crooked balloon, lips screaming, eyes dead but wide and asking Ephram something so he heard, "What, Daddy?" croak out of his throat. There wasn't a sound of water or frog or bird; death had drawn her chalk circle here and not a thing could breathe. Black flies covered his daddy's mouth like a blanket until Ephram saw the severed thing stuffed there.

Ephram wished he were a dog. Somebody's good dog with a mighty growl and bark. If he were, he would snarl and burrow his nose into the dirt, howl into the earth until it trembled on its axis. But he was only a boy so he buried that scream like an ax in his gut, where it remained to this day.

From far away Ephram felt Gubber's hands pulling, then hitting, then screaming something, then running. Then silence and him and his daddy staring into the holes of each other's eyes until another scream, this time it sounded like a sow at butcher time, then it was only Celia wailing, and more hands pulling at him.

Hands finally strong enough to pull his body away, but not the rest of him.

They laid his daddy to rest at the Piggly Service. The Rankins' cousin presided. By the time Ephram turned fifteen, he and Gubber were barely speaking to one another. Ephram watched Gubber swell and grow and strain against the fence of clothing, only to build a bigger fence, only to strain, again and again. Gubber wouldn't look at Ephram if they passed in school or at P & K, and worse, when circumstance threw them together, Ephram became the perfect foil for Gubber, a soft, weakened thing to point out when collective fangs were bared. The fact that he accomplished this with a chain of rebukes and thick jokes, and that those actions had done more harm to Gubber Samuels than himself, was not lost on Ephram. He'd watched Gubber swallow his kindness and shit it out until all that remained was the waste of a good man.

GUBBER BREATHED in the last of his cigarette and crushed it with his boots. He rose and pointed himself west, towards the Samuels's farm.

He spat out, "Watch your ass," then walked down the red road. Ephram sat and watched Gubber's back until it disappeared over the rise between a pair of pines.

Ephram lifted himself from the stump. His bones felt cold and ached just a bit at the joints. Celia would be rising right about now, drawing the water for his bath, then stopping herself. He felt a sudden longing for her grits and eggs made just how he liked them. For her coffee with a pinch of chicory and the psalm they would choose to read aloud every Sunday evening after dinner. They'd missed 124 last evening, which was one of his favorites. The road seemed to nudge him homeward. He took a step. Then two. Then he was walking, just to see if she was making out all right. Maybe he would knock on the door to say hello, or perhaps sit down over breakfast and talk it out with her.

A smattering of pine nuts rained down to his left. Ephram turned and saw the Bell graveyard, over the rise. And just that quick he knew that if he kept walking that's where his feet were carrying him. Into that grave of a house, that death of a life. Ephram saw his body cold and still, laid out on Celia's kitchen table waiting for the undertaker from Jasper to tote him off. He looked much as he did now, a fringe more gray along his temples. Then the picture was gone and he was left with the morning. She had unfurled herself fully and was waving her bright flag across the sky. He turned himself around and walked into Ruby's door.

Outside in a pine, just above a row of headstones, an old crow gnawed on a pine nut. She was the only creature to see the red powder, rife with ill intent, spread across the entrance of the Bell home. She was the only living being to see Ephram unwittingly step squarely into it and track it like evil into Ruby's house.

Chapter 16

Monday morning broke through, rubbing Sunday out of its eyes. All across town, coffee had been brewed and cups emptied. The crusts of toast and hardened grits had already been scraped into slop jars. By 9:00 A.M. Ephram Jennings's sin had already been stirred, baked and left to cool, its scent filling the air of Liberty.

The In-His-Name Holiness Church was bustling in preparation for the one o'clock service. Pastor Joshua was at his desk writing the eulogy, trying to avoid as many *R*, *M* and *T* words as possible, as they played the devil with his nearly conquered habit of stuttering. He wondered if Ephram Jennings would show his face today after the disgrace he'd laid upon Mother Celia. It wasn't just that he had taken up with another woman, because that was bound to happen in the life of a man given the temptation that surrounded him daily; it was that he had walked into a living room in hell and made himself at home. He was grateful Mother Celia had calmed the crowd, else they might have chased her out of town, like they did Sister Thelma after she took up with Supra Rankin's husband—and she was a churchgoing woman. Lord knows, he wondered, what they would do to a heathen. The Pastor looked at his paper and thought of how he could weave in Proverbs 29:3 and Matthew 15:22, but doubted that the Rankins would appreciate that many references to harlots and demonic possession during Junie's eulogy.

RUBY AWAKENED in a warm bed, sheets clean beneath and above her. Ephram was moving about her home so she watched him, in his undershirt, bringing in wood, lighting a steady fire in the stove. Ruby had only seen Ephram in ill-fitting shirts and suits. Now, in the morning light, his body was carved like hard oak—fine sanded, buffed, stained dark and polished. A watercolor tin of browns. She wondered what Billy would say if he saw her here in bed with this man. What would Mrs. Gladdington say if she saw Ephram? Met him, say, on Broadway and Fifty-third? Would she inadvertently try to put a coin into a paper cup filled with cola he'd just gotten from a hot dog vendor? What if Ruby stopped her, introduced them? Mrs. Gladdington could whip a word. Cut an object, a verb and a preposition, a beaker of adverbs, with the delicacy and skill of a cruel scientist. How easy would it be to wound this man, without him ever knowing that he had been hit?

Or what would any of the quick, darting people she had met, what would they *say*? The liberal world, the brave outsiders, and the wealthy philanthropists. So different, yet all could be depended upon for one common hypocritical judgment against this singular Black man. What disdain would tumble from their collective eyes, their taut, stretched lips?

The disapproval of class and race. If Ephram were a beleaguered member of the abject, illiterate poor, a recipient of their charitable largesse, flown in and trotted out at a five-hundred-dollar-a-plate banquet in their own honor—if he were in a suit purchased by them for the occasion, they would sit and chat and pose for snapshots in *Vanity Fair* and Page Six and pretend to be the type of people who didn't care about such things. But bring him to an upper East Sixties party as your guest and the socialite sea would part, leaving him alone with his canapés. Good? Hardly enough. Honest? Utterly boring. An aging East Texas Black man with slow speech and Sunday school clothes was beyond unthinkable.

Yet, there he was, making her a cup of coffee, a nervous start in his movements. She saw the nicks and scars that littered his body like twigs, little badges from a war he had not only survived, but won. Tall, proud, honest, brave. And when his friend had come to call him away, he had chosen to stay. Ruby's heart became soft like sweet potato pie and she couldn't wait to press against the man.

Close to eleven-thirty, walking up the narrow road to Bell land, came a migration of men, all dressed in their navy and black suits, nails and underwear clean. They smelled of Lifebuoy soap and Old Spice, except Chauncy, who led the pack, dabbed and splashed in Paco Rabanne, a gift from one of his lady friends in Galveston. Gubber trailed behind, head bowed, carrying a travel bag containing Ephram's suit, shirt and tie. He had thought to say no, but he wasn't a man likely to go against a strong woman, much less the whole of a town. Celia had given him Ephram's belongings with the charge of delivering a message. It was not one he relished. Not even a little.

By THE time the men reached Bell land, Ephram had already tracked the red powder all over Ruby's home—upon her fallen hair as he was sweeping it into a brown paper sack. He did not notice her watching eyes any more than the fact that he had tracked that same powder under her porch, where he hid the sack full of cotton candy hair until he had time to burn it, just as Celia had taught him to do his whole life to protect against conjure.

Then he'd unknowingly spread specks of the powder all about the kitchen and the bedroom. His belly had already wrenched and cramped and sent him running to Ruby's small toilet, where he rocked back and forth, grinding the red silt into the floorboards.

He did not know why he was suddenly aching and tired, not just his soles and the length of his feet, but his ankles and calves as well.

After he had shaved, brushed and washed himself off as best he could with the help of items purchased at P & K and a shallow small basin, the dull, exhausting pain seeped into his bones, making him have to sit down on the bed. When the malady reached his stomach again, sweat erupted in his temples and he almost doubled over. It was more than the usual pain; there was also a spreading sickly fear. It seemed to be pumping from his heart, through the smallest of his veins, so that it webbed through every part of him. He was empty and weak when the men arrived.

Chauncy, who didn't fancy himself an errand boy, sent Gubber to knock on the door.

Ruby opened it, a lift of fear catching in her throat.

Gubber and all of the men stopped dead when they saw her. The caramel glow of her skin, the curl of her black hair, rolling like a frothy river past her shoulder blades. They remembered the girl who had first arrived in Liberty and suddenly felt dull and thick.

Except Chauncy. He glared at Gubber and said, "Go get that boy."

Gubber, not knowing what else to do, nudged past Ruby and found Ephram sitting on the bed.

He walked to him, leaned over and whispered into his ear,

"Celia say if you ain't at Junie's funeral she gone send for the Sheriff in Newton to haul Ruby off to Dearing."

Ephram's eyes rested upon Ruby across the room fiddling with the crackers and peanut butter. He thought about his mama and the one time Celia took him to see her after their daddy died. The locked gate, and then the next—like a prison except everyone there with a life sentence. They had brought his mother down in a light blue gown with stains that had been washed and dried more than once. Ephram thought about her hair matted and high, the burn marks on her temples, and the needle pricks up and down her purple arms. He saw her eyes, scorched, empty things that only looked at the ground or just past his shoulder. She smelled.

She had seen him for an instant. A look of bittersweet relief visited her face, her shoulders sloped and her graceful neck rose. She tried to lift her hands, which is how Ephram noticed that they were bound. She seemed to notice it in that moment as well. She began to cry and so of course he did as well. An avalanche of shame seemed to turn her head and then her eyes became vacant and she rocked softly until they led her away.

She had never looked once at Celia.

Ephram took the bag from Gubber without saying a word and changed quickly. A pair of dress shoes was missing, so Ephram kept his on. Ruby walked closer. Gubber stood between both of them.

Chauncy called from outside, "That fool coming?"

Gubber hollered back, "Directly."

As the two men reached the porch, Ephram turned and looked at Ruby. The pain rose to his chest, making his breath shallow. She seemed as small as a child, standing in bare feet.

Questions were written on her face that he did not know how to answer. But his eyes softened and in spite of the fear corded through his belly, he couldn't help a smile stealing across his face.

He said, "Want me to pick up something on my way back?"

Ruby knew it was his way of telling her he was returning.

When he added, "Ice cream?" it felt like a declaration, an announcement that this was a place where laughter had plenty of water to grow, a bottomland for hope.

Ruby answered, "That would be nice."

Gubber nudged Ephram. "Come on, man." There was a general rustling outside.

Ephram then asked, "What flavor?" and something shifted inside of Ruby.

The idea of ice cream was more than she could imagine; choosing a flavor was like eating too much stuffing at Thanksgiving. She felt bloated and slow—suddenly exposed, instantly in danger.

Like a blast of heat burning through her, it was suddenly too much, this constant, unrelenting kindness, the gentle in the center of his eyes that never slipped and fell. His attention had filled the shallow bowl she'd set aside for joy. In that moment it cracked.

She leapt up, went to Ephram and kissed him, full on. Her hand sliding behind his neck, pushing her body against his, tongue down his throat.

Then she said, face inches from his, "Chocolate be nice."

She did all this before God, her babies and a pack of wolves. Although Ephram was more than a little surprised, Ruby could feel the men in the yard, their hunger rising, as if she were a wounded fawn.

The pack took it in, then, escorting a dazed Ephram, moved

away in unison. They pushed him towards the front. It was Chauncy who trailed behind, his eyes burning like a branding iron over her body. They landed upon her face.

Ruby looked right back at him, not saying a word.

Chauncy paused for another beat, long enough for Ephram to turn around. The men, then, walked down the red road, Chauncy uncharacteristically quiet as Ephram dropped flecks of red dust like bread crumbs along the way.

⁓

THE BODY of Junie Rankin was already laid out from the wake. The one person oblivious to the doings across town, Junie rested stiffly, a grin curling about his peachy lips, his wool navy duster and wing tips pressed and buffed to a shine. While everyone at the wake the night before had agreed that the Edwin Shephard's Mortuary/Ambulance Service always did a fine job, they worried about Junie going to his maker in August wearing wool. Chauncy had said that the Lord might take one look at him sweating and heaving and think to send him where he might fit in better. But as it was Junie's best suit and duster, everyone finally agreed that the Rankins and the funeral home had come to the right decision. Supra had put a small Bible into the casket with him just to keep on the safe side. This Monday the mortuary was represented by the junior, not the elder, Shephard. A slight, algae brown man with a drawn mustache, Edwin Shephard Junior bent low over Junie's shrunken form, reapplying a dusting of Max Factor's Fancy Pink blush. The Shephards were proud to be one of only two all-purpose ailment-to-bereavement transportation services for Negroes in the Liberty, Shankleville and Jasper area, answering police dispatches or personal phone calls when a loved one was in need of hospitalization, and then, depending upon the critical nature of the emergency, taking them to whichever destination was required, ER or the mortuary.

Several of the Church Sisters were plucking out the wilted flowers from last night's arrangements and peeking to see who'd spent what and who'd gone and cheated Junie out of his floral due. Righteous Polk and her sister Salvation had had conference with Celia Jennings at the break of day. They had sat in prayer and then helped her bring her pies, figs and cakes to Supra Rankin's home for the reception, where they had been added to the double-sided mountain of food that would become an avalanche after the burial. Now the two Polk women worked to add the perfect touches for the upcoming service. Righteous scooped a cup of pastel mints and poured them into the plastic crystal dish in the women's lavatory. Righteous tried on the face she would use when she fell out at the casket. When she had it just right she thought about what Sister Celia had said that very morning and knew that Celia was correct. It was fine to pray and mission folks in times of weak trouble, but when a wave was about to crash down on a person's head, that person would be a fool to hold out a flimsy umbrella. Serious action was needed, of that Righteous was sure.

It had been seven years since they'd had a case this bad—her own beloved daughter Honey, who had always had a sweet nature, until she rejected the church after getting pregnant by that Reverend Swanson. Righteous had tried to help Honey understand the nature of man and how it's a woman's job to hold herself above that nature, and then if she can't, to find forgiveness, especially for a man of God. But Honey had left the church anyway and the trouble started. She'd abandoned her own little boy, run off far from home and moved in with a female abomination of God, which had to be due to the drugs she must have been taking to do it. Righteous and her Church Sisters had done their very best by tricking her home with a story that Righteous was in failing health and then had taken Honey into the storm cellar, held her down and prayed over her for fourteen hours straight, not giving her leave to eat or evacuate her body, until she'd cried out for Jesus and spoken in tongues and had been welcomed back into the fold. But just like in Matthew 12:43, the unclean spirit left her, took tea in Hades, then came back with seven of his friends and possessed her again until the poor child drove that female abomination's car straight into a sixteen-wheeler two days later. No matter that people said the girl couldn't stop crying and drinking and crying some more, Righteous knew it was her own fault. The whole of the congregation's fault for not working harder to redeem her soul. Righteous tried her mournful face on again and was surprised to see the wetness of tears shining in her eyes. She quickly wiped them and went to join her sisters.

People started trailing into the church a little after noon, in order to get the good seats. Those closest to the casket and the family went first. Second were those next to Righteous Polk, as she always fell out with such grandeur and delivered dramatic screams and carryings-on both to and from the coffin. Celia arrived only fifteen minutes early with the certainty of one who knows her seat will be held for her. An eager group crowded near her, the clear star of the event until the Rankins arrived. Celia had chosen a simple black crepe skirt and jacket with a shiny teal mandarin collar blouse, pillbox hat with a black rhinestone flourish. Her eyes kept flashing to the church door anticipating Ephram's entrance. The men and women surrounding Celia let their eyes fly after hers like gnats over sugar, eager to alight at the very moment of contact.

She did not have long to wait. Ephram Jennings, who had milled outside as long as possible, stepped into the church that Monday afternoon and stood unguarded at the sanctuary doors. Celia shot tacks at him then made a big show of putting her hand over her eyes and turning away. Ephram, a riot of nerves and pitted fear, felt as if he'd been hit with buckshot. The crowd feasted upon this sweet exchange. Ephram absorbed the stares and walked into the church, tracking the powder from Ruby's, now wedged like glue into the tread of his shoes.

The Rankins, save Chauncy, who'd volunteered to retrieve Ephram, arrived in two baby blue stretch limousines hired all the way from Leesville. They crowded the doorway so Ephram cleared the way and let them pass. Despite the magnificence of their funereal finery, the black plume feathers in Supra's hat, the pressed straightness of the women's hair and the men's good suits, despite the severity of mourning painted on the faces of his kin, the tears already washing down Verde's slick cheeks, the genuine beauty of the seven Rankin brothers, and the heaving sobs of Junie's wife, Bessie, when Ephram sat down in the back and not in the seat next to Celia that he'd shared for two decades, the whole of the parlor turned first to Ephram and then to see how Celia took it. They found her with eyes closed in prayer.

Folks said later that the funeral of Junie Rankin was a good testimony to his life. It wasn't the best they'd seen, but it certainly wasn't the worst. The Rankins from out of town did find it a bit strange when the Pastor mentioned how glad he was that Junie had never been vexed by Jezebels or demons or lunacy. Everyone from Liberty had just turned around again and stared at Ephram Jennings for a beat. As the singing commenced, women fell out and had to be helped up. Men clapped and sang "Seraph!"

Righteous Polk did not disappoint and fell out so many times, shaking and weeping with such ferocity, that she had to be tended to in the Pastor's office by the recently widowed Deacon Charles. At the casket the competition had been fierce over who loved Junie the most, his wife, Bessie, or his sister, Petunia. Wail landed upon wail, followed by the thrashing and beating of flesh. Junie's framed photograph, the easel it was set upon, and two floral arrangements featuring calla lilies were casualties of the fierce rivalry. The service ended with no clear winner.

Ephram felt faint and his stomach flipped as he rose with the rest of the pallbearers, Chauncy, Percy, Gubber, Charlie and Sim Rankin. He took his place on the back left corner as all six men heaved poor Junie up and onto their capable shoulders. Ephram felt Celia boring into him the whole of the journey down the aisle, but some unnamed will would not let him meet her gaze. He left the church and climbed into the hearse with the rest of the men.

Then his bones began to tingle.

Edwin Shephard Junior drove them the four miles to Liberty Township Cemetery, where they unloaded the casket and carried Junie down to his plot. Edwin fiddled with the burial area while the six pallbearers walked into the heart of the graveyard to wait for folks to arrive. Between the family processional out of the church, the refixing of makeup and rearranging of undergarments, the heaving and sitting and gathering of strength and arranging themselves in limousines, the men had at least an hour of waiting ahead of them.

As soon as they had settled themselves on tombstones for a smoke, Ephram slipped his coat on and began walking down the hill, bound for Bell land.

Percy Rankin spit out, "I wouldn't go nowheres if I was you

until you get that meeting with Celia done and finished. Don't want nothing to happen to that gal." Ephram turned around, a weak terror gripping him, and rejoined the group.

Chauncy Rankin took off his jacket, looked at Ephram and busted out laughing. He laughed so hard he all but fell out on the ground then kept right on laughing. Side-splitting, tears-streaming-down-his-cheeks, ripping belly laughs. Percy and Sim turned away smiling as Chauncy quieted for a second, climbed his way up a tombstone, glanced back at Ephram and fell back to the ground howling.

Caught between shame and fear, battling the tingling in his joints and the flipping of his stomach, Ephram did not ask the question Chauncy's actions begged him to ask: *What you laughin' at?*

Finally Chauncy caught his breath and between gasps said, "Ooooooh, man! Ooooooooooo, man, I ain't laugh that hard since Gubber passed out and wet hisself at Bloom's last month."

Gubber spat out, "Only after y'all fool niggas stuck my hand in warm water whiles I'm asleep."

"I ain't saying who stuck what where, but *damn*, that was almost as funny as this here. What in God's name Ephram Roosevelt Jennings be thanking playing house with that, that—" Then he was off again, spitting out between guffaws, "Oh Lord!" and "Help me, Jesus!" until it became contagious and Percy and Sim let loose as well, followed by Charlie and finally, at long last, Gubber, the men giving one another fraternal handshakes and soldierly pats on the back. The cackling built like a storm brewing. When Chauncy had the pack of them howling and snapping, he grew quiet and glared at Ephram Jennings.

"Man, you should be 'shamed."

Ephram kicked his feet into the ground and to his great

shame said nothing. His stomach still turning. A little roll of thunder played in the distance.

"You a pitiful thing" was the worst Chauncy could think to say, but his eyes betrayed far more. Chauncy looked at Ephram with the utter disbelief that such a man could exist in their midst.

Then, leave it to Gubber: "Aw he ain't no different from us; we all looking for a woman just like our mama."

The crowd paused for a moment, deciding whether or not to draw blood.

Sim looked at Chauncy, then put the edge of a knife in his words, "My mama got straight teeth so I can't abide a gal with a crooked mouth, likewise Ephram wouldn't know what to do with no sane gal who keep her clothes on come Easter."

At that Chauncy sank into a wizened laughter. "Y'all *know* that's wrong." Then with a flick of his cigarette ash, Ephram was dismissed. Ephram tried to lasso the right words but they hurdled beyond his grasp. Then the moment was gone as Chauncy slipped on his jacket and turned to the other men, "Now which one of you men's fool 'nuff to think Cassius Clay got the stuff to win that there Thrilla in Manila?"

"The man's name is Ali," Percy corrected.

Charlie countered, "Hell, calling himself Mohammad like spitting in his mama's face."

Percy eased out, "Don't matter, he already whooped Frazier once."

"Fight was rigged," Sim countered. "'Sides Joe knock him cold that first fight."

"Truth is," Charlie shot out, "yella man born weaker than brown. Joe gonna peel that nigga like a gorilla do a banana."

"Yo' own daddy's a yella nigga," Percy threw out.

Chauncy cut in, "Then I guess he know what he's talking 'bout."

Sim tried out, "Maybe we should ask Ephram 'bout yella niggas."

Ephram leaned against a tombstone, great waves of self-disgust lapping against his heart. His insides twisted left and then right. He'd been called out three times in the last two minutes, he knew he couldn't live in the town if he didn't act now. He tried to muster his will, but something had cut into the trunk of his courage and he found his mouth flooded with saliva. Before he could stop himself, he'd heaved and vomited all over Weller Redding's grave. The men glared at Ephram.

"Damn, that's nasty," Percy observed. In response, Ephram's stomach pitched again and he heaved all over his shoes. The splatter deflected onto the cuffs of Chauncy's pants.

"*Damn!*" Chauncy shot out. "Watch yo' fool self!" and before anyone knew what had happened he'd shoved Ephram back over the tombstone. Legs akimbo, he looked too foolish to inspire laughter.

No one had seen the clouds overhead, but regardless of anyone's notice they had knotted in a soft, gray tangle and now began to rain. They sprinkled for a second and then, as if a faucet had been turned, they let loose a nice steady pour. Ephram felt the water splash off his upturned shoes, wet his ankles, his hands and eventually his face and hair. And without Ephram ever knowing it was there, the last of the red powder washed clean. Chauncy was cursing Ephram and the rain all at once, looming over him, fists tight. A new power and strength shot through Ephram, as if from the soil itself. He leapt to his feet and pushed Chauncy back. Chauncy staggered, disbelief splashing across his face.

"I was playing but now you done made me mad niggah!" He

charged, but a rivulet of water from Ephram's direction stole under his size 13 Oxfords and Chauncy, the most surefooted of men, slipped and fell, chest flat upon Ephram's vomit. The men exploded in rolling blasts of laughter.

Even Chauncy got the mean knocked out of him and surrendered to disgust. "Shit, man!" he said upon rising. "Shit! I got to walk home and change." To Percy he called out, "Tell Mama I'll be back directly." He headed down the small hill, to the road, and once out of sight, veered left, in the distinct direction of Bell land.

The rest of the men ran and sought refuge under the leaves of a barclay tree. Ephram stood his ground, getting soaked through to the bone, heaving and strong, all tingling washed away, a steady calm surging through his body.

Chapter 17

Otha Jennings's grave rested five headstones to the right and four up from where Ephram stood. A simple cement curved block with praying hands etched into the gray. Ephram tended it most Sundays after church, keeping the grass trim and flowers watered. The roots of buttercups and verbena wound atop the casket where Otha Jennings had been laid to rest. The coffin itself contained nothing of the woman, no bones, no teeth, not even a brush with a few strands of hair. Instead it contained her most dog-eared books, the *Complete Works of Emily Dickinson* and *Call of the Wild* by Jack London, a pair of her favorite gloves and her best lacing tat.

Ephram had been sixteen, Celia twenty-two when they had gotten the letter from Kindred Mental Hospital in Albuquerque, New Mexico, telling them of Otha's death in the hospital fire in July of 1945. The Colored wing had burned down to its pilings, leaving nothing but white ash. After Ephram had sent a total of twelve letters requesting her records, some kind clerk had finally sent them. Full of words like "psychotic break/schizophrenia" and "delusional episodes." A list of medications that neither Ephram nor Celia had ever heard of. When they showed it to Dr. Tully, the visiting Colored doctor from Beaumont, he'd never heard of half of them either. He'd closed Otha's file, shaken his head and said a little curse and the words "lab rats" under his breath. When Celia had asked him what he meant, he'd just pressed his lips tight and said to be grateful she'd gone to her glory.

Otha Jennings had been born in Baltimore, in May of 1900, to an educated father and seamstress mother. She came from a long history of freedom. No great-grand nor grandmother, aunt nor uncle, had ever lived under the trace and toil of slavery. There was at the time, a very small yet substantial legacy of landed Negroes in America, Negroes who had achieved the unthinkable and had become doctors, lawyers, politicians, scientists, college presidents, businessmen. No one in Otha's family had belonged to this group either. They were simple, striving people. Her father taught third grade at Washington Elementary, but before he died of consumption when Otha was fourteen, he'd already set aside enough money for her to continue her education at Fisk University in Tennessee. Otha was the only child of two only children. At seventeen she worked part-time with her mother after school and excelled in all things related to sewing, especially lace-making. Otha loved it so that she often dreamed in lace, delicate patterns covering her nighttime landscape. She was only a bit tall with skin as deep and rich as a plum. Her straight black "Indian" hair was from her mother's side. It fell to her waist until she cut it, the summer before college, like Claudette Colbert. The hair on the floor had made the beautician cry. The next day she met the Reverend Jennings, a man twelve years her senior, on her way to church. She had just made a navy low-waisted shift dress for school and was feeling very grown up when he told her she looked like a new penny. She was shy until he told her he was a reverend visiting from Texas and that he was guest preaching at the Jesus First Name Holiness Church on Tinkle Street. He invited her to that evening's revival. Since she was already on her way to a church choir meeting, Otha didn't see the harm and walked with him to Tinkle Street. Otha, who had always attended a calm, quiet Episcopal church, had never heard a first class Holiness preacher when he got riled. He slung words around her like comets soaring. She was in awe and waited for him after service as he had requested, so he could walk the star struck teenager home. He asked her questions about her life, her mama, her deceased daddy, her neighborhood, her friends. He asked her about the university when she told him she was to be the first Colored woman she had ever known of to get a college education. She told him of her plans to be a nurse in a Colored hospital. He listened with great earnestness, eyes deep and wide, nodding in tune to her yielding voice. He took her home and mentioned that he would be in town three more days until Friday, so she'd invited him to dinner the next night without asking her mother.

Marilyn Daniels disliked the man, but she was raised well and so she welcomed him into her husbandless home. She could see the loosely plastered desperation that hung over the frame of the man, the manners tacked on like pictures to hide the cracks. Worst he was a fly-by-night preacher, a man without a home except the one he wore on his back. And that, noticed the seamstress, was of shoddy cloth and make.

When he left for the evening, with a promise extracted from them to attend the revival the following evening, Marilyn could almost feel him marking her door like a male dog—done all the more easily because her husband's scent of tobacco and bay rum aftershave had long since faded.

Otha Daniels fell in love that next evening sitting in the third pew. Otha and her parents had always kept a quiet house. Reverend Jennings was a trumpet blasting into the tender space under her ribs. She could not understand why he was only the warm-up act for other, less worthy men. She was vexed by this, but knew that the injustice could be rectified—with her help. In that moment she ripped out the seams of her own dreams and patched them into his.

Her mother brought up ridiculous things like age and money. But when she mentioned Fisk and her daddy's dream, Otha felt the wind leave her sails for a moment. She had been her father's daughter and had believed and followed him in all things, but she was seventeen years old now, one month away from eighteen, and from everything she had learned of the world, everywhere she looked, women stopped being their father's girls when they became a husband's wife.

That next night the Reverend walked her home. There was not so much talking as they listened to their feet sweep along the sidewalk. They passed other Negro couples holding hands on the street and so he reached out and held her tapered, narrow hand in his. He began to talk about her hands, how long the fingers, how delicately they moved, how it had been one of the first things he had noticed about her. Otha had never thought of her hands as anything but agile tools to make lace and stitch. She felt a kind of magic running through her palms that made them want to dance like butterflies in the air.

They walked in circles, around parks, and dragged their feet long after the sun had fallen out of the sky. When they walked right by the graveyard where her daddy was buried, he'd kissed her so sweetly she melted into the earth. It was then that she had done it, given her daddy's dream back to him. She had done it with tears of sorrow but also with joy, because this new dream was filling her solar plexus like blown glass, scalding hot and liquid at the same time. So they walked back to the church where Minister Bowing made them man and wife.

Her mother had let out a small scream of agony when Otha told her she had married the Reverend. It was the loudest noise anyone had ever made in the house. Otha held her mother, her dark arms wrapped around the older woman's neck, wet cheek to wet cheek, both crying in the dim of the evening lamps. She whispered into her mother's ear that he gave her a reason to breathe in and out and that she would follow him and love him for all of her days.

Marilyn held her daughter. She would be hurt, of that Marilyn was certain. Helpless to protect her, Marilyn felt a wildness in her own chest, like a bird trapped behind a glass door. But when she looked in the girl's eyes she could see that she was already gone so she gave her words to help her in the dark days:

"Your daddy and me named you Otha. It means 'wealth.' You were your daddy's treasure from the time you were born until he died. He used to say there were rubies buried deep inside of you. Remember, baby, don't never let a man mine you for your riches. Don't let him take a pickax to that treasure in your soul. Remember, they can't get it until you give it to them. They might lie and try to trick you out of it, baby, and they'll try. They might lay a hand on you, or worse, they might break your spirit, but the only way they can get it is to convince you it's not yours to start with. To convince you there's nothing there but a lump of coal.

"Honey, one day I'm going to die, and that's not all, one day you'll die too. And between the here and the there, God sets us upon the business of collecting life's true fortune. I've gotten plenty: the way your daddy smiled when I met him; the apple pie your grandmother used to make, with whole cinnamon grated in with the sugar; the maple leaves in the fall and how that always meant your daddy's fig maple syrup would be on our pancakes. And you. You my big beautiful jewel baby. You my prize. And one day you'll have a child and that child will be your prize.

"Teach them to see it, teach them by doing. But if you can't, if you done give your treasure away, if you find it hard to make your way in the dark of your own soul, if you forget who you really are, know that it comes back to you when the lie they give you die. That lie don't die easy, and sometimes it take you with it. But for all that, your bounty yet waits for you to claim it.

"Remember and it will yet shine. Shine brighter when you let love touch you. Shine brighter when you love yourself. Shine on into heaven when you leave this old world.

"Remember what I say Otha. Remember to lay claim to your inheritance. Will you make that promise to me?"

Otha shook her head, eyes spilling with tears. "I promise Mama," she whispered.

Then she gave her mother a kiss on her dark cheek and went upstairs to pack her bags. She left that hour. Marilyn watched them drive away—the Reverend had waited in the buckboard, never entering her home again, not even to pick up her daughter's bags.

He was good to Otha for a month, and the days of that month were full of talk and big dreams and pictures the size of the sky painted with flourish. He told her of the South as they rode on his buckboard to Liberty, gentle breezes full of gardenia, and bluebonnets littering the sides of hills. He talked about seeing and knowing, how he was a grown man and knew what he wanted, how he wanted to shepherd the lost. He talked about the church he would have one day, and the rainbow glass with angel wings. He said how she was a little bitty thing who he would keep under his wing at least until forever.

The thirty good nights filled Otha with a kind of joy that broke her heart. It was too great a feeling to fit into her temperate body, her delicate spirit, so she had to keep breaking apart to accommodate it, only to glue herself back together each morning. By the time they reached Oklahoma she could no longer recognize herself. But Otha liked this new woman in the looking glass, with tired smiling eyes and world wise lips.

It would be years before he hit her. But in Texarkana, five days from Liberty, he began a covert assault on her judgment. It was little things, like how not to hang linen on the traveling line, what not to wear during Holiness service while he was guest preaching. When they arrived at the Jesus Hearth Church in Dearing and he gave his "Out of the frying pan, into the hands of Jesus" sermon with a 102-degree fever and chills to a decidedly cool congregation, he shamed Otha in front of the congregation by speaking about Northern women with shorn hair who thought the rib was bigger than Adam. By the time they reached Liberty his face was sullen stone that only cracked at night between white sheets.

When her mama got sick a year later, Otha didn't have the strength to tell her she had been right. She asked for money to visit Marilyn but the Reverend said train tickets didn't grow on trees. He gave her money for a trip to the funeral four weeks later instead.

The first two children died before they had fully taken root in her womb. Otha had wanted proper graves but the Reverend said that that was blasphemy as they hadn't come full term and hadn't been baptized. The next child was Celia and she was the

Reverend's child from the beginning, willed to life by the boom of his voice, smiling at his coos and tickles, crying even as she suckled at Otha's breast. Then five more lost children until her boy Ephram came in '29.

By this time the Reverend was hitting her good and proper when, he said, she deserved it. He hated to see her reading and would slap her whenever he caught her at it without first asking if she had finished her chores. He never let her cut her hair, but bristled if she primped in front of the mirror.

When Ephram was five, Grueber's mill went up in flames. It took three whole months before it was up and running, during which time the collection plates suffered greatly. So much so that Otha had to take a job in Newton making lace at Miss Barbara's Bridal Necessities. The Reverend had taken her there himself early one Monday morning. He'd said that Paula Renfolk, Miss Barbara's maid, had told him about the job, but when they got there, Paula seemed surprised to see them, and her husband and Miss Barbara were, oddly, on speaking terms. Even so much as for her to make a donation of fabric and notions to the children of his parish, and for him to follow her up the stairs of the shop to lift the heavy box, and then stay up there for a good twenty-five minutes.

Paula had leaned over and scolded Otha. She told her that she'd best keep her husband satisfied at home or deadly trouble would surely befall him. She'd told her that she'd seen Miss Barbara donate plenty to her husband when the shop first opened. Said no White fella would give her the time of day till she got those new teeth from Dallas. Even after they came in that blue medical box, she'd still made plenty of donations to the Reverend.

When Otha asked her husband about it that evening, he

slapped her so hard that blood filled up her mouth. After that, Otha kept her eyes on her work.

Which, truth be told, was not a sacrifice, because, besides her son Ephram, the beauty of lace was her one true love. Her mother had taught her how to move her fingers, how to stretch the wedge of the lacing tat and loop the fine silk thread. Her work was impeccable and soon she developed a reputation. Women from as far away as Pickettville and Beaumont came to Miss Barbara's because of Otha's intricate and delicate work there in the small dim room at the back of the shop. Often Ephram sat with her for hour upon hours, watching her work. Although the Reverend expressly forbid it, she silently taught him, stitching slowly when his eyes rested on her work, tilting the pattern downward if he leaned towards her. In this way they shared many evenings before getting on the Red Bus to Liberty.

The Reverend had taken to slipping out most nights. Otha assumed it was to see another woman—perhaps even, if Paula had been right, Miss Barbara, for which he surely would be killed. He had been betraying Otha for years with sisters of his own flock. She could always tell who by the way their eyes leapt and danced when the Reverend placed a hand on their arms or shoulders, by the sly cut of their smiles when they greeted her each Sunday. Otha expected and often found telltale signs on his person: a soiled handkerchief, the pungent scent of a woman, a stray pressed hair curling about a button or in his undergarments.

But Otha started finding other, more disturbing articles. She found a tiny Black doll with a pin through its neck in his breast pocket one evening. One night she found a small red velvet pouch filled with a smell so foul she almost regurgitated, another time some type of fang wrapped in sinew. She would come across bits of garlic tied to doorposts and small covered holes in her vegetable patch. When she dug into the earth with frightened hands she would always find a strange assortment of bones and nail clippings. But the last item she had found sent her into the piney woods in secret pursuit of her husband. It was the evening before Easter 1937. Ephram was only eight.

That afternoon, Otha had been going through the laundry basket. She had been unable to locate her good bottom sheet. The second best had been on the bed two days now and the Reverend was a stickler when it came to cleanliness, especially on a Sunday. She had searched high and low. It was not in the washroom, not on the bedroom shelves. The thing became a matter of pride for her, she simply could not have lost her single good bottom sheet. So she began looking in unusual places. She searched through the storm cellar, behind fig and peach preserves. Rising uneasiness caused her to ransack the attic and the smokehouse. Finally, balled in a gap of earth under the rotting wall of the unused outhouse, she found it. It was stiff with mud and something gooey dried hard like glue. It was not until Otha brought the sheet to her nose and smelled the low musk salt did she know it was blood. A chill circled her throat and grabbed her diaphragm. She smelled it again and knew that something had been killed there. She lay on the ground until her heart filled her brain with reason. Her hands were moving like air as she lay on the earth and it took her a moment to notice them. When she did she calmed them against her breast. She had been lacing. The movements always brought comfort. She stuffed the sheet back under the outhouse and went to find her children.

Celia, fourteen, was baking for her father, chocolate layer cake, his favorite. Celia was not a particularly inspired cook but she had an iron-hard will and determination to learn. Celia was fine. Then she went in search of Ephram. Her husband hated the boy with a deep, unruly passion. Otha feared the reason, but pushed it out of her head as quickly as it had come. She hunted in all of Ephram's favorite spots until she found him feeding fish at Marion Lake. She tried to quiet her heart at the sight of him, little legs curled under him, his breath so smooth and steady. But a bubble of fear stole up from her chest and she could not stop herself from crying when he turned to look at her. A small cloud of worry knitted across his face so she reached out and smoothed it down. She sat beside him and stared out at the water.

"You all right, Mama?" her son asked.

She ran her hand over his small square head. His father had kept his hair clipped so close to the scalp that it felt a bit like a new peach. "There's not even enough here for a part."

She watched her son smile. It was an old joke but he kept a fresh grin for whenever she told it. Dragonflies darted by, their wings catching rainbows. They sat so quietly that they heard the lean of the grass and the nuzzling pines. They were quiet people, always had been. He was her stock, had her daddy's brow and her mother's grace. There was nothing of the Reverend in him, which made it easy to pull him near. She wanted to tell him about wolves in the world and a gut-wrenching kind of danger. Otha could feel it rushing past the trees towards her. Her heart sped in her chest. Her son's eyes were so large and dark, his lashes so thick. He peered up at her and she leaned down and kissed him where the part should have been.

She didn't know that her fingers were moving until Ephram looked down at them.

Their eyes met for a moment. She smiled and shrugged. Then

he mashed his face into her, his spindly arms little spider things reaching to hold tighter. So she gathered him up in her lap like she had when he was a bitty thing, not the big boy he was now, and the two watched as evening crept in like a thief and stole the rest of day.

That night after the house was asleep the Reverend slipped out, but not before walking into his son's room. Otha was behind him, feet padding softly on the floor. She peeked in and watched her husband leaning low over the sleeping boy, rumbling strange words while his hands swept the air over Ephram's body. He left a red velvet pouch over the head of her son's bed. She watched as he went to the trash receptacle, opened his handkerchief and gathered tiny crescents of the boy's fingernails he had clipped after dinner. Then he started out. Otha ran like silent lightning and hid behind the closet door. He walked right by her and out of the house. She walked into Ephram's room and ripped the velvet bag from his headboard. Her boy kept sleeping. She sped in bare feet out into the night. She heard a twig break in the distance and she followed. The moon naked and whole above as she tracked noises so quiet that they registered in her unconscious. In this way she walked in her white gown, her hand tight about the red velvet. Where was he taking her boy's nails? Where? She felt the same danger rushing towards her like water. Like a flood rising as she crept after her husband. At one point he stopped and looked back. She ducked down and stopped breathing, then he was off again towards Marion Lake. She saw a glow in the distant clearing, a light flaring in the black thicket woods. Her husband was walking towards it with clippings from her son, and so she followed. As she got closer she could see the trees around it, some of the branches seemed to wave and move, until Otha got close enough to see that they were the raised arms of men, staring into the flames. They were waiting for something.

Otha crept closer, as quiet as the air. A wide pine ahead would hide her. She stopped and dropped to her belly, lifted by her elbows so she could see.

Her husband joined the group. The men dropped their arms and parted. He stood taller among them. Without moving a muscle they all seemed to bend down to him. Otha felt a flush of heat through her skin, as if she were standing in front of the pit fire as well.

From this distance Otha watched the men's blurred images take shape and form. Jaws and noses assembled into familiar faces. Otha's breath halted as she saw they were men she already knew. Friends—deacons from her husband's congregation. Men she had shared hymn books with for years, who had worn their Sunday best as they carried the brass collection plates. Men with patient smiles and familes. What were they doing standing before these flames? Otha lifted herself a bit more to better see their expressions. Even at that distance there was something in their eyes that seemed to crackle with the flames. Something she had never seen on Sundays or at P & K or at town functions. It sent her heart into her throat and made it hard to swallow.

In the red gold of the flames, Otha saw two men bring out a speckled calf, white with red dots—it looked like the Simpkins heifer calf not more than six months old. Eyes tender as creatures are who are new to the earth. The calf was scared. A baritone in the church choir, Josua Perdy flapped open a white sheet with strange markings on it—a black circle and twisting lines—and spread it on the ground. She watched as Deacon Marcus, the man who always bought his wife a bouquet of flowers on Friday, slowly tipped the calf over—it fell with a loud thump and let out a high, lonely mewl. Like a frightened child. Like a—and they bound its feet with a red rope. Tight, too tight, crisscrossed its legs. The animal began crying, long moans rising above the flames. Otha didn't know she was crying too, until she heard the soft drops on the leaves beneath her chin.

As if part of an orchestrated dance, men in slick city clothes and polished shoes stepped out of the shadows and joined the circle. Men she had never seen—tall, high-yellow Creole men who looked like they had come from New Orleans. As they joined the circle, one by one, they handed her husband what looked like folded cash, each nodding, until her husband's pockets were bulging and full. They were paying for something yet to come. Yet to—Otha felt the stars tilting, the world spin . . . it was too much, the thing to come.

She heard her husband speaking to the men. Their eyes rapt, alive. She could only make out a phrase here: ". . . at the peak of . . . ," then nothing, so she pushed against the wall of fear and crept even closer until the dangerous melody of his voice fingered the loose edges of her hair.

The calf's sides were rising and falling like a bellows, skin so thin near its ribs. The heifer began to quiet some, but kept a steady beat, its hollow call unanswered. No mama. No field of grass. Only fire and the eyes of those men.

"Welcome all. Welcome all. Obeah, will you draw the circle?"

Obeah, a squatted man, opened a heavy tan sack and poured red powder in a wide circle around the men.

Otha looked around the forest, hoping for something to stop.

This. To stop it. She looked up. The sky was heavy and a mist hung about the tops of the trees and the calf was groaning low. Nothing. No one was coming.

"We want to welcome our out-of-town members, come down here to experience the way we Sabine Negroes do our business." Her husband smiled so pretty at the crowd and gave off a little wink. She had never seen him look so handsome.

"Now y'all, we got us two initiates joining us today if they got the grist."

Two young boys, who looked to be about twelve, turned. Otha gasped as she recognized young Chauncy Rankin. His face fresh and upturned as if he was getting a medal. His younger brother Percy was the second. The men formed a tighter circle. Otha crept closer, and crouched lower still. Little Chauncy Rankin—he'd once stolen a pecan pie from her kitchen window.

All of them, all of the men began speaking into the flames, but they weren't words, they were chanting something that Otha couldn't make out. Words like snakes slithering from their mouths that made Otha's hands fly to her belly, where she imagined her soul to be.

Her husband lifted his hands with a wide embellishment he'd never wasted on his congregation. His voice rang clear through the air. "I speaks these truths, my brothers. They done come into they manhood high time, so I speaks to them and to the rest of you who done forgot."

Penter Rankin called out, "Tell the truth!"

The Reverend flashed the grace of his body against the flames and leapt up onto a stone. "Now Brothers, I was a little boy when my papa sat me down and tell me this. Just like his papa told him. Just like I'm telling y'all cuz I don't want you getting down on your knees asking no God for nothing, not no fine clothes or no grand house. Don't be asking for no wife to love you, or to feed your children neither. I seen men doing that whiles the whole family starve bug-eyed and them still down on they knees when they carried the youngest one out. I don't want no man on earth to be that kind of a fool."

Peeking through the brush, Otha watched her husband point his long, firm arm like an arrow into the sky and say, "That man up there? That one on his Roman chair? With his snow whiskers and his icicle nose? That White man what breathe out frost when he speaks, with them froze blue eyes like a lake in winter? You got to know he already done picked out who he favor and it ain't the likes of you. It ain't nobody with a lick a color spread over they skin. Not them he seen fit to drag down into four hundred year of slavin'. Not my grandpa who died in them salt swamps of Florida. It ain't your brother Tom got lynched over in Jasper, and dragged some twenty miles 'til they wasn't nothing left of him to bury."

The men started stamping. "Call it Brother Jennings."

"You ain't got to look far or wide to see whose ass he lean down and wipe anytime they ask him. God ain't nothing but a butt boy for rich White men. He let them do whatever thing they want, then make they way as smooth as glass. But White man, he ain't content with all that. He got to rule it all. God his mistress, but he wed to the Devil. How many times we find his workings in them woods? How much our blood he feed his soil, how many upside down crosses he be burning. They been courting the Devil since before Jesus walked the earth. And they doing it still. Back to the day Eve spawned them."

The men pushed closer, their faces hungry for his words like dogs waiting to fetch.

242 / CYNTHIA BOND

Otha watched her husband's eyes go black as he talked about Eve. He told the old story of how she alone baked evil in the bread of the world. Then he added, "Cuz who you think give birth to every nature of pestilence on this old planet earth? Locust and yellow fever—cotton blight and slavery—and when she took that bite of the apple, she open her legs and out come all of that, and worst of all—out come the White man!"

The Reverend looked at the two young initiates. "You just boys and just catching on to they curse. You got to know they born with it, but when they get they first blood it's too late. One day you'll find yourself wrapped up in knots for the want of a woman. You gone want her touch and she gone make sure you do by how she parade in front of you, but the second you reaches out she got to say no. Why? Cuz it's the nature of woman to make you shamed of the desires she done give to you in the first place. Cuz she carry evil inside her like a disease she don't never catch but can't help but spread.

"So hard as it might be for y'all boys to understand, we got to get them early. Got to snatch they evil when we can still use it against any enemy what come to cut us down.

"Some folks say slavery and the whip make us crazy. Some say we got so twisted up with pain and hate so we do this here. But is that true, brothers?"

The men screamed out like someone held a knife to their throats. "*No! No Brother!*"

"I say unto y'all, we as wise as Solomon and learn to use what we got, to take the reins of evil. We needs us some vessels to do just that!!!"

There was a pause in the crowd. Her heart pounding in her mouth, Otha watched as a giant of a man brought six little girls into the center of the circle. They were crying. Weeping. Little crumpled girls who looked like they had been kept in a dark box, cramped, wincing in the light of the fire. Next she saw Papa Bell's grandbaby, little Ruby so pretty, her face like a heart. She wasn't dirty, but had on a pretty blue dress. A blue bow in her hair. Why!! What are they gonna do to that girl? Those girls? *What are they–?* Otha almost stood. Almost. But God or the Devil held her tight to where she crouched.

"And these little ones here!" A practiced treble rang in her husband's voice as he preached hellfire. "Don't be mistook by they age, like a rattler and they poison, they come of age they gonna bite us."

The circle of men shouted out "Heya!" and "Speak it Brother, Speak it!"

Otha watched in horror as he pushed six crying girls forward.

A power surged through her husband so that he shook from head to toe, reached his hand into the heavens and screamed, *"And do you know how we take they evil?"*

The men answered, "Yes! We do, Brother Jennings!"

"How we do it?!"

A man hollered like a hammer. "We teaches them!!!"

"What do we teach them?"

A flurry of voices screaming on top of each other:

"How to use they lust to please us—!"

"—so we can take—"

"—take they power back."

"Yes, my Brothers! Take it back! And what Make They Power Stronger!!"

Obeah, the man who had poured the powder around the circle, answered. "The blood make it so." Otha didn't notice until he spoke that the man had a butcher knife. That he was standing over the calf.

The Reverend said, his voice as flat as death, "Them gals is for y'all to do with as you please. Them that paid go first."

Otha saw one of the girls run and try to break out of the circle, only to be grabbed hard and thrown back with the others, so she crumpled her body and stood still. One of the city men pulled her towards him and held her possessively, arms crossed over her chest.

"But this one . . ." Her husband gently took hold of Ruby. He held her face and gave her a smile. "This one belong to me. Ain't nobody else touch her. She a prize heifer, worth a-plenty. We send her out where she collect the White man's power and bring it back to me so's I can lead y'all."

The drums began. The girls were all crying, sobbing uncontrollably. Ruby looked glazed and accepting.

Otha heard a sound, a high careening cry, she looked and saw that the knife had been plunged into the calf's neck by Obeah. Its legs bucking, writhing, blood spurting on the white sheet.

She jumped, so that the branch broke that she rested upon. The Reverend peered in her direction and searched the dark of the woods. Otha watched little Ruby do the same. In a split second the child's eyes saw her. The Reverend took a step towards the woods, and Otha tasted bile in the back of her throat. She watched the girl Ruby take her husband's hand and turn him away from her. She saw her husband's face twist into a jagged grin as he called out to the men. "Now don't break 'em y'all! They for training! We gots to keep them whole!"

Penter Rankin ran up and threw an ale barrel full of white powder into the pit fire and the flames turned bright blue and green. A wall of blue smoke filled the clearing. It rolled so high and thick it seemed to cover the sky, so that Otha could only see shapes and bits and pieces of men and girls. Arms pulled, dragged off. Pants . . . legs running. Screams. Screams of the children. The dying heifer calf moaning. Pain. Red on one face. A child's cheek red. A man's hands.

Otha was frozen. She wanted to run. Wanted to tell. But who would she tell? Where would she—where would she?!? But she waited because, maybe, maybe one day she could tell God. He wasn't listening now . . . But later, when the blue smoke was gone. When he could see into the fire. See what they were doing. She would tell the Father so he could set it straight.

Then, then she couldn't wait—Otha lifted to go, to run, towards or away she did not know, but a hand slapped over her mouth. Another over her eyes. She fought, fought like life was a treasure that she would die to protect. Another set of hands held her down now. She tried to bite, and scream, she kicked into the hands holding her legs. She heard another scream pealing through the trees, a child was screaming louder, louder still. She managed to lift up, against the weight of hands—bodies. Someone punched her hard on the back of her head and she fell forward. In a second, a shock jerked through her, blocking all transmission, so that a jangle of images cut through her. She came to—minutes? hours? later, jerking on the dumb earth. They were still around her. Her hands were moving, moving against the carpet of dry needles, eating at the earth with her hands. Another jolt shot through her and scrambled the last of her reason. Time stopped and crushed in on itself, too too much for her tender spirit to fathom. Otha was shut down, and passed into unconsciousness.

She awoke the next morning while the sky was still gray. The sun was miles from the horizon. She leapt up and hit her shin against the log, reminding her of where she was. She had soiled herself. There were coals burning where the fire had been. They had—the men. The back of her head ached. They had—had someone hit her? They? Who? Something tilted inside her. She fell against the log. It was as if a scale had been tipped in the night. Something had happened, but she scratched in the ashes of her mind and could not remember a thing. Had there been a fire? Who stood before it? She had followed her husband? Or had she run from him? Little webs stretched before her eyes with spiders that devoured every thought before it could surface. Nothing remained of the night before so she walked in the dim gray pale of morning through the forest path; her reason snagged on a tree branch. She felt something tickling her thighs and saw that her hands were lacing again. She thought to stop them but they persisted against all signals to stop. So she walked home, opened her door. She scrubbed her privates with a soaped face cloth and climbed into her bed beside the Reverend, sleeping like death.

Easter morning found her awake under the three-star quilt she had made three falls ago, hands furious, her husband snoring beside her. She leapt out of bed and fell down again. Balance lost, the floor slanted until she slanted her head to meet the new angle and was able to walk that way. She put on her robe and fixed breakfast, glad to have something to occupy her hands; holding a spatula and flipping pancakes proved manageable. Keeping them busy was best so she cleaned while the household prepared for Easter Sunday. Otha looked at her husband and felt sick but she could not place where this feeling had been born. He chewed and swallowed and pulled back his chair and put on his hat. He always went early so she found the tail of a voice in her throat and croaked out, "Good day." He glared at her, but there was nothing unusual about that. She swept and scrubbed and told Ephram and Celia to go on without her, that she had plenty much to see to before the picnic. Ephram kept asking her what was wrong, what was wrong, until she was sharp with him and told him to go to service. Celia gave her her father's glare. Long a disappointment to her fourteen-year-old daughter, this was nothing new either. Once they walked away, what was left of Otha died right there on the kitchen floor. She felt all that was familiar: the heart that beat for her children; the morning quiet of her garden; even the ever-present low note of sorrow that ran through her marriage; the lavender scent of her mother; her daddy . . . every memory, every bit of her retreating, retracting. She burrowed like a parasite into little pockets in her body, then she barricaded them from the inside, until there was nothing, until all that she had been ceased to be.

Some new thing emerged that thought to lift her form and walk her into the bedroom. This new thing took off her robe and proceeded to get dressed. It tied her shoes and put on her hat. It decided that it would be best, if she could not stop her hands from lacing, to carry the lacing tat and pretend to work on it whenever someone glanced in her direction. This new being never considered not walking to the picnic because it lived under the sway of the Reverend's moods. He would already be livid that she had not come to the church. Why had she not come to the church? No, the floor had had to be cleaned and the breakfast dishes washed and so she couldn't go but she had wanted to, she would tell the Reverend when she saw him. She would explain to him very clearly, very slowly, so that she would make sure she was saying the words correctly because something was tilting her thoughts as well, mixing up the correct sequence. She was planning exactly what she would say as she walked over the hill, which is why the first scream was such a surprise. A little bug of memory collided with the web of her mind again. A child somewhere was screaming bloody murder, but it was devoured just as the Reverend punched her in the face.

The rest of the day was a blur of women and glimpses of Ephram sobbing. Her memory spitting out a dragonfly, in the form of her husband standing beside some girls, but why was he there and he wasn't really there but why did the girls turn into blue smoke? When she mentioned the girl in the forest he had begun beating her in earnest but even that felt distant, except she needed to see Ephram and tell him something about his bed, perhaps to take a red thing from there, but what, she could not fathom. And then she was too weak to stop someone from hurting her boy, and a pain ripped through her soul as she was torn from him, ripped like a spider from its web, and she was hit so hard the buckboard raced to her head and held it all the way to hell.

The sleeves they wrapped around her were too tight around her lungs so that she couldn't breathe in deep enough to sustain consciousness. She kept waking up gasping for air and then passing out again. Finally an angry White woman did something with buckles and she was able to stay awake, and then she wished she hadn't. She found that she was wearing a diaper and that it had been soiled more than once. She was in a room with four other Colored women all wrapped similarly. When she arrived the Reverend had taken her into a room and told a White woman that she had tried to throw her children down the well and had then run naked to the Easter picnic, that she was crazy and that he loved her but what could he do. The White woman had put her hand on her Black husband and patted his back then she had shoved Otha into another room, getting the little jacket over her bruised body. When she cried for her son the woman had pushed her hard against the wall.

By evening Otha's reason was slowly returning. She was terrified for her children. At the end of a week she began to smell again. She didn't realize that sense had been lost until she was assaulted by the stench of urine, waste and collective human sweat. She was moved into a great room with ten women and men strapped to beds. A very angry man said that her ribs were broken and she was wrapped up and left there where she developed sores on her ankles and skin burns on her vagina and buttocks from urine soaking and laying so close to her skin for so many days. After a month she was moved to a cell where human decency had long been forgotten. Twelve women shared a filthy room with a tin bucket for relieving themselves. Some women were strapped to their beds. Some screamed all day and wept. One woman played with her private parts until nurses slapped her hands with a ruler. When they were out of sight she would begin again. In spite of this Otha held fast to what was left of her sanity. She did it for one reason. Her son, Ephram. Besides the yawning pain of missing him she was terrified for him as well. She called out at night to speak about her children until two men came in and tied her to her bed with a leather strap over her mouth. Two days later a man came in to talk with her. They took the strap from her mouth then. She had not had water or food for two days. This man did not seem angry. He was a young White man, so young in fact that his face didn't look as if it would take a beard. He called Otha "Mrs. Jennings" and asked her how she was feeling, so of course she felt tears pushing against her eyes, she told him that she was very concerned about her son and daughter. She did not dare mention pit fires and young naked girls, not in the heart of this beast of a place, but she did tell the man that her husband beat the children in such a way that she was frightened for their very lives. The young man nodded and looked at a piece of paper in front of him. He said that he thought it would be best if she stayed with them for a while longer.

When she insisted that it would not be all right, that she was feeling much better and that the incident that had taken place was a thing of the past, that she was perfectly normal, he simply looked down at her hands and shook his head with a short little nod. Otha followed his gaze and saw that her hands were lacing. It was then that she realized they had been lacing since she arrived and had not stopped, not for one single moment. The young, young man said, "There, there," when she kept crying. He signaled for help as her cries intensified and left as they were strapping her in, telling her that he would be back to see her in a month. He lied.

Three months later when he returned Otha was barely human. She sat in a corner and laced the air around her. Every day or so someone would come by and tell her to stop. She thought to herself that she would have stopped by now if it was such a simple matter, but because they didn't realize this she often let a smile break onto her dull face. This always seemed to anger them and they would tell her to stop again and again, then drag her to a room somewhere to try some new horror on her body. They shoved her in ice water for so long that she contracted a fever when she got out that turned into pneumonia, which would have killed her if the janitor hadn't gotten one of the orderlies to take her to the hospital room. Another month in a bed while some flurry of strength kept her breathing until she was returned to the shared room. Next they wheeled her into a small tiled cell and shoved sour rubber into her mouth and exploded rockets in her brain. She forgot to use the facilities for two days, after which they sent her back to the ice water, for a shorter vigil this time.

When the young man reappeared he told her his name was Dr. Glass. He was wearing spectacles this time, which Otha suspected were more to make him look older than for any true ophthalmologic need. He did not apologize for his two month delay except to say that they had been very busy in this section of the hospital. Otha took every ounce of strength from not only her body, but from any God in the stars to keep her hands still. She managed it for five whole minutes. When they began again he glanced at them as if he had not been aware of their stillness. She talked about her children again. He nodded and said that they were going to try a new approach, that he would see her in a few days.

Days. The next day Otha's blood was taken and she was moved to a small room with only one other woman. She was given better food and the light was dimmed when it was time to sleep. She was given a larger room to walk around in at midday to keep her blood flowing. Then she was injected with something at the end of the second day that sent her into convulsions on the floor. The next day Dr. Glass arrived, looked at her chart and made some notations. That evening they gave her the injection again and she spasmed, but to a lesser degree than the day before. Dr. Glass saw her every other day and brought other men in to see her as well. Sometime during the third week her face and hands had swollen and puffed out. Her joints began to ache and the veins in her right and left arms collapsed, so they gave her the injection in her left thigh. Shortly after he left, swirls of rainbow light spun before

Otha's eyes. The walls seemed to breathe, then sweat black ink, which became oiled branches that crowded all of the air.

When Dr. Glass came back an hour and a half later, his head was a balloon floating above his body. When Otha asked why she was seeing such things, he told her that she was very brave and that she would be better soon. They gave the injections every evening thereafter until one night around three in the morning the Devil came to visit Otha while she worked.

He tapped on the door and then walked straight through it. His image fluttered in and out for a moment, like fighting through static to find a station on a radio. When he took form, he was holding a United States Postal Service bag, with a canvas strap that crossed his heart. Otha still dreamt in lace and eggshell silk, in top stitching and embroidered edges, and so the Devil's face was a patchwork quilt, with scraps of fabric from years of collecting and saving and sewing. There was a cotton bird print where his left eye should be and a zebra wool over his right. He smiled a thin swatch of teal and black check, and slipped two envelopes between her moving palms. In this new room no one tried to stop Otha's hands; they flew, long and dark, over her plum face, spinning lace webs over her head.

In spite of his observances Otha worked. She realized in that moment, that in the months she had been there, no one on earth knew what her hands were doing. She hadn't known either except that she had felt compelled to move them as if she were lacing at Miss Barbara's. Now as the Devil looked down at her work, she could see it as well. Reams and reams of lace filled the room, dangled out the window and unfurled into the sky. Her fingers had not moved in vain. She had been making lace out of night air and moonbeams, pine scent and starlight. She had made it frantically, feverishly. There was a piece made from morning dew and the tears of her son, another out of mother love. The stretch of sky and the corners of the ceiling above was her tat. She saw it reach out and cover a bit of the sky. It was a thin blanket of intricate cream, softening the rude sun. It was meant to calm the oceans and filter the oil from the skies. It was a net to save the planet, to catch the earth in her downward spiral and hold her safe. There was only a fragment of it finished, but its beauty was breathtaking; delicate, sparkling perfection. It was her offering to life.

Otha had to admit that it felt good to know that at least one other person could see what she had been doing, could see the importance of her work, even if that person was the Devil.

"Ma'am," the Devil asked, "are you going to sign for this?"

"Yes, of course," Otha said and set down her work. It was a special delivery. Why hadn't she seen that before? She reached out and his pen arranged itself between her fingers and she watched her signature spreading beneath her, while he rested in the doorway.

"What's it say?" he asked. "Don't see many with postage like that."

Then Otha felt the envelope flap tearing between her forefinger and thumb. The letter floated above her, the words moving like lice across the page. She saw that it was a list of names, alphabetically placed in a column. Halfway down she saw *Otha Jennings* written there. Then she looked up at the top. It was a death announcement, and the list grew longer and longer until it hit the floor and rolled onto the Devil's foot. He smiled as it lit like a fuse and leapt into flames. It caught the edge of the moonbeam lace; in seconds it had burned all that she had woven that night, then for the last month; it was racing out the window until Otha grabbed the tail of the fire and, burning her hands, threw it to the ground and crushed it between her toes.

"Doesn't matter. It still won't hold," the Devil said as he crooked his hat to the side. "It won't hold against the fire in the sky." She heard the comfortable gait of his step as he sifted through the closed door and left the room.

She began to work again in earnest. Night air and ephemeral light woven into the lace, into her Rapunzel lace rope that would save her and the world. The only difference now was that Otha knew she would lose.

OTHA JENNINGS remained in the Colored ward of Dearing State Mental Hospital for eight years until she was transferred to Kindred Mental Hospital in Albuquerque, New Mexico, in July of 1945, where she met her death. She received one visit from her son and daughter during her stay, after which she requested that no family members be allowed into the visiting area, especially her son. Her chart claimed that she was amiable and never a trouble. It said that she was, above all things, very quiet.

Chapter 18

Chauncy Rankin walked bare-chested along the back pathway towards Ruby's house, his soiled shirt and suit jacket slung over his arm, the rain soaking the weave of his slacks, his good shoes collecting mud. He marched straight towards Bell land. It was only two miles out of the way, but he figured he'd be home in time for the mourning meal and Junie hadn't really been his favorite great-uncle anyway.

Chauncy walked up to Ruby's door and knocked. The rain made the sound dull and hollow, so he peeked inside. The place looked like church, clean as a rifle in winter. He figured she hadn't gone far. Then, sure enough, just to the side, he saw her, hugging against an old chinaberry tree, naked except for a sheet wrapped around her. Chauncy was always amazed at Ruby's shenanigans. Once he'd come and she had piled a mound of dirt on top of her. She tickled him. He knew she only played at crazy, that it was a put-on thing that let her do the nasty things she liked to do. In all of his visits she'd never once said no.

Chauncy looked at Ruby clinging to the tree, wet sheet sticking to her body. She looked even better than she had that morning, too skinny, but legs as long as the River Nile. Ephram Jennings was no fool. He stood and looked at the girl's hair, all wet and moving like black oil rolling down her back. It was what folks called talking hair. Everyone had something to say about it. He leaned against the damp of the house and watched her quietly, his hand resting loosely against his crotch.

EPHRAM HAD let the rain wash him clean through. His clothes, down to his drawers, were sopping wet, and he didn't care. His shoes squished when he walked, his socks smacking against his soles. The Naugahyde bag he had packed hung easily from his left hand. Celia would notice the tracks he had made into her home. There was no way to avoid it. He had been compelled.

Ephram had watched Chauncy huff away, then suddenly he had felt as if the soil beneath him had all but lifted his feet and set them walking, Gubber and the rest calling after. Still he had walked back to Celia's and swiftly thrown his things into his only piece of luggage, the one he used to accompany Celia to the Holiness convention last April. He had packed like a man in a burning house, grabbing, stuffing only what he would need.

He was out of Celia's house in less than twenty minutes. The path was wet and in places the color of brick. He collected that good road in the cuff of his slacks, and nearly sprinted to P & K Market. He was glad that Miss P was either a good enough businesswoman or a bad enough neighbor to keep the store open during Junie's funeral. He would ask her to pack the chocolate ice cream in a plastic bag with ice. That way it would be perfect when he handed it over to Ruby Bell.

RUBY WAS once again the tree. She had slept morning into afternoon and had awakened to soft caws singing through the rain. She'd walked outside and luckily stepped over the streak of wet red powder on her doorstep, not in it, then she'd walked to her chinaberry and the old bird perched on high. She loved how winding and gnarled the roots were, how firmly they held to the soil. Again, Ruby felt her limbs and sternum twist and knot as they pushed deep into earth. A great bank of life rushed through her as she felt herself reaching up, until her branches trembled in the wind and soft rain, the tiny green beads quivering like bells, waiting for birds to pluck them. She felt the crow's talons holding tightly to one of her branches. The old bird said, *Child, I'd watch myself if I was you.* Which is how Ruby knew to turn around and face Chauncy Rankin, not two inches from taking off her sheet.

It took her a moment to remember that she was a woman. As a tree she had nothing to fear from Chauncy. The way he looked at her hair made her remember. He reached down and lifted a bit of the damp curls.

Ruby did not want Chauncy. What she wanted was to collect raindrops on her leaves and to nourish her roots. What she wanted was to stand with the wisdom of the chinaberry in her marrow and then walk into the door of her polished home. What she wanted was for the man Ephram to come back to that home and make her coffee, or dish up the ice cream he had promised to bring, or to put a comb through her hair. She wanted to smell the slight musk of him, and watch the purple she had discovered in his eyes. But Ruby was well trained in not following her wants and desires.

She lay upon the wet earth, still as the world around her. He slowly peeled back her sheet and draped it over a branch.

As CHAUNCY stood, watching the spindle of her sex begin to turn, he felt a prickling along the back of his scalp. He draped his shirt and jacket over a branch, and said low enough for only the nearest blades of grass and stones to hear, "Rub your nasty for me." She paused. For a moment. Then she pushed the palm of her hand down her body, stopping to slowly cup her breasts. He took a good long moment to admire her, as he grew thick and full. What with the house a clean and proper playground, and now that Ephram had trussed her up like a fat hog for a mayor's Easter supper, Chauncy would take her in ways he hadn't imagined when she was lying in ditches and peeing in streets. The burial would last a good two hours, given the hoots and breakdowns the sisters were sure to have. That would give them plenty of time.

The crow flapped above her in the tree, its caw mournful and plaintive.

THE DYBOÙ watched from the trees. The land was a banquet, sweet and salted. He saw his ox standing above the whore. Watched the way he savored, instead of wasting her skills with haste, as any other man might. He smelled the tall man's gluttony like bacon frying in cast iron, and he stretched across the sunless land until he reached the two.

RUBY THOUGHT of Ephram, the man who had lured her halfway out of madness, the sweet crook of his smile, and knew that he was best not here. None of the killing sweetness and respect ladled upon her, drowning her. She ignored the sob balled up in her throat as she let her hand fall lightly upon the soft black tangle. She knew through wizened experience not to enter, but to gently stroke in preparation. Then her hand, on its own volition, stilled. To her surprise she found that, try as she might, it would not move.

IN SPITE of the rain on his wide shoulders Chauncy felt the warmth of the pit fire. He felt the swell of shadow surrounding him. His arm, the one he must have bitten while having a nightmare, ached. The bandage had begun bleeding through in his fight with the fool Ephram. It did not matter. He felt his might and strength as he watched her hand hovering, tempting. He held on to that—the painful sweet of waiting. Then a misted weight dropped upon him, pushing into him. He remembered in flashes. The Dyboù filling his firm muscles the night before, wearing him like a well-made suit. Chauncy suddenly realized that Ruby had actually stopped. A strength jolted into Chauncy as he swooped down, grabbed Ruby and pulled her up by her hair. He gave her a good slap across the cheek and pushed her to her knees. The Dyboù was fully inside of him now.

RUBY FELT blood in her mouth and suddenly saw the clouded emptiness of a ghost filling Chauncy. The scent of smoke. She had felt the Dyboù inside of her before and knew he wanted more than her body, so she began to fight. Hitting, trying to stand.

The Dyboù and Chauncy pushed Ruby down again; a dot of red wetted her lip. They would as soon kill her if they hadn't wanted her mouth on them—taking them, drinking them. Chauncy swiftly unzipped his pants.

In one gliding rush, Ruby felt the Dyboù falling through her, melding, joining, reaching for the graves of her children. Ruby pushed with all of her might and Chauncy fell back. The Dyboù was clinging to her, threading through her as she jumped onto the porch, then leapt, sailed into the house, away from her children. Chauncy was on her in seconds, hooking his elbow through her and crashing her to the floor. He did not hit her. He held her shoulders down against the clean wood and simply said, his voice like iron, "Quit."

Her children safe, Ruby did just that. Her back on the kitchen floor, Chauncy straddled her face, pinning her with the weight of his body. He was angry. Ruby knew it would be difficult to breathe in this position, with this much rage, but certainly possible.

Seconds before he pushed into her mouth, Ruby heard her name in the air. It took her a moment—then she knew. It was Ephram.

Chauncy leapt up and zipped his pants. Remarkably unscathed, he wiped his mouth as the Dyboù slipped from his body. Ruby scrambled into the bedroom, blotting the mud from her skin. The Dyboù hovered against the ceiling, then pulled back, seeped out of the front door and drifted back into the piney woods.

Chauncy tipped carefully over the entrance, then walked leisurely into the yard. Ruby wrapped the robe around her that Ephram had bought at P & K, then went to the doorway as she saw Ephram turn the corner.

He walked towards the yard, suitcase and plastic bag in hand. His face seemed to fall into confusion with each step. By the time he reached them, Ruby saw his arms taut, his jaw tight. Chauncy stepped right up to Ephram, his hand outstretched, a look of sincerity painted across his face.

"Hey man I was hoping to find you here."

Ephram just stood there waiting, letting Chauncy's hand hang in the soft rain.

"Yeah man, figured you wasn't stayin' round there with all that foolishness."

Ruby saw Ephram set down his bags as he listened.

"I come out to 'poligize for all that 'bout your mama. Men

gone be men but don't nobody need to be draggin' all that back out to light. It ain't right. Me, I'm gonna have a talk with both Sim and Percy. They ought to know better."

Ephram turned to Ruby and said low and steady, "What's he doing here?"

Before Ruby could answer, Ephram hauled back and hit Chauncy square on the jaw. Chauncy staggered back, a look of shock washing over him. Ephram charged again, punching Chauncy in the face, once, twice, until the two men went tumbling.

Ruby rushed to them, screaming, "Y'all stop! *Stop!*" She turned to Ephram. "Ain't nothing happen! *Stop!* He come here to see you about something so I wait inside."

Chauncy jumped in, honesty stirred into every word. "Man, hold on now! I was trying to get you to come back with me for the reception. Damn! Ain't no need for that! Past is past with us. What kind a' man I be to trespass in the here and now." He gathered himself and added the truth that always makes a lie more plausible, "Mama asked for you special. 'Sides, I needs you to explain to her why I ain't there at the burial on account how you got sick all over my shirt!" He strode to the tree, grabbing his shirt and jacket, proof of his sincerity. He waved them about as he walked back. "Look what you done, man! Now you know some-body's got to answer for it. You know what she's like. She ain't gonna believe nothing I say. Gonna have my hide. Hell, she try to cut a switch for Percy just yesterday."

Ruby looked at Chauncy and realized that he was the best liar she had ever seen. Even she almost believed him.

Heaving, Ephram looked into the man, searching, then he calmed and said, "Yeah, Supra don't play. But I can't help you. I wasn't there neither. Left right after you."

"So you coming?"

"No, I'm done for today."

"Don't make me beg."

"I can't help you," Ephram said.

"All right, I'll have to settle for that." Chauncy said finally, "I was wrong today, man, at that grave. We all was. I'm sorry for that."

When Ephram turned away, Chauncy winked at Ruby. He then half trotted down the road past the bend and was quickly out of sight.

Ephram looked into Ruby. "What happened to your face?"

"I fell against that chinaberry while I was playing with my babies."

Ephram took a step back so she answered his feet, "Hell, man, I'd tell you. I've got nothing to hide. You ain't my boyfriend or nothing. I do as I please, so why wouldn't I tell you."

"You—he didn't do nothing?"

"Ephram, I swear, he was knocking on that door two minutes before you came. I've never said two words to that fool."

He sighed like air leaving a tire, and Ruby learned that quickly, how easily lied to Ephram Jennings was.

CHAUNCY RANKIN ran like a colt down the forest road. At forty-seven he still felt the raw power in his easy movements. He was just the kind of man he admired, tall, good-looking and clever as hell. It didn't hurt that God had gifted him with length where length was most needed and the width to strike an ax hard enough to fell a medium-sized tree. Chauncy broke into a fine sweat, pushing his body a little bit harder. He knew he would have her again and soon by the looks of it, and damned, if messing with Ephram hadn't turned her out. She looked good enough to eat. He felt a burning pride that he had been chosen, of all the men, to be welded to the Dyboù. Only the best and strongest were picked, so of course, it had been him. He would rage with might over the pit fire. He would rule.

Chauncy would have laughed out loud but he didn't have the time. There truly was going to be hell to pay for not being at the burial. The best he could do was blame it on Ephram and his fall into damnation and sin. Why else would he pick a fight in a graveyard? Hell, the mood folks were in, Chauncy figured, he could say just about anything and they'd just *tsk-tsk* at the stealing of a good boy's soul. Ephram Jennings deserved all of it and more, being with a born whore, a *woman* who had laid not only with him, but with half the parish. More than anything Chauncy was grateful that the Brothers had never invited Ephram to the pit fire. A man like that wasn't worthy to gather their kindling.

THE PINES towered high above Ruby and Ephram as they stood in the front yard, looking at each other in the haze. It was as if the clouds couldn't decide whether to finish the storm properly or just leave it alone, so it lived a kind of half-life over their heads. It was Ruby who reached her hand through that uncertainty and pulled Ephram towards her.

In spite of the lie or maybe because of it, she felt the soft of the man like a balm. Lying was the shield she had picked up against the hate of life. It would save her still. It would keep this man beneath—no, beside her. She put her head against his chest and heard the steady beat under his sternum. She was a used thing. She was nothing, except his arms wrapped around her, and she felt her heart squeeze in her chest.

Ruby felt the dirt and terror of the afternoon melting.

Ephram looked down and saw shame covering her like a bushel. He lifted up her face.

Ruby saw something in his eyes. It was akin to respect, and shone like a candle. It was so bright, the light entered her, so she couldn't help but look around. In that instant Ruby saw the walls of her own soul, saw things sparkling there she had never thought to look upon. Pictures of women, old, ancient with eyes like eagles, hands with love burning. She saw Maggie. There were sparkling lights lining the walls, gemstones gleaming. There was a lifetime of learning scribbled there, and a march towards life in spite of the hell that had been dealt her. Ruby blinked against it and then quickly the light went out. She looked away from Ephram, but she knew, knew in that moment that she had seen it, that she could never again pretend she had not felt her worth. It would always haunt her, tug upon her in her darkest moments.

So Ruby kissed Ephram. She had to stand on tiptoe to do it.

Ephram felt her hand glancing the back of his neck and then, soft like the mist around them, Ruby held her lips against his. His hand found her hair and let his fingers rest in a tangle. The other barely touched her waist. She did not press or move, but still Ephram felt a rush through his chest, a steel in his legs, and then she held his lower lip between hers and suckled softly. Then the tip of his tongue. Had she become sugarcane? Did she know the secrets of the stalks? He felt their syrup in her kiss.

Ruby breathed in the man, his salty scent, the faint odor of his aftershave. She took his air into her lungs and held it as he began kissing her, his hands firm now, in her hair, on her back, fingers tight against her ribs. Some powdery feeling collected at the back of her throat and her chest rose too quickly and released with a moan. When she pulled away her eyes were wet.

She looked down at the earth because she couldn't look directly at the man. She could not give her heart to him. She could never hand over what had been ripped away so long ago. Still, she could stand shoulder to chest beside him. She looked up at the sky. It had made a decision and suddenly poured full and free about them. They did not move.

Ephram almost reached out to touch her cheek but a flash of lightning stopped him. He counted silently and the thunder rolled when he reached nine.

Together like children they waited and counted the next flash. They stopped at seven. The storm was coming closer. Ruby felt the urge to leap against Ephram and hold him too tight, to weep into his collar and thank him for her salvation, but instead she punched his right arm and said, "Nice suit."

"You like it?"

"Sure do." Ruby stepped towards the house then turned around. "If you've got any others like him at home tell them they're welcome to come over and stay awhile."

Ephram smiled. "Six at least. But they don't go nowhere without their shoes."

"I suppose the shoes don't go nowhere without them socks."

"They're pushy that way. Matter of fact, they so presumptuous, they jumped in that there bag and dragged me all the way here."

"Did they?"

"They sho did."

"Well, if they went to all that trouble, no telling what else they likely to do. I 'spose we best let them on in."

Ephram went to get the bag. The ice cream was a bit mashed, but still cold in the sack.

They were both grinning when they reached the porch.

The rain fell so hard it started singing. They were almost at the door when they both saw the last traces of the red powder streaking in front of the door. Ruby took a step back. The sight of it sent a spark of anger across Ephram's chest; he bent down and sniffed. He thought of the stories he'd heard since childhood, of hexes and spells and curses under the blood moon.

"Foolishness." Then to Ruby he said, "Wait here."

She leaned against the porch and watched the dark woods as Ephram ducked inside. A quiet terror washed over her. The scent of Aqua Velva lifted with the wind tinged with tobacco. It lasted for only a second. Ephram came out with a scrub brush. He made quick work of finishing what the rain had started; when he was done he rinsed his hands at the pump and put the bags in the house. He lifted Ruby by the waist and easily carried her to the door's threshold, then paused as the crow started fussing again in the trees, soaked and angry. It cawed, *Child, I'd watch myself if I was you.*

Over Ephram's shoulder, a soft outline formed in the dark, and for a moment Ruby saw the Reverend Jennings like a puff of smoke. In the warmth of Ephram's arms, Ruby tucked it away as a trick of shadow.

"Shut up Maggie," she whispered, as Ephram carried her into the house.

Chapter 19

Celia walked into her silent home after the Rankins' reception. The fact that Ephram had left during the burial was embarrassment enough, but when he failed to make Junie's reception, Celia had felt a shame she hadn't known since her mama rubbed her nakedness in God's face. She had kept peeking towards the door when it opened, certain that the men and women of Liberty, that threats and plain decency, would have waved Ephram's little boat home. When it became clear that it had not, she had burned inside of her skin. Supra's smirk when she handed Celia a piece of Verde's lopsided coconut cake crushed Celia's chest in on itself. She stooped just a bit from the effort to accept it.

Now, alone in her home, the empty pans in the shelves and unused plates in the cupboards, brought their daddy, the Reverend, to mind. The slice of loneliness heaped upon her plate when he was killed by those White men from Neches came back to her. The food she'd kept on hand for him, the smoked ham and salt pork, the pickled trotters and the hot peppers in vinegar for his greens, all waited for years until the twisted lids grew mold. Neither she nor Ephram had found the gumption to go near it.

Thirty-three years later, Celia knew that the food waiting in the refrigerator for Ephram would soon start to curl and lose its crisp. The mountains of his favorites sat in new Tupperware: fried chicken and pork chops, okra with tomato and corn, fresh yeast rolls, collard greens, black-eyed peas with butter rice, potato salad, lemon meringue pie, sweet potato pie, blackberry cobbler and more. All made with a certainty that Ephram, hungry and guilty, would surely be home by sunset with his tail on a plate.

As she looked about the house the practical business of life without him began to unroll before her. Without the new bags coming home every day from the Piggly Wiggly, her larder would soon run low. And what was she to do? Walk the mile to P & K and tote her own bags home? Past the Rankins' land and everyone wandering down to Bloom's Juke come evening? Even paying some young man to do it would have proved shameful, as if she had no family, no relation who cared enough to tend to her needs. Where would she get her stamps? Who would post her letters? Who would accompany her to purchase her wigs in Newton and so much more?

Celia sat upon the plastic slipcovers on her mint velour sofa. It was not only the loss of him, but who had gained. Ruby Bell was not just a girl. Celia knew what she was and how she had become that way. Celia was one of the few women in Liberty who knew about the pit fires. Others whispered over white ashes, but she had been there. She had seen the thing one evening and seen the girl who took delight in sin and debauchery. That girl was Ruby Bell.

Celia felt her stomach grip and churn with fear for her boy. A hunger rose from her body, and she crept into the kitchen. Bowls upon bowls of a glistening Sunday repast waited. Celia ate. She gnawed chicken to the bone and scraped the cartilage. She gulped unchewed mouthfuls of perfectly seasoned okra, corn bread found near the back, rolls crammed too full in her mouth for her molars to bite down. She stuffed and stuffed until food fell down her gown, pushing the handfuls almost to the back of her throat, so that her breath was labored and the food locked in her throat. Then she padded to the bathroom, knelt down on the pink shag throw rug. Her hands met her lips, her fingers white from pressing together. She let them part and slid two fingers into her throat. She pressed a secret button and up it all came in a gush. In a matter of seconds it was done. Her body shook like a train screeching to a stop. Then she was empty. After she washed her hands, she used the same two fingers to pull the lever on the toilet. She turned away as it all swirled down.

It had been years since Celia had prayed on the bathroom floor and her throat burned from the effort. At fourteen, after her mama left, it had somehow helped her to manage the business of living and raising Ephram and taking care of her daddy—but it had begun when she was twelve, the night Ruby dragged her daddy into hellfire, where he swam, and eventually drowned.

In those days, Celia trailed after her papa. She didn't know why, except that he needed looking after. Her mama kept her eyes on Ephram and didn't seem to care much about Celia, much less her own husband. Celia had noticed how she always looked down at the ground when he came into the room, or busied herself with the wash—any little thing to keep herself too high and proud for her daddy. Being educated like she was, she liked to lord it over him.

Everyone in the house had picked their partners. Ephram and her mama. The Reverend and his church. Celia was left alone, so she followed her daddy.

First she started walking behind him when he went to the church some off days to help the head of the Women's Auxiliary tend to some chores. She made sure he didn't see her; still she would wait for him in the thicket of trees. She would take little things she imagined might come in handy. A tea cake wrapped in a napkin, if he found himself out somewhere hungry. A canteen with sweet water—she'd even measured the sugar in herself. Smelling salts, a toothpick, a pack of matches and sometimes a fresh pair of socks. She invented all types of instances when he might do something like step into a mud puddle on the way to a meeting with the Church Board, and she would show up out of nowhere to clean up his shoe and hand him the socks. He might faint from all of his work, and there she would be, with sweet water and reviving salts.

So one night, when she heard her daddy going out, Celia followed after him. Her mama and Ephram fast asleep, she had thrown on her waiting school dress and shoes, then walked out into the pines. She had known he did work out in the back woods, where some folks believed in conjure and went to a Godless woman named Ma Tante.

Celia thought, *That is where he must be walking, to minister to the heathens*, who, she had heard, prayed to something other than Jesus. She was well practiced at walking silently behind him, and he never turned once, but walked proudly through the trees until he reached a glowing fire surrounded by men.

Celia watched her daddy smile big and set the men at ease. Some Celia knew and she was shocked to learn that they were heathens and would therefore be left behind during the rapture. She was too far away to hear him, but she watched her daddy speaking in earnest, trying to save their souls from purgatory, and sure enough, they were listening—each and every one. They nodded and Celia knew that come Sunday they would be in Marion Lake, being baptized by her father.

Then something strange happened. The flames seemed to grow larger and the wind picked up, then came little girls. Celia figured they had been sent there to bring their daddies home, until she saw Ruby Bell, who didn't have a daddy at all—at least not one who would show his face.

When Ruby stepped out her daddy stared at her and all of his words just fell to the wayside. Celia could tell something was wrong with her daddy. The other girls started crying—but not Ruby, who stood still as anything. Celia wanted to know what was behind that fire, what was hiding out in those woods she couldn't see. The men started shuffling too. Without her daddy's words to stop them, they started pounding on some kind of drum and moving their lips all at the same time.

Then Celia watched a type of bedevilment take hold of her daddy. He started swaying with the drums, started moving his mouth with the other men. Celia began praying for him. She pressed her hands tight together and called on Jesus, and the Father. It didn't help.

It seemed like her daddy, the one she poured coffee for every morning, because her mother was too slow about it—it seemed like he was gone, and this man, looking dead-eyed at Ruby, was all that was left. She wished she had brought something to help him, but nothing in her little bag would help, not even the salts.

So she began whispering her daddy's favorite, Psalm 23, into the quiet night while tears slid down her face.

It seemed to Celia like something made her daddy hand off each child to men she had never seen, picking up a tiny wrist and laying it in a grown man's hand.

"He maketh me to lie down in green pastures: He leadeth me beside the still waters."

Celia felt a fist of anger and sorrow ball up in her throat.

"He restoreth my soul: He leadeth me in the paths of righteousness for His name's sake."

It seemed—it seemed to Celia like he was giving those girls away, like you would if somebody won a raffle at a Fair.

"Yea, though I walk through the valley of the shadow of death, I will fear no evil: For thou art with me . . ."

What would make him do such a thing? What force? What—then Celia looked at Ruby Bell, who seemed to be just smiling through it all. Other girls crying, being led off like they had gotten a new master. Ruby Bell hadn't been passed to anybody. Who hadn't shed not one tear.

Then Celia watched in the smoke and black night, as Ruby turned to her daddy, and seemed to will him to her. He marched towards her like a puppet, and when he reached her, seemed to hug her near, hug her close, closer than he had ever held his own daughter. Then something happened that Celia did not understand—how they stayed that way too long, too close. How they seemed to be swaying with the beat of the evil drums . . . and how her papa never danced, but now, somehow, Ruby's head rocking, her daddy's hips shifting, he was doing just that. A kind of dancing. Were his pants brown? She had been sure that they were black when he walked in there, but now, were they the same color of his skin? What—what had happened to his pants?

Celia let out a scream that began in her belly as she turned crashing through the branches. She pounded the earth all the way home and slammed the door to her room. She shook in bed until morning, knowing, knowing, knowing that her father was a good man—that God had singled him out early to do his work, to rattle the Devil's cage. She knew that old Satan had to work hard. Very hard. Very hard with such a good man. Must have hammered his spike long and hard to find the key to his undoing. It had to be hidden where her papa would never think to look. Inside of a child.

From that day onward, Celia never, ever followed her daddy again. Instead, Celia watched Ruby. Watched her coming back from that White lady in Neches, acting better than everybody. Watched her sparking that Wilkins girl like she would have a man, with nobody saying a thing about it. Watched her move on up to New York City where her kind of evil banded together, and later she'd watched her slide across town filled with demons, begging bread and sympathy from Miss P, and drawing good men from their wives' beds. Now she was trying to steal her Ephram, as she had her father. She saw Ruby as a red beacon washing over Liberty. For some reason Celia had seen fit to let that live untampered. She regretted that now. First, she would try to cleanse Ruby's soul. If that did not work, Celia would get ahold of the Sheriff and put that girl somewhere she could only tempt lunatics and those who minded them, down in Dearing.

Chapter 20

The pines had been watching men and their fire circles since they were saplings. For nearly two hundred years they had seen upside down crosses glowing red in the dark, long before men in white sheets ever rode the horizon.

Dark cloaks donned, secret chants and the pealing screams that followed. The slaves of these men had hidden in the shadows and witnessed the unthinkable. When morning came, the tall trees watched the men, brown and black, scrubbing blood from the knives of their masters in the cool river and kicking dirt over stiff maroon soil, cleaning quartered animals missing hearts and heads. The great pines had stooped in sorrow when they saw these slaves learning in the thick brush, the source of the White man's might, then mingling their own ancient homeland rites, magic and shadow secrets with the new, until they began gathering about their own fires and driving their desires into the roots of the world.

The Dyboù had been walking through the same piney woods for the past thirty-seven years. He was earthbound. His soul had been stitched to the land with a curse made moments before his destruction. It had been spit over his body as he lay bleeding, and then cemented as the bones in his neck snapped one at a time like dry twigs. Then the circle had gathered around him, crying, some wailing, just as the Apostles and the whore Mary had wept over Jesus.

But those were the thoughts he'd had while breathing. In death it had become much simpler. Jesus was a fluff of tobacco smoke. God was a figment of distilled whiskey. The name his mother had given him, Omar Jennings, and the name he had forged, the Reverend Jennings, both were dust in the crack of his shoes.

He had gathered at the pit fires since he was thirteen, nearly seventy-five years before. Then later, as a man, leading the circle, fear and awe freshly painted on every man as they looked upon him.

But first he had been a boy and the whole of his life had been spent sleeping in the corner of a one-room dirt cabin. His daddy had been too useless to feed all twelve of them so Omar had taken to stealing chickens before he turned six. He brought them home to his mama, beaming, and she would slap him to the ground for thieving. But when she served that chicken plucked, cleaned and fried, her eyes would land soft over his features. It was the one moment of joy he remembered in all of his young life.

His daddy drunk up any two pennies his mama found to rub together, then got mean and limp, eyes blood red with raw hate piercing through. He was too lazy to stand up and beat a boy, but if one happened to be wandering too close to his spider hands he would snatch arm, leg, hand and start beating with whatever was handy—broom, stick, frying pan, hammer. He would say his son's name with heat and spit, "Omar, Omar . . . you a low-down piece of donkey shit." Or "Omar, you the asshole of a maggot."

If it bothered Omar Jennings as a boy, he had no recollection of that fact. Certainly he could recall the physical pain of the beatings. The hiding his face from his friends. His arm in a sling. He even remembered getting on his knees in church, with a hollow nothing for his efforts.

So when the old man was killed after passing out near Master Gibbs's cotton fields with his pipe burning too close to the twenty-pound gas tank, Omar wasn't particularly troubled. Even later, when he heard how they found his father, writhing on the earth, every stitch of clothes and skin seared right off his muscle, Omar took the news in stride.

A week after his daddy died Omar Jennings, feeling far older than his twelve years, put the other children to work. The girls to Miss Sybil the laundress, the boys collecting scraps at the mill. He organized and planned and collected all the money from his siblings and put it in his mama's apron come every Friday night. Now she didn't slap him. Instead, with the children out playing where she had sent them, she took his hand and guided it under her skirt. Told him when he held it back that he had grown plenty big, that he was the man of the house now and had to perform certain duties. How the first time they rutted, she ate him whole in the dim of that shack, on the pallet where she and his daddy had slept, on top of the dirt he had watched her sweep. How his mama worked against Omar's fear for the first ten minutes and then, to his young shame, in spite of it for the next hour. Availing herself of his embarrassed reflexes like a bear waits for salmon. Until, exhausted and spent, she nudged him from her mat as the girls stumbled in, complaining about the dark.

That whole next week Omar kept his eyes tight on the floor whenever his mama was near, pulling up a root, specializing on a pebble. But by the time Friday found its way back to his doorstep, the steel his papa had beat into him held Omar in good stead.

When she spread her apron out for his collections, he slapped her hard across the face and took her by force instead, pushing and beating until they were the two of them beasts in the night, thrashing like hooked fish on the dry, hot floor.

Things went on like that for another two years, Friday nights coming and going like swallowing a briar patch dipped in chocolate. Until his mama came up pregnant. When he asked about sin, she threw back her head, mouth wide, teeth white. She laughed until she choked on her spit, then coughed and laughed some more. She rolled from him and a chuckle burped from her throat. What she told him next was worse than all the rest put together. Her eyes glazed, she leveled them at him. "You a worse halfwit than your daddy. He weren't much, but at least he was a man. You ain't nothing but a woman's whore, and give her money besides. You leaving come morning and Ernest Meagers moving in. He think it's his and you ain't standing around moon-eyed to tell him no different."

Face wooden, Omar said, "But I looks after things round here."

She was lying down limp when she grinned. "You ain't nothing but a tadpole wriggling in the mud, 's time fo' a bullfrog."

Some people said it was the chain gang that had escaped from Tallahassee that had done it. Most thought it was Gibbs's poor relations or the Klux, but the way they found Sofia Jennings cut up like a prize hog was the shame of Jessup County. Both White and Black talked about it for years. White women from the Ladies Sugar Beet Society brought Omar and his siblings cake and round bread for weeks, mashed potatoes over cauliflower and beets with crinkly onions. He took it and pained his face according to their needs. He took their money too when it was offered and still set his sisters to work. He took their money come Friday and from the middle girl, Betty, who'd just turned ten, he took more than that in the outhouse while the rest of his siblings slept.

When he left Jessup three years later he had $400.45 rolled tight in his knapsack, every nickel in the family bank.

Omar also left with his mama's pallet folded in his knapsack, brown with years of sweat, and a few remaining bloodstains his able sister had not been able to wash clean. He left with the ax handle he'd buried in the thick of the forest the night his mama had forced him to kill her. And the same pack of matches that had proved so useful some two years before, when Omar had found his daddy passed out from drink, tied him to a mule and dragged him two whole miles to the Gibbs plantation, and set his past aflame.

As he walked away he could almost hear them screaming just under the loom, their souls blocked from rising by the lodestone he placed over each of their graves and the cold ice terror he'd frozen in their eyes at the moment of their death. Omar learned one thing for certain. Not all souls rose.

Chapter 21

An entire week had passed after Junie Rankin was laid to rest, but the porch at P & K still chewed on the fat of the funeral. How Sister Celia had taken the high road and how Ephram Jennings had vomited all over Chauncy Rankin's new suit.

Plenty had made their way out to Bell land to inspect the sinful goings on. Each acting as if they were wandering that way on some errand or another, after which most had come knocking on Celia's door reporting, as she had requested, on the things they had seen.

Verde Rankin came to Ruby's door for her mother's dishes and had seen Ephram breaking the hard sod in the yard with a hoe, seeds at the ready, while Ruby was sitting next to that chinaberry tree talking to the wind.

Cleary had seen Ruby and Ephram walking around hand in hand down by Marion Lake while Moss Renfolk had caught sight of Ephram nailing fresh lumber from the mill onto Ruby's roof.

Minnie Hardy, K.O.'s cousin visiting from Beaumont, got in on the act and said while she was taking the bus from Newton she had spied Ephram holding red roses, no less, tucked under his arm with a big white bow. She had also peeked and seen that he was carrying two bags full of groceries with things that looked like Vienna sausages and two big rib-eye steaks.

Righteous Polk and her cousin Grace reported that Ruby's clothes, even her drawers, were out on the clothesline when they stopped by to drop off pound cake and, *Lord*, if they hadn't seen Ruby walking around in clean clothes, with her hair braided and put up, looking for the life of her like a normal girl.

The worst of it, Supra gave over with a snide grin, was how they were keeping house like a Christian married couple, but how her son Percy had told her he'd gone by late one night and still seen Ruby cooing and petting little piles of dirt by the chinaberry tree.

Tressie Renfolk concluded that Ruby Bell looked good enough, but crazy still hung around her eyelashes.

IN SPITE of all of this, Ruby and Ephram kept right on living. While Ruby hid the sweet ache Ephram's presence gave her, she would turn over a small smile or a gentle look now and again.

That first night in the rain, with the door fresh and scrubbed, with her standing, confused, not knowing what to do, Ephram had told her, "Ruby you got to know I'm marriage bound, and I aim to treat you like the lady you is until that day offer up its glory."

She had to give a bored shrug to keep him from seeing the gratitude in her eyes.

Mornings gave way to afternoons with Ruby drinking coffee and eating the scrambled eggs and toast with raspberry jam Ephram cooked for her, then watching him as he walked off to the Red Bus to go to the Piggly Wiggly in Newton. Each day Ruby stopped to look at the world the man had made for her. Fruit sat in a bowl on the table. There were clean plates with tiny blue flowers on them, and matching blue placemats, napkins and true-life silverware.

He brought her the Beaumont *Bugle* and she stepped back into time and learned about: the new speed limit, Nixon and a hotel called Watergate. He brought a transistor radio and she heard a woman named Roberta Flack sing "Killing Me Softly" on an FM station. She had cried hard into her sleeve and was grateful that Ephram had not been nearby to see it.

Every morning Ruby did the unthinkable, made up her own bed, then walked into the spinning day to tend to her children. They glowed, the sun gleaming on their faces, their bodies waving in the light, making rainbows that flashed on the earth. They often hopped upon her and followed her into the pristine house, tugging with hundreds of hands on her clothing. They hid under the bed and under her skirt; in the beams of the ceiling and inside the sink. They drifted and skipped and jumped Mary Mack with an invisible rope. They loved the home almost as much as the chinaberry and Ruby played ring-around-a-rosy with them late into the afternoon.

While they napped Ruby would wander into the thick of the piney woods and let nature rush through her. Tuesday she washed against the sand of Marion Lake and felt silver fish swimming in her belly. Wednesday and Thursday she waved as a field of bluebells, letting the bees tickle her fingers and toes. Friday through Sunday were for the earth—the black gumbo clay with its pill bugs and wriggling worms.

When she made it home she would wait for Ephram. When he arrived she would quickly lean down like she was wiping away something on the stair, or picking at the hem on her dress, then she would step into the house with only a tired look.

Each day he brought her gifts. She barely nodded thanks when he brought her roses on Tuesday. On Wednesday, she took the small bottle of perfume from Avon but accidentally knocked it into the woodbin, where it cracked—the smell filling the house with sickly gardenia sweet. She drank his chicory coffee with rich cream because she loved it so, and held his smiles because they tickled something in her chest. On Thursday he brought her glazed doughnut twists for Friday breakfast. She felt saliva arc from her mouth before she could devour five of them.

Still, if he had so much as lifted her shirt, stroked her leg, she would have settled into herself, but night after night he lay next to her like a deacon. Friday he brought her maple syrup for Saturday pancakes; Saturday he planted sweet peas in her front yard. As she watched him sweating, something perched upon her like a dove. She shook it off, but on Sunday as he hammered her roof it came back and decided to nest.

Monday evening it rained as he toted home a bag of fresh apples from Jordon's Orchard in Jasper. He laid them at her feet and against her better judgment she circled his neck with her arms. They stood together like that. The woody scent of him entered her lungs. She pulled him tight until they pushed into one another, kissing, with the smell of wet earth rolling over their toes from the open doorway, the scent lining the floor and playing in the folds of their clothes. The bag of apples resting just inside the house.

When their breath came in hot gusts, Ephram bent his head down and held her like she was a cloud he couldn't squeeze lest it disappear. He stepped back and looked at her grinning. Her beauty shook him: the smooth tan of her skin, her collarbone and shoulders, her neck as graceful as a queen's, and her eyes—her eyes were where her heart lived.

"What chu got there, gal?" He let his fingers linger on her cheek.

"Just a mole," she answered.

"Naw, it ain't. That there's a beauty spot."

"It's just a mole."

"Yes, Ruby, it sure is." He held her face, as soft as a peach, and turned it up to the single light. "It sure is. Looka there. Somebody round here got them a beauty spot where anybody can see it."

"Do not." He saw a chuckle rising from her chest.

"So do. Miss Beauty Spot."

"You better stop it."

"Cain't stop it when it be right there staring at me."

She mock-slapped him against his chest and began to turn. "Now that's enough."

Ephram wouldn't let her leave. He spun her softly in a bitty two-step. "All right then, Miss Beauty—"

He kissed her again and Ruby felt the rock inside of her begin to crumble.

He held her so firm and so long her chest ached and a pinch in her throat came out in soft sobs. She cried into his open mouth. Now inches away but still crying, she pulled him down to the floor with her and she let her salt mix with his old sweaty collar.

She sniffed in deeply. "See! I open up for one drop of good and out come all this."

He softly joked, "All a' what? That ain't but a little faucet . . . Miss Beauty Spot."

And she began laughing.

"I don't know what happens now," Ruby whispered.

"Well, that one ain't so hard."

"What do you mean?"

"Cuz we can sit here, or we can stand up, or we can walk outside, or we can lay ourselves down, or any hundred number things what come to our mind. What you feel like doing, Miss Ruby Bell?"

"I don't feel like doing . . . anything."

"Nothing?"

"No. I can't say one way or another, so nothing suits me fine."

"I can tell you what I want—and it ain't nothing. I want something from you, Ruby."

"What you want from me?"

"I need you to look at me. I need you to see me, right here. Right here. I ain't nowhere but here. I need you to see that."

Ruby stared at the man in front of her. "I see." Suddenly she did. A good man sat before her, strong and patient. She had thought not one existed in the entire world, but here he was, looking right into her, skin still wet with rain.

"Thank you." He paused, then, "What do you want Ruby?"

So she told him the truth. "I want you with me in sleep every night. And when I wake up, every morning, I want you there too."

"So that ain't so hard is it?"

Ruby shook her head no. Ephram rose and offered her his hand and they walked to the bed.

Ruby smiled. Ephram took off his shirt and slacks and shone like dark wood against the white of his undergarments. They sat on the bed, brown against caramel, breathing in the scent of gardenia as the rain began to rage.

NIGHT TOOK hold and the storm became alive. The sky was charged and crackling. Up high in the pouring black, a cluster of clouds paused above the world. They tingled with ions and unleashed great claps of sound and fire bolts along their path. The Dyboù let the clash of wind and rain lift him. He watched the deluge beat upon the little graves near the chinaberry, rivulets of topsoil running down the small hill, leaving small waxen faces bare to the wind.

Inside the house the girl was lost in the gold of love. Through the window his idiot son lifted up from the bed and handed her his shirt to wear then turned his back as she slipped it on. He watched the boy fiddle with the girl's hair as the rain poured harder, little spirits lifting up against the whip of the storm. The light of the house was like sunlight cutting through the dark woods. The girl Ruby was eating an apple his boy had cut with a pocketknife. One child started whimpering softly as he approached. The crow was cawing as the girl popped a slice of apple in her mouth, the wind screeching through the pines as he reached the graves and in one easy move lifted a tiny, wriggling six-month-old and opened his mouth.

Maggie the Crow lifted against the storm, rain pelting her eyes, and screamed like a siren, an earsplitting caw that cut through the air currents and fell like an ax onto the floor of earth. The sky split open in answer and hurled a bolt of lightning close, too close to the house, 'til the spirit dropped his prey. To the uninitiated it was only the twist and turn of nature, but Maggie watched as Ruby Bell burst out the front door, hair flying, and ran to the graves of her children.

Ruby's feet pounded in time with her heart as she leapt from the porch, Ephram's pocketknife in her hand. It was hard, cold, sure. She had grabbed it as she swept out of the house. All of her children were crying as she raced towards them. Lightning had struck the chinaberry tree and one massive branch lay smoldering on the ground like a severed arm, flames flowering only to be smothered by the rain. The ghost children saw Ruby and hurled themselves towards her, knocking her to the ground. They each knew fear, had lived and died with it collecting in cold sweat against their skin, but still they scrambled towards her, tripping and falling, getting back up and running into her arms. Ruby lifted up and saw the thing they ran from. It moved in the dark, held at bay for a moment by the burning branch of the chinaberry. The rain fell in sheets across Ruby's face, her eyes cutting between the heavy pines. Ruby had felt him for too long, had taken him to her bed. There he was, perched and waiting for her to lower her vigil. Her children knew like lambs sense a wolf prowling, and they pressed closer to her, limbs flowing through her chest, heads buried in her legs, her shoulders. Soft little shoes stepping onto her calves and pausing for a heartbeat before falling through her body like sand. The sky flashed bright with lightning and then growled low and hot. Ruby knew Ephram was watching her from the porch. She knew he was afraid of her, she knew it did not matter, she would not budge until her children were safe.

Ephram stepped into the rain, his chest bare under his suit jacket. He walked to Ruby and stood above her on the wet earth. That is when he saw the knife in her left hand.

"Ruby?"

She looked up at him through the reaching arms and heads of her children, and for a moment in the shadow and blackness, she forgot there was a man named Ephram, she held her knife tight until the sky flashed again and she caught the soft of his eyes.

"Ruby, come on inside."

"I ain't going nowhere." The New York woman had washed away, leaving the girl from Liberty.

"Come on in baby, you getting wet. Ain't nothing out here won't keep 'til morning."

The sky rolled thunder like a pair of dice. Ruby bored holes into the black of the woods and mumbled, "Man get back inside, you—you a good man, but don't mess with things you don't understand."

"School me."

Ruby looked up again and shook her head in futility. The rain grew thin for a moment and he knelt beside her, put his suited knee into the mud. "Didn't nobody ever teach you to test a bridge before you cross it? Try me."

Ruby pointed her knife towards the dark woods and growled, "*Git back!*" Then she whipped around and snarled at Ephram, "You spoiling my concentration. Sit down or get back inside."

So Ephram sat on the earth and got wet. Wetter, as Ruby stood the night vigil, knife at the ready. Finally she said, "You think I'm crazy."

"Naw, I don't."

"Well, you wrong. I'm crazy, but that don't make me stupid."

"Then tell me what you're watching."

Without turning her head she took one step onto a bridge named Ephram. "A man. One without benefit of flesh and bone."

Ephram stared into the black dark.

"Who is he?"

She paused, then whispered, "Don't know."

"What does he want?"

Ruby glanced quickly at Ephram. "My children."

Ephram sat quietly. He wanted to reach out to her, touch her free hair. Instead he put both of his pinkie fingers into his mouth and whistled, sharp and clear through the rain.

"What—?"

He stopped for a moment. "They say haints hate the sound of it." Then he resumed. It was a sweet, clear warble that sang through the raindrops and echoed against slick trunks. Ruby watched him, whistling in waves and crescendos, and sure enough the thing waiting in the woods slowly ducked back and slunk away. Her heart slowed in her chest and she looked at this man. After a good long while she said, "You can stop now."

So he did. "Did it work?"

Ruby let a smile tremble on her lips as she nodded yes. The rain moved off to the southwest while the wind blew in warm, and carried a bit of lilac along its edges.

"Good."

Ruby looked at the waving sky. Ephram reached his open palm to her. "Come inside?"

"I'm staying out here on this hill tonight with them."

"Then I am too."

"No," New York crept back, clipping at the heels of her words, "they need my full attention."

"Maybe I can help."

"You can't."

"Maybe I can."

"You don't know nothing about them."

"You could tell me." He reached out then and brushed back a ringlet of hair from her cheek, slipped it behind her ear. He caught hold of her eyes and said, "Ruby, tell me about your children."

"I'm cold."

Ephram stood and went into the house.

The truth was that Ruby had stories decades old that she had folded up and tucked away between her spine and her heart, tears she had shed in silence, private moments of pride. The truth was that she wanted to share the burden. Ephram came back and held a blanket between them. She unbuttoned the shirt he had given her and let him drape the warm blanket over her shoulders. The night air dried like sheets on a clothesline, crickets commenced their nightly song and lightning bugs sparked in the distance. Ruby began to speak. The waxing moon lit the small graves that covered the land.

"They're tarrens. Spirits of murdered children."

"How—where they come from?"

"Different places. They's too many stories to tell. Some found me. Some I watched the crossing. One hundred thirty-seven stories in all."

"Tell me one." Then he gently brushed his hand over the top of the nearest grave. "Tell me this one."

Ruby let out a low breath and looked at him, unsure.

Ephram nodded.

"All right then. All right then." She paused a good long while. "You remember Miss Barbara we talked about so long ago in Ma Tante's house?"

"The one my mama worked for?"

"That's her. Well, you know I worked for her too."

"Yes."

"You know how churches have bake sales to raise money?"

"Yes."

"Well some of the people who hurt me, hurt my children, they had sales too, 'cept they didn't sell cakes."

"Tell me who this child is Ruby."

"I'm telling. But it's hard to grab ahold of where to start."

Ruby felt Ephram slide closer and pet her tenderly on the forehead, then along the turn of her neck. "I ain't goin' nowhere, Ruby. You spin it how you see fit."

SHE MADE several stops and starts, then, since there was no nice way to start, she just told him. About the place in Neches. About where she went when she left town. About Miss Barbara's Friends' Club and the change she collected in the candy dish. She told him about the first man, she told him about the last and the many in between. She told him what a quarter could buy.

She told him about when the little blond girl had run off and Miss Barbara had had a fit. How they had each of them been questioned until the rumor spread she'd run off with one of her "friends," the one who liked to hit, hard. How Tanny and Ruby had talked about it and how they feared for her life. The two girls talked about a lot of things during the morning when they were supposed to be sleeping. Tanny would sneak into Ruby's room and paint the world on the white of the ceiling. They talked about what they would do when they left, where they would go. Tanny said Albuquerque because she liked the way it sounded and she had seen a picture postcard of it once. Ruby said New York because that's where she knew her mama had gone. Then Tanny said if that's where Ruby was going she supposed she'd have to go with her.

In the four years Ruby had been taken to Miss Barbara's, the girls had become something more than friends. Ruby was ten now, Tanny eleven. Some lucky days Miss Barbara put them together as a team. Those were the best because it wasn't so bad to have company when face-to-face with a friend. Tanny would wink to her during the worst of it and make it pass all the better. The thing Ruby loved most about Tanny was that no one had taken the time to break her spirit before she got there. After four years she still stuck out her chin, still giggled with Ruby about the funny frog men.

"We lucky they keep us together sometimes," Tanny said one evening after a man with a bad cold had left.

Ruby nodded, putting her tip in her dish, then handing Tanny hers.

Tanny smiled. "Ole Mr. Fart Face so ugly his mama slapped herself when he was born!"

Ruby laughed. "You really do remind me a' my cousin Maggie. Maggie fights all the time."

"Mama usta say I come out her with my dukes up." Tanny smiled softly to Ruby. "It ain't so bad, though, least these men got a time limit. Ain't like we livin' in they house." Tanny leaned into her, eyes flashing. "But I tell you what. They send in another one sneezin' all over me I'ma knock!" Tanny played like she was a boxer. "Him!" Fake punch in the air. "Out!" She held up her hands in victory. They laughed, leaned against the wallpaper.

"Damn, they's a hole in the window in my room. Can't tell shit time in here, day or night."

"Seem like night."

Tanny looked over at Ruby. "You know what? You sure pretty, girl."

"Ugh ugh." Ruby shook her head no. "*You* is," Ruby answered back.

They were quiet for a moment.

"Sometimes I wonder if that's why they pick us. Cuz a' how we look."

The girls were quiet for a while. They heard footsteps. The door opened and a man looked into their room, paused, whispered to Miss Barbara, then walked ahead and stopped.

Miss Barbara poked her head into the room, and smiled especially wide and sweet. Ruby noted that she had taken to doing so ever since she'd gotten what seemed to be new perfect white teeth. She spoke to them slow, as if they were cats, "Well, we got ourselves a very special friend who done paid extra for y'all two. So do exactly what he say and two big scoops of chocolate ice cream after, all right?"

Ruby nodded dutifully. Tanny just grinned. When Miss Barbara walked away Tanny turned, crossed her eyes and stuck out her tongue.

Ruby laughed. The man poked his head into the room, "What's so funny?" He was tall with round features. He wore a smooth brown hat. His eyes were soft and kind. Different. So different that Ruby wondered if he was a spy sent by her lost mama.

"Hmmm? What's so funny, girls?" He walked into the room, took off his hat and hung it on the coatrack. Ruby still looked at him hopefully. He knelt down in front of them, face open and smiling, his eyes bright water blue, the black in the center of his eyes big.

"Hmmm?" he asked.

"Nothing," Tanny finally answered.

"I don't believe it!" He tickled Tanny. Ruby's hope cracked like a sour egg.

Tanny didn't giggle like he wanted her to. She sensed his strangeness too. So he reached out and tickled Ruby. She laughed dutifully. He pinched her cheek. "Aren't you a sweet little thing." The strangest thing was that he did not avert his eyes. Ruby realized what it was that made him unlike the others. He didn't have shame.

Then the man started patting his pockets and smiling until he reached into his back pocket and retrieved a Hershey bar. Ruby couldn't help but beam. The man grinned back at her, unwrapped the bar and broke it right down the middle, handing half to Ruby and half to Tanny.

"My name's Peter Green. You can call me Peter," he volunteered. Ruby and Tanny chewed in quiet. They weren't used to men at the Friends' Club giving over their names.

Then the oddest thing of all happened. Mr. Green started asking them questions, normal questions that regular folks might ask. What games did they like to play? What was their favorite color and why? Tanny answered quick and short, but Ruby talked about freeze tag and fishing, bluebells and yellow sun.

He told them about other little girls he'd met in his travels, in places just like Miss Barbara's. How they told him their favorite game was "Queimada" in a place called Brazil, and "I-Wen Hu" in Taiwan and "Eun Suk Ji" in Korea. He said there was a game like hide-and-seek in Germany that sounded like a fish, "Sardines." He said it so funny it made Ruby laugh. How there was "Ampe" in Ghana that was something like playing Simon Says. He named other towns and games and talked about all the pretty, good little girls he had met and how nice they had made him feel. He smiled so big and sweet while he talked. He said how of all those girls Ruby and Tanny were the prettiest. Ruby liked him talking about playing and faraway places. She liked thinking about how there were girls playing all over the world even if they had to do what she was about to do, what she had been made to do for four years now. Still she liked talking before best, anything to stretch out the candy-eating time. When the man looked away for a moment Tanny snuck a wink to Ruby.

"Now," Mr. Green smiled broadly, "which one of you is in this room originally? Is in it most of the time?"

He looked at Ruby. "Is it you?" She nodded. He smiled warmly at her. "Good for you, sweetheart." He rubbed her back and whispered, "There's my good girl." It was the first time Ruby had been called a good girl since Papa Bell died. Then he turned to Tanny. "And that means you are usually in room number twelve?" Tanny nodded yes.

Then Mr. Green walked over and sat on the edge of the bed. He motioned to Ruby. "Come here, sweetheart." And Ruby did. "My good little girl sits on my right, like Jesus." He pulled Ruby beside him. Then he looked at Tanny. His face twisted as he said, "And the other one on my left." Tanny cut her eyes to Ruby for a millisecond. His voice shook, "*Don't* look at my good girl." And he pushed Tanny down between his legs, unzipped his trousers and forced her mouth onto him.

All the while, Ruby felt transfixed by the gentle of his voice. He was no worse than the others, and he had brought them candy.

He leaned over and whispered to Ruby, "My good girl doesn't have to look. Cover your eyes princess." Ruby did, until she heard Tanny gag. She opened her eyes to see Tanny looking about in horror, a thin black wire about her neck. Mr. Green held it looped like a tight leash as he plunged into her mouth. He was trembling.

"*Look* what you're making Daddy do!" Tanny's face grew dark, dark. She vomited the chocolate.

Ruby felt a snap inside of her. "*Miss Barbara!*"

She beat against Mr. Green with her fists. She leapt on his

back and grabbed at his face. Tanny's eyes walled back in her head. Ruby screamed, "Miss BARbara! MISS BAR-BA-RA!"

Mr. Green spun on Ruby like a snake. Eyes too black. Blue too narrow. He hissed like razors, "Little girl, I am the Devil. I know everything about you. I see who's good. Who's bad. But sometimes I make a mistake—did I? Maybe you're the bad one. Are you?" Ruby looked at the girl who used to be Tanny. The girl struggling for breath. Then the man removed the snare from Tanny's neck. She fell to the floor coughing, gasping, and he brought it over Ruby's head like a black halo. He lowered it and pulled. Ruby could barely breathe. She urinated.

"Did I make a mistake?" He pulled the cord tighter. Ruby felt the world spin darkly.

"Did I? Did I?"

Ruby spit out, "No."

"No? You're sure? You're sure now?"

Ruby nodded, unable to speak. "So you are my good girl. You are she." He loosed the cord a bit and added, "And good things don't mind when we punish bad things, do they?"

Again no.

"And if they do, then we know that they are bad too. Don't we?"

Ruby nodded yes.

So the man removed the cord from Ruby's neck and turned and lifted Tanny from the floor.

Tanny cried out when he put the cord around her neck again. She coughed and pooped, as the man dragged her all about the room, Tanny trying to fight, Ruby saying nothing. Then she hated Tanny for being so evil with the Devil. And then she did not. As he put himself in Tanny's mouth again, Ruby shot silent words into her friend's heart, *i'msorryi'msorrysosorryiloveyousorry*, until Tanny hung limp, and the man's body trembled and jerked. When he was done he dropped Tanny to the floor. Still. Too still. The entire world slowed up then stopped. Her chest did not rise. Did not fall. Her face was plum dark, fat. Her ankles were too twisted under her waist. Her body like an empty sack.

So Ruby died with her. Where was she? Ruby looked wildly around the room. Then high up, she saw Tanny shooting up through the ceiling, and she wailed, *Wait! I'm sorry! Sorry!* So Ruby lifted up, spirit to spirit, up above the tin roof, out of the gray. *Where . . . where to go. Where . . .* Then down, Ruby looked down and saw herself sitting on the bed, pink dress, pigtails, and sadly guided Tanny back. Down into Ruby's own body. Invited her inside, to live in there with her, to take root. There was no place else to go. No God, no nothing else. Couldn't be. So she swallowed Tanny in deep where it was safe.

Because Ruby knew in her evil, evil heart that the Devil had indeed made a mistake. That Ruby was the bad one and Tanny the true. She knew it as the Devil stood gasping in the center of the room. He walked to the door, placed his hat on his head and said, "Be good now," and left.

Then it was like a rubber band snapped inside of Ruby. She let out a scream that exploded out of her chest, ricocheted against walls until it busted out of the crack in the door. Ruby heard feet running but she could not stop, the air sucked in her lungs too fast. Spit fell from her mouth. Miss Barbara swung the door open. Looked at Tanny. Walked over to Ruby and slapped her in the mouth. Slapped her silent.

"Shut the fuck up."

Then sweet as cotton candy she explained, "You see, baby,

he ain't rent your friend there," she motioned to Tanny as if she were a dead mouse, "he done bought her fair and square, and paid plenty, so he could do what he liked with her."

Miss Barbara smiled, showing her shining square front teeth. "We ain't about to let that happen to you. That is unless you curry mischief like your friend done." She looked at Ruby hard, then stretched her lips into another smile. "If you stay a good girl and do exactly what our friends ask you, you gonna be fine."

Then Miss Barbara patted her on the leg and said, "Come on and get that ice cream while we clear this here up. You got another friend, going to be here in two shakes, and he asked for you special."

R UBY SAT beside Tanny's soul, her fingers sifting dirt and patting the small mound. A sob bubbled up from her chest but she'd long ago learned to swallow those back down. Ephram hadn't, he wept openly beside her, so she reached over and wiped his tears.

"Shhhh." She whispered. "It's all right."

A rush of longing stole through Ephram and he took Ruby in his arms and held her, the blanket folded between them. He held her so long and so tight that the bubble in her chest found its way into the night air and she let it go, one long deep sob that echoed into the woods. A cloud of bats rose into the air before settling again in the pines, an owl let out her *hoooo*, and the crow flew out of the elm's hollow and landed on the earth, strutting and pecking at the ground.

Ephram found his voice. "That's one story?"

Ruby nodded. "You ready to leave yet?"

He brushed her hair and found the dip of her temple. He

pressed his lips against it. Then her wet cheek, he kissed there as well, the cut of her jaw. Her long turning neck, the hollow between her collarbone. He kissed until he uncovered her heart and then he pushed the flat of his palm into it and held. His lips found her mouth and entered there with his pain, his desire. He whispered into her ear, "I ain't going nowhere. If you brave enough to live it, the least I can do is listen."

Ruby fought against the rise of hope. She lost when he said: "Girl, you a miracle of nature." Then, "We got to find a way to keep these souls safe 'til they can make it home. And they will make it home, Ruby. They will make it home. We'll make sure of that."

Ruby nodded.

"Then you got to tell me what on this earth you believe in."

Ruby scanned the dark sky. "Only two things, that chinaberry and that old crow."

"Then move your children up high into those branches. I'll build a house for to keep them dry. And you ask that crow to keep an eye. I'll watch over them too, Ruby, you tell me how, give your mind a chance to rest. Give your body a chance to sleep. You been holding up the whole world, girl. Let somebody help you out."

So Ruby said a prayer to the tree and it waved against the stars. The old bird stopped its scratching and before Ruby could think to ask, the creature bowed its dark head and flapped its large wings. *Thank you, Maggie . . .*

She stood and said, "It's Monday." From Ephram's questioning look she continued, "No ox."

He grinned sheepish and rose to his feet. "No ditch."

He couldn't help but gather her in his arms, then hoist her up, cradling her like a baby, like a child, like the woman she was; he rocked her in his arms and somehow found the courage to kiss his Ruby again.

The night leaned in as somehow Ruby found a way to accept that kiss and, in so doing, dipped her big toe into life.

OF COURSE she didn't hear the knock on the door ten yards away. Or the second. In fact, ten people had gathered on the front porch without Ruby or Ephram hearing a sound. It was not until Celia, the Pastor and the rest of the congregation surrounded them on the small hill that Ruby sensed an inkling of danger and looked away from Ephram. She let out a short scream and slipped from Ephram's arms, feet weak beneath her.

Ephram stepped up bravely. "Y'all best get—"

Five grown men tackled him, including Sim and Percy Rankin. They pulled him out of the door, down on the wet ground, while the Pastor began, "Ephram we come here to re-re-re-re-reclaim your soul in the name of Jesus."

Ephram pushed against them with all his might. "Damnit! Y'all *stop* this foolishness and let go of me!" But they pressed him harder into the mud.

Sim slapped his hand over Ephram's mouth. Ruby hung back, unable to run, unable to fight. Two strong Rankin elders gentled her onto the land as the congregation began to pray over Ephram. *Release this child of God. Release this child of God.* Over and over. Soon, the congregation whipped up a froth of hails and hosannas. The Pastor yelled above them, "'For G-G-God so loved the world that he g-g-gave his only begotten Son, that whosoever b-believeth in him should not perish, but have everlasting life.'" Amens leapt up from the circle like flames. Pastor Joshua continued, "We are g-gathered to cast the unclean spirits from our

Brother Ephram Jennings." Ephram struggled against the men sitting upon his chest. He flipped over onto his stomach and broke free for a moment. The men yelled, *Whoa there! Git him! Hold him,* until he was once again conquered. They sat again, this time upon his back, his stomach pressed into the mud. Celia stood holding a Bible, eyes closed in apparent meditation, but there was a steel girder in her jaw. Ruby was frozen. She wanted to run but was held in place. She tried to speak, but terror caught in the back of her mouth.

Finally she scratched out a whisper, "Ephram . . ."

Celia let her left eye slide open, then her right and a grin tugged at her lips as she started walking towards Ruby, left hand holding the Bible, right palm raised against the night, "Lo, be free of the inciting words of Jezebel," and the women called out, *Jezebel! Jezebel!* Celia sang louder, "Jezebel, what called her man from the righteous path. For she will not sway thee, for her is nothingness against the wall, food for dogs!" Righteous Polk found the one dry spot of grass and fell out on it, her body writhing, speaking the gibberish of tongues.

Gertie Renfolk began singing, *At the cross, at the cross where I first saw the light,* while Celia advanced upon Ruby. Ruby heard the growl before noticing that it was coming from her own throat. It built in size and stature as Celia and the women closed in. Celia's voice rose over the rising sound, "I command ye out! Out of this woman, you unclean demons. 'Ye are of your father the Devil, and the lusts of your father ye will do.'" Ruby crouched against the ground and somewhere under the rubble of men she could hear Ephram calling for her. The world began to sway for Ruby, as if she were in a tire swing, up and down, up and down. *And the burden of my heart rolled away.* Ruby swung her open fist at the women before they reached her, falling off balance from her own momentum, from the sway of the earth. She overheard one woman whisper, *You sho was right, Sister Jennings, them demons got hold of her for sure!* Then a chorus of *You sho was. Tell the truth and shame the Devil. Amen!* Then from Celia, "Child, accept the Lord, renounce the sin that opened the doorway to the unclean spirit." Ruby's growl was a roar now, she heard a song bitten off in a crush of voices. Ruby could see through the legs of the women. The Pastor was bending over Ephram, throwing something down on him; he yelled out. Someone grabbed at her left leg and held it tight so she kicked the right with great might as the tire swing looped over and over, spinning the hands and the stars, and her growl had turned to biting snarls and oil was on her forehead, now her right arm was held when she looked down in the mud and saw the pocketknife; she grabbed it in her left hand and swung. It caught the fleshy part of Celia's thumb. The Bible went flying. The world fell silent as the women backed away. Ruby leapt to her feet, the knife thrown into her right hand. She stood like a beast. Celia was scrambling up, up, then running, then tripping over Righteous Polk's brown legs and falling flat, and Ruby was over her and she was screaming, blubbering something about her thumb, about not to cut her, please God, yelling, *That crazy bitch is gonna kill me*, as Ruby towered over her, knife pointed sharp against the wind. The thumb squeezed out blood that fell on the earth and Ruby's children scrambled away, scrambled into the chinaberry, scrambled into the tip-top branches. Then the men were all up, running towards her, *She's got a knife. Gonna hurt Sister Celia! Tryin' to kill her. Grab her! I ain't 'bout to get myself cut. Jump her back. You jump her back, fool, don't be telling me what to do.* The roar was bellowing from Ruby's chest, the knife pointed at her tormentor when some man came up to her, his voice was soft like she had heard in a dream and he was saying her name, saying, *Please don't hurt my sister,* saying, *Please, baby, give me the knife, they done now, ain't y'all done?* And a chorus of voices agreeing that they were done. But done is a cake, like the one some man brought her days before, done is a cobbler like the kind some women stuffed into her mouth, done had nothing to do with this she wanted to say but the sound from her mouth mixed with saliva dripping. Then someone was reaching out to her, some hand was on her wrist saying, *Baby, stop Ruby, please, for the love of God,* so she threw the knife back into her left hand and cut into the air only it wasn't air, it was soft, and then it was hard and then it was wet warm wet warm warm wet sticky warm and a man was falling like a dove to the earth and then everyone was gathering and blood, blood hitting the earth. Dark wet spreading from the belly of his shirt. Then they were lifting him, all of them, the woman and her fat thumb screaming and crying, tears flying hot under the trees. There was a parade of men and women screaming, directing, saying to put pressure, to move, to—but words were a rumble in her head as she fell to the earth. Now the growl of a broken spent thing oozed from her mouth. Somewhere in the distance they carried a man, a man spilling blood, spilling hope, spilling a name over and over and over again, a name she had forgotten was hers.

Alone on the hill the black book flipped wind-thin pages, spine open on the earth. Ruby lay on her side and watched as they flipped this way and that, this and that, catching the moon in their white. Her body was untouched, unharmed, still she did not move, could not move, only watch the wind and the paper for hours, her heart pounding soft in her chest, until the black night became gray, and gray became the pink of sunrise, and pink became yellow, which became hot white and the pages dried from morning dew and started turning again. She heard a buckboard easing down the road, some kind of tittering as it rolled steadily by. Lucky that it was a back road, lucky not one single human paused at her door. Finally, as the evening settled, Ruby heard the black bird cutting the air with a gentle clucking. She crawled towards it, then discovering the knife still in her hand, brick brown sticking between her fingers, she plunged it into the earth and dragged her body after her. It seemed impossible to use her legs, unthinkable to stand. In this way she made it to the china-berry as the sun was dipping over the western horizon, orange and plum streaking after it.

The crow stood stock-still on a low branch. One night, one day and another evening with no water, no food, barely taking in enough air. The crow would wait like that until the next morning, not breathing too deeply, lest it ruffle the air around the girl. Ruby wrapped herself about the tree trunk and did not cry.

Chapter 22

It was Miss P who found Ruby after three weeks and one day of being lost to God and man. She found her half alive by Marion Lake. Chewed dandelion greens in her mouth, hair twisted with twigs and pebbles. She had wasted to nothing but still held tight to the knife. Miss P had been scouring the woods every evening where she imagined Ruby might hide. When she saw the girl, she eased the knife from her limp hand.

Ruby felt like air against Miss P's side as she walked her back to P & K Market, and she fell like cotton onto the little cot kept inside the market closet. She gave the girl dandelion root tea with a touch of ginger, and sweetened it with honey. She watched Ruby take a sip without fully waking. She saw the warmth spread onto the child's lips, her face. Then Ruby was asleep again.

Next, Miss P gave her a spoonful of chicken broth, with big chunks of celery and clear onion. Ruby swallowed it down, then leaned up sharply, eyes jutting about the room. Ruby looked down at her hand, then began feeling for her knife.

"Ain't no need for that, child."

Ruby jerked up from the bed. Panic streaked across her face and Miss P tried to calm her, told her that she was perfectly safe, that nobody was going to hurt her, but Ruby stood and tried to run to the door. She fell against the frame and sunk to the floor.

She did not escape until the fifth day, after she had regained some small bit of strength. Miss P did not try to stop her, just as she had not tried to stop her mama, Charlotte Bell, forty-one years ago, when she ran from rape, from hate and a small brown baby named Ruby Bell. Ran to Newton, to Beaumont, and eventually to some old city folks had thought to call New York.

RUBY RAN down the road to Bell land, stopping to catch her breath, then running on. She wanted her knife. The guns pointing in a circle like they had at her Auntie Neva, the cord wrapped around Tanny's throat, Abby Millhouse's missing kneecap, Ephram Jennings being dragged away from her home. Ruby knew she needed her knife as a small little match against the night.

The road cut into her feet. The road was her enemy as well, dragging against her, pulling her back to P & K, back to the wolves. She fought her way home, fought her way to her children.

When she reached Bell land she stopped dead. There were no mewling whispers, no cries, no little hands reaching through the soil. The ground was as hollow as an empty womb. She leapt onto the rises, digging furiously, yanking up tufts of soil, huge gulps of dying grass, soft clay and mud; she tore earthworms from their home and cast a dozen roly-polys out of the crumbling brown.

"Where? WHERE? ARE? THEY?"

Even the crow was silent in the tree. Even the pines turned away. Ruby knew they had been powerless to stop him, powerless to save all of the children who landed in the Dyboù's gullet while she rested on a soft bed only a mile away from home.

She let out a scream, a mighty screech that boomed up to the treetops, careening so that it pierced the tangle of branches and flew out of the piney woods, out of the burning atmosphere, bolting into space.

Ephram heard her from the road he had been walking to Bell land. He gingerly, carefully picked up an ounce of speed and made it to his Ruby.

He had been dragged away over three weeks ago, the night Ruby had cut into his belly full up to the knife's handle. The night the congregation nearly killed him, dropping him on his head while trying to drag him away. Over three weeks in the Jasper County Hospital due to an infection, due to the fact that his liver had been "lacerated" and his bowels nicked. He had lost so much blood, the White doctor said, not particularly interested in looking Ephram in the face, that he should, in fact, be dead. It was Miss P's call that pushed Ephram out of the bed. Away from the smooth brown faces of the Women's Auxiliary, who plied him with fried chicken and pound cake, even though the nurses insisted he eat soup and crackers until his belly healed up. Away from Celia, who, despite his objection to her presence, stayed every minute of posted visiting hours, and sometimes beyond, propping up his pillow, slipping on clean socks and combing his hair. All the while humming the tune of "At the Cross, at the Cross Where I First Saw the Light."

The walk had been a hard one. While his stitches had been removed two days before, he was still weak.

Ephram stood over Ruby. He saw the narrow spokes of Ruby's legs, the reed crook of her arms. She wept as if her entire body were the rising heaves and scratching sobs.

There was nothing to say and so he just stood there, letting the soft of his eyes gently stroke her hair.

She spoke to him, without turning, without moving her lips from the earth, "They all gone."

"Tell me—"

"My babies. *My babies* . . . They gone."

Ephram felt the air leave his chest. He breathed in her sorrow, and knelt beside her.

Her eyes leveled at him. "Get away from here."

Her words pushed him back like a fist.

"Go on. Get."

"I ain't, Ruby . . ."

"What else you want?"

"I want you."

"And what it gone cost?" Hot tears ran down her cheeks. "What I gotta pay to have you?"

"They was wrong, Celia and them, they was worse than fools. But it weren't me. You put a knife in me." He lifted his shirt and showed the bandage looped about his right side. "And I'm yet here. Let me help you, baby. Let's find your children."

She said it flat and deadpan, "I'll do it again."

Ephram stood very still and looked at her. She was broken, more than broken—her eyes were empty, deathly.

"No, you won't, Ruby."

A cord snapped inside of Ruby. She threw buckshot and nails in Ephram's direction. "*What else* you come to take? You got what was left of my mind. You bring them here to take my children. What else you want?"

She slammed into him, scratching at his neck, grinding against him. Ephram tried to push her away but she hung on like a panther, face-to-face, yanking his hand between her legs.

"You just a man! Can't even admit that you came here to get your dick sucked."

Ephram pushed her back and held her at arm's length. "*Stop it!*"

"You hang-dog country motherfucker. I like to spit after you first kiss me."

Ephram broke through. "You kiss me, woman! Don't let sorrow steal 'way truth. Don't blaspheme who we is."

"You right. I kiss you. After I fucked Chauncy," she lied.

Ephram stood with his hands about her rib cage. A part of him froze.

"You walk up right after we finish. Remember? How we—Chauncy and me—laughed at you. Lord, I needed a real man after being around your limp punk ass."

Ephram shot out, "You think I'm a fool? You think I don't know what you been doing since you come to this town? What you doing now? You think I like it? Naw! *Naw!* But I know how life don't teach you no different. Like a fox can't stop chewing at his own leg after it been in a trap."

He watched her anger as it began shaking her center, breaking apart. "*Ain't no trap but the one you fixed for me. You dress it up with marriage, pancakes and maple syrup! Fix me up so you can bend me over! Act all deaconly and holy but I know what you come for! Even if you don't! And you don't! Can't admit it now!*"

Ruby fell down onto the ground and lifted her dress. She spread her legs and pushed down her panties. "*This* what you *want!* Don't be afraid to take it like Chauncy and all them other men you call friend. You only here for two reasons—cuz I'm a crazy cunt like your mama, and cuz you want to fuck me. I know you. I see you. Seen men like you since I was six."

"I ain't none of them men."

She leapt up. "*I ain't nothing but a whore!* I want your food, your money—that's all. I can pretend like I want anything, even a moose in heat. Ain't you been laughed at your whole fucking life! There's good reason for it. You a servant to your own sister? Cuz you a coward and a fool."

Ephram started, "Ruby—you care for me. I feel it like an ax in my chest."

Ruby screamed the knot from her throat. "Why you think them flowers and blue napkins do shit for me! Why you think building me up like a queen what I need! Doing every little thing before I ask and never letting me give nothing back. That don't make me no queen. That makes me a cripple. But you need to fuck broken. You need to love crazy. Right? Right!"

"Ruby . . . I know what you doing. I know—"

"What do you know!"

"I know you love me." He was gulping for air, sobs catching, then breaking free.

"*So what if I love you? I'm the fucking fool for it. You got the kind of love that keeps me from rising. That make me take my eye from my children, make me lose my children. One of us got to die we stay together . . . by my hand. You want that? So you get from here before I kill you. I see you on my land again, I'll kill you.*"

Ephram took one step back, then two. The knife had hurt less. He turned and stumbled, then he began to run. He ran past P & K, and past the whole congregation of men on the porch. He felt every eye on him, judging and laughing at him. He ran collecting shame and self-hate like pollen on a daisy hill. He ran all the way to Celia's house, where he stepped in the door, walked past Celia, straight to his bedroom and lay down on the chenille spread.

Celia stood just outside his door, her hand soft on the wood. Ephram was safe. All that she had done was to keep him safe from the pit fires of life. Safe from the haints killing souls in the woods. From the Devil, who walked the earth. Safe from Ruby, who had dragged her papa to hell, who had cut her brother—her boy— and nearly killed him. Ruby Bell, whom he would learn to love a little less every day . . . every day he was with her.

Celia said calm as a still sea, "I done made your favorite, Ephram, fried pork chops, greens and corn bread with a pinch of sugar—just the way you like it."

In less than ten minutes Ephram would wash his hands. He would dry them on Celia's dress towel, with the pink ribbon stitched on. He would sit at her table and eat every scrap of her food along with the yellow cake with chocolate frosting she had made just that morning. He would hand her his plate and let her wash every dish and clean every sign of life from the kitchen. Then he would bathe and dress for bed and read marked passages in his well-used Bible.

Once he had done all of these things, Celia came in and sat beside him on the bed.

"How you feeling, boy?"

It felt as if a stone had set upon his chest. All he could manage was, "I ain't no boy, Celia."

"I know that Ephram."

She placed her hand on his forehead to make sure he didn't have a fever.

"Let me see your dressing."

"Not now."

"Doctor say we got to change it every day."

He looked straight at her, "Not today, Celia."

She backed away and stood.

"I go to Jasper tomorrow, get me some more of that gauze and iodine. And that special grease they be rubbing on your scar."

Ephram said nothing. He simply set his Bible down and turned out his light.

Celia almost said, *Glad you home*, but decided to let well enough alone. But she thought it so loud, Ephram heard it anyway.

She slipped out of the door as Ephram lay atop his bedspread, too tired to crawl under the covers. He turned to his side, ready to bide the years until he slipped into grateful oblivion.

Chapter 23

Ruby no longer wandered through the piney woods. Instead she hunted, searched, ripping away branches until her fingers scraped and bled. She knew their souls were still alive. She heard them on the wind at times like flutes, until they faded around a bend in the trees. Ruby felt them—held, bound like a spider's feast.

Ruby called to them as she walked until her voice became sandpaper. She returned home each night to eat the bread, fruit and beef jerky Miss P left her during the week. Not to satisfy any hunger. There was no hunger. There was no pain nor joy. She ate to keep walking. She ate to sustain her breath. She ate so that she could find her babies before it was too late.

So when Chauncy came looking for her early one Saturday morning, she picked up the shovel Ephram had brought and hit him upside the head. Hard, so that he fell out cold in her front yard. When Ruby came back that evening, fingers bloody, he was still there in a heap on the ground. As she stuffed food into her mouth he came to, stumbled home, weaving and leaning in the dim evening.

He came back the next day with a nasty lump on the side of his head and a package of mean stowed in his gut. This time when Ruby swung the shovel Chauncy caught it and threw it to the ground so hard it broke in two. The tail end of a shadow flapped behind him, which is how she knew the Dyboù was living inside of the man like a dead rat poisoning a well.

Ruby felt a fear spread hot in her belly. Still she asked with the weight of a stone, "Where are my children?"

Chauncy and the Dyboù walked slowly towards her.

Ruby stood like a tall pine. "*Where my children!*"

His hands were taut, his arms like springs. "Woman, you too crazy to live, God knows."

Ruby grabbed one of the large stones and hurled it at him, hitting him on the dimple he loved so much. He swooped down and picked it right up.

Next Ruby pitched a gray rock onto Chauncy's broad chest. It tore his shirt. He—they—roared towards her and she took off running, but screaming, blasting, "*Where my children!*"

She sprinted like a wild deer through the piney woods. He was a bulldozer, tearing away branches and kicking away low brush. Ruby turned back and saw the rock still tight in his hand.

Ruby leapt ahead. The forest pushed her along ahead of the man—the men—who chased her. They meant more than to take her, to push her down, they meant to steal her soul even if they had to kill her to do it.

Her lungs were aflame and sweat poured between her shoulder blades and breasts. The world was the rising smell of mud and pine, the dank salt of her body and the sweet cologne that Chauncy Rankin must have bathed in, getting closer.

As she approached a circle of pines, she spied a thick branch. She swooped it up as she ran.

Chauncy reached her just shy of the clearing. His arm caught her wrist and flung her to the ground behind a low line of briar bushes. A trickle of blood mixed with sweat and began winding down his nose, catching the crease in his lips. The Dyboù reaching, corpulent, stretching through Chauncy, inches away from her as if he wanted her to know. In that moment, Ruby saw him, truly saw him. The Dyboù—the man who had taken her to the pit fire, who had sold her to Miss Barbara, who had branded her with his hate—now glowered above her. The Reverend—he was the Dyboù who had taken her children.

She reached for the dead branch but felt only pine needles and dirt, so she used her legs. She connected with the kneecap. Chauncy staggered back then fell on her, crushing her. The Reverend was dead-eyed, grinding her down. She bit him on his jaw and drew blood, then fought from beneath him.

The spirit and the man hopped up, face twisted almost beyond recognition, and they lunged towards her and punched her right temple. Hard. The world warbled into slow motion. As she dropped back, they hit her again across her jaw, hit her like she was a man, and she fell to the empty earth.

But what Chauncy could not know, what the Reverend could never fathom, is that they would never be strong enough to fell a mother in search of her children.

Something bolted through her body, from the earth, from the roots of the trees, from the sun slanting into the clearing. She reached again and felt the thick handle of the branch. The trees were spinning into black, but some force kicked it through the wind and it landed like a boulder, crashing into Chauncy's right shoulder.

Chauncy screamed, loud. He then fell back, clutching his arm. It sloped at an odd, loose angle as he yelled like a boy whose mama had taken a switch to him. The Dyboù—the Reverend— jolted out of his body as Chauncy whimpered and whined. The

Reverend spinning into the black of the trees, and Chauncy was running away from the clearing, away from her.

Ruby lay down her head on the soft earth. It was only then that she knew. She listened with her whole being. She no longer felt her children in the wind. She had only felt an empty, gaping hole when she looked into the Dyboù's eyes. He had been bloated and fat. The silence in the trees was deafening. She realized she had known the moment she had seen that they were missing. That is how Ruby knew she had lost. She wept. She had lost them to the ether. Tanny. Her own baby. All of the murdered, twisted, broken children of Liberty. Gone. Every last one of them.

The forest swirled as Ruby passed into the starry night.

WHEN SHE awakened Ruby could not remember anything but the weight of her head on the clearing floor. An alarm ringing through the cotton. Her heart exploding with pain. Loss. She could barely move. Clay and a smattering of stones lined the exploding pain of her cheek. Her left eye was hot and swollen shut. Her right creaked open and through the grog of sleep, Ruby saw where she was for the first time. The clearing. She had run straight to the clearing like a child coming home. The alarm grew louder.

Ruby tried to rise—she had to lift her head, but a blackness fell like down upon her. And that quickly, she was six again. The last thing she remembered was drinking a bitter cup of milk the Reverend had given her on their picnic. She had felt her eyes heavy and she hadn't been able to feel her mouth. She had awakened in front of a giant pit fire, like the one Mr. Rankin used for barbecue on Easter. She was small, too small and limp on hard dirt. Heat and air pressed down on her and she felt her mouth open. She was embarrassed at the drool that soaked into the ground.

A hot fear rose in her throat and she threw up her chicken lunch, her body pushing, gagging. Someone's hands were on her, large and lifting her, dragging her to the brush. The last of it heaved from her belly onto a small briar patch. The clearing pushed up and tilted. Feet stomping. Drums. Crackling. Fire. They moved her to the heat but she was shaking. Unable to move but shaking from some awful knowing. Someone held her up, petted her head. Fire too close to her skin. Skin hot like Crisco in a pan. Hot like frying chicken. Through warped air Ruby saw the men. More skin than she had ever seen. Something was coming. A terror wrapped around her throat as she saw the dark low fur on each man and private secrets that she knew she should not see.

Hands picked her up. She could barely lift her head to look around. There were white fuzzy circles around the fire, the stars that spun up when her head fell back and the moon. Like a nightmare, like the hell Jesus talked about, the hands were not connected to arms, nor bodies. They were large and lifting her too high. Words, all said together like a Bible verse, but it was not a verse. They reached her, rolling inside, like her grandmother kneading dough. Someone was taking off her dress. Her hands were too weak. There was no fight in her arms. Her tongue too thick to speak so she screamed. It came out as a croak.

She thought about Maggie and what she would do, who she would fight. She tried to find an ember in the ice of her body, but she wasn't like Maggie, she was a scaredy-cat. She was more scared than could fit into her body. Something was cutting her in half, in four parts. She started bucking, convulsions moving through the dead weight of her body. Then she heard a warm voice, deep, familiar, family-like. Gentle. His voice entered with the other words, but it seemed to hold her. It had sugar stirred in like sweet tea. It stroked her, seemed to anchor her, so in the empty she grabbed ahold.

It was a trick. His words carved out Maggie's face and Papa Bell's corncob pipe. They gutted the carnival she had seen when she was six. They sliced out blackberry cobbler and warm milk with honey and the thin skin on top. Then they bound her hands with a damp red strip of fabric and poured her onto the ground, crying, crying as the men circled her. She could not catch her breath. They came closer. She could not breathe. She felt some horror rising ready to crash and flatten her. Their hands like lightning jerking back and forth. So fast like a race. Like a dark blanket falling. She still could not move, yet a part of her was running. Climbing a tree. The Reverend's voice yanked her back hard into the earth of her body as something hot was spit onto her. Again. Again. Slipping wet down her body. Slick like white poison, like warm glue on her skin. Again and again. Her neck, her back, her belly until the men almost growled over her. Then they were rubbing their sticky hate into her body, into every corner, her legs and arms, her chest, her toes, her privates, pushing their fingers into her mouth. The Reverend kneeling over her, chanting, strange garbled words that felt like a rope wrapping around and around her, binding her to him.

The thought of death smoked around her. Of dying like a snail poured over with salt, like a black bird Maggie had found—stiff and hard. She knew that if he let her live, if her heart kept beating, that any life she lived, any road she took, would always lead her back to them—back to him. Like a rotted seed taking root, burrowing through her belly, her gut, his eyes whispered that she was their thing now. They owned her.

The Reverend unwrapped the red cloth, petted her hair then slipped something round like baby aspirin onto her tongue. Then he closed her mouth and stroked her throat until she swallowed. He put a satchel under her head, and threw a rough blanket over her. Ruby watched sideways as the men became human again. As they put on their clothes and began to chat about early harvest and the size of a catfish Sorrell Wilkins had caught. Now that they had faces, she saw that some were men she knew. Men who walked to church on Sunday and sat and played checkers at P & K. Mr. Rankin and Mr. Simpkins. Daddies with four or six children, with little babies at home learning how to crawl. Men who worked at Grueber's Saw Mill, or waited on the bus to Newton. She felt so small. Like a bunny falling to sleep in a circle of wolves. But she saw before she drifted away that the wolves were also normal men, which made it the most horrible of all. A man with a smile and a soda pop for his daughters, with a tub of melons at the church picnic, with a handkerchief to give out if you had a runny nose—that man could eat you whole before you could say "boo." Those men were a part of the wheel of the world and helped it turn. The same wheel that Ruby knew would crush her every time she rose up to fight. Even a finger. Even a thought.

THE ENTIRE congregation stood in white at the southern shore of Marion Lake. The sound of Verde Rankin bludgeoning the hymn "His Eye Is on the Sparrow" filled the air. Ephram Jennings stood, the fourth in line, behind Chauncy's drunken uncle, Mandy Petty's seven-month-old son and a woman from Nacogdoches. Ephram was to be the last and final baptism of the day.

The choir blended in at the chorus, "*I sing because I'm happy!*

I sing because I'm free!" One or two angels' voices rising above the pool of wispy notes of old women and the booming off-key singers cramming every note into God's beleaguered ear. Verde was only one. Moss Percy's wife, Clara, was another. Women for whom tone-deaf and well-meaning family members had mistaken volume for talent and praised them thusly, and so both Verde and Clara sang even louder, each trying to top the other.

Ephram did not look at them. He kept his eyes on his bare feet, stoic and silent. A hangnail on his left baby toe was red and swollen. He wondered what the muck at the bottom of the lake would do to it.

When Celia had first suggested, over pork chops, grits and scrambled eggs, that Ephram be reborn through baptism, he had said no. But she had nagged so, every day another drop, until, to spare himself years of erosion he had complied.

He was to be the slow-cooked pork roast of the evening. The rest were only yams and corn and okra. Chauncy's uncle was the Tabasco sauce.

Ephram could not help but think of Ruby. She entered him like a taste at the back of his throat—the memory of his mama's peach cobbler. Now, Ruby would be only a yellowed recipe to be hidden away, slipped into his shirt pocket. He would unfold her on the way to work or when he was sitting on his bed alone.

A few pines clung to the banks of the lake, dipping their branches into the murky green. Reeds rose and clustered as the sun dipped and painted the world a twilight blue. Ephram took in the whole of life around him, the hush of the forest, the slant of the sun hiding behind the pines. It was as if a banquet lay before him, but it became sawdust in his mouth.

The Pastor entered the water and walked until it rose to his thighs. He spoke in a rich, low tone, stumbling only here and there. Chauncy's uncle, all in white, was the first.

"B-Brothers and Sisters, Matthew chapter twenty-eight, verses nineteen to twenty, say: 'G-g-go ye therefore, and teach all nations, b-b-aptizing them in the name of the Father, and of the Son, and of the Holy Ghost: T-t-t-teaching them to observe all things whatsoever I have commanded you: and, lo with you always, even unto the end of the world.' Amen."

Then he took the man and dunked him backwards in the water. The man came up sputtering and coughing, his hand high in the air, followed by general hallelujahs, and made his way to the shore.

Ephram straightened the baptismal robe he wore over a white cotton T-shirt and shorts. He felt naked each time the wind blew the light fabric against his body. Ephram imagined the discomfort of rising from the water in soaked garments, all but transparent, as he walked back to the shore. He noted that the congregation was always a bit richer with husbands and grandfathers when an attractive church sister was set for baptism.

The third acolyte inspired such attention. Her white gown was flowing as some of the gentlemen from the congregation crowded closer. Her hair was newly pressed. Ephram imagined, knowing the workings of woman's hair, a good three hours' worth. She seemed to have felt it was a worthwhile sacrifice in the face of eternal salvation.

Celia stood proudly at the forefront of the congregation. Her Church Mother sash satin white with glittered letters. Her shining Page Boy wig, and crisp white jacket and suit with tiny false pearls along the collar. Ephram could see that she had never been happier in her life.

Ephram felt something like steel in his belly as his turn approached, a firm anger churning, for to do this thing, to take the walk to Marion Lake Celia had bade him take, Ephram had had to leave pieces of himself along the open road. Celia, plump and grinning since he arrived home, seemed to have collected them in her apron.

Verde was about to start another hymn when K.O.'s wife, Evelyn, had the eternal mercy to push out in front. She began, *"Oh Happy Day..."*

The choir gently echoed, *"Oh Happy Day..."*

Next the preacher sprinkled lake water over the baby and recited,

"Mark chapter one, verses four and five: *'John d-d-did baptize in the wilderness, and preach the b-b-baptism of repentance for the remission of sins. And there went out unt-t-t-o him all the land of Judea, and they of Jerusalem, and were all baptized of him in the river of Jordan, confessing their sins.'*"

"Oh Happy Day . . ." Evelyn's voice sailed through the air, *"When Jesus washed..."*

Softly behind her, *"Oh when he washed..."*

"He washed my sins away..."

A familiar gush washed through Ephram. He had stood on these banks his entire life, his papa's voice thundering across the water, his real mama standing to his left, her hand gentle upon his shoulder, so close her perfume, sweet and lemony, seemed to settle on his clothes. He had fallen to his knees and the hands of the congregation had stretched around him when his mama had died. He had passed into the void and felt something holding on to him, holding him tight.

"When Jesus washed..."

"Oh when he washed ..."
"He washed my sins away."
"Oh Happy Day! Oh Happy Day!"

The church sisters, their aroma of Royal Crown hair oil and baby powder, were all he had known. The pride in their smiles. Pride, he knew, that only Black women can have in pointing out a good Black man. Their arms that had held him in esteem for decades.

He had sat in the pews, seasoned with the salt of sweat and tears for forty-five years. But that was not Ruby. It held no wildness, no talking hair and whisper kisses. No magic bolting through the world. But it did not cut him. It did not blind him with pain.

The woman from Nacogdoches stepped onto the shore and fell onto the thin sleeve of sand. She began jerking and speaking in tongues and the whole of the congregation rushed to her, placing their hands upon her body. Ephram passed the time looking at the moving lake. Her salvation could take more than a little while.

Then, Ephram knew that soon it would be his turn to step into the waiting water.

RUBY LAY with her back flat on the ground, the pines stretching high above her. She could still remember, still feel the slick on her body. She could still hear their chanting. Then, her cheek against the forest floor, Ruby realized it was singing. Someone was singing. *"Oh Happy Day . . ."* Sailing wisps of cotton. *"Oh Happy Day..."* The song gliding through tender, new saplings. There was a rumble of hope somewhere in the world. Not here. Here, she had led other children to the pit fire. Here, she had pointed out Otha to the Reverend with a glance and they had caught the woman and done the unthinkable. She had let Mr. Green take the cord from her own neck. She had watched in silence as her friend was murdered. She had allowed all of her spirit children to be taken. Taken and swallowed into the oblivion of the Dyboù.

Her own child had also been taken because Ruby had never fought. Not once, not the whole time she was at Miss Barbara's.

Ruby knew all that she had done. All that she had allowed. She had blood under her nails, up to her elbow.

The song danced above her bowed head. Her tears dampening the ground beneath her. She understood then there was another reason she had never run. The Reverend Jennings. He had not swallowed her down as he had her children. Instead he had braided their spirits one to the other, then threaded them through her body. Each step she took away pulled the Dyboù closer.

Then in the distance hundreds of branches quivered. Ruby felt him moving towards her as if he had been called. She tried to rise but in seconds he fell on her like a block of timber. Ruby felt the flash of his teeth, the gutted rub of his breath above her. The heft of his shadow pressing her dress, her hair close to the ground. Her scalp twisted, throbbing. The pine needles flew and swirled around her. Clouds of dust whipping in her eyes. She felt as if a lit match had been thrown under her. A sickly fire warmed her pelvis. Then, in spite of everything he had done, her body moved with him.

She slapped at her face and pulled her black hair. Her breath pushed, forced out of her lungs in hot frenzied blasts. She shifted her legs to allow.

He entered her completely. Sliding, filling. Then everywhere, under her fingernails, through her tear ducts, her eardrums and open mouth, like swallowing a hurricane. They joined, merged.

Ruby saw the shrunken raisin of the world through his eyes. The surety that all men were lined in tar and pitch. They were not different. They breathed as one. Rising and falling. She too hated. Hated like a jackknife slashing the canvas of the world. Hated the men who had taken her. Hated the fire. Hated the hands. Hated the clink of every damned quarter. Hated Peter Green and Miss Barbara and in the great swirl of it all—hated her own sinew and bones. It was the hate that joined them.

It had ruled her. Even her children had not been bigger than this hate. Ruby knew then that she had never nursed her children with hope. She had nursed them with fear and death. She had nursed them with evil as truth. She taught them not to rise, not to fly, but to crouch, to hide. She had fed each the poison of self-hate and they had grown weak because of it. Weak enough to be taken.

The Dyboù's voice growled through her as she pushed her hips into the crackling air. She felt herself build, build, rising. *Bitch. My little whore. Little cunt.*

Ruby became that.

Ruby's back scraped on the earth as he moved within her. She felt the sorrow of the soil beneath her. The grieving roots of a dogwood tree holding her. The sweet bay magnolia soothing the wind with its fragrance. The ticks of the crows pausing in the branches and what was left of the sun leaning to warm her twisted face. Ruby felt the red clay pulse around her.

A chain saw screeched through her like at Grueber's mill. Still, she knew she was not alone. A red oak stood proudly beside a thistle blossom. And the pines, the pines towered above her. They were older than her and everyone she had known, older than the Dyboù.

The Reverend growled, buckling the thin skin of her shins, her thighs. Then Ruby remembered. She saw the lampshade and heard the squeaking bed at Miss Barbara's and remembered she could hide in the chinaberry tree while the world was thundering overhead. As she had so many times as a child, she sat under the umbrella shade, the berries green and hard enough to roll between her fingers. She felt a soft weight upon her shoulder and Maggie was by her side. Sharp as razors, sweet as taffy. Her arms held Ruby close, "You listen to me. Listen now and don't you forget. Ain't nothing you ain't a part of. You want to know about that sky, then you feel it swimming in your chest. You want to know about them life tall pines, then feel they bark on your skin. Ain't nothing you ain't and can't be a part of. You already got honeysuckle in your breath. Already got them roses on your lips."

The Dyboù yanked her back to the forest, lifted her inches above the soil, the clearing rumbling, the trees bending. A branch cracked and sailed through the clearing. So Ruby prayed. The spark of life that was still in Ruby answered. A firefly was flickering. It landed upon her finger . . . like a flare it took hold. Next, it fanned to her wrists and arms. The circle of her waist ignited, along with her long legs and toes. It leapt to her shoulders, set the edges of her hair aflame and poured from her open mouth.

Ruby began to fight. She called on the roots for help. The water winding under the earth and into Marion Lake. Ruby prayed to the dome of life around her. She felt the invincible black walnut growing wild. The might of the golden oak. The lavender foxglove sprinkled near Rupert Shankle's hen house. The spark inside of her flared. It began to smoke, then burn, then rise.

Ruby started kicking, arms flying against the gray nothing of the Dyboù. He faltered for a moment so Ruby scrambled back. He roared through her, but she somehow, pushed herself up to standing and screamed into the thick air with all of her might.

"I ain't yours! I ain't your whore! I ain't your nothing!"

She began to push out, with her hands. Her feet stomping hard on the ground. He held on, held on, until Ruby felt the tug, the anchor of the rope that bound them.

She looked at him, the fire of spirit burning through her eyes. She felt the tether weaken.

"I'm not meant for using! I never was! Never was! I ain't never never going to be used again!"

She felt the rope burn to cinder. He paused, then flew out of her. He seemed to shake, then fall away, swirling into the shadow of the forest until he became too small for Ruby to see. She sat in this new silence. Felt a new freedom in her bones.

Then she remembered Ephram. Not at all like Maggie. Not sweetness and golden bluster. Maggie who would have fought armies for her, if only they had shown their faces. Maggie, so grand that she painted the sky with stories of catfish and heaven. Ruby had loved her for all of that, more than her life.

Ephram was different. He did not fight the world, he moved through it. He watched life marching before him and watched the beauty and the foolishness. Then he stepped, gently into the noisy, pounding fray. He had found his way to her door. He had tended her. He had stood right alongside her, not in front with his dukes up. Perhaps that is why Ruby learned that she could protect herself. Say "no" herself. Cast out the Dyboù herself.

Ruby then remembered the periwinkle ringing the earth brown of Ephram's eyes. His walk, as smooth and easy as Marion Lake. She then thought of his smile, and the way the corners of his mouth curved to accept it. She thought of his heart and the way he had loved her. Seen her. Helped her see her own worth. Her own treasure. She had never been his whore. She never would be. Not if they did not see each other for a thousand years. She would always be loved.

Ruby knew then that a lie could only control a person if they believed it. That all of the work the Reverend, Miss Barbara—all of them had done. All of the spells they had cast. All of it had been to convince her of a lie.

The song she heard was louder, it lifted high above the horizon. Ruby looked up and listened. It was coming from Marion Lake.

—

EPHRAM STOOD at the shore. The woman from Nacogdoches had finally, at long last, finished and stepped out of the water. The men seemed dismayed as Supra Rankin quickly ran up to her with a towel.

Ephram paused and took in the lake in the dimming light. The Pastor was kindly waiting, yet with a smug look of victory tugging at his lips. K.O.'s wife had not stopped singing "Oh Happy Day" for fear Verde might cut in. Ephram was glad. She did the song justice. So much so that frogs began their nightly serenade early. The crickets joined in along with a bold mockingbird. Ephram took a breath, lifted his foot when he felt the push on his back. He turned around. It was Celia. Not content to allow him to walk unescorted into his new life, she had walked past the congregation to the shore and given him a little nudge.

Ephram stood still as a pine. He did not turn his head either way. So she pushed him again. Harder this time. So Ephram spun around and grabbed her hand.

The singing stopped.

He looked firmly into her shocked eyes and said simply, not raising his voice, but loud enough for every person on the banks to hear, "Celia, you best stop."

Then he let go of her hand.

She stood there, a rush of anger flashing.

Ephram turned from Celia and walked into the water towards the Pastor. It was cool against his legs, then his pelvis and waist. The Pastor put out his hands as Ephram walked right past him, slipped off the gown and began swimming towards the middle of the lake. His legs powerful, his arms dipping into the dark green water and lifting back again. He filled his lungs with air as he swam across the lake.

Then his heart filled with the thought of Ruby as he swam, the amber of her skin and the frothing black waterfall of her hair. Suddenly he wanted to pull out all of his Mama's old recipes and cook them for her. Smothered chicken and okra, corn bread and pecan pie. He did not know what would happen. For now, it just felt good to swim under the white of the moon. He would figure out the rest when he reached the other side.

R UBY STOOD in the forest. The song seemed to enter her. Night had almost arrived. Ruby watched the stars dotting the sky far to the east. The west still held on to twilight.

She did not know which way to walk. She did not know where to go. She wished she had told her children so many things. She wished she had told them that it was their birthright to rise. That nothing could hold them. That anything the Dyboù said was a lie. She wished she had told them to fight—

Then she knew. Before she could teach anything, she had to know it herself.

Night had almost arrived. Ruby watched the moon rising and saw a crow making lazy eights high above her.

SHE LOOKED up high and saw that the top of the pine had turned black with shining wings for leaves. There were hundreds of crows perched on the narrow branches.

Another landed, closer than the others, upon a new pine cone peeking from the needles. The weight of the crow loosed a mist of green dander that dusted from the tree. It lightly rained upon Ruby's face.

Ruby wiped her cheeks, and another cloud floated down, sticking to her hair. It felt like a baptism, washing away the day, the weeks and the years of crazy.

A silence settled over the crows and Ruby saw them, wings fluttering, dancing above her. That is when the first of her children peered behind the great outstretched black and tumbled down into her lap. Then the next. Then Tanny, climbing down, laughing. The crows had had them all the time, keeping them until it was safe. The Spirit had lied. Her children all came, like baby spiders on silk strings. Ruby called them to her.

They gathered close under the pines, the wind playing with her hair. She smelled the honeysuckle and the dry dust of pine needles.

Then Ruby stood and walked, all of her children around her giggling, running ahead, swinging from the low branches. Ruby walked all the way to Bell land, into her door, and looked about the place. She lit the lantern. Then two, then five, until the place was golden and warm. She noticed that a bit of dust had blown into the kitchen so she picked up her broom and began to sweep. Next she would wash the curtains. The bedding could use boiling as well.

Ruby walked to the window and looked. There was the ripe scent of something coming through the woods. It was sweet and salty, like pomade and sweat. Tears of gratitude wetted her eyes.

She turned to her children. She had so much to teach them. To stand. To fight. To believe in rising. She would teach them. She would teach herself. She felt her heart beating steady in her chest. She could give each of them this knowing. She would give it to them like angel cake.

Acknowledgments

I'D LIKE TO THANK the talented Cole Rucker, Beth Collins-Burgard, Lorrie Feinberg and, of course, my mother, Dr. Zelema Harris, for finding me lost in the thicket of the piney woods, time and again. For resetting my fractured spirit, for warming me with gumbo, tales of mugwort; sharp, pointed wit; and the sweet balm of trust, then guiding me, with love, back to the waiting road. For teaching me, by their magnificence of character, how to live. My agent, Nicole Aragi, for first, choosing my manuscript, which changed the course of my life, then with patience and astounding equanimity gifting me with a sturdy map and compass to help me track a clearer, more meaningful path. For answering every lonely, anxious call with knowing kindness, and for having a belief in my work, so sturdy and firm, that it slipped past my doubt and into my heart. Thanks to my editor, Lindsay Sagnette, who bore gentle witness to both horror and joy. Who led me to blue smoke, clouding the pit fires, and the wind carrying the scent of sweet and salt. Whose stunning insight made all of my waking, walking dreams a reality. To the undaunted, torch bearer, publisher, Molly Stern, for leading not only me, but so many writers, towards the northern star. To everyone at Hogarth, for shaping a trudging hope into a firm reality. To novelist John Rechy, the late James Pickett, playwright and activist, and Henry Kisor of the Medill School of

Journalism at Northwestern University, for giving me the necessary tools and supplies for the journey. To my sister, Narissa Bond, who has held my hand since childhood, and whose inspired voice and music echoed through to my marrow, reminding me of timeless earth and the waiting horizon; and my big little brother, the indomitable Jay Harris, who survived the unsurvivable with such grace and dignity, that he strengthened my resolve to live. Who has always kept my feet buoyant and parted the thickest branches to let in the sun. To my dear Billy Wright, whose brilliant writing and wry Texas humor has kept me laughing for twenty-eight years, even through moonless nights. Whose face is, and always has been, family. To Jason Ellenburg for warming me with the irony of his art and ginger sweet potato mash. To Terry Wolverton and the late Ayofemi Folayan for legitimizing veracity and providing a sacred clearing for women to shatter the silence. To the late Harryetta Peterka for infusing my heart with fearlessness so many years ago. To Peggy Medina and Judea Cavoto and the Blackbird Writing Collective for cradling my soul and reminding me of magic. To PEN USA for providing much needed support, and for creating a sacred circle of Fellows, including the late, great, Qevin Oji. To JB Blanc for the unyielding beacon he held throughout the years. For perfect French, the steadfast anchor of logic, and enduring the trail writers must take. To copy editors Carolyn Clark and Jan Simon for providing expertly crafted guideposts. Thanks to Greg Grant of the Piney Woods Native Plant Center for helping me to stop and gather dogwood and honeysuckle along the way. John Imig, Damon O'Neil and Jason Parker of Swork Coffee, for the life-sustaining elixir, and for allowing me to rest, type and weep for hours into months into years. To Lindale Banks and her great-grandmother's healing hands.

To Duvall Osteen, for skillfully scouting the path ahead, and reporting back, that I might not stumble along an unknown terrain, and Nora Evans-Reitz, for deciphering unbelievably cryptic codes and travel notes. An inexpressible gratitude to my late grandfather James Marshall, 16 deceased aunts and uncles and a phalanx of ancestors for whispering hope through the roots and clay. To my talented father, the late Horace Bond, who taught me forgiveness. Special thanks to the courageous, lost children of Hollywood—those who ran away from monsters, hiding in shadows, and those who, sadly and unwittingly, ran towards them. Thanks to the many social workers and organizations who catch these brave, young people, when the bough breaks, including, but not limited to, Children of the Night and the Kruks/Tilsner Youth Shelter. My heartfelt, humble gratitude to my beloved and gallant partner La Tina Jackson, for teaching me about a phenomenon called gravity, for welding love to truth, and with heart-stopping wonder, always welcoming me, at long, long, last, home. To Avrie McKinley-Jackson for stoking the hearth fires and spinning beauty and love out of whole cloth. To Julie Curtis, Josh Raisin and Sonia Martinez, for standing vigil, teaching and cherishing my greatest treasure. Most of all, my deepest, forever thanks to my brilliant, beautiful and utterly hilarious daughter, Malia Jay Bond-Blanc, who came to me on the wings of a thousand prayers, who arrived in my arms, slippery and crying, and has in nine years, answered every single Mother's wish, and others I could never have imagined. Whose shining face, dancing walk, and contemplative joy allowed every breath, every step, every single day.

RUBY

A Reader's Guide

A haunting debut novel from gifted storyteller Cynthia Bond, *Ruby* brings to life a suffocating all-black community in East Texas. When the glamorous Ruby Bell returns to her hometown of Liberty Township after living in New York City, her sanity unravels as she faces the secrets of her past. The townsfolk enjoy spinning vicious gossip about Ruby—the way she screams each night like a distant train, entertains the "good men" of the town, and whispers to ghosts that dwell upon her land. At the root of her pain is a tale that no one dares to hear. The only one courageous enough to try is Ephram Jennings, a wounded soul himself, who has loved Ruby all his life.

An inspiring tribute to the human spirit, *Ruby* will captivate your reading group. We hope this guide enriches your journey.

QUESTIONS AND TOPICS FOR DISCUSSION

1. How did Ruby's story change the way you view the world? What does the novel show us

about the nature of trauma and the power of compassion?

2. Celia copes with tragedy by putting her world in strict order, from her family life to her church life. But Ruby becomes lost to disorder. What accounts for their different approaches to emotional pain?

3. At the heart of the novel is Ruby's vision of her children, and her vision of herself as a mother. How is she able to respond with a nurturing urge although no one nurtured her? Discuss the roles of mothers and fathers in Liberty.

4. How did your understanding of the Dyboù shift throughout the novel?

5. What protection do you think Ma Tante gives to young Maggie, Ruby, and Ephram? Are they comforted by her powers, or does she only stoke their fears?

6. What fuels the racism depicted in the novel? Do some of these factors persist today? Discuss Ruby's different experiences with racism in East Texas, New York City, and on her trip back to Liberty.

7. As you read the story of Ruby's aunt, how did you react to the notion that the past is still present? What does it take to overcome the Bell family's legacy?

8. What role does Christianity play in Liberty? Does faith enhance or hinder Celia and her congregation in their attempts to heal Ruby? What does Ephram's baptism mean to him?

9. Discuss the irony of the township's name. Is

there any liberty for the novel's black characters there? How do their experiences compare to the freedoms and shackles Ruby encounters in New York?

10. Otha Jennings and Ruby both lose their sanity as a result of Reverend Jennings's actions, while Chapter 20 reveals the Reverend's own tormented past. In the novel, how do women and men react differently to trauma? How are the expectations for Liberty's girls different from those for the boys?

11. The author gives us vivid scenes of the night on which Ruby's fate was hinged. What were the Reverend's motivations that night? As you read the scene from the perspective of different characters, how did your perceptions change?

12. Evoking the image of a precious gem, why is Ruby's name appropriate? Throughout her life, what is she taught about her beauty and her value?

13. What common losses do Ruby and Ephram share, from childhood to adulthood? What opens their eyes to the possibility of peace? What do you predict for their future?

14. Although *Ruby* is a work of fiction, the situations it describes are very much a reality. How can you and your community help protect the most vulnerable?

Guide written by Amy Clements

A Conversation with Cynthia Bond

Q. There are elements of *Ruby*—locations, characters, stories—that have come from real life. Can you tell us a bit about this?

A. It's a bit like a pot of gumbo. There are moments, spices, that have been stirred in slowly—from my life and from the stories of others.

Some of my first memories are of listening to my mother tell stories about her childhood home, a small, all-black East Texas town. A stunningly beautiful and nationally recognized academician today, my mother grew up on a little farm in the piney woods. She has a collection of tiny scars on her body that illustrate her journey. Stepping on a rusty nail and having to wear a slab of salt pork wrapped around her foot for an entire summer. The elbow where a teacup was hurled at her as she bolted out of a door. As children, my sister and I would point to each of these scars, these "chapters" in her young life. In many ways, this is how *Ruby* began.

As my sister and I grew older, my mother shared more of her story. Of her beloved sister being murdered by the sheriff and his deputies, of so many other siblings who, because of their skin color and the dehumanization of racism, made the decision to flee up North and pass for white.

More than anything, my sister and I grew to love our grandfather, Mr. James Marshall, the son of a slave master and a slave, who became Mr. Bell in the novel. Mr. Marshall, who was so light in complexion, whose eyes were so blue and hair so blond, that he was mistaken for white. However, he always corrected the misconception. Upon stepping onto a bus, and being told by the driver that he did not have to go to the back of the bus, my grandfather would turn around and say, "No, sir, I'm colored."

My own history of abuse informed this novel, as well. As a victim of human trafficking as a child, these stories and images filled my chest with horror, rage, and fear until I picked up a pen and placed it upon the blank page. Writing *Ruby* became my salvation. When I taught writing to homeless youth in Hollywood, I found that most of my students had themselves run from abuse. Somewhere along the way, living with my own abuse, and hearing stories of such pain and torment, I thought, *If you can bear to have lived it, I can at least bear to listen.* Ephram Jennings says that in some form to Ruby later in the novel. I asked that of myself while working on this book.

I read books about conjure and ancient spiritual beliefs, about both healing and destructive magic in the Deep South and throughout America in both white and black communities. I have, as a writer, taken all of the facts I have gathered and woven them together, along with images and voices, with the ephemeral thread of fiction.

Q. At its heart, *Ruby* is a love story between Ruby and Ephram. Which aspects of their characters do you think draw each of them to the other?

A. I think they both see the magic sparkling around the edges of the world. They both see life in all things and notice the unseen. They both have felt a hollow in their chests, deep, as if they were made of hardwood that had been carved through to the center ring. I suppose they are both so broken as well.

On a deeper, more spiritual level they are perhaps the only two people on earth who can truly see the other person. She will never be a whore in his eyes and that knowledge saves her. He cannot be his sister's "child" when he is with Ruby. By taking one step onto her land, he becomes a man. They can be a salve to each other, but that same combination of ingredients can also be incredibly combustible.

Q. From the red East Texas dust to the crow in the chinaberry tree, the natural world plays a major role in the novel. What inspired you to ground *Ruby* in this imagery?

A. This is one of the surprises of writing. After moving from Texas as a child, I became a bit of a city girl—I have lived in Chicago, New York, and Los Angeles—but I suppose I believe that nature is the truest, most empirical evidence we have of the force of life. Of hope. Life fights its way through concrete, barbed wire, and landfills. In time, it pushes beauty through any obstacle built to deny it. A seed never pauses and contemplates not taking root. It may not, that is true. But it will try, against all odds, in drought, in floods, in waste. It may live for only a second before getting yanked out, but it does not fear life—it reaches for the sun, or the moon, wherever it gains sustenance.

Q. You've been working on the story that became *Ruby* for over ten years. How do you feel about finally putting forth your novel into the world?

A. It's been in fits and starts. Working on scenes, a short story, then stopping to devote myself full-time to being a social worker, then working again, then winning a PEN/Rosenthal Fellowship while being pregnant, then having a child and learning to juggle writing with motherhood. I've often imagined how amazing it would be to have a little cottage somewhere and contemplate the horizon, while a sweet somebody gently knocked on the door, gave me steaming Yorkshire Gold tea with a pinch of raw sugar and milk, not cream. I would nod, then furrow my brow, focus, and begin writing once again. Virginia Woolf's quote, "A woman must have money and a room of her own if she is to write fiction," is the ideal. I do believe that many beautiful books and poems and essays are lost to stirring oatmeal and trying to get the mystery stain out of a child's shirt. They can also be lost to working over forty hours a week, parent or not, and coming home too tired to raise one's hand to lift the remote, much less to perch on a chair, fingers poised to write. They can also be lost to mental illness and homelessness. To slavery and oppression. How many gifts spilled, bled out, and thrown into unmarked graves—it is too difficult to fathom.

The toughest thing is letting go—you can ask my mother, my friends, my agent, and my editor. More than anything, I am excited that my nine-year-old daughter will be able to see her mother achieving her dream. That means more than anything.

A Recipe for White Lay Angel Cake

INGREDIENTS:

1 1/2 cups all-purpose flour

1 cup confectioner's sugar

1 cup caster sugar (baker's sugar)

12 egg whites (reserve 6 yolks)

1 tablespoon melted butter

2/3 cup vegetable oil

1 tablespoon baking powder

1 1/2 teaspoons cream of tartar

1 1/2 teaspoons salt

1 teaspoon lemon juice

2 1/2 teaspoons vanilla extract

2/3 cup cold water

Preheat oven to 325 degrees Fahrenheit.

1. Sift flour, confectioner's sugar, baking powder, and salt three times. Set aside.
2. Separate 12 eggs. Set aside the whites in a bowl. (It is best if they are room temperature.) Save 6 yolks; put them aside as well. Stir vanilla extract into egg yolks.
3. In large bowl combine the egg whites and cream of tartar. Beat with an electric mixer on medium setting until foamy.
4. Beat 2 tablespoons of caster sugar at a time on a high speed until a stiff, shiny meringue forms. Be very careful not to underbeat.
5. Add lemon juice, water, butter, and oil to egg yolk mixture. Whisk ingredients together.
6. Alternate folding in yolk mixture and flour mixture, beginning and ending with the flour mixture. Sprinkle in flour by hand, one small handful at a time. Pour in yolk mixture 1/4 cup at a time. Make sure you fold, not stir.
7. When complete, pour batter into an angel food tube pan.
8. Bake for 45 minutes, then increase the heat to 350 degrees and bake another 15 minutes, or until done. You will know that it is done when the top is golden brown and when the top springs back when gently touched. You

can also use a straw from a cake broom.

9. Immediately turn pan upside down onto heat-proof funnel. Let hang for about two hours, or until the cake is completely cool. Loosen side of the cake with a knife. Remove from pan, turn over gently with hands.

10. Lay your burdens down and enjoy!

About the Author

Cynthia Bond has taught writing to homeless and at-risk youth throughout Los Angeles for more than sixteen years. She attended Northwestern University's Medill School of Journalism, then moved to New York and attended the American Academy of Dramatic Arts. A PEN/Rosenthal Fellow, Bond founded the Blackbird Writing Collective in 2011. At present, Bond teaches therapeutic writing at Paradigm Malibu Adolescent Treatment Center. She is also an advocate for the victims of human trafficking; to learn more about organizations related to this cause, please visit www.cynthiabond.com. A native of East Texas, she lives in Los Angeles with her daughter.

cynthiabond.com
facebook.com/cynthiabondruby
twitter.com/cynthiabondruby

Stories ... voices ... places ... lives

We hope you enjoyed *Ruby*.

If you'd like to know more about this book or any other
title on our list, please go to www.tworoadsbooks.com.

For news on forthcoming Two Roads titles,
please sign up for our newsletter.

enquiries@tworoadsbooks.com

TwoRoadsBooks